Louisbourg

The Novel

Live the past as it was...

Guy Wendell Hogue

Guy Hogue

PublishAmerica
Baltimore

© 2004 by Guy Wendell Hogue.
All rights reserved. No part of this book may be reproduced, stored in a retrieval system or transmitted in any form or by any means without the prior written permission of the publishers, except by a reviewer who may quote brief passages in a review to be printed in a newspaper, magazine or journal.

First printing

ISBN: 1-4137-1766-7
PUBLISHED BY PUBLISHAMERICA, LLLP
www.publishamerica.com
Baltimore

Printed in the United States of America

Dedication

Heartfelt appreciation is given to Dr. E.E. Reimer of the University of Winnipeg, whose encouragement and editing made this book possible. Pride and gratitude I give to my son Al Hogue, who painted the wonderful cover art, and to son Terry, who digitized and made the art into a book cover. My beautiful daughter Sandra, as always, offered her cheerful love and assurance. But most especially this book is dedicated to my wife Nita, whose patience and encouragement endured through many long months of solitude as words formed pictures in the wee hours of many and many a night.

Acknowledgments

It is said that you can't judge a book by its cover, but if you could, this book would be a classic. My son Al Hogue, alhogue@alhoguetheartist.com , painted the wonderful cover. Terry Hogue, his brother, thogue@serenityart.com, did the scanning and layout work that brought it together as a book cover. The seascapes of Al Hogue are admired and collected by art lovers around the world. He and his brother market art prints to galleries in the U.S. and Japan.

Dr. David Owens of Sam Houston State University accepted the challenge of separating the wheat from the chaff in my voluminous manuscript, while making the text less offensive to lovers of the English language.

The most difficult research for this book was done by Keiko Fukumora, a graduate student in Paris at the time, who spent many hours researching and translating French naval archives. The staff of the British Naval Museum in Greenwich were very patient and helpful with technical questions regarding the Georgian Navy of England.

The Wooden World, an anatomy of the Georgian Navy, written by Dr. N.A.M. Rodger, WW Nortion & Co., was a helpful aid in technical questions during the writing.

Last, but not an invaluable resource was *Louisbourg, From its foundation to its fall*, by J. S. McLennan, published by The Book Room Limited.

Author's Note

By the mid-Eighteenth Century, old rivalries of religion and economics reached an eruption point. Wounds from The Wars of Succession festered in Spain, Austria, and even in Britain, where Royalists sought to crown a Catholic, Charles Stuart. In Europe, the great powers aligned into opposing forces to fight what would be called the Seven Years War. In America it would come to be called the French and Indian War.

With the aid of their Indian allies, France sought to protect the Ohio Valley from encroachment by English colonists.

Britain chose to fight France at sea and in their colonies, leaving the great land battle in Europe to their ally, Frederick the Great of Prussia. He battled Prussia's old enemy, Austria, as well as France. Outnumbered by his enemies, King Frederick showed his military genius in the first *blitzkrieg*.

Most scenes in this novel are fiction, but they are true to the history, and most events described actually happened at sometime or another, but certainly not to a single ship or person. Most characters are fictitious. However, words spoken by actual historical figures are based on historical accounts or inferred by recorded actions. Most prominent of these figures are the Chevalier de Drucour, Governor of Louisbourg during its siege in 1758, and his wife, Madame Drucour. The exploits of the fictional French character, Captain Renau, are based upon the real heroics of Brevet Captain Jean Vauquelin, whose story deserves a future telling of its own.

Chapter One

The year was 1755 as Lieutenant Charles MacGregor pushed his way through the crowd at Boston's harbor. Over a muscular shoulder he carried a sea bag. Seagulls, white against the blue sky and screaming for spoil, darted and hovered over the waterfront where ships unloaded baskets of silvery fish. Carts rumbled over cobblestone streets. Cargo handlers, merchants, seamen, hucksters, and children added their voices to the din. The young man measured the height and breadth of warships in the roadstead, his anxious eyes seeking a frigate. His blue coat with white facing identified him as an officer of the Royal Navy. An ancient sword hung at the young man's waist, his grandfather's Scottish claymore.

MacGregor stopped, looking up at the tall masts of a frigate tied to the wharf. He set his sea bag on the rough planks and stood looking at H.M.S. *Grenadier*. The warship was a bustle of activity. Men shouted and blocks squeaked as ropes lowered supplies into the ship's dark, cavernous holds. Orders echoed from the master's speaking trumpet. Sailors caulked the hull with smelly tar pots and heavy black mops. Carpenters hammered treenails into planking torn loose by cannon balls. Saws rasped and sawdust flew. A blacksmith hammered red-hot pieces of steel on his anvil with sparks flying, while a boy pumped the forge's bellows. Everywhere on deck men sweated, except the small group by the gangplank. A boatswain, identified by his tin whistle hanging around his neck and the short length of bamboo rattan under his arm, chatted with his mates. They joked and chatted as other men labored. Working on deck, MacGregor saw two sailors in kilts; they were squat young men, bare chests and bare feet, with red hair and beards. There were yellow men and black men. A few wore baggy black pajamas and some were covered only by rags. The British Navy of 1755 did not provide uniforms for ordinary seamen, only officers. It was still essentially a civilian navy, just making the transformation to an arm of the military. But British sailors prided themselves as such and could usually be recognized by their clothing. They favored a checkered shirt, a neckerchief or scarf, and a very short jacket, usually blue, known as a "bum-freezer." Sometimes a red or other colorful waistcoat was worn under the jacket. The bum-freezer was as practical for climbing the masts as it was distinctive. Their trousers had short, wide legs, almost like a skirt, unlike the tight breeches worn by most men of the period. If a man had to swim for his life, these bell-bottoms could be removed quickly. Some wore a natty little hat with a ribbon and most men were barefooted. Any man who might be ordered to climb the masts high above the ship wanted his feet bare.

Young boys of nine or ten clambered over the foot ropes, high above the ship. As a young midshipman, MacGregor remembered his fear looking down from the tall masts. Those years as a young midshipman led to this coveted assignment as first officer of a frigate.

Officially, Britain was not at war in 1755. But on the seas, an undeclared war raged, thundering toward America like an approaching storm. The British Navy and H.M.S. *Grenadier* were on a full war footing. MacGregor felt especially privileged to be assigned to the *Grenadier*, a frigate, a fast raider of the sea, eyes and ears of the fleet, scourge of England's enemies; this ship took more prizes than any other. He rested his hand on the cold metal of the heavy sword swinging from his side. His grandfather's claymore, he had carried it since he was given over to the English navy as an apprentice. The feel of this steel at his side had given him confidence as a young midshipman. Never mind that, in his grandfather's hands, it had cut down many Englishmen, enemies of the MacGregors. He thrust back his shoulders and lifted his chin. He would master this British ship just as he had the colonial revenue cutters and coastal packets.

MacGregor hefted his sea bag, thinking to himself, *Royal is my race! That's what my family taught. The MacGregors' descended from kings, even though we are now poor and landless. But I'm no king, and I'm not even considered a gentleman, until now. Now I'm a British officer and a gentleman. I can prove my loyalty to King George and maybe win prize money and respect for the MacGregor name, whatever.*

He saw the boatswain and his mates watching him from the spardeck. Casually, the young man mounted the heavy wooden gangplank, feeling the bounce of the planking as he made the steep climb. MacGregor balanced carefully; it would not do to make a fool of himself by falling in the salt-chuck his first day aboard. MacGregor doffed his hat at the red, blue, and white Union Jack fluttering on the bowsprit. While surveying the rigging above he said, "I'm Mister Charles MacGregor, your new first officer. I'll be needin' someone to take me to Captain Walshingham."

HMS Grenadier

As if seeing him for the first time, the boatswain looked over MacGregor's salt-stained, black hat, veteran of many watches in sea spray, adorned with a brass badge of strawberry leaves and then his gaze fell to the officer's sword. With a crooked smile he took the pipe from his mouth and said, "Our Cap'n don't like to be disturbed this early in the mornin'. Besides, Mister, your ol' sword makes you look like one o' them ol' Jacobites an' Cap'n Walshingham sure don't like no Jacobites." The crewmen behind the boatswain chuckled nervously. The boatswain looked into MacGregor's eyes with a wry smile on his face and rapped the rattan against his leg.

MacGregor thought, *Many times I have practiced drawing my sword quickly. Now I'll use that practice.* He pushed his seabag into the arms of the surprised boatswain whose rattan clattered to the deck. With the man staggering backwards, MacGregor drew his sword from its sheath, cold steel scraping shrilly against metal. The boatswain jerked his head backwards to avoid the hilt, his clay pipe falling from his mouth and breaking on the deck into pieces. With eyes narrowed, the young officer spat out the words, "Bosun, this old claymore serves King George... and keeps his tars in line." While continuing to look into the boatswain's eyes, he twirled the sword downward and dropped the point into the deck with a thud, an inch from the boatswain's bare toes. Jerking his foot backwards, the boatswain stepped on a live coal from the broken pipe and danced with a burned foot.

MacGregor said, "You take me to the Captain, whatever." The boatswain tossed the bag to one of his mates and led him aft across the deck, past sailors on bent knees, smoothing wooden decks with holy stone. Seamen looked up in surprise to see one of the boatswain's favorites carrying the young officer's bag. With a swat from his rattan, the boatswain sent a sailor hurrying away from the companionway, spilling a pail of water in his quick retreat. The three men descended the short stairs to Walshingham's cabin just below the poop deck. There a smartly uniformed marine dressed in his bright red tunic with crossed white belts and gleaming buckles stood guard. He moved his bayoneted rifle to the ready and barred entrance to the door.

"Lieutenant MacGregor reporting to the captain," MacGregor called out as he stood before the marine. Marines were new to the sea service in 1755, but this man had been aboard long enough to recognize the familiar face of the boatswain. He knocked on the door, all the time keeping his eyes on the waiting men. They stood in silence as footsteps sounded from within the cabin. An iron bolt scraped steel and the heavy wooden door creaked open. The small, wrinkled face of the captain's servant peered through the crack in the door.

He opened his mouth to reveal a few yellowed stumps of teeth. His Adam's apple bobbed on his skinny neck as he turned back into the room and repeated, "A Lieutenant MacGregor to see you, Sire!"

From deep within the cabin a throaty roar emerged, "By God, he'll soon learn not to come groveling at my cabin before I've had my breakfast! Send the blighter in here and I'll give him the word straight from the poop." The boatswain's scowl eased to a smile as he turned to survey MacGregor's face for any sign of discomfort. Boldly, MacGregor pushed the door wider, jolting the boatswain, and stepped inside. As the captain's servant moved aside, MacGregor saw Captain Walshingham. The rotund man swayed with one foot in his trousers and bare legs beneath his nightgown. Walshingham's bloated, ruddy face grew redder. His eyes sparkled beneath bushy eyebrows. The captain's hair protruded beneath a powdered wig sitting askew on his head. His fat belly seemed to sway him off balance and his upraised foot slapped hard on the cabin floor. His attendant rushed to his aid. Captain Walshingham pushed the little man aside and kicked the trousers across the floor. Now clad only in his nightgown and wig, he surveyed MacGregor from head to toe.

MacGregor's eyes inventoried Walshingham's cabin of gleaming oak. An ornate candelabrum glistened over his desk. Where gilded leather-bound books failed to cover the walls, expensive oil paintings in gold-leafed frames hung. Gleaming silver vessels held water and fruit. A Greco-Roman bust on an ornately carved pedestal served as a holder for Walshingham's best wig. Polished lamps of copper and brass, candlesticks of silver and gold, stained glass windows, a bed with a silk canopy and high side boards as well as various musical instruments made the cabin look like the home of some nobleman.

MacGregor removed his hat and lifted his chin, saying, "I'm Mister Charles MacGregor, late of His Majesty's Sloop *Siren*, reporting by admiralty orders as first officer of H.M.S. *Grenadier*." He extended his left foot behind him and slammed the door with a heavy kick, almost breaking the boatswain's nose with the noise reverberating through the cabin.

Wide-eyed, Walshingham padded across the oak cabin sole, his thin, hairy legs protruding beneath his silk gown. His face red and with hands clasped behind his back, he marched around MacGregor. Walshingham's gaze paused at the sight of the Scottish claymore. He repeated aloud, "MacGregor… Scotsmen of that name are banished from England, as I recall. I have heard ye MacGregors are rebels against the King, murderers, brigands, horse thieves, border raiders, bloodthirsty savages, and… and Jacobites. Why does the admiralty send me a God forsaking Jacobite?" Walshingham positioned himself in front of MacGregor with his eyes burning beneath his eyebrows, his fists on his hips.

Lieutenant MacGregor's eyes narrowed. "Captain, my family is outlawed in Scotland and England, whatever. But not in the colonies. Here we are free men and loyal subjects of King George."

Walshingham looked at him with a glassy, fishy stare. He lifted his right hand toward him and held it with the palm up. MacGregor lifted his hand to shake the outstretched hand of Walshingham but hesitated as he realized Walshingham's intentions; he then quickly reached inside his coat pocket to withdraw his orders. They trailed a long red ribbon. Looking just over Walshingham's wig, he laid the scroll in the captain's upraised hand.

Without taking his eyes off MacGregor, Walshingham ripped the red tape off the scroll, threw it on the floor, and held the scroll open. He stood for a moment watching MacGregor then moved his eyes down the paper. Scowling, Walshingham read, pausing at times to look up at MacGregor, often mouthing a phrase. "... Scottish father, banished to France, mother French noblewoman... speaks fluent French... educated at the French court... apprenticed to the English Navy in America... nine years at sea... knowledge of local waters... high marks on the admiralty exam... served with distinction... excellent navigator... marked for advancement."

The Captain wadded the paper and tossed it on the floor. "Serving with distinction on a halfpenny sloop is not the same as command on a blue water warship." Walshingham rocked back and forth on his bare feet, his hands locked behind him, his eyes surveying MacGregor from head to foot. Walshingham spoke slowly and deliberately. "I despise Irishmen, Scotsmen, Jews, papists, and colonials. As a matter of fact, there's damn few I don't despise. But ye are a witch's broth of all I detest. Ye are an affront to my command. Alas, my enemies in the admiralty have outdone themselves. Oh, yes, I expected they would sift through the bottom of the list and give me the dregs. I expected they would embarrass and discredit me. Always the admiralty sends spies and saboteurs against me." He turned away, stroking his chin. Walking slowly across the cabin, he stood for a few moments looking out the stern window, then quickly strode back before his new executive officer. "Well, Mr. MacGregor," he rolled his R's contemptuously and slurred the name with a falling inflection, "Ye will find me a hard nut to crack. This is no revenue cutter and I'm no mud flats pilot. I'm the most envied officer in America. No stooge of the admiralty nor spy in my ranks will tarnish my exalted reputation. No fumbling incompetents will impede my glowing success."

Walshingham's frown turned to a sinister grin. "They try but fail! Before ye attempt it, think on the fate of my late first lieutenant… let me see, what was his name? Oh, yes, Joshua William Coldwater. One of *the* Coldwaters of Chelsea, no less. Whitehall could not help him when a musket ball ripped open his guts. Now the crabs feed on his eye balls and nest in his empty rib cage where Norman blue blood once ran." Walshingham smiled and searched MacGregor's eyes. "Mind ye, the blood did not look blue as it spilled on deck. Nor, I wager, did his excrement look any different!"

MacGregor replied, "I'm no, whatever. I've never been in Scotland. I don't know anyone in the admiralty. I sailed under Captain Benjamin Sedgewick, twenty years a master of a sloop on the American station. Under Captain Ezra Hooker I patrolled American waters and was not found wanting, whatever."

The corners of Walshingham's mouth turned down and his eyes sought eagerly to see inside MacGregor's mind. All Walshingham saw was his steady eyes and a determined jaw where the muscles were set so tightly they seemed apt to break the teeth. The captain sighed. "Ye Highlanders are known for fightin'. So be it. Let's see how ye fight. Fight ye well, keep to my lee, and I'll tolerate you. But remember this, Scotsman, ye may have the title of first lieutenant and ye may be first lieutenant in the ward room, but ye are nothing to me. Ye are the lowliest man on this ship so far as I'm concerned and don't ye forget it. Have someone show ye to yer quarters." Walshingham padded across the polished floor to his ornate desk, mumbling, "I'll be needing a new midshipman as well to replace the incompetent little bastard killed in the last battle. God only knows what worthless wastrel he'll be."

Taking Walshingham's last word as his dismissal, MacGregor reached for the heavy door, but before he could draw it open, it was quickly thrown open by Walshingham's servant, his bald pate revealed as he bowed. Stepping out into the hall, MacGregor hardly broke stride as he called to the waiting boatswain, "Show me to my quarters, Bosun."

MacGregor followed the sullen boatswain and his grunting assistant laboring under the weight of his bag. The trio clomped down the stairs to the main deck and processed to the wardroom just below the captain's cabin. When they reached a small alcove on the portside at the stern of the ship, the boatswain opened the alcove door, snatched the sea bag from the attendant and slammed it to the floor inside. There was another alcove across, on the larboard side, which MacGregor knew would belong to another lieutenant if there was one, or a warrant officer if there were no other officers. Both alcoves were separated from cannons just a few inches forward on either side.

There was talk that the admiralty might soon remove the privacy walls now enjoyed by the officers and replace them with a curtain which could be lifted to provide more room for the guns.

"Thank you, Bosun," said MacGregor as he looked around the tiny cabin, his new home. "I'll let you know if I need your services again."

The boatswain sneered, "Our previous lieutenant lasted only one cruise. He got a ball right in his belly... kickin' and screamin' on the deck with blood pourin' everywhere. It was a sight to behold. Our good captain pulled out his pistol and put him out of his misery, with a lead ball in his skull. I hope you don't carry on like that, Mister." With a toothy grin the boatswain quickly shut the door behind him.

MacGregor sighed and tossed his hat on the swinging cot, at least it was better than a hammock. A tiny port hole admitted light into the cabin and provided a view of the wharf behind the ship. His eyes shifted to his sea bag on the floor. He looked quickly at his personal security knot tied into its duffle for any signs of tampering then surveyed the other things in the cabin. Beneath the swinging bed was a dented and soiled chamber pot. There was a broken locker made of oak with its brass hinge pried loose. MacGregor lifted the lid of the locker to reveal a worn Anglican prayer book and a book of poetry. Obviously, books did not interest the thief who cleaned out the dead lieutenant's locker. Even the linen lining of the locker was slit in a search for valuables. Besides a broken comb there was nothing more. MacGregor was surprised that they had not taken the locker too. He tried to picture the young officer's family. *Did Walshingham send the man's sword home to his relatives?*

MacGregor dumped his own belongings out of his sea bag and into the locker. He picked up a miniature portrait of his parents, the small, gilded frame carefully wrapped in a stocking. He removed the protective coverings from the portrait while he looked around the rough, wooden wall. From deep in the bag he found a bent and twisted nail. With the handle of his dirk he pounded the nail into the wall above his bunk. There he hung the picture on the nail and took one and one-half steps backwards before colliding with the opposite bulkhead. MacGregor put his hands on his hips and looked fondly at the portrait of his parents. It showed a kilted Scotsman with a lovely French lady by his side. He dusted his hands with satisfaction and turned back to his bag. MacGregor stood, and buttoned his woolen jacket. Slapping his hat on his head, he walked out the door, touring the ship and asking questions. Just forward of his cabin were the curtained quarters of the midshipmen and warrant officers. He saw the off-watch sailors' hammocks hanging in the gun deck, fore and aft in close lines of fourteen inches per man. However, the two watches alternated so that when the larboard watch was sleeping, the starboard watch was on deck, thus each man had, in practice, twenty-eight inches.

MacGregor's neighbor on the starboard side was, as usual he supposed, the second lieutenant. An elderly man named Black, he had been a second lieutenant for almost as many years as MacGregor had lived. MacGregor found that the boatswain berthed as usual under the forecastle, along with the carpenter. This was a highly desirable location because the open gun ports provided ventilation in the summer and the galley stove found just below them provided heat in the winter. The nearby sick bay sheltered men under the forecastle to take advantage of fresh air and to be close to the head for those with diarrhea.

On the lower deck of the ship, just aft of the cockpit, the ship's surgeon and the purser berthed. Here on the orlop deck, below the water line, it was dark and damp but a safe place to be when cannon shells began to fly. These were the only men who permanently berthed on the orlop deck among the cordage, casks, and supplies of the ship. In a nearby space, the surgeon, a warrant officer, did his bloody work on the torn and twisted bodies brought down from the fighting decks. However, on a small frigate, the surgeon more often tended the sick. In these times more men died by disease than wounds. Treating the sick would have been done on a larger ship by a physician who was usually a commissioned officer, but on a small frigate a man was lucky to have anyone at all.

In the orlop deck the purser was near his inventory of cable, sails, salted meat, hard tack, and all the items he must insure are available to operate the ship. These supplies, like the warrant officer's cabins, did not extend all the way to the ship's hull. A space was left so that the ship's carpenter and his mates could repair damages.

MacGregor went up on the spar deck in the bright sunshine and walked the ship from stem to stern. At the bow, the head served as a toilet for the enlisted men. It was little more than slotted rails open to the sea below on either side of the bowsprit. As an officer, MacGregor had an enclosed bathroom near his quarters, which he shared with the second lieutenant, and had privacy few others aboard enjoyed.

As a sixth rater of twenty-four guns, *Grenadier* usually carried ninety-one seamen, not including the ratings, officers, marines, and idlers. Even the so-called idlers were busy with their specialties, preparing the ship to sail: mending sail, repairing the hull, preparing food, and the other essential tasks to keep men at sea. Only the marines wore smart uniforms of bright red tunics and white trousers. There were thirty-nine, including their sergeant, a big Irishman named O'Bannion, and two corporals. With fifteen officers and midshipmen the total complement totaled one hundred and seventy-two souls. Not included in this number were several so-called widow's men listed on the payroll. Pay was issued but the men were not present, a practice common in the British navy to provide a pension for widows… but evolved into other convoluted uses. It was sometimes salary for new recruits and other unseen needs of the crew and at rare times, a license to steal. Walshingham liberally availed himself of widow's men, including a personal orchestra for his entertainment.

Since hard working sailors need fresh meat, a few goats roamed the deck and sailors ignored them as if they did not exist. Even chickens clucked and roosters crowed from pens in front of the quarterdeck. A pungent odor told Lieutenant MacGregor that pigs were also penned somewhere nearby. He introduced himself to the sailing master and found his place and time on the larboard watch.

Later that evening, MacGregor found his way to the ward room for the evening meal. He had brushed his jacket and his hair was tied by a ribbon in the back. As second in command of the ship, he walked to his place at the head of the officer's table, standing beside the ancient second lieutenant, Mr. Black, third in the chain of command. Black's wrinkled neck fell in folds over his soiled, white lace and one eye looked strangely toward heaven. Scurvy had long ago claimed most of his teeth. His white waist coat and the white facing of his jacket showed the stains of many meals that followed the spittle that now glistened at the corners of his mouth. Mr. Black stood and introduced the other officers, pausing briefly to be prompted for the name of the younger midshipmen. All eyes surveyed this new first officer with curiosity. MacGregor nodded, smiled, and sought to remember their names and titles.

MacGregor found a steaming bowl of soup placed before him by a cabin boy. Lifting a spoonful, he paused. All officer's eyes watched him. He returned the soup to the bowl, thinking for a moment. At last he lifted his wine glass and said, "To the King, God bless him."

With a scuffing of chairs and the rattle of dinnerware all officers lifted their glasses. They answered, "God save the King," thumping their glasses down on the table. In a din of noise they all fell heavily into their chairs and began to eat. With the rattle of spoons against chinaware and the tinkling of glass, they attacked their food.

Midshipman Collingwood watched with the enthusiasm of youth. A younger son, his wealthy family in Sussex had sent him to sea. Long before Collingwood could achieve maturity, an older brother would be called upon to manage the family fortune. Young Collingwood must seek his future at sea. He eagerly tried to please everyone.

Just newly arrived from England, Midshipman DeWitt was little more than a child. His fine clothing showed he, too, was from a wealthy family. A Manchester stepmother sent the boy to apprentice at sea upon the death of his father, while her own son was tutored at home. Quiet and shy, it was probably his first time away from home and his large, watery eyes seemed ever ready to cry.

Life on board a British warship was a reflection of English society of that period. Thus, a gray-haired man with twenty years at sea would not find it strange to take orders from a mere child if he were an officer, just as he would from the Lord of the manor's young heir back in England.

Sethford, the big sailing master, ate his dinner in total silence, his huge head leaning close to ham-like hands that moved food swiftly to his mouth. Dr. Abrams, thin and pale, swallowed large gulps of wine and small bites of food. With skin exceedingly white and black eyes looking under bushy black eyebrows, he surveyed MacGregor in silence.

The midshipmen interrupted their eating with banter. Midshipman Thomas, his blonde hair tumbling down in his eyes, turned to Collingwood to say, "I've bet twenty pounds on the fastest filly at Newmarket. Just you wait, when word comes from London my horse will have made me rich. I'll leave the navy and buy myself a brothel in London. Then I'll make a fortune on the likes o' you before I fornicate myself to death."

Dr. Abrams raised his wineglass and interjected, "That's right, my friend. Just send your money to Newmarket and stay away from the boatswain's scurrilous friends. You've a better chance to win on the races at Newmarket than playing dice on this ship."

Farwell, the purser, pouring his tea into his saucer, looked at Dr. Abrams with narrowed eyes. He blew his tea several times and slurped it noisily. Wiping the tea from his chin, he said, "If the boatswain were so scurrilous as ye say, our good Cap'n would no' keep him aboard. There's no cap'n more popular in the navy than our Cap'n Walshingham. Our sailors eat better than most men in England. Every man gets one and one-half gallons of beer every day. That's more than any other ship, by damn! Our Cap'n pays the extra cost from his personal share of prize money." Farwell quickly folded his napkin and rose from the table. "By yer leave, gentlemen, duties beckon." Without awaiting a reply, he hurried out the door.

MacGregor looked around the table and said, "I expected to see the boatswain at this table. Is he on watch?"

Lieutenant Black quickly answered, "Our boatswain ain't no warrant officer. He takes his mess with other ratings. He wuz' once a warrant officer a long time ago but kain't hold that rating no more. He does a purty job here, and our Cap'n pays him fine in other ways."

The surgeon looked away from the second lieutenant, saying, "The other ways would distress the conscience of honest men."

Lieutenant Black cleared his throat and said, "Rekon I'll be turning in soon." He rose from the table and followed the purser out the door.

Dr. Abrams watched the lieutenant as he left the wardroom. "I suppose none of us are any better." The doctor was beginning to slur his words as he spoke. "Just a little more rum every day and a romp in the bed once in a while with a pretty whore makes everything tolerable."

Young Midshipman DeWitt looked up at MacGregor. Embarrassed, looking down at his soup, he said, "Sir, I don't drink rum and I shan't be seen in a brothel. I am a blue blood."

"Well, your blood may be blue but your snot is the same color as our servants. You should go to the brothel," further rejoined Thomas, the older of the crew's midshipmen. He emptied his wine glass again. "A romp in the bed with a buxom English whore would put warmth in your cold, blue blood, Mr. DeWitt. I'm sure some of your old Norman ancestors dipped their wicks at the cat house. That's where they got the courage to conquer our poor savage kinsmen. When your time comes to lead a boarding party, Mr. DeWitt, you may wish you had fortified your courage with a philosophical exchange in a brothel." Midshipman Thomas looked up at the lamp swinging above the table as he continued, "Ah, me, I'm just afraid I may have to meet my maker with not enough sins to atone. I simply must have a few more fornication marks against me when I arrive at the Pearly Gates. I've far too few as it is. That's why I should own a brothel. My problem is, I would never allow any whores on my payroll to entertain other customers. I could never become wealthy in such a business. Perhaps I'll have to find another enterprise for my winnings at Newmarket." Midshipman Thomas turned to MacGregor. "Lieutenant MacGregor, did your service in coasters provide prize money?"

MacGregor spoke over his spoonful of soup. "My second officer's share of illegal tobacco failed to provide a fattened purse. I'm more familiar with the practice of thrift."

Dr. Abrams looked at MacGregor under droopy eyelids as he listened to MacGregor's reply. "I can assure you, Sir, as first officer, you shall earn prize money aboard this ship... so long as you live. You'll get one-eighth of some very lucrative prizes. However, living long enough to enjoy it will be another matter. Your predecessors spent little of their prize money. You can be sure there will be a betting pool with the boatswain on your longevity."

MacGregor's face flushed until he mastered his emotion. *I must tread carefully here. I do not know the ropes aboard this ship.* He asked, "Should I enrich my estate by betting against my survival?"

The surgeon smiled. "Other than widows' pension, we have no compensation for kin. Dead men's money goes to surviving crewmen, who promptly gamble it away to the boatswain's dice games. Some dead men's share comes to me... the ship's surgeon. While others are killed and maimed on deck, I stay below the waterline, sawing off limbs and getting richer. That's why I spend every farthing of prize money on those conscious-cleansing elixirs sold in pubs and taverns. I rid myself of the tainted money as quickly as possible. What I do not drink I share with every little wench I meet. And I'll try to spend your share of the prize money more quickly, lest miserliness subverts my carefree nature."

Midshipman Thomas rejoined, "Mister MacGregor, pay no attention to Dr. Abrams. He is not always so disagreeable. His interludes of sobriety, rare though they may be, interfere with his good humor. Give him more drink and he's much more agreeable. He's best as a surgeon when he's in his cups."

MacGregor lifted his wine glass to Dr. Abrams, saying, "Dr. Abrams, I'll buy you a jug of good whiskey from my share of the next prize my boarding party takes. Since everyone thinks I'll be coming back feet first, I'd like a good surgeon waiting."

Dr. Abrams smiled at MacGregor and returned, "The drinks will be on me, Mr. MacGregor, any time you care for one. If you do not find me in the sick bay, you will find me teaching the ship's boys in the orlop deck, as I have inherited that job too. It's good to know I'm preparing young boys for cannon fodder." As the surgeon drank copious quantities of wine, other officers took out their pipes. Soon, a blue haze of tobacco smoke filled the wardroom.

* * *

While dawn was orange against the black horizon and stars still twinkled in the sky, Lieutenant MacGregor took his station on the quarterdeck. *HMS Grenadier* lay anchored at right angles to the shore of the Charles River. He looked at the short, black snouts of their cannons, aimed down the river. They were manned and ready, their crews lounging about the guns. Their sister-ship, H.M.S. *Gladiator,* was similarly anchored nearby; her cannons also pointed down the river. These two smaller warships of the British fleet lay anchored fore and aft across the river, stern to stern, a cable length apart. They were ready to fire on any enemy trying to reach the main British fleet anchored farther up the river.

MacGregor looked at the anchorage and the sleeping town of Boston. *I was only thirteen years old when my uncle brought me here. He used five pounds from his dwindling funds to bribe Captain Sedgwick to take me on as a midshipman. What a poor lot we MacGregors are.*

Maybe it was my mother's prayers from heaven that gave me a benevolent master at sea. Captain Sedgwick said later that he accepted me because I was Scot. By his good graces and only with his patronage, I became a midshipman. He gave me my uncle's five pounds when I left to become a second lieutenant on a revenue cutter. Lifting his hat toward the orange-red sun peeking over the horizon, he looked across the water toward the commodore's flag ship. There was movement on her deck as officers disembarked to boats. Lifting a telescope from the rack, he watched the commodore descend into his boat. When the boat set its bow toward *Grenadier,* Lieutenant MacGregor rattled the telescope back into its rack. He turned to the other men on deck. "My compliments to the captain, and tell him the commodore's barge approaches. Bosun! Assemble a side party to receive the commodore." Men scurried in many directions at MacGregor's orders. Soon big Sergeant O'Bannion clomped on deck and assembled his marines. In their scarlet coats they moved into line, adjusting their hats and straightening their white, crossed belts. The drummer boys took their places, quietly tapping a practice roll on the wooden side of the drum. A piper softly practiced notes on his flute. Captain Walshingham strode quickly on deck, his short legs pumping under his portly figure. He took his place on deck with his officers assembling behind him with the barge drawing alongside. Lines flew up from the barge and eager hands pulled them taunt. The boatswain's pipe shrilled loudly. The Commodore climbed over the bulwark, standing before Captain Walshingham as pipes and drums filled the air with their squeals and staccato. Behind the commodore, staff officers climbed on deck, each acknowledging the flag flapping on the bow. All the visitors shook hands with Captain Walshingham and his officers.

Captain Walshingham

Pausing by MacGregor, the commodore examined his face carefully. In faultless French he addressed him: "You would be young MacGregor? Welcome to my service, young man. I approved your assignment here myself." The commodore turned to look at an expressionless Captain Walshingham who understood little French. Dismay contorted his face. The commodore continued, "You have an excellent record, young man. Your service with our American coasters and knowledge of the French language will be helpful in our blockade of Louisbourg. It could be more so as hostilities with the French escalate.

"By your name, I take it you are descended from the rebel MacGregor clan. Everyone knows them to be rebellious. But that interests me little, not if you fight as well as your Highland MacGregors. All my life I have heard of the courage of your Highland clans; that is another reason I selected you from the list. In my fleet I tolerate men who have been murderers, brigands, and thieves, so long as they are models of piety in the King's service. I care nothing for their past reputation; I care only how they conduct themselves aboard my ships. Here we have only loyal, dependable, fighting sailors; the best in the world. Some men murder for good reason. But one who murders aboard my ships is speedily tried, bound to the body of his victim and keel hauled until dead. A thief's hand is quickly cut off, and he is cast adrift. A brigand is lashed with the cat until he becomes a pussy. No matter what your past or your ancestry, Mr. MacGregor, you are not an outlaw in my service, but a loyal and respected officer of the king… until you prove otherwise." Again the commodore looked carefully into MacGregor's eyes before continuing, "It is said that you MacGregors are a most proud people… that you consider yourselves to be of Scottish royalty. If that is what you believe, so be it. Keep your pride, and let no one subdue it. Serve King George as your ancestors served their lairds and you will always find my door open to you."

The commodore turned to look pointedly at Captain Walshingham. He was almost smiling when he said for Walshingham's benefit, in English, "Proudly do your duty, Mr. MacGregor, and we shall get on well. So long as you do your duty, you will be royalty in my eyes, just as the lowliest man in our navy is a hero when he spills his blood for our cause. You, like the lowliest sailor, will enjoy riches from prize money… and what is more valuable… the stamp of my approval and, thereby, the gratitude of your king."

The commodore turned to Captain Walshingham. "Captain, I have orders for you. Let us go to your cabin and look at your charts." With those words the staff officers trailed after the Commodore, and he led the way to

Walshingham's cabin.

Lieutenant MacGregor stood the side party at ease and waited in the now blistering sun. He could not help thinking of Lieutenant Black standing in the shade of the poop with the boatswain and his mates. With perspiration running down his back, MacGregor squirmed inside his woolen jacket. It was almost an hour of perspiring torture before the Commodore and his entourage emerged from below.

MacGregor called the side party to attention as the Commodore turned again to Captain Walshingham. "Good hunting, Captain. I will expect to hear good things of you in the coming months. One other thing, Captain… I expect you to take good care of your sister-ship, H.M.S. *Gladiator*. An inexperienced captain commands her with a green crew; watch over them, as I have watched over you and nurtured your career, often to the detriment of my own!" The Commodore turned an embarrassed eye toward those who might have overheard and continued more softly, "Captain, I remind you again, this is the *King's* ship, and not your private yacht. You may only serve yourself by serving the King. Follow your orders exactly and you shall continue to prosper. Defy me and I shall drop you like a hot coal." With those words the commodore led his staff over the side.

A scowling Captain Walshingham, watching the Commodore's boat depart, said, "All right, Mr. MacGregor, yer royal highness, make ready, we sail on the next tide."

Chapter Two

At the same time, in French Canada, young Marie Gauthier stood near her crude, hastily built log cabin which she shared with her aging father. Nearby stood the brown, rough hewn, log palisades of Ft. Beausejour, flying the white Bourbon lilies on the pale blue flag of France. Marie's life had been torn apart by the undeclared war between England and France. It seemed that war would soon engulf the world. In America, the Iroquois, a French ally, committed unspeakable horror against English colonists seeking land in the Ohio Valley. French privateers seized any ship on the ocean not protected by King Louis. In retaliation, British warships laid claim to every French vessel in their sight. Now, expanding English colonialism pushed Acadians from their ancestral homes on the isthmus of Chicgnecto at the north end of the Bay of Fundy.

From her one room cabin Marie could look east and see, on the distant plains of Beaubassin, where her ancestral home once stood. The British had built Ft. Lawrence there, across the Missagaush River. With hostilities in view, the Acadians of Beaubassin were forcibly resettled only a short distance across the Missagaush River, to the French side. Now the two fortresses faced each other like two gladiators, waiting for a sign to begin the fight.

Her home on the other side of the river had been a large house, once filled with music and laughter, graced with all the amenities bought from sale of goods produced by the Acadians. Her home had served three generations of the Gauthier family who settled the area in 1685. Like his father before him, her father had been a successful trader, exchanging the farm produce of the Acadians for manufactured goods in the ports of Quebec, Boston, and the Caribbean. He bought the farm produce of hard-working farmers who raised flax, hay, cattle, sheep, and hogs. Having developed their skills in the lowlands of France, these industrious farmers had diked and drained these lowlands. The rich land produced a bounty not often found in Europe.

Now this undeclared war had ruined his business and destroyed their lives as it had other Acadians of Beaubassin. They had all been forced west of the Missagaush River by a militant churchman and his Indian allies. All this, even though the British had acknowledged their land rights on the east side of the Missagaush in exchange for their pledge of neutrality. Now they lived as wards of the French government, performing menial labor in exchange for their livelihood.

Marie looked toward the Bay of Fundy, shining in the sunset. She shaded her eyes from the sun's glare and saw a line of tired men returning from the fields. Her aging father would be among those Acadians conscripted to work in the fields and dikes. Marie saw another British ship recently anchored in the Bay of Fundy. A troop transport, its tall masts reflected in the golden waters, discharged red-coated soldiers that swarmed ashore like a horde of red-backed beetles. Fighting must surely begin soon. Why else would the enemy bring so many soldiers?

Back against the sunset Marie saw the column of Acadian men growing closer. They walked with tools over their shoulders, casting long shadows in the evening sunset. Near the end of the column, she saw her father forcing one tired foot ahead of the other.

Father is too old for such labor, but stubborn. He will not run away with me to Miramichi, and he will not admit he is too old for work on the dikes. He grieves for my mother and my brother but will not discuss their deaths, always losing himself in the thought of regaining his lost wealth, a wealth that can't be recovered in his lifetime.

Hurrying inside their little one-room cabin, she stoked the coals in the fireplace, adding split wood. To a pot of thin soup hanging over the coals she carefully rationed a handful of peas. Marie looked over the rough hewn table now covered with a fine linen tablecloth rescued from their home. Expensive crystal glasses, imported from France, held small portions of dandelion wine. A silver vase of freshly-picked flowers graced the table. Silver rings held linen napkins, vestiges of the earlier, happier time. Confident that everything was as pleasant as she could make it, she pushed her hair in place and straightened her apron.

Marie met her father at the open door of the cabin. His dusty clothing hung loosely on his small, thin frame. He removed his cap, slapping it against the knee of his trousers to remove the dust. Marie poured her father a basin of water. Her words erupted angrily. "Work on the dikes should be done by younger men."

Gaston Gauthier splashed the water on his face, replying slowly, "True, and it would be if there were any young men, but the Abbe' LeLoutre took them all away with his Indians to fight the English. We are now only old men and little boys." He sat heavily in the roughhewn chair.

Marie's thoughts turned darkly to her dead brother, killed while serving under that mad priest. Facing away from her father, she quickly wiped the moistness from her eyes. She turned with a forced smile, saying, "Look at the lovely flowers in this vase, like Mother had on her table. At least flowers bloom here, if nothing else. They can't take those away." Marie ladled the thin soup into bowls.

Her father smiled thinly. "Things will get better, my dear. When the harvest is in, the authorities should allow us to return to our homes."

Marie angrily slapped a knife on the table with the rattle of dinnerware. "Father, another English ship arrived at Fort Lawrence today. I saw them rowing more soldiers ashore. What will it take to convince you they will never allow us to return to our homes? There will be war, Father. That is why so many English soldiers come."

Gaston Gauthier looked up at Marie. "Marie, my child, I know you want to walk the trace to Miramichi. Please, let's not begin that subject again. So what if another shipload of English soldiers come here? There are many Englishmen at their fort across the river while only a handful of French soldiers guard Beausejour. That makes it even less likely to be war. Our leaders will not fight the English with so few soldiers. They are not so crazy like Abbe' LeLoutre. The French Army will go back to France like they did before and leave us alone in this land. Then we will make friends with the Englishmen like we did before. The English are anxious to buy our produce and sell us their wares; they only want us not to fight them again. I didn't mind taking the Englishmen's oath; I never fought them anyway. Why should I? War is not good for my business. Trade with the English settlers in New England is better than trade with France. I speak the Englishmen's language, and I have business associates in Boston. New Englanders would rather trade with us than the English. Perhaps if the English take over, it will be easier to trade at Boston and Halifax. We will have no more interference from France. The colonies of Boston and Halifax need our food and livestock, and our people need their bricks and planks. I will be in business again trading with both. We will no longer live in this miserable cabin; I will again make a comfortable living, and Beaubassin will prosper once more." The old man shook his head and sighed. "Then I will quit grubbing in the mud with sticks! I look forward to that day, and I expect it will come soon." He lifted his spoon and noisily slurped his soup.

Marie finally lifted her spoon. "Father, before one army sails away, there will be war. And the Beaubassin you speak of no longer exists. In its place are these two forts filled with soldiers waiting to fight each other. The Abbe' LeLoutre says the French will fight to the last man against the Englishmen, and he is prepared to see the last Acadian killed in his demented cause. Father, please, let us slip away and join the Acadians who go to Miramichi. It is not far; we could hide in the daytime and walk at night."

Gaston Gauthier waved his hand without looking up from his plate. "Bah! The French Army will not listen to that mad priest, LeLoutre. He can't dictate to the officers at the fort like he does to our Acadian boys and the Indians. No, our army will be sensible as they have always done in the past. The French Army will surrender the fort. They will march down to the boats with their weapons and flags. They will sail back to France. No, Marie, you are always too fearful. You must have more confidence."

Marie thought of the warrior priest who had taken her brother away. "Suppose the French Army leaves," Marie persisted. "Abbe' LeLoutre and his Indians will not leave. His killing will continue, and the English will forever distrust Acadians."

Her father held up his hand. "Without the French army to supply him shot and powder, that crazy priest and his Indians will be helpless. The Englishmen will hunt him down and shoot him like a dog," he replied. Looking down he added, "And I will not shed a tear."

Marie angrily held her fists in the air. "The English will shoot other young Acadians he has conscripted too, just like they did Pierre." The anger drained from Marie's face as she realized she had called her dead brother's name. It was not done in their house.

Silence followed her mention of Pierre. Gaston Gauthier rose slowly from the table. He stood quietly, filling his clay pipe with tobacco then chose a twig from a cup on the mantle. Painfully, he bent low to hold the twig in the fire. Slowly, he stood with the glowing ember from the fireplace and lit his pipe, bathing his head in blue tobacco smoke. Marie knew his dewy eyes were not from the smoke. Taking her father's pewter mug from the mantle, she poured a measure of rum and plunged a red-hot poker into the mug. Returning the poker to the coals, she placed the mug of hot rum before her father. Gaston leaned back in his chair, smoking his pipe and sipping hot rum, silently.

Softly, pleadingly, Marie continued. "Father, I am afraid. If the French soldiers leave and the English put an end to LeLoutre, I would not worry. But, Father," she continued, laying her hand on her father's, "I fear we will lose the little we have left, each other. You are all I have in this world. Let's do as other Acadians have done and follow the trace to Miramichi. We must escape before something dreadful happens to us. I have a bad feeling. It is something I can't express, but I know it in my heart."

Gaston laid his pipe aside and took his daughter's hand in both of his. "My dear, you are the most important thing in this world. That is why I want to do what is best for you, but what is best? If we go to Miramichi, then what? We can't stay there. Would we live in the forest like Indians? If we go to Quebec, what would we do? We have no money or credit there. There would only be menial jobs for us; you might be someone's house servant. I want to provide for you as I did your mother. You should have a beautiful home with pictures on the walls, stained glass windows, and another harpsichord to play. I want you to have a cellar stocked with food, wine, and fine linen on your table. No, it is better to remain here. The French and English will maybe shoot at each other a little, but then they will make peace. They always do. The Englishmen will rule this place as they always wanted. Perhaps English rule may bring peace. Then we will return to our land. I still have credit with a wealthy merchant in Boston; it's a lot of money he owes me, eh? My business associate will pay, and I will be in business again. Again I will ship Acadian produce to Boston, Virginia, and the Islands. France will no longer stop me. I will rebuild our home and more young men will come here for you to marry. One day you will give me grandchildren, and we will have a big family again."

"Would you have me marry an Englishman? Did they not kill my brother? There will be no young Frenchmen left here when the English rule!" Marie turned her head to hide anger.

Her father's eyes softened as he spoke. "There are some good Englishmen. You did not think the young officer who rescued us from the sinking ship so bad; what was his name, MacGregor?"

Marie replied quickly, "Charles MacGregor is no Englishman. He is Scottish and his mother was French."

Gaston Gauthier replied softly, "He serves the English, perhaps as he must. Perhaps as we must. And perhaps he finds it not so terrible. The English pay their seamen well and respect their naval officers as gentlemen. I came to know men in their colonies who are just like you and me. Some feel the same about their government across the ocean as I do about ours." Gaston Gauthier puffed on his pipe. "If they could, they would as we would do, have our own government here and not send our profits back to the old country."

Marie turned to washing the dishes and thought of Charles MacGregor, the handsome young man who rescued them from the raging seas. *Young though he was, his orders to the older sailors were quickly obeyed. All the men seemed to know he knew best... and he spoke French like the army officers at Fort Beausejour. He was strong, yet kind. I could tell that he liked me. Shall I ever see him again? I would not mind to see him again.*

Chapter Three

After three turns of the half-hour glass on the binnacle, the stern anchor had been recovered, yellow morning hues filtered through an orange horizon, and the ship rode to a single anchor. Her cannons were secured and the gun doors tightly shut. Gaskets held the sails loosely on the yards and men stood high aloft, ready to let the sails go free.

After two more turns of the glass, First Lieutenant Charles MacGregor noted the slack anchor line. The tide was turning and could take them out to sea. MacGregor turned to the sullen man standing beside him. "Bosun, my respects to the sailing master, and ask him to join me on deck! Pipe the men aloft and call the idlers on deck. Ready the stream anchor. Mr. Collingwood, hoist the Blue Peter and signal for the pilot." Men scurried about the deck, experienced and able for the tasks ahead. The boatswain's pipe screeched a high undulating call across the decks and top men sprang into the ratlines, climbing high in the rigging with an enthusiasm not seen on deck. The boatswain himself flew into the rigging behind them with unexpected energy, pausing to whip out his rattan and swat any man across the haunches he found to not be moving at top speed. Any man who paused to seek a better toe hold on the foot ropes could expect a sting from that cane.

Landsmen and ratings rushed across the gundeck to brace against the long wooden stakes of the windlass, where any slackness there might also merit a swat from their second lieutenant's rattan. With groans and shouts, the creaking windlass began to haul the anchor line on deck.

From the quarterdeck MacGregor noted their sister-ship followed the same movements and the blue signal flag with the white rectangle rose up her signal halyard as well. The sailing master took his place beside Lieutenant MacGregor. Sethford had spent fifty years at sea. Built like an oak tree, with an enormous girth, his body was straight from the wide shoulders to his hips. His gray hair protruded from beneath his wide brim hat and bushy, gray eyebrows surmounted rheumy red eyes reflecting his many years at sea. He wore a sea-stained hat and a blue coat over patched breeches which may have once been white. His stockings had been darned many times and his shoes were scuffed and worn. The man rattled the speaking trumpet from a perch near the binnacle and looked aloft.

MacGregor turned his attention to a commotion alongside. An elderly pilot, leaping to the boarding ladder with an agility befitting a younger man, pulled himself over the bulwarks and slowly hobbled to the quarterdeck, taking his place beside the officers, ready to direct their helmsman on a course down the river.

Calmly, as he had done a thousand times before, Mr. Sethford raised his speaking trumpet and shouted, "Brace the main yards 'round starboard." A drumming of bare feet sounded on the deck as men ran to take up their position. More sailors scampered across the deck and freed the halyards. High above the bow men climbed the foremast. "Stand by the outer jib," Sethford called. More sailors dashed toward the bowsprit at his order. "Weigh anchor," he called and men resumed turning the windlass, winding the anchor on the big wooden spool, lifting it from the muddy bottom. With grunts and groans from the men on the windlass, the heavy rope was followed by the massive, dripping, muddy anchor.

From the bow Lieutenant Black, that aging man who had long ago reached his pinnacle in rank, stood like a scarecrow with his rattan under his arm and cried, "Anchor aweigh," and the ship began to drift slowly with the tide.

While the quartermaster and pilot watched closely, the helmsman turned the spokes on the big ship's wheel. Mr. Sethford raised his speaking trumpet to shout, "Loose gaskets, set lower topsails and jibs." Great sheets of flaxen sails came billowing down. Loosed from the constraints of the gaskets, the sails popped, slatted, and thundered, then caught the breeze to form a rigid sheet against the wind. A rippling bow wave formed as *Grenadier* moved down the Charles River, standing out to sea. Soon the ship leaped through the swells of the ocean, her bow sending a shower of sparkling salt water into the glassy sea. Land's greens and browns fell behind with the musty smell of earth and their sistership sailed in *Grenadier*'s wake, a mile or two astern. With a northwesterly wind filling their sails, the flaxen canvas stiffened like sheets of hammered iron, and the two frigates cleared the headlands, bounding out into the North Atlantic.

MacGregor stood in command of the quarterdeck. *The open sea! My open sea, the fresh air, the salt spray, life is good, and I'm earning four schillings a day, not including my pension. I'll get one-eighth of all prizes, and one good prize could make me rich; maybe I'll be a landless no more. A MacGregor with land has not been seen in this world for many a year. If not landed, then I'll still have become a gentleman, a station I would never have reached on land.* He reflected on Captain Walshingham's custom of having dinner with the officers on their first evening at sea. It was then they always learned their impending mission.

Later that evening, he made his way to the wardroom. There he found their captain's arrival anticipated, as many candles bathed the room in a soft yellow glow and the polished oak table reflected the candlelight. It was resplendent with fine silver and china, all gleaming and bright. MacGregor surrendered his usual head seat in the wardroom and sat beside Lt. Black. Dr. Abrams, sitting across the table, seemed bored already, his brooding eyes locked on some distant thought. The white shirt of Dr. Abrams was soiled and torn, looking as though he had slept in it, which he likely had. His blue coat was threadbare and soiled. Nearby, Sethford silently watched through placid eyes.

The room became quiet as a cabin boy thumped the deck loudly with a broom. Another threw open the cabin door as the marine guard rattled his musket to the salute. Walshingham swept into the wardroom, clad in an immaculate dress uniform of his own design. Complete with brass buttons and gold braid, the coat sported sparkling medals of Walshingham's own choosing and a red silk sash from China. With a twinkle in his eye and a cheerful smile on his face, he looked around the table and room, inspecting every item that saluted his superiority.

Chairs scuffed across the floor and dinner ware rattled as the officers stood. Captain Walshingham took the usual place of the first lieutenant at the wardroom table and stood beaming as he looked around at the officers. With a flourish he lifted his coat tails and sat heavily. There was more scuffing of chairs and clinking of silver as the other officers took their places.

Captain Walshingham picked up his glass of wine and held it aloft, sweeping his gaze around the men at table. "Gentlemen, fortunate are ye to be alive this day! Fortunate we are all to be English." He face fell and his smile faded as his gaze fell on Lieutenant MacGregor. Recovering, he continued, "We shall lift those noble crosses of our King above all others. That red cross signifies English blood shed throughout the world, and from every spot on Earth touched by that precious nutrient, seeds of civilization grow." He then smiled sweetly toward Lieutenant MacGregor. "And those other crosses symbolizes our dominion over the uncivilized clans of Scotland and Ireland." MacGregor's face grew red and his eyes narrowed.

Again sweeping the officers with fire in his eyes, Captain Walshingham lifted his wine glass higher and said, "Gentlemen, I give ye the King! May God bless him." Captain Walshingham quaffed his glass of wine. With exuberance the officers called out in unison, "God save the King!" But Walshingham's attention had already wandered from the subject of the King. Hearing the toast to the King, cabin boys had rushed in with hot soup, setting it before the eager officers. Walshingham sat looking over the food being placed on the table. He swept up a bottle of wine and examined it. Lifting it to his nose, he sniffed. "Ah, a fine bouquet!" Walshingham thumped the bottle on the table and rattled the lid off a tureen of steaming soup, leaning over the steam and sniffing. "Excellent, ambrosia for the Grecian deities," he exclaimed. The captain shoved his already empty wine glass in the direction of a cabin boy and drummed a spoon against the table. He watched impatiently while the boy poured more wine. Another steward ladled soup for the captain as Walshingham held the wine glass under his nose. "Ah, nectar for the Gods on Olympus," he exclaimed before sipping the wine. He closed his eyes, opened his mouth and let the wine dribble from the corners of his mouth before swallowing. Slurping loudly, Walshingham devoured his soup, his eyes roving about the room, watching the food being placed on the table. Walshingham's hand shot forward to retrieve a long loaf of bread. Reaching under his coat, he withdrew his dirk and sliced off a piece. He thrust the dirk into the fresh butter beside him, slathering it over the still warm bread. His eyes looked heavenward as he munched the freshly buttered bread and gulped the wine. He belched loudly and looked at the officers. "Eat, lads, 'tis a fine meal. Soon we'll have French food and wine, which will make this taste like swill." His eyes held a shank of lamb captive as Walshingham continued to talk. "Gentlemen, we are not at war with France, but last year they captured our Fort Necessity in the Ohio Valley, not a great military feat, of course. It was commanded by a mere colonial named George Washington. Had they put a British officer in charge, the outcome would have been far different." MacGregor's jaw muscles rippled in his face. He glanced at Dr. Abrams who winked.

"For sure, lads, war is just around the corner," Walshingham continued as he picked up the lamb shank and sliced off a slab. "In anticipation of war, Whitehall ordered a quarantine of the French fortress Louisbourg. Ye'll be rememberin' that just ten short years ago our brave lads wrested Louisbourg from the French. Our glorious fleet swept the ocean clean of cowardly Frenchy ships. In due time, strangled by our navy, Louisbourg was stormed by our lads and surrendered. Unfortunately, the treaty of Aix-La-Chapelle returned it to those hated papists. What our brave lads won by bloodshed and toil, those bumbling politicians in London gave away in their inept snuffing and writing." With grease on his chin Captain Walshingham leaned forward on one elbow and lowered his voice. Looking intently from one officer to the next he said, "But now, we are going to blockade Louisbourg. We are to seize any ship bound for Louisbourg or Quebec." Walshingham leaned back in his chair and smiled knowingly as he continued. "And by God, as far as I'm concerned, any French ship anywhere on this damned ocean is bound for one or the other, and we'll seize 'em, by God! Rich, ye'll be."

Dr. Abrams smiled at his captain's reference to riches. Walshingham was one of the wealthiest captains afloat. His home at Greenwich sported an addition resembling a ship's poop. Filled with expensive furnishings and art, his home boasted the finest library in Greenwich. Prize money allowed him to live better than many landed gentry. Meanwhile, captains with far less skill and daring than Walshingham rose to command a battleship while he languished on the lowly frigate. That lowly frigate, however, alone on the open sea, was much more likely to capture a prize than a battleship. Battleships travel in fleets, meeting the enemy in battles which often pound opposing battleships to pieces. Through rich shares of prize money to his commodore and the admiralty, Walshingham insured his tenure and ever growing fortune.

The captain continued. "Yesterday, Wednesday, June fourth, the year of our Lord, seventeen hundred fifty-five, Lieutenant Colonel Robert Monckton led three hundred British regulars against Ft. Beausejour on the isthmus of Chicgnecto in Canada. Oh, yes, two thousand American militiamen were taken along, perhaps for fighting Indians. But they are, as most of you know, useless in war. It is as General Wolfe has said, 'The Americans are the most cowardly dogs a gentleman can conceive. There's no dependin' on 'em in action. They desert by battalions, officers and all. Such rascals are more an encumbrance than strength to an army.' They are, as Brigadier Wolfe has said, 'Worthless as fighting men.'[1] Walshingham looked at MacGregor, saying, "But Wolfe praises Highlanders, like our new lieutenant here. We must all watch MacGregor to see if he measures up to the Highlander reputation." Lieutenant MacGregor glanced at Abrams, who watched him with a little wink. MacGregor's eyes glowed and his face muscles rippled. Walshingham continued. "Only two hundred French regulars and a few Acadian farmers defend Ft. Beausejour."

He concluded, "Wealth awaits ye lads, at forty-six degrees north, sixty degrees west. There, on the banks of Cape Breton, where all the fishes in the ocean come to watch sailors battle the world's worst weather, ye will become wealthy." He lifted his glasses. The officers lifted their glasses to toast their new fortune, and Captain Walshingham digressed into a monologue. "Tonight, gentlemen, it is fitting my orchestra play Handel's *Music for the Royal*

Fireworks. It commemorates the treaty of Aix-La-Chapelle in which our stupid politicians gave Louisbourg back to the French after our bleedin' lads captured it ten years ago. We'll take Louisbourg back, and the devil can burn that worthless treaty in hell!"

With two violins, a cello, and a flute, a group of rather unlikely looking sailors, widows' men all, filed into the wardroom. The musicians entertained them with Bach and Handel. Captain Walshingham beamed as his musicians looked to their instruments, tuning them to plinks, plunks, tweets and hums.

Late into the night the drinking, eating, and merry making continued. At last Lieutenant MacGregor excused himself and rose from the table. He made his way to the dark quarterdeck where he stood under a panoply of stars twinkling in the heavens. *Soon I'll be fighting the French... my mother's people. The French aided my Scottish ancestors who fought for the Stuarts along with my father and grandfather. But now I have sworn an oath to fight for King George of England.*

And then there's Marie Gauthier. I remember that cold day five years ago. We were patrolling the seas off Cape Cod in a gale when our lookout spotted their floundering ship. Awash in the tossing seas, the wind had carried their mainmast away. The ship drifted before the gale, trailing fallen rigging and sails behind. Waves swept over their stern and filled their holds. The ship was sinking. Cows, sheep, pigs, and even a sailor were washed overboard and drowned. It was a heart breaking sight in the wake of their ship as our cutter sailed to their rescue. I remember their red ensign flown upside down as a signal of distress. Captain Ezra Hooker ordered me to take a boat with sailors and axes across to the sinking ship. We fought our way through the rough seas and chopped away the trailing rigging. Coming up in the lee of the floundering ship, we boarded her. There I found Marie Gauthier and her father, who had chartered the American ship to bring his produce to Boston.

We rescued Marie, her father, and the crew of the sinking ship, taking them back aboard our coastal cutter to safety. After a few days at sea with Marie, I could not take my mind off her. Oh, the lovely Marie Gauthier. Why can I not take my mind off her? But I could see something in her eyes as I took them ashore in Boston. Can I obey my oath to King George and fight the French? Marie is French. My mother was French. I am half French. How can I fight them?

The ocean breeze blew cool and fresh in MacGregor's face as Bach's Concerto drifted up from the stern windows. Beneath him *Grenadier* heeled to the fresh westerly winds. MacGregor's thoughts turned to the ocean's peace and beauty. His troubling thoughts washed out the scuppers and floated away in the wake of the ship. *I'll think about those problems tomorrow. Perhaps the solution will be easier then, whatever.*

Chapter Four

Gaston Gauthier arose early. The cool, gray dawn filtered through the little cabin's front window. With a hand on his hip, he slowly stood with a groan. Across the room Marie breathed heavily in her bed. *I must keep her safe from danger. Mary, Mother of God, she is all I have.* Gaston slipped quietly to the door in his night shirt and lifted the latch. It opened silently on its leather hinges, revealing the misty morning pastures still slumbering in dews and damps. Only the calling of a sea gull and the distant bleating of a lamb in search of its mother broke the morning's stillness. The scanty heard of cattle, so plentiful in years gone by, had not yet begun lowing for relief of their full udders. Gaston slipped his feet into wooden shoes and walked outside, stooping painfully as he picked an armload of kindling from the woodpile. Straightening slowly, he started back to the cabin when an explosion shattered the silence. Gaston dropped some wood and stood listening as another explosion echoed across the valley. That explosion was followed by the cries of thousands of sea gulls rousted from their resting in the tidal damps. Dogs barked in the village. A cannon volley thundered a ripping series of explosions in the distance that echoed over the river and disappeared in the woodlands. Exploding geysers of dirt and smoke rose into the air on the French side of the river. White smoke drifted from the trees across on the British side.

Marie sat upright in terror. She sprang from bed and ran outside. Clutching her nightgown around her neck, she pulled her father inside the door with firewood falling to the ground. Before they could close the door, another volley of cannons thundered across the valley.

Disbelieving, Gaston Gauthier watched the war erupting before his eyes. The dust and smoke from the cannons drifted away slowly in the gentle morning breeze. A bugle sounded in the distance, filling the silence between explosions. Its notes echoed across the morning stillness to be consumed by another cannon volley that crashed and thundered over the pastoral landscape, only to be followed again by the quietness of the morning.

In the direction of Fort Beausejour, hoof beats sounded. They pounded closer with the jangle of horse harness. A French officer mounted on a big bay horse galloped past their cabin. Cursing, whipping and spurring his horse, he rode over the pasture and disappeared through the trees. "Father! Come inside and lock the door," Marie urged.

As Gaston closed the door, another cannon volley erupted. Behind them drums rattled and bugles blared from Fort Beausejour. Excited voices called from afar, issuing instructions. Marie threw a shawl over her shoulders, closed the door, slipped the wooden bolt to a locked position, and looked out the window at the war engulfing their peaceful countryside. Smoke and dust now created a yellow-orange haze across the eastern sky as cannons boomed and thundered. Between the cannon crashes, a new sound arose, the sharper, high pitched rattle of musketry.

Throughout the morning Marie and her father huddled in their cabin. At noon Marie and her father sat at their crude table having their midday meal when a heavy knock shook their door. Hesitantly, Gaston Gauthier eased himself up from the table. Cautiously, he opened the door to peer out the narrow opening. A hand pushed the door open and two French marines stood before him. They were dressed in blue uniforms and carried long muskets with bayonets. The younger of the two marines asked, "Are you Gaston Gauthier?"

Gaston looked at the men curiously. "Yes, I'm Gaston Gauthier."

Again the man spoke, "Gaston Gauthier, in the name of His Christian Majesty the King, you are hereby ordered to take up arms in defense of the realm. Bring your weapon, if you have one, and come along with us."

"No! I must not bear arms against the English," replied Gaston. "I swore an oath to them after the last war that I will never again fight them."

"Yes, yes, you and everyone else here, old man. Your oath means nothing. I have been sent to fetch you and I shall, voluntarily or on the end of a bayonet. Now come along peacefully, and quickly."

"Please," begged Gaston, "my daughter is here alone. She needs me to look after her."

The older marine stepped inside the cabin. He looked at Marie like a fox eyes a chicken. Putting his arm around Marie, he said, "Ah, yes, and a lovely little wench she is, too. Don't worry, old man, I will come back and look after her. All of her!" The marine's hand slipped off Marie's shoulder, sliding down to fondle her breast. Instantly the cabin rang with Marie's slap of the marine's face.

Anger flashed in his eyes as he held his hand against his stinging cheek. He doubled his fist and shook it at Marie as he swore, "You little bitch, I'll teach you respect!" He reached for her throat.

The younger marine stepped between them and shoved his partner out the door, saying, "Not now, Andre, today we make war, not love." He turned back to Marie's father. "Mr. Gauthier, thousands of Englishmen crossed the river.

You know how they rape and pillage. You can protect your daughter by coming with us to fight them. Get your gun and come along. We have more Acadians to round up."

"I have no gun," replied Gaston. "I'm not a man of violence. Please leave me in peace."

The younger marine stepped into the room and stripped a blanket from the bed, tossing it at Gaston. "You have no choice in the matter. Take a blanket. You will likely sleep on the cold ground tonight, if you sleep at all." The younger man lifted Gaston's dark coat from a peg beside the door and thrust it into his hands. Gaston grabbed his black hat as the other marine shoved him toward the open door.

Marie, with tears running down her cheeks, ran after her father. "Please, please, don't take him away. He is too old to fight."

Grabbing Marie by the shoulder, the older marine pulled her away from Gaston. "Now, now, little chicken, don't interfere. He must go kill Englishmen. If you're afraid, I'll come back and look after you later." As he spoke, he slipped his hand down over her breast again with a wicked squint in his eyes.

Marie pulled away, her hair falling down over her face. With hands over her mouth and tears glistening on her cheeks, Marie watched the marines push and shove her father away. Sobbing, she fell against the cabin and pounded the rough logs with her fist, hearing only musketry and cannons.

Shoved and prodded, Gaston Gauthier stumbled in Fort Beausejour's gates where he found many Acadian men gathered, but only old men and a few young boys. The young men of fighting age had long before been conscripted by the Abbe LeLoutre to fight with his Indians. Gaston looked around him to see all the familiar faces of his old village of Beaubassin. They were grandfathers and grandsons–too old or too young to fight. Only a handful of the men in the group could provide more than canon fodder. Standing out from the group was a tall man in buckskins, his long white hair flowing from beneath a blue toque. It was his old friend, Henri Ouilette, trapper and fur trader who had sold Gaston many a bundle of furs for trade in Boston.

The French commander stood before them in a splendid uniform. Gaston noted, absent-mindedly, that the officer spoke to the Acadians. "To fight to the last…" he was saying, then something about "…His Christian Majesty Louis XV…" Gaston cared little for the officer's words, but the part about fighting to the last man, Gaston heard clearly those words. The officer said an order came from Governor de Menneville in Quebec. Gaston understood very well that order. "Under penalty of death you will serve the King, disregarding any illegal oath given the English aggressors."

Gaston Gauthier's thoughts were not long off his daughter. Exploding cannon shells again brought pictures to his mind of the little cabin disintegrating and Marie trapped beneath the rubble. Gaston hardly realized he now held a musket in his hands, put there by a soldier as his thoughts drifted far away. He stood like the other Acadians, waiting for their names to be called. A uniformed officer called names for assignments. Mr. Gauthier would have missed hearing his name had it not been for his old friend Henri Ouilette. The big man slapped Gaston on the back. "Gaston, my friend, when these little soldier boys get in trouble, they have to call on us men, eh?" Gaston looked up at the big man with broad shoulders and massive hands. Ouilette's eyes smiled at him from a lined and chiseled face. He looked at ease leaning against his own long rifle, not one of the French muskets. His long, gray hair spilled from beneath a long blue toque. He wore a fringed, buckskin jacket and breeches with knee-high moccasins. A blue sash around his waist held a skinning knife and tomahawk. Straps crossed his chest, holding leather shot and powder bags while a goatskin water bag and blanket roll showed he was ready to campaign.

Gaston's low spirits rose again at the sight of his old fur supplier. "Henri, my friend, they have taken you to fight too? You are probably the only man here who has experience in fighting the Englishmen."

"*Oui*, I have fought the Englishmen, fighting beside the *Mi'kmaq*s. But we did not fight like these little soldiers here. They fight silly, eh?" With an outstretched hand and wide smile he continued, "They stand up and let the enemy shoot them. I'm not going to stand up and let them shoot me. Better you sit down and be comfortable while they shoot you, eh?"

Gaston smiled for the first time that day. "But, Henri, Marie is alone in the cabin. The shells… they explode everywhere and soldiers gaze at her like a bull at a heifer. I must get her to safety."

"You two, there! Stop talking and pay attention," shouted a sergeant, giving Gaston a shove. "You two follow me. I'll take you to your positions." He mounted a big bay horse and said, "Come along now."

The two Acadians followed along behind the sergeant's horse. Henri whispered, "Gaston, you must be patient; don't try to go to Marie. They may shoot you, eh? We must bide our time. A chance will come, probably after dark tonight, then we'll go and find Marie." They walked glumly behind the big horse while it switched at flies with its tail. Occasionally the tail brushed their faces.

"Cheer up, Gaston," said Henri. "Look," he continued, pointing at the horse's buttocks, "you should be happy to be following our King into battle, eh?" Gaston managed a thin smile. "*Oui,* Gaston," Henri continued, "careful you don't step in a royal edict."

Skirting the marshes, the three men climbed up to a brush-covered rise. Artillery boomed and thundered in the distance. They came to a place where the trail was flanked by high brush. Here the sergeant reined his horse to a stop and dismounted. At the hill's edge he showed Gaston and Henri two marines. They stood beside a swivel gun mounted on an iron stake. Anyone approaching from the front would not see them, but they could be seen easily from above. The sergeant pointed to a shallow ravine beyond the swivel gun and said, "You'll be forward pickets there in that ravine. We do not have enough regular soldiers to guard all the approaches. You farmers are the forward defense in that area. If the enemy succeeds in getting past you, he will be killed by this swivel gun loaded with grapeshot. I suggest you not think of running away. Our marines have orders to shoot deserters. If you see anyone, anyone at all, attempting to come up the hill, you shoot them. If the enemy attacks here, you must drive them back or at least hold them here until help arrives. You must not let them pass. You may take turns sleeping but don't be caught off guard. Now, hurry quickly down the hill and take your place before you're seen by the enemy."

Henri nudged Gaston, and with a twinkle in his eye, said, "Sergeant, don't you think it would be better if Gaston and I walked slowly down the hill? If the Englishmen see Gaston and me running down the hill at them, they will panic. We could cause some terrible calamity, eh?"

With disgust, the sergeant said, "Stay at your post until relieved!" He spurred his horse while pulling the reins across the horse's neck. The horse trotted away up the hill with the soldier shaking his head.

Henri said, "Come, Gaston, it is dangerous here. You could get kicked by a horse." Henri led the way down the hill. They made their way slowly toward their position. At the eastern brow, they arrived at the position of the swivel gun. Henri paused to attempt a friendly chat with the men, but they proved to be unfriendly, so he gave up the effort and stood looking down the hillside he must cross. He saw a ravine overlooking the enemy positions across the river, marking it in his memory. Henri selected a route down to the ravine giving him the least exposure to the enemy. Instructing Gaston to follow him when called, he picked up his long rifle. He moved carefully down the hill in a low crouch. Climbing to the opposite side, he rolled over in a prone position. With his gun pointed toward the enemy lines across the river, Henri lay ready to shoot. The woodsman lay watching the enemy positions, then signaled for Gaston to follow. Gaston stumbled awkwardly down the hill, slipping and falling several times as Henri lay watching. Breathing heavily, Gaston dropped beside Henri. While Henri carefully scanned the terrain, Gaston sat upright, brushing dirt and grass from his clothing. Henri pulled Gaston down in the grass then watched until satisfied all was well. Contented, Henri rolled over on his back. He laid his musket aside and propped his head comfortably on his bedroll. Crossing his leg over his knee, the woodsman took out his worn clay pipe. He lay chewing on the stem. Henri put both hands behind his head, closed his eyes and said, "Gaston, I think maybe no one will be so crazy to come up that hill in daylight. My friend, you keep watch for a little while, eh? After all this work, I need a little nap."

Gaston lay in the grass with his musket at the ready just as he had seen Henri do. Looking toward the English lines Gaston asked, "Henri, should I load the musket?"

Surprised, Henri removed the pipe from his mouth, turning toward Gaston with one eye open. "*Oui*, Gaston, maybe a little powder in the musket would help wake me, in case the English come." Henri closed his eyes with a smile on his face as Gaston fumbled about loading the musket.

Gaston poured in powder, wondering if he had added enough. He sat looking down the barrel thoughtfully, then added more powder, still wondering if he had added enough. For good measure, Gaston added just a touch more. He chose a ball from a pouch in his pocket and dropped it down the barrel. Awkwardly, he removed the long ramrod from beneath the gun, thrusting it down the barrel. With a grimace on his face he seated the ball with the long ramrod. Gaston pulled the hammer back and set the rifle on half-cock. Satisfied, Gaston settled down comfortably in the grass. Nervously, he watched the enemy positions for more then an hour, then his eye lids grew heavy. In trying to keep awake, Gaston saw Henri's pipe had fallen from his mouth and his heavy breathing told him his friend was asleep. Gaston rubbed his eyes and tried to stay awake.

Time passed slowly as Gaston looked for the enemy, dozed, and awoke to worry about Marie. Rifle fire occasionally rattled from the trees farther north, but the war seemed to have abated.

After another short nap Gaston woke and sat in the quiet evening, admiring the valley's beauty. The sun, low in the west, bathed the landscape in a reddish yellow sunset, casting long shadows behind the low bushes and trees. Except for the occasional explosion of artillery shells near the bay, the world of Gaston Gauthier and Henri Ouilette remained peaceful. The two Acadians rested as gathering darkness extinguished the red hues of sunset. Gaston watched the night shadows form like a black apparition and creep stealthily down the hill. Early evening stars winked brightly in the clear night sky. Crickets chirped in the nearby grass. As a loon called to its mate on the bay, Gaston saw shadows sway. He rubbed his eyes. Was someone moving up the hill toward him? Gaston raised his musket and pulled the hammer back to full cock. At the hammer's click Henri Ouilette raised his head quickly. In an instant he lay beside Gaston with his rifle at the ready. "What have you seen, my friend?" he whispered.

"I thought I saw something move in the darkness," whispered Gaston, pointing down the slope toward the river.

"Don't shoot, Gaston," whispered Henri. "Maybe your eyes play tricks in the dark, eh? We will watch. You must watch in the darkness like the Indians, Gaston. Keep your eyes moving. You will see danger best from the side of your eyes, not from looking directly at it."

Both men watched the slope intently for several minutes, seeing nothing. Satisfied all was well, Henri pulled the goatskin water bag from beneath his bed roll. He pulled the wooden bung with his teeth and handed the bag to Gaston. Gaston turned the bag up and took a long drink. As Gaston passed it back, Henri gave him moose jerky and they lay chewing the hard, dried meat and talking softly. "Gaston," Henri began, "I think maybe I'll have to slip around behind those two marines with the swivel gun and kill them, eh? If we are to find Marie, we must be gone from here before the English attack, which I think will be maybe just before dawn. I think they will cross the river tonight and attack in the morning with the sun at their backs. I'll work my way across the slope…" Henri stopped talking in mid-sentence. He pressed his hand against Gaston's shoulder and motioned for Gaston to be quiet. "Maybe I thought wrong, Gaston," he whispered. "Lie still, maybe the enemy comes to visit us early." Henri watched the defile carefully. He shifted his gaze to one side of the defile, as he had been taught by the Indians, allowing him to better see an object in darkness. The minutes past slowly. Henri's limbs ached, but he moved not a muscle. As he watched, the silhouette rose slowly in the darkness. The dark figure rose to reveal a big man in buckskins with a coonskin cap. The man slipped quietly up the defile toward him, walking in a crouched position, placing heels down first on the ground, gently, like an Indian. Henri pulled the hammer on his rifle back to full cock. Instantly, the man dropped out of sight. Henri motioned for Gaston to train his rifle in the direction of the man. Henri quietly laid his rifle on the ground, waiting a few moments, then eased himself out of the ravine, moving slowly. Creeping through the grass, he circled to the side of the defile; his movement was so slow it was hardly perceptible. He slipped his skinning knife from its sheath and held it in his right hand, with the blade forward. Henri stopped. He fought to control his heavy breathing, crouching silently, like a coiled spring, ready.

Motionless in the darkness, Henri watched as the silhouette rose again from the defile and moved upward. In what seemed like an eternity, inch by inch the man moved, slowly, silently. The dark figure grew closer and loomed above him. Henri looked up at the man from waist level and sprang like a lion. In an instant his big, strong hand clamped over the man's mouth while the hand with the skinning knife darted back and forth into the man's buckskin jacket like a viper. The man twisted as he sank to his knees. His fingers dug into Henri's face. Henri dropped on top of him, continuing to hold the man's mouth as he twisted his knife and felt the warm life flow out of his opponent. The silence was broken by the sound of the man's gasp and the noise of his rifle rattling to the ground. Henri rolled quickly away from the lifeless body. The big woodsman heard a rattle of stones and wheeled around to receive either a headlong charge or the impact of a rifle ball in his chest. Another black silhouette charged him with an upheld tomahawk, buckskin fringes flying. Behind Henri, Gaston's musket roared with a flash of light in the darkness. A rifle ball caught the running man solidly in the chest, slamming him backwards. He fell heavily into the bushes. His tomahawk rattled on the rocky hillside as his legs and arms jerked in death. Henri's ears rang from the blast. The shot echoed across the valley, diminishing as it reverberated in the darkness. Then, once more, the dark valley was as silent as the grave.

Henri stood for a few moments, hearing only his own breathing and the ringing in his ears. He wiped the blood from his knife on the dead man's buckskins and sheathed his knife. Returning to Gaston, Henri knew at once something was wrong. Gaston lay motionless, his legs cocked crazily, his arms outspread. Henri felt the warm, sticky blood on Gaston's head and found the shattered musket lying beside him. He pressed his fingers against Gaston's throat and felt the pulse, weak and irregular against his skin. Holding his friends limp hand, Henri knelt beside him, wondering what to do. Looking up the hill, he considered the big swivel gun concealed behind the barricade, capable of cutting down twenty men in one blast. Henri thought of Marie alone in her cabin. He remembered the promise made to his friend on the ground beside him. The woodsman looked up at the sky and watched the dark clouds floating past the faintly glowing stars. He swore under his breath, then quickly crossed himself. With his skinning knife Henri cut a crude bandage from Gaston's shirt, wrapping it tightly around his head. He wrapped Gaston's blanket around him and tied it too.

A golden moon penetrated the darkness as Henri lifted the bundle that was Gaston Gauthier to his shoulders. He picked up his rifle, slipping out of the ravine. Henri's back and legs ached under his friend's weight, small man though he was. Moving in short, quick intervals from one dark shadow to the next, Henri waited, listened, and watched as he regained his breathing. Occasionally stumbling, he slowly moved across the hill in a wide arc, circling behind the swivel gun. Getting closer to the gun position, he moved more slowly, approaching from the rear, fighting for breath. He carefully laid Gaston's unconscious body on the ground, then examined the frizzen and pan on his rifle while recovering his breath. Henri checked to be sure his knife was ready. Inching his way forward, he slowly parted the grass to look down into the moonlit barricade. It was empty. There were no marines and no swivel gun. Henri eased himself down into the trampled grass inside the barricade, resting against the logs as he caught his breath and considered what to do next. *The marines are gone, but where have they gone? Did they return to the fort or merely move to a new location farther up the hill? If they had been only a little farther up the hill, they would surely have seen me crawling into the barricade.* Henri stood up to look around him. The moon illuminated the landscape and turned the river into a silver ribbon winding its way to the sea. All was quiet. He returned to Gaston, put his hands under his limp form, and straining, lifted him to his shoulder. Slowly, Henri set off toward Fort Beausejour, staying close to dark shadows. Expecting a rifle shot at any moment, Henri trudged through the tall grass and low trees, breathing laboriously with Gaston's body heavy on his shoulder.

He stopped suddenly. A soft sound, one that should not have been heard, jolted his mind. He stood motionless, his breathing heavy, his heart pounding. At last Henri's eyes found the location of the sound in the darkness. In a little willow thicket he saw something—a form he decided was a horse—tied to a tree. Quietly, he gently laid his rifle in the grass and walked that direction. Soon he perceived a French soldier, his chin on his chest, his hat over his eyes, his rifle laying in the crook of his arm, snoring loudly. Henri moved very slowly, inching toward the horse. The horse neighed; the soldier stirred in his sleep; Henri froze. Afraid to move, hesitant to breathe, he watched and waited. The woodsman waited a long while after the snoring resumed before feeling free to move forward again. Slowly, he approached the horse. Henri reached out to pat the animal gently on his withers. Slowly, carefully, gently, he eased the burden of Gaston Gauthier's limp body across the saddle. Henri untied the horse from a tree and rubbed the animal gently between its ears. He led the horse away while the soldier continued to sleep peacefully, stopping to pick up his rife.

Henri led the horse out of the valley and toward Fortress Beausejour. Slowly, they approached the clearing near the fortress where Henri paused. Concealed in the darkness, he stopped to formulate a plan. He removed one of his blankets and drew his knife. Carefully, he cut the blanket into strips. Laying Gaston across the saddle, Henri tied him securely. He then tied the horse's reins around its neck. Quietly, he moved back to the horse's rump and drew back his hand. Like a thunderclap Henri's hand sounded against the horse's rump. The horse reared, whinnied, and set out across the moonlit landscape in a gallop, its hooves rattling on the stones, running toward Fortress Beausejour. Henri yelled loudly. He then hid in the dark bushes and watched as soldiers rushed to the palisades, their silhouettes clearly visible in the moonlight. One man shouted, "Halt! Who's there?"

Henri heard them talking quietly between themselves and saw them pointing down at the ground. The men discussed the horse with Gaston's limp form tied to the saddle. In a short while the wooden gate creaked open and several men walked out, guns at the ready. Carefully, they approached the horse. One man lifted Gaston Gauthier's head. "He's been wounded," the man said. "Come, let's take him to the doctor." As two men stood with their muskets at the ready, the other men lifted Gaston and carried him inside the fort. Henri waited until the men disappeared then quietly moved away in the shadows.

Meanwhile, Marie was alone in her small cabin. *I must do something. Anything! I must keep my mind busy. I can be ready to leave Ft. Beausejour when Father returns.* She opened her mother's trunk, carefully removing and sorting the contents. Her most precious items she packed in an old seed bag. Marie returned the other items to the trunk and waited once more, long minutes becoming hours. At last she went to the hearth. Taking tender from a bag near the fireplace, she kneeled and struck the flint against steel. When a small flame ignited the tender, she blew until a tiny fire erupted. Marie laid birch bark shreds across the tender and followed with a few sticks until a roaring fire bathed the dark cabin in flickering light. Marie added logs and stood back, satisfied with her effort. With a burning taper from the fire she lighted two candles, twice as many as normal. Tonight she wanted light and would indulge herself.

Marie put on her apron. She opened a bag of dried beans and rationed them carefully into a pot. Marie added lard, salt, and a little dried codfish. With care she hung the pot over the fire. From the box she took a precious loaf of bread and laid it in a dish in the center of the table. By the light of a candle she opened her mother's box of silver. The forks, knives, and spoons glistened and sparkled in the candle light. Humming softly, Marie set the table with her mother's finest silver. In the wine goblets she poured dandelion wine. With hands on hips Marie stood, looking over her handy work. *What else?* Marie remembered her father's evening favorite, a cup of hot rum. It helped him sleep, he said. She fetched a cup from a peg in the wall and lifted the little rum crock from its place in the corner. Pouring a small amount into the cup, Marie stopped, and considered the measure. No, this has been a terrible day for father. She poured the cup almost full. *The evening is cool, and Father will enjoy the hot rum.* Lifting the fireplace poker; Marie placed the long, steel rod in the fire. She had done all she could think to do. There was little food or she would have prepared a feast. Removing her apron, she sat before the fireplace, waiting. Humming the tune to *Plaisir d'Amour*, she imagined her fingers running across the harpsichord keys, playing as her mother had taught her, playing as she had done many long winter evenings before the war. Her thoughts drifted back in time, across the river, at Beaubassin; how wonderful it was where families lived with plenty and peace abounded. Marie closed her eyes and dreamed of days gone by.

When the fire had burned down to embers and the candles burned low, when the food she had prepared for her father was cold, she stood up and looked outside into the darkness. Marie picked up the heavy steel poker and stoked the coals in the fireplace. She added more water to the soup and returned the poker to the flaming coals. Again, ready for her father's return, Marie slumped in the rocker, a hand to her throbbing temple. She sat rocking very slowly before the fire until the blaze waned to glowing embers once more. Catching herself nodding again, and feeling very lonely, she decided to sleep. The guns were almost quiet now; she could hear crickets outside. Marie stood and stretched.

Meanwhile, a French sentry stood quietly in the moonlight looking down over the Acadian cabins. Scattered musket fire sounded faintly in the distance where isolated fighting continued into the night, but between shots, crickets chirped. Occasionally a dog barked. The marine leaned against his rifle and rubbed the whisker stubble on his chin. He thought of the young Acadian girl. The man remembered the fairness of her skin and the silkiness of her hair. She smelled clean and fresh. He remembered the pleasure as his hand slipped across her firm young breast. Oh, how he would love to open her dress and run his hands over the bare flesh. His breath quickened. He visualized her standing before him in nakedness.

The marine looked out across the land and picked out her cabin in the moonlight. Maybe her old man is dead by now; along with other Acadians, he had been put in the front line. She would be alone in the cabin. He looked around to see if anyone might be watching. Dark clouds glided slowly across the moon, obscuring the countryside in darkness as they passed. The marine walked slowly, his big shoulders drooping as he carried his musket loosely in his hand. His hat shadowed his beefy face in the moonlight. Only the white shirt collar was clearly visible above his dark jacket.

Somewhere far away a dog barked again. The marine continued to walk slowly through the grass to Marie's cabin. *I need a woman*, he thought. *I may be killed tomorrow so what difference does it make?* The dog stopped barking as the French marine made his way past the first two cabins. Slipping quietly to Marie's cabin, he saw a faint glow coming through the little window near the door. Creeping closer, the man looked inside. Marie stood in the candle light, preparing for her bath. As he watched, she lifted her dress over her head. Removing all her clothing, she stood before him in nakedness as she bathed. Her firm young breasts, warm and aglow in the candlelight, kindled his passion. Her slim young body glistened as the droplets of water ran down her flat abdomen. His hand trembled and his breath came quickly. The marine reached for the door, then withdrew his hand quickly, almost in panic. *She might scream*, he thought, *waking every damn Acadian in the village.* Marie dried herself. The man watched excitedly as she drew her nightgown over her head and blew out the candle. He stepped back away from the window, standing in the shadows with his back to the wall, breathing heavily. *I must wait until she is asleep*, he thought. The marine sat quietly in the shadows and removed his hat. Leaning his head against the rough-hewn logs, he ran his trembling fingers through his damp hair as his mind wandered over Marie's body. A smile crossed his face as he shut his eyes and dreamed. He quietly laid his musket aside and slipped off his boots. Mosquitoes hummed around him. *Damn this hell hole*, he thought. *When will I ever get back to France?*

Looking up at the moon, he saw dark clouds scudding past. Picking out a nearby treetop, he decided to wait until the moon had risen over the top of that tree. *She will be asleep by then.* The man wondered when another marine would come to relieve him. Would the officer of the guard come to see if he was performing his duty? *Damn those officers... I wish the moon would hurry past the treetop… Oh, to hell with it.* He stood up and slipped his knife from his belt, creeping quietly to the cabin door. Slipping the blade between the door and its casement, his knife slipped down until it sliced through the leather hinge. Slipping the knife farther down the door, he sliced through the lower hinge and sheathed the knife. He slipped his fingers through the door, pulling it outward. The opening was so small he had trouble squeezing through. He pushed harder. With a loud crack, the wooden door's bolt snapped.

Chapter Five

Meanwhile, off Louisbourg that evening of 1755, *Grenadier* sailed in moonlight under silvery clouds that illuminated tossing seas with their brilliance. Only waves slapping and lapping against the ship and the creak of oak broke the silence until lookouts above called, "Deck there! Sail ho!"

Lieutenant MacGregor lifted the speaking trumpet from its rack to ask, "Where away and course?"

With eyes uplifted to the crow's nest he heard the faint answer, "Abaft the starboard quarter, course west-southwest."

MacGregor called the sailing master on deck and sent a message to the captain that a sail is sighted, bound for Louisbourg. "Wake the larboard watch and send the boatswain topside. Make ready to wear ship." He walked to the quarterdeck's windward side and swept his telescope across the dark ocean until he found a light speck across the flashing waves. His mind was busy calculating the distance and angle of tack when Captain Walshingham hurried out on the quarterdeck.

Captain Walshingham strode to the quarterdeck's windward side, his black cape flowing in the cool wind. He lifted his long telescope and glassed the darkness until he caught sight of the sails. "Mr. Sethford, wear ship." Captain Walshingham's orders rang across the decks. "Brace 'round the main yards, hand the jibs. Raise the courses."

From above came another report. "A snow, makin' fer' Louie'burg," the lookout cried from the main top crow's nest. His observation put a grin on the faces of seasoned sailors for they knew a snow would be easy pickings. There would be no eighteen-pounders smashing through the bulwarks, crushing bone and bodies.

"Ready the bow chase," ordered Walshingham quietly. Midshipman DeWitt relayed the order below with his eager young voice.

Lieutenant Black echoed the order. "Ready the bow chase!"

A flurry of activities brought clanking, banging, and then silence, as men removed restraints from the forward gun and made ready to fire. Silence hung over the gun decks as everyone waited. Silently again, *Grenadier* raced through the moonlight.

When the bulwark of the snow showed above the waves off the starboard bow, Captain Walshingham ordered, "Ready a shot across his bow as he comes in range."

Forward, on the gundeck, Mr. Black sighted the six pounder and responded, "Starboard bow chase ready." Time hung suspended as the two ships bounded across the gray seascape on converging courses. With spars, courses, and ratlines now visible in the moonlight, Mr. Black removed the telescope from his eye, snapped it shut, and ordered, "Fire a shot across his bow."

The cannon belched fire and smoke with a thunderous boom shattering the silence. A geyser, white in the moonlight, lifted in front of the snow as the sound echoed across the waves to be swallowed in the darkness. The snow sailed through the falling spray of the shot and continued its headlong run toward Louisbourg. Captain Walshingham opened his telescope and again aimed it at the snow. Slowly, he lowered his telescope, walked to the taffrail overlooking the spar deck to order, "Aim and fire the bow chase at her sails."

Black repeated his orders and the stillness was ripped by another cannon blast. Presently another geyser erupted just before the snow, and the ship sailed through the falling water. Now it slowly turned its bow into the wind, its luffing sails popping and snapping. It loosed a topsail, the international signal of submission. The snow now lay idle in the water, rising and falling on the silvery swells, moonlight dancing on its flapping sails. No flag or bunting marked its home port or master. H.M.S. *Grenadier* sailed slowly toward the suspicious ship. At seventy-five yards Walshingham ordered the bow back into the wind. "Heave to!" As the sails were backwinded, the warship slowed to a stop and Walshingham said, "MacGregor, speak to him in that fancy French of yours. See how he answers."

MacGregor rattled the speaking trumpet from its holder. He called in French, "Ahoy, what ship and where be ye bound?"

Their English answer returned, "The snow *Sarah Goodley*, Liverpool to Salem."

Captain Walshingham snatched the speaking trumpet from MacGregor's hand. He yelled, "In the name of King George, prepare to receive boarders, *Sarah Goodley*."

Walshingham ordered, "MacGregor, ye'll lead the boarding party! Pistols and knives for our lads and rifles with fixed bayonets for the marines. Find out what that ship conceals in her orlop."

Sailors rushed to the weapons lockers where the master at arms rattled firearms from the locker, passing them to eager hands that quickly loaded them. The ship's boat dropped from davits into the sea. Men tossed lines and called directions. MacGregor pulled his hat down tightly, feeling for his dirk. He shoved a loaded pistol under his belt while feeling for his claymore. Ready, he motioned for Sergeant O'Bannion. Sailors with pistols in their belts and cutlasses swinging from their waists climbed down into the boat. Sergeant O'Bannion led his red uniformed marines over the side. The coxson handed a lighted signal lantern down to a sailor's waiting hands.

MacGregor covered his pistol's priming with oilcloth and thrust it back in his belt. He hitched up his big sword and swung a leg over the side. With cloak flowing over his shoulder and blowing in the breeze, MacGregor descended the ladder, taking his place in the sternsheets. A sailor in the bow stood and shoved the boat away from the frigate while the coxswain's mate shoved astern. Sailors pulled at the oars and the boat moved away through the tossing waves. With long, smooth oar strokes, the sailors coursed the distance to their quarry.

Lieutenant MacGregor swung onto the rope ladder as his boat brushed the snow. A hand reached down from above and took the lantern. In an instant he found himself being helped aboard the ship by a bearded man in a black hat. "We welcome ye aboard, King's man, and bring all yer' friends," he said. "We are loyal subjects of King George, we are. Honest, seafarin' men, we are."

MacGregor lifted his lantern toward the man. "That's hard to believe, Sir. We watched you reaching into Louisbourg, and we know there's no loyal merchantmen sailing to Louisbourg these days."

"Oh, I was not going to Looie'burg, never. I was jist followin' the coastline down. Tryin' to avoid running aground on Sable Island, I was. Many a good ship foundered on Sable Island, ye know."

MacGregor signaled for his marines to follow him on deck before turning back to the man. "You almost ran aground on the mainland while skirting Sable Island," replied MacGregor. "And why didn't you heave to when we first fired a shot across your bow?"

"Pirates," the man replied. "You can never be too careful. I thought for sure you were pirates, I did. Them pirates sometimes fly the King's X over 'em too."

As Sergeant O'Bannion and his men trooped on deck, Lieutenant MacGregor said, "Now, let us have a look at your log book, and we will inspect your cargo."

"Well, now, it's a strange thing about our log book," the man replied. "My first mate left it in Liverpool, he did. I skinned his hide within an inch o' his life, but there was nothing I could do, a hundred miles out o' Liverpool. Nothing!"

Lieutenant MacGregor hesitated a moment. It would be unlikely the log book would leave the ship. And secondly, it was even more unlikely a captain would sail the Atlantic without a log. "Sailing without a log violates not only the Navigation Acts but all common sense on the sea. Let us go directly to your cargo, Captain," answered MacGregor. "May I see your manifest, please?"

"Why certainly," he answered. "It so happens I have the manifest right here in my pocket," he answered as he unfolded a piece of paper.

MacGregor took the paper. "Do you always carry your manifest in your pocket?" Without waiting for a reply he read, "Woolens, topes, calico, and hand tools. Is there anything else aboard, Captain?"

"There's nothing else, lad. Pretty cloth for the ladies to wear and hand tools for their men to earn the money to buy 'em."

"I've never seen a miracle before, Captain, but I'm expectin' to see one if there is only what is shown on your manifest," answered MacGregor. "Let's go below and have a look at that miracle. Come along with me, Captain. Sergeant O'Bannion, I will take two men while you remain on deck with the others. Bring our sailors aboard from the boat."

With the lantern in hand and the captain leading the way, MacGregor and his two marines followed to the cargo deck below. They walked down a narrow aisle between stacks of cargo wrapped in jute. Lieutenant MacGregor lifted his lantern high and pointed to a bundle, saying, "Remove that one, and expose the goods inside."

MacGregor looked into the captain's eyes as the two marines removed the bundle and began opening it. "Don't bother opening that one," MacGregor said. "Remove the one behind it."

The captain moved forward in an attempt to stop the marines. Hesitating, he rubbed his hand through his beard. "Lieutenant, there's no need for armed marines here. I'm a peaceable man and you can send them above while we discuss things below. I have here some other papers you ain't seen." The captain took a small bag from his pocket, holding it carefully so that only MacGregor could see the gold inside. It would be easy to slip the gold into his coat pocket; no one would be the wiser. *MacGregors are descended from kings,* he thought.

Standing erect, he lifted his chin and with sharpness to his speech, said, "Captain, I suggest ye' put those away and hope I forget I laid eyes on 'em. You're in a mite 'o trouble already, I'd say. Now, open *that* bundle." MacGregor said, pointing to the bundle below. Quickly the marines ripped it open, removing the jute covering and revealing a roll of calico cloth.

"Calico," quickly said the captain, "fer them lovely little fillies in Salem."

But the bundle's weight suggested there was more than cloth within. MacGregor ordered, "Unroll the bolt of cloth; there is more here than calico for the ladies." Behind him MacGregor noted a marine had leveled his Brown Bess at the sailor.

As the marine unrolled the cloth, a rifle clattered to the wooden walkway. MacGregor lifted the rifle to his lantern and slowly read the French inscriptions on the breech. Slowly lowering the rife, he said, "These rifles are the property of King Louis of France, Captain. You didn't buy these in Liverpool or Manchester. I've seen enough; we can go topside, Captain."

As MacGregor gained the spar deck's fresh air, he turned to the coxswain's mate and ordered, "Mr. Murphy, take two sailors with you to the captain's cabin. Find his log book and a true manifest, if there's one aboard." Reaching the snow's quarterdeck, MacGregor clanked the shutter on his lantern back and forth, sending a coded signal back to Walshingham. In a moment a flash of lights from the *Grenadier's* signal lantern returned his answer.

MacGregor said, "The Royal Navy will take your ship and cargo to Boston. The King's counsel will decide there if the vessel shall be seized with all its cargo. He will also decide what shall be done with you. Good luck to you and may God have mercy on you, man. In the meantime, you will be confined to your cabin and your crew will be confined below deck."

By sunrise a prize crew sailed away to Boston with the captured ship.

Chapter Six

That same night, Marie turned fitfully on her straw-filled bed in the lonely cabin near Ft. Beausejour. She shut her eyes and tried to ignore the popping and rattling of muskets in the distance. But suddenly, there was a different sound. A sharper crack sent fear through her body. She opened her eyes. There was a rustling noise from the door. In the ember's glow she saw a moving, dark form. Marie looked up as the silhouette loomed over her. A scream formed in her throat, but the sound was cut short as a sweaty hand clamped over her mouth. Terror filled her throat; her heart pounded; she twisted her head to the side and screamed. Her scream trailed into silence as the big hand slipped down and squeezed her throat. Marie felt the man's heavy body astride her. She scratched and clawed at the hands squeezing her throat. *I must breathe!* Her lungs were bursting, and her heart was pounding in her chest. Marie felt her consciousness slipping away. *Oh God, Mary, Mother of God! Don't let this happen. I can't die. It must not happen. My father needs me...* Her bursting lungs ached and stained for air.

The terrible pressure in her chest, her heart pounding, the throbbing in her head, and the pain in her throat all faded away into blackness. She struggled to push with her arms, but they were like lead and slowly fell to her side. Even her eyes failed. Only her ears continued to report the heavy breathing of the monster above her. Darkness slowly overcame her. Marie's struggle ceased as she plunged into a pit of blackness.

From the dark pit she heard her lungs gasping for air. Consciousness crept slowly into her mind as air filled her lungs. She felt her nightgown being lifted, but her arms seemed so far away... they would not move. With burning lungs and aching throat, Marie moved a hand, but her heavy arms would not respond. Marie stopped, lying still and quite, waiting for death as the man lifted her gown over her breasts. Rough, sweaty hands pawed her body and a foul breath filled her nostrils. *I will not die,* she thought as life-giving air flowed into her lungs. *I'll do what I must to live. Think! What can I do?* She fought to control her emotions. Marie lay still as the coarse hands squeezed her breasts. Fighting back an urge to scream, she bit her lips as his hand wandered her body. *I will survive*! *Think! What can I do?* Slowly, Marie lifted her hand and began to caress the sweaty, stubbled face of the man above her.

"Ah, ha, the farmer's girl maybe likes a little sex, no?"

Marie tried to speak. Her voice failed her. Marie struggled with her mind. *Think! Oh, God, think! I need time to think.* With a trembling voice, she said, "First, before we make love, let us have a drink of father's rum. It will put us in the mood for... love."

The marine replied in a shaky, panting voice, "No, no, I must hurry. My replacement comes soon to relieve me on the guard. If you scream, I'll kill you, you bitch."

"J-j-just one quick, little drink," Marie rejoined as sweetly as she could in her shaky voice, stroking his rough beard with trembling fingers. "Who will know you are here?" In a voice she hoped had not betrayed her, she said, "My father has good rum. I will fix you a hot cup of rum to drive away the chill." Marie gained courage as she felt the rough hands relaxing from her words. "Besides, you must get up and remove your clothing. It will be better without your clothes. I will pour your hot rum while you undress."

"Yes, yes, I will remove my clothes," he said in his husky whisper. "Fix me some of that rum but be quick about it... and no tricks!" To emphasize his last statement, he gripped her throat in his hand and raised his heavy fist, shaking it in her face.

As the big man lifted his weight from her body, Marie considered her adversary. *He is big and strong. Can I escape from him alive?* The big marine lifted his body from astride her. Marie stood on weak legs and caressed his cheek. Struggling to remain calm, she made her way to the hearth. Her hand trembled. Aided by the ember's soft red glow, Marie lifted the cup with a trembling hand. She walked toward the man and held it to his nose. Her courage mounted as the marine sniffed the rum. She forced a seductive smile, hoping he did not see her trembling lip. Marie watched as he removed his coat. With shaky hands he unbuttoned his shirt, fumbling with the buttons, as his eyes devoured her nakedness. The man squeezed her breast painfully, and she loosened his belt. Overcoming a scream, Marie turned her back on the marine with a shudder running down her naked back. She held the cup of rum and sought the iron poker in the fireplace. Praying it was still red hot in the coals, she saw the silvery handle. Yes, it was where she had left it earlier, ready to heat a cup of rum for her father. Marie lifted it with an unsteady hand, watching through the corner of her eye as he threw his shirt on a chair. He began removing his trousers with fumbling hands while keeping his greedy eyes on her naked body. She measured the distance to her adversary. Her heart beat rapidly in her chest; the blood pounded in her temples. She took a deep breath to speak without her voice cracking. "You will love this hot rum," she said. Marie carefully drew the hot poker out of the fire. The long iron poker glowed red, its tip yellow, with rising waves of heat. She lifted the glowing steel rod and held it swaying over the mug of rum. Marie looked over her shoulder to see the man bending over, with his trousers down around his ankles, lifting one foot off the floor. He struggled shakily to clear his uplifted foot from his trousers. Marie covered the distance in one stride, whipping the red hot poker ahead of her. She struck him in the face with the glowing iron. The marine recoiled in a searing, steaming, hissing instant of agony. He grabbed the poker with his hands and again raw flesh hissed on hot metal. Staggering backwards, the man swept the air with his hands as he fell. A scream filled his throat. With his feet tangled in his trousers, he fell on his back, rolled over, and raised himself to look at Marie with one wide, staring eye. A nauseating smell of burning flesh filled the little cabin. His vicious scream erupted and trailed off into a snarl as he raised himself to his knees. The marine lunged at Marie. His trousers again entangled his feet and he fell headlong before her. With both hands wrapped around the handle, Marie repeatedly swung the poker against the man's head, using all her strength. She heard the sickening thump as the poker struck the man's skull. She smelled burning hair and flesh as he raised himself again. Again and again she struck his skull. The man fell flat against the floor, his legs and arms moving jerkily. Tears welled in Marie's eyes as she continued to strike him with the poker. She cried hysterically as she stood with the poker raised above her head. Slowly, her strength ebbed away. The poker waved in her hands and clattered to the floor. Sobbing, Marie pulled a blanket from the bed and staggered into the corner of the cabin. Trembling, she wrapped herself in the blanket and collapsed on the floor, crying hysterically.

Meanwhile, Henri moved past the Acadian cabins as quickly as he dared. It had taken him several hours to travel from the ravine near the fort. Dawn would soon be breaking. He stopped in the shadows to catch his breath and watched the Gauthier cabin for signs of movement. Dogs barked in the distance. The northwesterly wind blew gray clouds across the dark sky. The air was cool and fresh. A rooster called for the sunrise. Henri moved silently out of the shadows, crossed the open ground, and pressed himself against the dark wall of the Gauthier cabin. Hugging the rough logs, he slipped around the corner. The toe of his moccasin touched a boot on the ground. Henri froze stiffly and listened as he saw the rifle beside the boots. He pressed tightly against the wall. Laying his rifle on the ground, he rose with his skinning knife drawn. Inching closer to the door, Henri held his breath. He listened. The door stood ajar and Marie's sobs sounded from within. In an instant Henri stood inside the cabin, his feet wide apart, his body low, his knife held ready, rapier-like, blade forward. In the dim light he saw the French marine's body. In one quick step he stood over the man, and in an instant, he flipped him on his back, holding the point of his knife at the man's throat. With a sigh Henri looked down at the dead man. Sheathing his knife, he eased across the room to Marie. Gently, he lifted her. Taking blanket and all in his arms, Henri laid her on the bed and tucked the blanket around her. Marie, wide-eyed, sat up with the blanket hugged around her, sobbing. Like a father, Henri held her closely, speaking softly into her ear.

Gently, he lifted Marie's head and wiped away the tears. After a few minutes she turned her wide frightened eyes toward Henri as if seeing him for the first time. "Henri, what will become of me? I have killed one of the King's soldiers." Not waiting for an answer, Marie continued weakly, "Father? Where is he? Is he... hurt?"

Henri turned his eyes away from Marie's as he answered, "Gaston is a little bit hurt, maybe he get hit on the head a little, but I think he will be all right. I took him to the fort so the doctor could look after him. I said to myself, I better let the doctor look after my friend Gaston, and I better go look after Gaston's little Marie. So I hurried over here as fast as I could. Now I think we better leave this cabin, eh?"

"Henri," she sobbed, "we must find Father and walk the trace to Miramichi. If anyone can get us away from here, you can. Please, you must go and take us with you."

With sadness in his eyes, he looked at Marie and answered, "My child, your father is in the Fort. The English will soon be at the walls, if they are not already. We can't go to him now, eh? I will take you to Miramichi, and after you are safe, I will return and find him. Now you get dressed. I will look after this fellow."

Henri walked to the door and looked out the cabin. He surveyed the area around the cabin in the semidarkness and seeing no one outside, walked back to the dead marine. With his hands under the man's arms, he dragged the body outside. Puffing and pausing to rest, Henri dragged the body far away from the Gauthier cabin. He placed it in the shadows, a short distance from a deserted cabin with its roof caved in. Henri gathered the marine's rifle and boots, dumping everything on the body. Resting momentarily, his hands on his hips, breathing heavily, he looked down on the near nude body. Satisfied that he could do no more, Henri returned to Marie's cabin. He paused outside the door and raised his hand to knock on the door.

It was then he felt the cold muzzle of a rifle behind his ear. The telltale click of its hammer sent chills down his spine. Henri froze. He held his breath and heard his heart thumping in his chest. He waited for the musket's roar to take his life. Instead, he heard a voice speaking in a language he did not understand. "Easy there, old man, don't move too fast, or I will blow your old gray head off."

Henri turned slowly to see a man in a fur cap with a rifle pointed at his head. Dressed much the same as Henri, the man wore buckskins. His rolled blanket tied across his shoulder showed he was a woodsman. His powder horn hung from a strap across the other shoulder. A beaded belt adorned his waist, supporting a shot bag and skinning knife. Henri watched as another man in buckskins appeared. The second man spoke softly to the first in English as he cautiously lifted Henri's knife from its sheath and placed it in his own belt. "This old geezer can't be too bad; he kilt' a French soldier. I saw him hiding the Frenchman's body in the bushes over there."

Inside, Marie stood dressed and waiting for her journey to Miramichi. Her tresses, neatly combed, flowed from a white peasant's cap and tumbled over a blue woolen shawl. A long, blue dress fell over the wooden shoes on her feet. With her most precious belongings packed inside a seed bag, and a blanket beneath her arm, Marie waited, ready for the journey to Miramichi. She stood anxiously, holding her breath, listening to voices outside. A shudder of despair swept over her, and her eyes swept the cabin for the poker.

Moccasin clad feet moved to the door. With Henri in the lead and a musket at his back, the three buckskin-clad figures moved near the cabin. A ranger pushed the door open with his foot, holding his rifle at the ready. The other man shoved his gun muzzle against Henri's back, forcing him inside the cabin.

They found Marie standing in the doorway with the poker lifted high above her head. Defiance drained from Marie's eyes as she stood looking into the muzzles of the two guns. Slowly, Marie lowered the upraised poker and closed her eyes with a prayer on her lips.

The two men spoke in English; Marie could not follow the conversation very well, so strangely did they speak the English language, not as her teacher had taught. One of them motioned Marie and Henri to sit on the floor against the back wall. He guarded them carefully while his friend kept watch through window in the door. The two men smelled of spruce smoke and sweat, and it was obvious they had not washed in many days.

The man near the door opened a pouch on his belt, removing jerky. He popped a piece in his mouth with dirty hands and began chewing as he watched

Henri and Marie. Cautiously; he offered a piece to Marie and Henri. While Marie declined by dropping her gaze to the floor, Henri quickly accepted a piece and happily chewed it. He uncorked his own water skin and drank. Henri opened a leather pouch of his own and offered the two men some parched corn. They readily accepted with nods of approval and with the sound of teeth gnashing loudly on the dry, hard corn. One man looked carefully at Henri as he made a sign motion, drawing his finger across his throat. He then jerked his thumb in the direction of the dead marine outside and sat looking expectantly at Henri. Henri solemnly nodded his head. The American smiled and made a sign of friendship.

Marie stood cautiously and walked to the fireplace. She stoked the fire, placing a kettle over the flames. With jerky, rice, and dried vegetables, she soon set bowls of steaming stew on the table. She poured cups of rum for them. Marie dared not speak. With trembling fingers she picked up a spoon and sipped the stew. Henri and the American Rangers picked up their bowls and wolfed down the stew, noisily nodding their approval. Soon Henri put his bowl away and sat sipping his rum. As he did so, he signed to the American Rangers. The woodsman took a pouch of tobacco from his belt and stuffed the bowl of his pipe. When Henri rose to take an ember from the fireplace, both Americans moved their hands to their knives, but Henri squatted before the fire and lit the pipe. With tobacco smoke swirling around the cabin, Henri first offered the pipe to one American and then the other. Soon the men passed the pipe from one to another; they smoked together and an animated conversation in broken English, fractured French, and Indian sign language turned to laughter.

Later Henri told Marie, "They have little love for the English and would do to some of the English what we did to the French marine. They are waiting until it is safe. Then they will take us to Fort Lawrence, across the river where all the Acadian civilians are being taken. Ships will come to take the Acadians away, they say."

Marie asked, "Where will they take us?"

"He does not know," Henri replied. "Maybe, across the ocean. To France maybe. Others say to an English colony. He does not know."

The sounds of a flute and drums signaled the approach of a regiment of red-coated English soldiers. In a long line of battle they marched under their colorful banners with rifles and bayonets reflecting the morning sunshine. The occupants of the cabin watched from the cabin door as the soldiers marched past, proud and disciplined in their scarlet tunics in the dawn.

With the last soldiers marching out of view, the two men directed Marie and

Henri outside. Slowly, they walked toward the Missaguash River with more Acadians joining them along the way. Mostly women and children, the Acadians carried their meager belongings with them. Soon they joined a long column of people marching toward Fort Lawrence, herded by American Rangers.

At the Missaguash River, the man with the red beard handed his rifle to his partner and picked Marie up in his arms, wading across the shallow ford. He deposited her safely on the other side, and they continued their walk to Fort Lawrence while the cannons thundered in the distance.

Crowded into crude shelters at Fort Lawrence, the Acadians waited for the fall of Fort Beausejour. The siege was short and casualties few. The French marines, almost one hundred and fifty strong, marched out the front gates of Fort Beausejour to surrender. Carrying their rifles, and with banners held high, they marched to drums and flutes. Behind them shuffled some two hundred Acadians men. Red coated English troops replaced French marines on the ramparts of the fort. The red, white, and blue Union Jack replaced the white *fluer de lis* on blue over Fort Beausejour.

At Ft. Lawrence Henri found the crude shelter where Marie huddled with three other women and six children. "Marie," he said happily, "it's over. They have surrendered, eh?"

Marie jumped to her feet. She ran to the door. "Now can we see Father?"

Henri replied, "The Englishmen say everyone in Fort Beausejour is a military prisoner. They can't mix with civilian prisoners, but an officer says maybe we can inquire about your father."

* * *

Weeks later, an English officer allowed Marie and Henri to visit Gaston. Marie put on the better of her two dresses. Happily, she bartered a little rum as a present. With the sun high in the sky, Henri and Marie left Ft. Lawrence, walking past the soldier's tents. The sight of Marie walking through the English camp brought hoots and whistles from lonely soldiers. They crossed the crude wooden bridge over the Missaguash River, walking past Acadian cabins, most now looted and ruined. Showing their pass to the red coated soldier at the fort, they were not admitted until Marie parted with a bribe of her father's rum. At last they found Gaston Gauthier in the hospital, sitting on his bed with his head wrapped in bandages. Tearfully, Marie embraced her father. Gaston closed his eyes tightly and his hands trembled as he held his daughter in silence. Later, Gaston asked, "What happened to me, Henri? I remember shooting the gun but nothing afterward. They found me tied to a horse."

Henri Ouilette smiled. "Gaston, when you loaded the rifle, you put in so much powder, the bullet crossed the ocean and fell in the English king's porridge. The rifle broke your head, I think."

"I never did much shooting before," replied Gaston. "But, why am I a prisoner and you are not, Henri?"

Henri lifted his big hands skyward and a broad smile spread over his face. "Gaston, the Englishmen find me with Marie and the other civilians. They find you in the fort with the soldiers. Maybe you went to fight the English, but not Henri Ouilette, no!" Henri asked with a wink, "You do not think I would fight the English, eh?"

Gaston smiled thinly. "Henri, thank God you are with Marie. You can look after her better than me, I think. Please stay with her, Henri, and watch after her."

Henri clamped his hand on Gaston's thin shoulder. "Gaston, just you get well and we will all look after each other, eh?" He leaned closer and whispered, "We will go to Miramichi when you get better."

Gaston looked thoughtful. "I'm not sure, Henri. Perhaps it is too late now. We should have listened to Marie and left sooner. The soldiers say we are to be taken to France in exchange for English prisoners. I will talk to them; perhaps they will allow you and Marie to come to France with me, maybe."

Marie took her father's hand. "Father, you are not a soldier. They should not take you to France with the French soldiers. What would you do in France? This is our home. We must stay here somehow."

"Yes, my dear. The French soldiers made me fight; I did not want to fight the English. But the English say that I have broken my vow not to fight the English." Gaston Gauthier lowered his head in his hands. "Now they will deport me. This is our home for generations, and we know no one in France. What would I do there, and what would you and Henri do in France? I must think. If only I could get my hands on some gold, but that is not possible here. I will sleep on the problem, surely I can do something."

Marie put her arms around her father. "Wherever they take you, I will find a way there myself. I will not be separated from you, ever."

Henri stood up. "I will see no one harms your little girl, Gaston." He whispered in Gaston's ear, "Maybe we escape and come for you when you are well."

It was several weeks and Henri came often to the tent where Marie stayed with two other women and their children. Marie knew by the way Henri held his head and by the sad look in his eyes that he had bad news to tell her. With his cap in his hand, he moved nervously. "Marie, my little one, I must talk to you. You must not be alarmed…"

Marie interrupted him. "Henri, I know you have bad news for me. Just tell me. I have become accustomed to bad news. What is it?"

Henri changed hands holding his cap and brushed the hair back from his eyes. He looked up and smiled self-consciously. "Maybe I don't have to tell you… you always seem to read my mind." He looked down at his feet and lowered his voice. "I have been to Fort Beausejour and looked at everything. I have talked to guards and other prisoners." He looked up at Marie with a pained expression on his face. "There is no way I can free your father from his prison in Ft. Beausejour. The English will not let any prisoners from Beausejour escape. They never take their eyes off those prisoners; they are not allowed outside the fortress walls. I have nothing for bribery. I thought of digging under the palisades… Gaston cannot climb over the walls, eh? Now it is too late; my friends say the French soldiers are to be taken away on a ship. My friends do not know where… maybe the English do not yet know where, eh?" The wrinkles increased across Henri's brow and his eyes looked as though he carried a heavy burden. "Marie, maybe I take you to Miramichi, alone. Gaston can come later. It would be easy to take you. You are young and pretty; a smile would take you past most guards. We could meet on the trail in the forest and easily walk to Miramichi. We can stay with Indian friends along the way. The English will never catch us." Pleadingly, he added, "You could maybe go to Quebec… maybe your father can talk the English into letting him go, eh?"

Marie held her hand to Henri's lips. "Henri, do not speak to me of leaving without Father. If we left here, I might never know where they have taken him. No! I will not leave without him. Wherever they take him, I will go. He would be heartbroken without me." Marie's eyes glistened. "Surely, heaven will not forever deny my prayers. We have suffered for more than six years. I think God must soon show us mercy." Marie sighed, her eye softened and she put her hand on Henri's sleeve. "God will make things better for us. I will stay here. If the English move Father, I will follow. I can't ask you to stay too, Henri. You must escape to Miramichi alone."

Henri smiled. "Now, why would I want to go to Miramichi? I know no one there. As for me, I can leave anytime I like, eh? I can live in the forest with the *Mi'kmaq*s or build myself a cabin anywhere I like. No," Henri continued, "I will keep my vow to your father. I will look after his little girl. Where you go, I go and where you stay, I stay. But I tell you truly, I have it on good authority from an American Ranger, who heard it from a friend who knows the Governor's secretary that they are coming with ships to take all of us away. I don't know where; they don't know where. The English are angry that the Acadians did not keep their vow, eh? They promised not to fight the English. That's why I want you to come away. It's possible you may be sent to one place, I to another, and your father to another."

Marie's eyes sparkled; she looked down, speaking softly, "I refuse to believe that God could be so unkind." Tears welled in her eyes when she looked up at Henri. "He has taken my brother and mother. He will not take Father too."

Chapter Seven

A few days later *Grenadier* sailed into Boston to retrieve her prize crew. Walshingham said, "MacGregor, I'm entertaining an aide to the Admiralty along with my friend, Brumley. He is a wealthy Boston merchant but a colonial like you. I think your presence at our dinner may impress him. You will dress in your best uniform and join us at dinner. We must entertain them tonight for we will sail to Halifax on the morning tide."

The sun was low in the west when Lieutenant MacGregor hurried on deck. MacGregor scanned the harbor to see a long boat approaching with Captain Walshingham's guests. The overloaded boat moved slowly, plowing deeply in the water with its gunnels almost awash. As it eased against the ship, MacGregor nodded at the boatswain. The boatswain snapped his rattan under his arm and lifted his pipe. With his face turning red, a trill from his tin pipe echoed across the water. In the boat below a portly lady, filling the boat's thwart from gunnel to gunnel and twirling her pink umbrella, waited to be hoisted aboard. Sailors moved according to plan. The bosun's chair fell quickly into waiting sailors in the boat. They loaded a passenger in the chair and sailors on deck heaved at the cathead. With squeaking blocks, groaning ropes, and heavy breathing from the sailors, a hefty lady rose slowly over the bulwarks, swinging in the bosun's chair. Holding her pink umbrella with one hand, the lady squeezed her eyes tightly shut. Over the bulwarks rose the swinging chair. Ten hands reached every part of the lady's anatomy. Wiggling and giggling, she allowed a sailor to guide her feet to the deck, holding her ankle and thigh. Other hands slipped the bosun's chair over her head while lifting her dress high over her waist. She continued to stand, eyes tightly shut, with a grin on her cherubic face. "Oh, my! I think I'm in good hands!" Down onto the deck the bosun's chair rattled as she giggled, "Can I open my eyes now?"

"Yes, Ma'am, you are safely aboard His Majesty's frigate *Grenadier*," answered MacGregor. "And the safe hands will now see to the other guests," he yelled sternly at the grinning seamen. Smiles faded and men dutifully hurried away.

The lady looked at MacGregor with eyes wide in pleasure. "Oh, you must be the handsome young Scotsman I heard about," she giggled. With thick arms she pulled MacGregor's face down and planted a wet kiss on his lips. From between the cleavage threatening to flow out of her bodice, she drew a fan, spreading it over her ruddy face.

MacGregor turned to help the second lady now arriving on deck in the bosun's chair. He elbowed the disappointed sailors aside and guided the chair ropes himself. The bony looking woman was hardly on deck before one gentlemen climbed over the taffrail, followed quickly by another. MacGregor shook their hands. "Welcome aboard His Majesty's frigate *Grenadier*. Follow me, please. I'll escort you to Captain Walshingham's cabin."

The marine guard opened the door to Walshingham's cabin and snapped to attention. As the guests hurried into the cabin, Walshingham bowed. Side boys stood attentively as the cabin blazed with the light of a dozen candles in the candelabrum and oil lamps lit every wall. Walshingham's little chamber orchestra played a fanfare from Handel. Walshingham strode forward, his portly body resplendent in a fancy red uniform of his own design, featuring a bright yellow sash covering his rotund waist and shining medals clinking and rattling on his chest. Most medals were liberated from captured French officers. Captain Walshingham tugged his lapels as he spoke. "Tonight's dinner, my friends, will be a farewell dinner as well as a reunion, for His Majesty's frigate sails again on the morrow to do the King's bidding."

Mr. Brumley's interest quickened. "And what might be the King's bidding? What is your destination? Does the entire fleet sail or only your frigate?"

MacGregor wondered about the merchant's volley of questions on the fleet sailing. Many local merchants made rich profits, he knew, from dealings in contraband. If Brumley, like most American merchants, violated the Navigation Acts, he would certainly be interested in the fleet's whereabouts.

Captain Walshingham smiled. "Ah, careless lips sinks King's ships!" They smiled at the familiar admonition as he continued, "Ladies and gentlemen, I have a special treat for ye. My orchestra will play a flute sonata by our new ally, King Frederick of Prussia, written by his own hand. He is as talented in music as he is in war!" Captain Walshingham turned to his musicians and waved his hands like an orchestra conductor as his guests listened to the flute sonata.

With the music's conclusion, side boys put glasses into waiting hands. Brumley raised his glass to Walshingham. "Good hunting, Captain. May fortunes await you in French ships."

Mr. Whitham lifted his glass also, his narrow eyes impassive. "He already holds the attention of the Admiralty with his captures. His name is on every lip there."

Walshingham hung his head in a display of modesty. "I regret, Mr. Whitham, that French prizes escape while we waste time enforcing Navigation Acts on American vessels."

Abraham Whitham waved a hand in the air. "There was a time when we knew how to handle scofflaws. There's nothing like dancing at the end of a rope to take the devil out of those who violate the Navigation Acts." Brumley smiled and patted Whitham on the back, nodding his head in agreement.

Captain Walshingham smiled over his whiskey glass. "There would be few left to hang in America and no one to hang them."

Whitham turned to Brumley. "The King's colonists should trade only with England. When I return to Whitehall I shall propose stern measures to enforce our tariffs."

Brumley replied, "Our Crown might profit by listening to the colonials. A little fair trade between colonies will do nothing but strengthen the colony, which can only be good for England. High tariffs discourage such trade, making everyone the poorer. The colony could eventually fail. Where would England be without her colonies?"

Like a teacher, Whitham returned, "England will not be without her colonies. The Crown will not allow the failure of her colonies and would make short shrift of any insurrection. Once a colony of England, always a colony of England."

Brumley tossed down his whiskey and smiled broadly. "I've heard how Indians in baggy bloomers imprison our soldiers in the Black Hole of Calcutta."

"Oh, posh," replied Whitham. "We will send our man, Clive, back there. He will put an early end to the Bengal business. Besides, it is the French who make trouble there, as elsewhere. We must do something about the French."

Brumley responded, "The French make trouble everywhere. You can't kill a snake by striking at his tail; you must strike his head. Never mind Calcutta or America, England should strike in France."

"Yes, yes, I agree," replied Whitham. "We should invade France and put an end to this nonsense once and for all."

Walshingham held up his hand in protest. "I'm afraid England is not up to that task. Let's leave that messy business to our friend King Frederick of Prussia. We will defeat the French at sea, that is our strength and their weakness."

Whitham dabbed at his lips with a linen handkerchief. "Captain Walshingham, why is it the navy cannot stop the flow of supplies to Louisbourg with their blockade? The French should have abandoned Louisbourg by now.

I've seen the maps. It seems to me very simple; all supplies must enter the narrow harbor entrance to Louisbourg. The navy need only sit there with their battleships and prevent the French from entering."

Walshingham looked condescendingly at his guest. "Weather isn't shown on yer maps. Louisbourg fogs are so thick, ye can't see yer ship's bow, never mind a Frenchman a cable distance away. He may as well be on the other side of the world. Gales lash the coast with onshore winds. Such storms keep our ships far out to sea while French ships run Louisbourg's safety. In spring, great icebergs drift down from the Cabot straits. Unseen, they can crush a ship and send it to the bottom."

Whitham looked blankly at Walshingham. "That Scotsman, Commodore Holmes, has kept us liberally supplied with excuses such as you have described. We would welcome a report describing something other than the inclement weather, maybe victory at sea?"

Walshingham lifted his wine glass and held it aloft as everyone followed his action. "Victory at sea and glory to the King!"

"Just a moment," Abraham Whitham interjected before the other dinner guests could respond. He looked suspiciously at MacGregor. "Let us remove the finger bowls before toasting our king. You know, the Jacobites hold their wine glasses over their finger bowls as they toast their king over the water, meaning that Scottish pretender Charles Stuart who hides at the French court."

The other dinner guests, with embarrassed glances at each other, shifted their finger bowls to the side. They responded in subdued voices, "Victory at sea and glory to our king."

Whitham set his wine glass on the table and leaned back in his chair, looking at Walshingham. "Perhaps our ally, King Frederick of Prussia, might give us some pointers at Louisbourg, Captain?"

Walshingham looked at Whitham under his bushy brows and smiled benevolently. "King Frederick is rather busy with Austria. He guards his flank against France and hopes to keep the Russians out of the war. But his niece, Sophia, perhaps soon to be Queen Catherine II, tries to persuade Russia to aid him. Frederick is outnumbered wherever he turns. Alas, Lloyds would never insure King Frederick."

Mrs. Whitham ceased fanning herself. Holding her fan in the air to gain attention, she gushed, "Oh, I do so wish King Frederick would come here. I would ask him to play some of his music. I just love it. Your orchestra played beautifully. Captain Walshingham, King Frederick must be a genius like you."

Walshingham smiled demurely, replying, "As long as he orchestrates against the papists with his cavalry, I will recognize him as genius too."

Walshingham turned his attention to the food. From beneath his coat he drew his dirk, slicing a piece of roast beef. He said absent-mindedly, "The Swedes and the Russians may enter the war against Prussia while Spain joins France against England. As more colonies become involved in America, Africa, and India, the whole world may be at war. We may find Prussia our only ally, fighting with England against everyone." Walshingham waved the speared beef on his dirk as he continued, " I hope ye enjoy this roast beef; it is marinated in a special wine I liberated from the enemy near Madras."

Whitham persisted, "France may invade England. What are their chances of succeeding, Captain Walshingham?"

From his dirk point Walshingham stuffed a piece of roast beef in his mouth; he chewed for some time before replying, "None! Do ye think French soldiers can swim the English Channel with their cannons? Bilge-rot!" He waved his knife in the air. "French ships can't take them across; our navy would blow them out of the water. It would be the end of France. I would to God they should try."

Whitham turned to MacGregor with piercing eyes. "But if France should invade England, Ireland would certainly rebel. And what of your Scots, MacGregor? On which side would your Highlanders fight? Would they not invade England from the north?"

MacGregor looked up quickly, his jaw muscles rippling. "I've never been in Scotland, Sir. I'm a loyal officer of King George and don't know how the Scots may feel."

Whitham addressed the others. "The French often try to force a Catholic on our throne. It's not only the French that concern me. Armed Highlander regiments are in all our colonies. They could turn our weapons against us, making Jacobite fiefdoms of every British colony, especially here in America."

A fork clinked noisily in the quiet room. MacGregor measured his response. "Correct me if I speak not the truth, Sir, but I believe many Scots died fighting for England at Culloden. Is that not so, Sir? Now Highlanders spearhead most attacks of the British Army. How much blood must they shed to prove their loyalty? It's said by some that using Highlanders as cannon fodder is a clever English solution to the Scottish problem."

While slicing off a piece of onion, Walshingham waved his knife in the air, his blazing eyes piercing MacGregor. "Bah! Highlanders die because they like to fight. They love war. It is a man's vocation, and there's no more noble endeavor than combat. I, for one, would not care to live in a world without war."

Walshingham smiled graciously. "We have much heavenly music for ye. But first, I'm sure that we older folks must be boring our young Mr. MacGregor. Keen officer that he is, he's anxious to do his rounds. Ye are now excused, Mr. MacGregor," he concluded with a sweet smile.

MacGregor carefully folded his dinner napkin and nodded at the guests. He stood and nodded at Walshingham, saying, "By your leave, Sir, I am indeed anxious to make my rounds." He forced a smile and stepped briskly out the door.

With MacGregor's departure Walshingham struck up the music while his guests drank and listened to Bach's *Brandenburg Concerto*. Afterward, Walshingham resumed. "I suggest Mr. Brumley should be appointed Prize Commissioner for Boston. A colonial prize commissioner would send a strong message to the colonials that America is a part of England. And since he is well known to ye, Mr. Whitham, his fairness in prize distribution could be explained at the Admiralty as well as Whitehall. Ye can be confident that prize captains will be anxious to share their reward with such fair and objective judges as yerselves."

"I agree," said Whitham. "Appointing a local commissioner here would be a stroke of genius to mollify our colonials. And you can be sure I will be an assiduous servant before Whitehall in earning any stipend that might come my way."

"Such an appointment would be well received here in the colony," rejoined Brumley. "I will work hard to make the office appealing to my fellow Americans. At the same time, I can allow my colleagues here in Boston to purchase French booty for resale. A little profit goes a long way in winning allegiance."

With a scrape of his chair Walshingham stood, his eyes glowing, and lifted his glass. "Wonderful! Then let us drink a toast to this infant genie born here tonight... a servant who shall grow tall and strong in our service! He shall provide rewards while strengthening the colonial alliance. Let us drink to our success!"

Whitham stood slowly, inclining his head toward Walshingham, and then turned to Brumley with uplifted glass while he responded, "Our success! You can be assured that the appointment of our new prize commissioner here will be the first item in my report."

The next morning *Grenadier* again eased out on the tide, a grey ghost slipping silently across a black harbor, her tall masts silhouetted against the sky.

She ghosted in the ebbing tide until a zephyr caught her limp sails. It became a breeze and filled those sails as the rising sun turned them to a golden hue. Finding the open sea, the fresh wind propelled her forward, and the New England landscape slipped away behind her. Cold gales blew from the northwest, sending tall waves with horses manes leaping over the frigate's decks while steadily they sailed toward Nova Scotia.

There, *Grenadier* and *Gladiator* plied the Grand Banks and blockaded Louisbourg. Three weeks later, they responded to a call from the Commodore and rode gently at anchor; their images reflected in the smooth water of Halifax Harbor. Sailors in a dozen small boats ferried supplies and foodstuffs aboard the ships in quantities never before seen. All day long they transported barrel after barrel of salted beef, lashing them into every crevice of the ships. Workers hastily constructed pens on the spar deck and sailors filled them with squealing pigs, sheep, and even goats. Six head of oxen, prodded by sailors in boats, swam reluctantly out to the ship. With much shouting and cursing, slings were forced under the panting beasts, and they were lifted out of the water by ropes strung over derricks from the windlass. Then, with sailors grunting and pulling ropes and with much bellowing of the oxen, the great beasts were lowered one by one into stalls constructed on the gun deck.

Goats bleated loudly from makeshift pens on the quarterdeck, leaving only small passageways to conn the ship. Never had the crew seen so much food. Sailors chatted eagerly of the upcoming journey. They would eat like kings, with their choice of meats at every meal, they said.

For every lighter of supplies loaded on *Grenadier*, its sistership, *Gladiator*, received an equal load. At last, when it seemed the ships could hold nothing more, when their water lines were almost below the safety limit, men built additional wooden enclosures on the forecastles and filled them with more chickens. One old salt observed, "If we don't keep those chickens flying all the time, this ship will surely sink." Farther away, almost out of sight of the two frigates, a troop ship was being loaded with far more produce and animals than both frigates combined.

After days of preparation *H.M.S. Grenadier* rode low in the water off Halifax Harbor. She was full to the brim. Sailors joked that by the sounds and smells they must rename the frigate Noah's Ark.

The next morning Walshingham ordered boats to ferry sailors to the Halifax parade grounds. Officers stood in two short ranks behind Walshingham. Four long ranks of sailors, most barefoot and hatless, stood before their captain. Smartly uniformed marines stood in two short ranks to the side, armed only with belaying pins as they guarded a stack of kegs. Nearby, tethered to a stake by his hind leg, a large billy goat with big curving horns bucked, kicked, and snorted. In a cage nearby a pig squealed and shook his cage, trying to escape.

Captain Walshingham was in a jolly mood. Smiling, nodding, patting his belly, and strutting in front of the assembled men, he said, "Lads, today I have a treat for ye. We are having a jolly good party before we depart Halifax. There will be plenty to eat and drink." His smile turned to an angry glower. "But by God don't kill each other partying! Good seamen are hard come by." His scowl quickly faded and his pleasant smile again spread over his face. "Ye shall have all the vittles ye can eat, and ye may enjoy killing yer own meat. Then I personally shall cook it for ye." A great cheer rang out from the men. Walshingham lifted his hand for silence. As men's cheers died away, Walshingham drew his sword, pointing to the billy goat. The animal struggled at the stake binding his leg. It lowered his head and charged toward Walshingham. At the end of his tether the rope pulled the goat short of striking him. He bowed to the goat. Sailors cheered happily until the captain raised his hands to silence them. "This goat is part of yer dinner, men. Ye may use no weapons on him, no stone nor club nor dirk. Only yer head and yer hands. Those are the rules. The man who kills the goat wins a bottle of my good whiskey and can keep the goat's hide and horns." Again the sailors cheered wildly.

"The pig will be well greased and a turpentine plug shoved under his tail. He'll be fast as lighting and difficult to catch. The man who returns him also wins a bottle of my whiskey! Go at them, lads, and have fun! But keep yerselves in condition to serve the six fine whores of Halifax I have procured for ye aboard our ship. They will be waiting when ye return, and I shall be sorely disappointed if any woman can walk when my sailors are finished." Cheers erupted; hats flew in the air; men leaped and slapped each other on their backs. Walshingham yelled, "Now, have a drink of ale, men, and we'll start on the goat."

In a crushing mob, sailors invaded the ale kegs, each struggling for a larger share. To prevent toppling the ale kegs, marines whipped the men into lines with belaying pins. When every man held his ale in his hand, they marched toward the bleating goat. Gleeful sailors formed around the goat as a balding man with a long, red scar across his face quaffed his ale and tore off his shirt. Snorting, he crouched low, facing the billy and pawing the ground with his bare foot. The goat lowered his head. With his head lowered too, the sailor charged the goat. With a resounding "thwack" they collided. The sailor fell backwards, shaking his head, but smiling broadly. Twice the goat struck the man as he attempted to rise. Sailors laughed, made bets, and cheered. Time after time the sailor crashed into the goat, but tiring, with his nose bleeding and one eye swollen shut, the big sailor fell backwards. Another husky sailor grabbed the man and slung him aside, rushing to take his place.

With scuffling and arguing over whose turn was next, fist fights erupted. Again, marines waded into the sailors with belaying pins, flailing the men across the back and jabbing them in the stomach to restore order. The more belligerent felt the oak on their skulls. Reluctantly, the sailors formed a line. Then sailor after sailor lowered his head and charged the billy goat, thrashing and sweating in the dust. The men dragged an unconscious sailor from the ring as more men happily rushed the tiring animal. With cuts, scrapes, and bruises, the men watched with disappointment as one man drove the exhausted billy goat against the stake with his head. The sailor repeatedly battered the dying goat against the stake.

Captain Walshingham walked into the ring, holding his sword aloft. He circled the exhausted goat. With a deep bow Walshingham held both hat and sword aloft. He twirled the sword downward, plunging it into the writhing goat. The sailors cheered hysterically as he withdrew the bloody sword. Walshingham wiped the blood from his sword on the clothing of an unconscious sailor lying nearby. The captain stood with a boot on the dead goat, his sword high in the air. "Cooks! Take this tasty morsel for yer fires. There, I personally shall prepare a feast for the best damn sailors in any navy!" The men cheered hysterically.

Captain Walshingham raised his voice above the din. "But first, follow me, men, the play is not yet over." He led them to the pen with the squealing pig. Walshingham nodded at the sailors, holding the pig. Released, the squealing pig dashed away, pursued by a thundering herd of shouting, shoving sailors. While the melee thundered around the parade ground after the pig, cooks skinned and quartered the goat. With the goat roasting over a fire, the frightened pig ran all over the parade ground, chased by the band of screaming, yelling, shouting, cursing, falling, fighting sailors until the pig too roasted over the fire.

Scratched, bruised, and bleeding, sailors limped happily back to the ale kegs to refresh themselves. With Walshingham himself serving food, the men ate, drank, fought, and sang. They feasted on goat, pig, beef, ducks, and geese with lots of gravy. At sunset, herded by the marines with belaying pins, men limped back to the boats, carrying comrades unable to walk. Some injured and drunken sailors required a sling and tackle to board the ship. However, most flew quickly up the boarding ladder to find the six whores of Halifax waiting aboard. Beefy-faced and grubby but beautiful in the eyes of drunken sailors, they waited in the infirmary. At the door, the boatswain stood, collecting tolls. He left his station only long enough to rout any sailor overstaying his allotted time or causing problems for the women.

    The next morning, a limping sailor, his broad smile displaying a missing tooth, hoisted the Blue Peter on the signal halyard with a bandaged hand. He was assisted by a comrade with one eye purple and swollen shut. Sick, injured, but happy ship mates cheered as they saw the colorful signal glide up the mast and flap merrily in the breeze. Contented, bruised, and penniless sailors marched around the windlass, hoisting the anchor from the Halifax mud. They watched the northwesterly breeze slowly turn their ship seaward. Sailing much more slowly than usual, they sailed past the high cliffs overlooking the harbor. *HMS Grenadier* lay several inches deeper in the water than usual, so heavily she was loaded. Elsewhere in the harbor, *Gladiator* and the troop ship made sail, only more slowly.

    Grenadier sailed sluggishly, but morale was never so high. Sailors' laughter and banter often drowned out the bleating sheep and squealing pigs. No seaman knew their destination, but everyone knew they had never been so well prepared for a voyage. When they turned south, the sailors at the scuttlebutt[2] reported their destination was the East Indies by Cape Horn. Young Midshipman Collingwood, standing on the quarterdeck, cleared his throat. Summoning his courage, he ventured a statement. "Mr. MacGregor, I'm looking forward to serving with the East Indies Squadron. Surely, Sir, we must be going to India, since we are obviously supplied for a very long voyage."

    MacGregor turned to look up at the men setting the topsails, diminutive on their lofty perches high above the deck. "Likely we'll know our destination this evening, Mister Collingwood. But there are many merchant ships in this roadstead. I suggest you concern yourself with insuring we do not collide with one on our way to sea." Midshipman Collingwood pulled his hat down on his head and bounded down the steps.

    Grenadier sailed slowly south, past Pennant Point while their sister frigate and the troop ship were mere splotches of sail behind them. With *Grenadier* sailing the vanguard, the three ships proceeded south. Acres of canvas caught the westerly wind, driving the heavily laden frigate on a sea churned white with tossing waves. Steadily, the ships sailed as pigs squealed, sheep bleated and roosters crowed. Hours turned to days and on Sunday, as they sailed past Seal Island, Captain Walshingham mustered *Grenadier*'s crew on the sun-baked deck. It was time for Walshingham's Eventide Service. With his officers and midshipmen behind him, he opened his prayer book to the service. Awkward and uncomfortable, the men stoically resigned themselves to the usual Sunday sermon, just another hardship to be endured in service to the Royal Navy and not nearly as dangerous as some. The Royal Marines stood smartly to the side on the spardeck.

Walshingham read the scriptures in a voice befitting Westminster Abbey. Only the crowing of roosters, bleating of sheep, and squealing of pigs subverted the service from becoming a monument. His sermon was short and to the point. "Lads, papists and heathen hold sway in many lands, and by God, the Royal Navy will change that. It's up to ye lads to rid the sea of infidel ships. We shall sink them wherever we find them... after we liberate everything worth taking. Amen!" The sailors cheered and their amens resounded across the deck. Walshingham stood, arms folded, rocking from heel to toe, smugly nodding to the men. Every sailor's happy face reflected admiration for their captain. They sang Walshingham's favorite hymn, Bach's *Fire of God*, and were dismissed for warm beer and a Sunday feast with fresh meat, bread and cheese.

The successful service seemed to bring fair winds until Wednesday dawned hot and still. With no breeze to ripple its surface, only a long, low, swell rolling into the Bay of Fundy from the Atlantic ocean furrowed the glassy water's surface. The swells rocked the ship slowly from side to side, slatting the empty sails and creaking the timbers. As the morning wore on under the hot sun, odors from the animal enclosures hung languidly in the damp air. Perspiration washed down mens' faces. Their clothing looked as though they had been overboard. Walshingham posted a marine guard at the scuttlebutt to ration water.

At noon Captain Walshingham assembled the men on the hot, blistering deck to perform the "wind ceremony." Under the broiling sun the ship's officers stood on the quarterdeck. Beneath their woolen coats perspiration slipped down their backs in rivulets. On the spar deck, sailors formed long rows on both sides of the foremast. Old sailors watched knowingly as the sailing master slowly descended the steps from the quarterdeck, his heavy shoes sounding loudly on the stairs. With uplifted chin Mister Sethford walked across the deck, his hands clasped behind his back. In that tradition of the sea, Mister Sethford stood before the foremast. He rubbed the gray stubble on his chin, looked aloft, and lifted a dirk from his belt. Gripping the knife in his fist, Sethford held it aloft. Puckering his dry, cracked lips, he practiced a whistling noise. The sailing master lifted his knife higher and plunged it into the portside of the foremast in a thump heard across the quiet ship. Sethford removed his hat, wiping the perspiration from his brow on his woolen sleeve. He moved his puckered lips near the knife handle. Confident he had found the correct musical key, the sailing master pursed his lips and began to whistle. As Sethford's raspy melody drifted across the decks, no other sound could be heard save the creaking of the ship and slatting of the sails. Hushed and superstitious sailors stood on tiptoe, straining to see Sethford's actions. Old hands watched critically to see that no conventions were omitted. A few men glanced at the sky, hoping to be the first to see the heavens parted by wind.

Captain Walshingham kept the men standing in the broiling sun for almost an hour as Sethford's monotonous tune drifted over the empty ocean and foul odors from the animal pens offended the nostrils. A midshipman lost consciousness and fell to the deck, but no one risked interrupting Sethford's rite. The sailing master carefully whistled on all sides of the knife, leaving no part of the ritual undone. At last he doffed his hat to Captain Walshingham. The captain nodded at the boatswain. The boatswain lifted his tin whistle, blowing a long, high-pitched trill. Reverently, the sailors broke ranks, moving away from the ship's mast to the rails where they engaged in hushed conversations, waiting for the expected wind. That night, many sailors kneeled on unaccustomed knees to add their own petition to the force of the sailing master's ritual.

Wednesday morning dawned hot and still, with their other two ships far astern. Walshingham assembled the crew on deck. "Men, we have business on behalf of our King. We can't sit idly in the Bay of Fundy. I want two boats over the side with twenty men each and a thirty-fathom tow. Lieutenant MacGregor will command the boats, and every man on this crew will have a turn at the oars. The Lord has shown his displeasure at this crew's wicked behavior by withholding the winds from the sea. Now ye must do penance. All ye sinners will serve a turn at towing *Grenadier* from a ship's boat. Perhaps the Lord will be satisfied and return our wind."

Privately, he whispered to MacGregor, "I want a steady twenty strokes per minute. Change the boats every two hours.

"Mr. Black, yer station shall be on the forecastle with the sand glass to apprize MacGregor as to timing and change of boats."

Under the blazing sun, sailors lowered boats onto the mirrored ocean's surface. With throbbing heads and bleeding hands, the sailors pulled at the oars, twenty strokes per minute as MacGregor sat stiffly in the sternsheets, sweat pouring down his back. Several men lost consciousness and dropped to the bottom of the boat while their mates rowed harder and faster to maintain the pace.

Animals died in the sun's heat. Their bodies, swollen and smelling, were dragged from their cages. Sailors with handkerchiefs tied around their faces threw the rotting carcasses in the sea where they seemed to follow the drifting ship. Late in the afternoon, when the sun hung like a blazing ball of fire, the lookouts spotted a line of squalls to the northwest. MacGregor altered course toward the dark clouds. The men pulled at the oars with renewed vigor, an end to their agony in sight. Rowing hard for three hours, they intersected the squall but found only a fleeting breeze and a few drops of rain. The paltry breeze failed to drive the sails. Disheartened men again bent their backs to the oars, rowing through the heat of a brilliant orange sunset, pulling into the stillness of a windless night. After dark, MacGregor stood for a few moments on the quarterdeck, watching the occasional faint glow of lightening on the horizon. Relieved on the watch by Midshipman Collingwood, he walked wearily to his berth and fell asleep in exhaustion.

The next day their sister ship and the troop transport had disappeared from view. MacGregor returned to the stern sheets with salt stains on his woolen coat. In the broiling heat, a semiconscious sailor lay at MacGregor's feet, his teeth chattering and his body shaking. There was nothing MacGregor could do for the luckless man until it was time for a crew change. All day sailors toiled at the oars as the sun dominated a cloudless sky.

It was long after dark when Mister Sethford's whistling finally produced results. A gentle breeze drifted across the water with the smell of rain. Lightning flashed and thunder rolled loudly across the black sky. Squalls filled the sails with wind. The rain started an hour later. With blistered and bleeding hands, sailors fought to recover the boats in tossing seas. They suffered more injuries as the waves smashed boats and limbs against the ship's hull. By midnight *Grenadier* thrashed through six foot seas and a driving rain under full sails. Tired, weary sailors, freed from their oars, stumbled to their bunks. Before they fell asleep in their wet, salt-caked clothing, they rejoiced that Mister Sethford's ritual had brought them wind. At midnight the wind rose to gale strength. The boatswain hurried between the bunks, blowing his pipe and prodding men with the rattan. "Awake, ye' little darlin's! It's on deck with ye' to reef sails. There be a gale a'blowin'. Mister Sethford whistled too long a'fore the knife I rekon." The exhausted men climbed out of their bunks and out on the rain-swept decks. With salt water stinging their cut and blistered hands, the sailors climbed up the ratlines and out on the slippery foot ropes to take in sails. By daylight the gale had blown itself out, and *Grenadier* again wallowed on a windless sea. Again, the boats were ordered over the side.

Carpenters, sailmakers, cooks, riggers, and gunners took their turn at the oars. Everyone labored in the boats, except the boatswain and his favorites. Even Farwell the purser sat in the sternsheets of the long boat and counted cadence. Again they toiled under a hot, cloudless, silver sky.

Late in the afternoon, when the sun hung low over the Bay of Fundy, appearing to resist setting, little breezes stirred the white ensign hanging from the stern of *Grenadier*. A tiny cat's paw of wavelets wrinkled a small patch of water near the towboat, stirring hope in the men. Soon every man lifted his head and opened his senses to the wind. The faint breath died away into stillness and then reappeared as a genuine breeze. The white ensign lifted and fluttered. Men in the boats almost held their breath as they felt for the wind. Captain Walshingham placed his hands on his hips and rocked backwards, sniffing the air. With his eyes shut he lifted his left arm and pointed toward the southwest. "Southwesterly," he stated. "Make ready the sails, mainsail, haul!"

Men who had slumped about the deck like empty sacks now jumped eagerly to their duty, bare feet pounding the decks. They braced yards around to catch the southwesterly breeze. Empty jibs blossomed with wind. Sailors in the towboat rowed faster to keep ahead as the towing line went slack. Men in the tow boat cheered. When the grey-green twilight surrendered to darkness, the wind lifted even more and *Grenadier* bounded along under all sail. A billion stars twinkled and sparkled from the heavens but few men on board noticed. Slouching tiredly below deck, the men collapsed in their bunks and sleep claimed their weary minds.

The sun dawned blood red on a canvas of orange. Mister Sethford stood by the big ship's wheel aboard *Grenadier*, looking at the sun. "Red sky in the morning, sailor take warning," he said. "Bad weather is sure to come with a red sun and my rheumatism confirms it."

By midmorning the light wind that had blown all night from the southwest began to back. Then it blew strongly from the southeast. With the wind gusting near gale strength, Captain Walshingham ordered the topsails reefed on the heavy ship.

Just before noon, a lookout from the main top spotted their other two ships bearing dead astern. In the early afternoon heavy gray clouds rolled across the sky, and the wind rose to gales strength. *Gladiator,* sailing in front of the troop transport, gradually gained on Walshingham's ship. Soon they both stood a few cable lengths from *Grenadier*'s stern as the trio of ships pounded through the wind tossed seas. Hour after hour, the English ships raced up the Cumberland Basin, riding a flooding tide. *Grenadier* rounded into the wind in the roadstead off Fort Beausejour, followed by the troopship. Meanwhile, *Gladiator* continued past Ft. Beausejour a few cables east and dropped her anchor off Ft. Lawrence.

MacGregor lifted a telescope from the rack and looked at the crowds of people waiting to come aboard the two ships, throngs of poorly clothed refugees, eyes wide, their paltry possessions clutched in nervous hands. He rattled the telescope back into its rack and stood thinking of Marie Gauthier. *This was her home before the British Army came. Now where is Marie and her father? Would they have fled before the invasion, or do they stand on that beach, waiting to be taken away?*

When the anchor splashed down, Captain Walshingham addressed the officers. "Gentlemen, remember, the Bay of Fundy has the most treacherous tides in the world. Within the hour we will crest on a high tide and then the ships will fall forty feet on the low. Forty feet, gentlemen, think about it. We do not dare to anchor any closer to shore, lest the falling tide deposits us high and dry. The glass is falling and a storm is blowing in upon us. I do not intend to be caught by a storm on a lee shore. Our cargo shall be discharged in record time, then our flotilla will load the enemy for transport to Boston. Lieutenant MacGregor, ye will go ashore and explain our need for haste to the officers on shore. Ye will commandeer every boat and every spare man ashore to discharge cargo. When our deck is clear of cargo, returning boats will begin bringing French Army officers and a few others on board. *Grenadier* will transport only military prisoners, mainly officers. Prisoners will be held on the forecastle under guard by our marines until the holds are ready. French enlisted soldiers will be taken aboard the troop transport. *Gladiator* will transport Acadian civilians. Our three ships will convoy to Boston. Now, let us be about our business quickly, gentlemen. The wind is rising; the tide is falling; we are on a lee shore, and by God, we shall not lose this ship on this forsaken land."

Quickly, all *Grenadier*'s boats headed for shore. MacGregor was the first officer ashore and quickly commandeered every available boat on the beach after winning the argument with an officer off the troop transport that French officers should be loaded before enlisted men. MacGregor enlisted every idle man he could find to row the commandeered boats. With conscripted boats from shore, a small armada plied back and forth between *Grenadier* and the beach, busily moving their cargo. Pens arrived on shore filled with pigs, sheep, and chickens. Sailors rowed quickly from the ships, and when the boats came close to shore, they leaped into waist-deep water, pushing the boats in water too shallow for rowing. *Grenadier*'s sailors found other eager hands waiting to take the cargo. With the supplies unloaded, men made the difficult row against the wind, back to the ship for more.

MacGregor walked along the beach, supervising the exchange of supplies and prisoners. He constantly stole glances around him, hoping to see Marie Gauthier or her father. At a distance he could see the women, children, and elderly men assembled on the beach in front of Ft. Lawrence. He knew they were waiting for transport on H.M.S. *Gladiator. Likely, Marie and her father will be with that group. I will ensure that my frigate arrives in Boston ahead of them and will be waiting when they arrive.*

Chapter Eight

Farther down the beach that September day of 1755, Marie Gauthier stood beside Cumberland Basin with other Acadian civilians, waiting to be forcibly resettled. As the British ship anchored, she heard the anchor chain rattle and splash in the water. She even heard voices across the water from the ships. A setting sun hung in the west, and the stiff wind kicked up sand from the beach. With English guards, they waited while boats discharged food stuffs for the English occupation force. Casks of salted beef, crates of chickens, live pigs and sheep were unloaded from the boats and taken away to the fort. The Acadians must wait to be taken away, they knew not where. Mostly women and children, they clutched their remaining precious belongings in uncertain hands. Children chattered, babies cried, and dogs barked, but it was a quiet group of adults who waited with hushed voices. Elderly men, even older than Henri, were among the women; there were a few boys. They looked apprehensively at the dreaded ship that would take them away, sometimes glancing over their shoulders at their homeland. Other anxious eyes sought the group of Acadians captured at Fort Beausejour. They waited with the French soldiers. They appeared as dark silhouettes waiting a short distance to the west. English guards with glistening bayonets formed a barrier between the two groups. Marie shaded the setting sun from her eyes and stood on tip toes in an attempt to see her father. Like a few other Acadians, Marie called out her father's name and soon loved ones shouted for each other from both groups. Boats began taking the people to the English ships laying at anchor a few cables offshore.

Henri Ouilette stepped out of the group, shouting, "Gaston, Gaston! Are you over there, Gaston?" Henri looked over the heads of most. "There, eh?" Henri was sure he saw Gaston Gauthier waving at him. He moved quickly and hurried toward the soldiers where he had seen Gaston. Henri had taken only a few steps when a red-coated marine stopped his advance with the point of his bayonet against his belly. Another soldier slammed his rifle butt into him.

The English soldier yelled, "Stay with your own group! And quit your bloody gibberish." Henri crumpled to the ground, his hand over his kidney.

Marie rushed to Henri's aid, helping him to his feet. "You stay here, Henri. Perhaps they won't hurt a woman." Marie dropped her belongings and kicked off her wooden shoes. She lifted her skirts and rushed away toward the men waiting to board the other ship. Her quickness eluded her guards. Running as fast as she could, Marie crossed the beach with a guard running after her. "Father, Father," she called as she ran. "Are you there?"

Yelling between the two groups engulfed Marie's calls to her father. Gaston Gauthier tried to look for his daughter but was stopped by a guard. Marie ran closer to the military prisoners when an English marine rushed out to her. She attempted to run around the marine, but he quickly enveloped her in his arms and lifted her off the ground with her legs kicking. "Help me, please, help me," Marie called.

The panting guards from the civilian group caught up with her at last, and the two men began roughly hauling her back to the civilians. A French marine broke from the group of prisoners and struggled with English soldiers before one of the Englishmen landed a blow to his head. Seeing one of their comrades clubbed, several French marines bolted toward the English soldiers. With bayonets the British soldiers turned to meet this French attack, and Marie broke free.

On the beach Lieutenant MacGregor ran to the gathering melee. He foresaw a riot. Drawing his big Scottish claymore, Lieutenant MacGregor ran across the beach, with the sound of steel scraping against steel. He ran between the opposing ranks, pulling French soldiers backward. In French he said, "Civilian prisoners cannot mix with military prisoners. Just return to your ranks and all will be well. You will all be reunited in Boston." He turned to the English soldiers and ordered them to place the girl on the ground. They put her kicking feet back on the ground and shoved her roughly in the direction of the watching Acadians. Stopping the red-coated soldiers with a wave of his hand, MacGregor ordered the young lady to stand still. His voice was gruff, but his eyes were kind. He spoke in Parisian French. "*Mademoiselle*, please, you must stay with your own group." Only then did realize it was her. *Do my senses betray me? Is it really Marie Gauthier?* He asked, "Marie, is it you?"

Marie struggled to free her hands from the English soldiers as she saw MacGregor. "You?" she asked in surprise. "Charles MacGregor? Have you come to take us away as your prisoners?"

MacGregor fought the urge to touch her, even the thought of hugging her crossed his mind, but it would not do. *No, I do not know how she feels about me, and this is not the time. She is afraid. I will talk to her and maybe calm her.* "Marie," he said, "all of you are being taken to Boston. These are military prisoners. They can't go with you civilians. Both ships will go to Boston. I will meet your ship in Boston, there we will find your father."

Her eyes quickly turned away from MacGregor, excitedly still seeking her father. She ceased struggling to exclaim, "My father is with that group of men in that boat, there." With a trembling finger she pointed at the departing boat and continued, "My father is in that boat. I want to go with my father."

MacGregor replied, "All three ships are going to Boston, Marie. I don't know why your father is with the military prisoners, but you will be together in Boston. But you must hurry to the other ship. This one is for military prisoners only. Please, Marie, go to your own group. We must load the ships quickly and leave before the tide goes out. A storm is coming. We must not be caught in these shallow waters by the storm. I will be waiting at the dock in Boston when you arrive, and I promise I will have your father with me."

A marine from HMS *Grenadier* took her by the arm, more gently than had the others, moving her slowly toward the Acadians. MacGregor stood watching as the marine led her back to the women and children, with the young woman still looking back over her shoulder as the boat carried her father to *Grenadier*.

Lieutenant MacGregor raised his voice so the civilians could hear. Speaking in French he said, "All ships are bound for Boston, and you can be reunited with your loved ones there. Now, we must hurry for the tide is going out. The sooner you get on the ship, the sooner you can be reunited with your loved ones at Boston." His words helped pacify the people. They reluctantly followed his instructions.

MacGregor oversaw the final loading then hurried to take a place in the last boat returning to *Grenadier*. His heart felt heavy for the refugees looking over their shoulders, perhaps the last longing glances at their ancestral homeland. Later, he reported to Captain Walshingham, "All prisoners are aboard and all boats recovered, Captain. There is just adequate depth to allow the ship to follow the tide out to the Bay of Fundy."

Walshingham stood looking over the side at the rocks exposed by the falling tide. "Mister MacGregor, ready the spar deck." He turned to his sailing master. "Mister Sethford, take us to Boston."

Lieutenant MacGregor watched *Gladiator* attempting to recover her boats in a wild, disorganized melee as the wind freshened and the tide fell. With his hands on the bulwark, MacGregor called to Captain Walshingham, "*Gladiator* is having trouble recovering her boats. Shall we assist her?"

Captain Walshingham did not hesitate. "Of course we shall not assist the idiot. It would be foolhardy to risk a good frigate sailed by competent officers for a ship of fools filled with French peasants. Besides, I have no intention of allowing the charlatan to make Boston before me. Make sail, Mister Sethford." Walshingham descended the quarterdeck steps and watched while his marines herded the prisoners below the deck.

MacGregor watched *Gladiator* attempting to recover her boats. *I will see we reach Boston before them, and I will be waiting for Marie when she comes ashore. I must find Mr. Gauthier if he is aboard. But how will I free him?*

Under Mister Sethford's experienced hand, *Grenadier* clawed her way out of Cumberland Basin and began the long tack up Chignecto passage. At last MacGregor saw *Gladiator* make sail, a speck of white in the gathering darkness. With nightfall the storm failed to materialize and the wind even abated; light rain fell in the darkness. Captain Walshingham called for more sail and the boatswain hurried his men up the rigging high above the ship. With hands still blistered and stinging from the salt on the rigging, they added more sail. The frigate beat laboriously up the Bay of Fundy, and MacGregor watched the progress with satisfaction.

Late that night, when everyone but the duty watch had gone to bed, Lieutenant MacGregor walked down into the dark orlop deck. He stopped before the marine guard. "I'm here to check the prisoners." The guard removed the bar from the door, holding to as MacGregor entered the dark hold where only a lantern's glow provided light. He stood a moment, looking down the stairs at the prisoners, then spoke, "I'm Lieutenant MacGregor, first officer of this ship. I seek a Mr. Gaston Gauthier. Is he here?"

An Acadian with a bandage on his head approached him as he descended the stairs. "Lieutenant," the little man began in accented English, "my name is Gaston Gauthier."

MacGregor answered in French, "Mr. Gauthier, perhaps you remember me? It was I who assisted you when your ship was swamped off Cape Cod."

"Perhaps, I think your French is better than my English," answered Gaston Gauthier, with the trace of a smile creasing his wrinkled face. "My daughter..." Gaston asked. "Marie... my only daughter, my only blood, they have taken her from me. I think they put her on the other boat."

MacGregor replied, "Don't worry, Sir. The other ship sails to Boston just as we do. You will be reunited with Marie in Boston. You and I will be waiting when her boat arrives. Just how we will do it, I have not thought just yet, whatever, but it will be." MacGregor lifted his voice to the other men in the ship. "For those of you with loved ones on the other ship, please don't worry. You can be reunited in Boston." MacGregor repeated the statement louder. "We will be sending you drinking water tonight and food in the morning. Officers, as gentlemen, have vowed not to support further insurrection and will be allowed on deck, but others must remain below. Do not attempt to gain the deck, or you may be killed. But if you need anything, ask the guards for me, I'm Lieutenant MacGregor."

To Gaston Gauthier he said, "I must return to my duties, *Monsieur*, but I'll call on you again as time permits. We will find Marie as soon as we reach Boston." As MacGregor made his way up to the next deck, he noted a change in the ship's heel. There was also a different pitch on the waves. He climbed past the gun deck and up the stairs to the spar deck. A cool, wet wind struck his face as he emerged from below. Rain spattered against his face while his nose detected that musty smell of land blown over salt water. Holding his hat in his hand, he crossed the spardeck and climbed the stairs to the quarterdeck.

Mister Sethford stood in the darkness beside the helmsman, his collar turned up and his back to the wind. Sethford pointed aloft. "I've ordered a reef in the topsails, Mister MacGregor. A fresh wind blew up a few minutes ago and now seems to be backing around to the east. I'm mighty glad we've cleared Cape Chignecto. I'm thinking the wind will be blowin' from the east before morning."

MacGregor felt a chill down his spine. Cold replaced his earlier perspiration as the wind howled through the rigging; it made a lonesome moaning call, answered by the creaks and groans of the hull. Crashing waves sent a salt spray rising over the forecastle, reflecting the rays of the navigation lanterns in the foremast ratlines.

"Mister Sethford, I'll go below for a little sleep. Send for me when you go below at the mid watch; I'll join Midshipman Collingwood on his watch."

"Aye, Sir," Sethford replied, "and I'll sleep better knowing you'll be with the lad should something go wrong. I'll take in more sail before I leave if the wind continues to rise."

It seemed MacGregor had just crawled into the warm blankets of his bunk when his name was called. "Mister Sethford's compliments, Sir, and he is changing the watch." MacGregor pulled on his clothing and threw on an oilcloth before braving the storm. On deck he found Midshipman Collingwood shivering in the cold night air, his oilcloth cape flapping in the wind. Rain blew horizontally and spattered like metal pellets. When sailors could no longer see the bowsprit in the darkness and rain, MacGregor shortened the tacks. He tied men in the chains where they swung the lead line, feeling for bottom, and hoping to avoid disaster of running aground on the rocky shoreline.

Chapter Nine

Marie Gauthier sat on the tossing floor of the dark ship's hold. She was seasick. She leaned her aching head against the tossing bulkhead with her knees drawn up under her trembling chin; there was no room to lie down. Two hundred and seventy-five Acadians: men, women, and children huddled miserably in the lower-deck between casks of shot, cordage, spare sails, spars, rats, and smelly bilge water.

They were seasick in the dark, rolling, stinking ship. Henri Ouilette, who would never have complained on land if his guts were on fire, moaned, lamented, and wished to die. The ship also groaned as it rolled in the swells, to join the moaning Acadians. The damp, fetid air filled the farmer's nostrils. Two lanterns, swinging back and forth with the roll of the ship, cast a dizzying light of moving shadows to compound the sickness. Up above, English sailors avoided the prisoner's deck because of the stench. Only the ship's doctor spoke to the Acadians on the way to his quarters in the orlop deck and sometimes did what he could to comfort them.

The little Acadian priest stood, swaying in his long black frock and flat hat, his wide eyes looking out from dark shadows in his gaunt and ashen skull. After a very short prayer the little priest succumbed to his churning stomach and hurried to the overfilled pail.

Marie Gauthier summoned her courage, thinking, *"I must take my mind away from this place or I shall die."* She freed her memory to wander to happier times in her village of Beaubassin. Marie shut her eyes, remembering her home as it had been before the coming of Abbe' LeLoutre. *Our's had been the finest house in the village. Its high dormer windows made the gray winter light more cheerful with stained glass of red, green, and yellow. Its thatched roof was cool in the summer, and the stone fireplaces drove out the winter's cold. Every night a dozen candles cast their warm glow over fine furniture and paintings from France. Milk, butter, eggs, cheese, stone ground flour, and wine filled our cool pantry. Our farmers' harvests provided a surplus for export. My father traded the surplus produce from Beaubassin with merchants in Quebec, the West Indies, France, and even Boston. Cattle fattened in our pasture and frisky young colts pranced about the fences. Grapes, transplanted from the vineyards* of France, provided wine for our dinner. Homemade ale sparked our parties with much music and dancing. When the winter was unusually long and harsh and food became scarce for the Indians, Acadians shared their food with the Mi'kmaqs, who appeared like ghosts out of the forest.

Marie's eyes sparkled as she remembered the day her father returned from a trading trip to Boston. *Father brought gifts for everyone in the family. They had laughed as he made everyone guess their gift. Only her brother Pierre had correctly guessed his gift at the outset, for he knew there was only one gift he would consider. Pierre, young and confident, seemed never to have had a doubt; his father's gift would be the violin he had always wanted. He had been only five years old when he announced that some day he would accompany his mother on the violin while she played the harpsichord. His mother would again hear the violin, he said, as she had in Paris. He had been twelve years old when his father brought this reality to the boy's life. Marie remembered the joy that danced in his young eyes. Mother taught Pierre to play the violin as she had taught me to play the harpsichord.*

The harpsichord opened a new world for me. Soon my faltering notes became cords and the cords cascaded into beautiful melodies. With a few years practice, the compositions of Europe's great musicians flowed from the harpsichord.

Marie shuddered as she thought of her burning home. *It was five years ago when the missionary priest, LeLoutre, appeared at our door. Leading his band of Mi'kmaq warriors, the priest came upon the Acadians quietly in the dark.*

It had been a warm summer night with peace settled over the forests and fields. Marie's family sat around their dinner table in the flickering light of oil lamps, their heads bowed as they said prayers of thanksgiving. Suddenly, loud pounding sounded on the door. Father opened the door to the priest, Jean-Louis LeLoutre. Behind him, fierce Indian warriors, smelling of bear-grease and spruce smoke, peeked inside the cabin. Their bare skin glistened in the light of burning torches. Human scalps, some with freshly dried blood, hung from their belts. With faces painted for war, they carried muskets, tomahawks, and bows. LeLoutre's Indians stalked a plentiful game, English settlers.

"You must leave your home and move across the river," the Abbe' LeLoutre said.

"But why?" Father asked.

"The English are coming," the priest replied. "The new treaty gives them this land. Now all Acadians must move across the river where we build the new fort. When the English come, they will find only scorched earth."

"There's no need for me to move. I don't fear the English," her father argued. "We will stay here. I speak their language. They have always treated me fairly. When the English came in forty-eight, my neighbors and I swore not to take up arms against them ever again. So now that the English are here again in fifty-five, the war with England is none of my concern. I think they will not harm me or my family. I only want to live in peace."

"I know about you, Gaston Gauthier!" The priest shouted. "You deal with the devil! It is because of unpatriotic Frenchmen like you that France does not prosper from the investment made in this colony. Trading with the English should be a crime of treason! You should trade only with Quebec and France. Have you no love for his Christian Majesty, Louis XV, who nurtures this colony? You should be hanged for trading with the heretics."

The French priest's eyes burned like embers. "Gaston Gauthier, my warriors would be happy to tie your bloody scalp to their belts. Be thankful I'm a priest, or I would allow it. You are a disgrace to France, to your King, and your God.

"Now, load only your necessities in your wagon behind your oxen. You will leave all the other ill-gotten gains from trading with the enemy here, where it will be set in flames. You may think of it as a burnt offering for your sins. May the Lord forgive you.

"Take the wagon and your family across the Missaguash River. Take only the bare necessities, for there will be little room for anything where you go. You will live in French territory, poor like everyone else, in a cabin which you can build yourself. Under the protection of Ft. Beausejour you Acadians will build new dikes and farms to preserve this colony for France. From there you will fight the English until our land is free of those heretics."

I shall never forget sitting on that wagon behind a yoke of oxen with Mother sobbing and crying. The warriors set the torch to our house, and I will always remember the tears on Mother's face reflecting the oranged-red flames as they consumed our home... no, not just our home, our life. The beloved and priceless harpsichord, brought by ship from France, *was burned forever.*

Marie tired of sitting in the cramped space. She wiped tears from her eyes and pulled herself erect. With difficulty Marie threaded her way through the Acadians. Lifting a crying baby from a mother's arms, Marie sat holding and rocking the baby as the tired mother succumbed to sleep. Later, she helped a child to an overflowing toilet bucket in a corner behind a blanket. Many needed assistance and it helped pass the time. When at last Marie returned to her space near the moaning and seasick Henri, she sat exhausted, tired beyond caring about her soiled clothing, the discomfort and stench. She drifted off to a fitful sleep of nightmares.

Marie awoke to the first lurch of the ship. She sensed something was wrong. She sat stiffly upright, clutching her seed bag. Again the ship lurched, and those who stood fell on others nearby. There was a bigger lurch with crashing noises. Screams pierced the darkness. People tried to stand but toppled over as their world tilted sharply. The starboard side of the hold lifted as people fell away into a mass of tangled arms and feet on the opposite side amid spilling pails and flying bundles.

Henri Ouilette leaped to his feet, his sickness forgotten. He struggled to the stairs leading out of the orlop deck, pulling Marie with him. With an arm around her waist he held her tightly against the steps as people battered against them in their slide down the orlop deck. The ship creaked, groaned, and timbers crashed beneath the terrified Acadians. On the larboard side, seawater flowed around the screaming, writhing mass of humanity in that darkness. Fear became terror. As people struggled around the stairs, Henri made his way to the top and pounded on the locked hatch. After some time a compassionate sailor shoved the latch from above and lifted the hatch. Terror-stricken Acadians erupted in a rush up the stairs, led by Henri Ouilette. Survivors struggled up to the higher level of the gun deck, calling down into the orlop deck to lost loved ones. Below, seawater boiled into that lower deck, rising to the opening of the gun deck on which they stood. Acadians who could not make the rush up the stairs drowned in the dark, swirling water. Cold seawater rose to waist depth. They looked for escape to a still higher deck. Marie found herself struggling along behind Henri in an uphill climb toward the stairs leading to the spar deck. Henri pulled Marie along while other Acadians slipped and fell in their wooden shoes, his moccasins allowing him to walk where they could not. A young Acadian boy in bare feet dashed past Henri and bolted up the stairs. At the head of the stairs a belaying pin whacked the boy's skull, swung by a husky British sailor. The boy toppled backwards against Marie with blood streaming down his face. Descending the stairs with the club again cocked in his hand the sailor said, "Stay below! Get ye back where ye belong. Ye dumb farmers are safer here than on deck. We've run aground, and the ship's rigging is falling. Men be killed on deck by falling yards. Stay ye here or be ye kilt'."

Henri could not understand the man, but it was obvious to him the sailor would not allow them to climb the stairs. Henri moved toward the sailor. The sailor swung the belaying pin in a wide arc toward Henri's head, narrowly missing him as Henri ducked under the swing. Henri rushed in under the swinging club and clamped the sailor in a bear hug. But the sailor was no novice in a fight. He jerked the back of the belaying pin toward Henri, catching Henri over his kidney with the handle of the club. Henri dropped to his knees in pain as the stick of oak crushed muscle, flesh and bone. Marie held Henri as she translated the sailor's words. "Everyone must stay here. It is safer because the ship has run aground, and the tall things are falling on deck, killing people." She knelt over Henri as dozens of people crowded around the stairs.

The sailor swung his club and yelled over the shouting Acadians, "The Cap'n sez' ye stay down here where it's safe. Now back off or I'll split more skulls with me belayin' pin."

The Acadians turned to find another place to escape. They wrestled with a gun port and a shaft of gray light penetrated the darkness when it opened. The Acadians saw an avenue of escape, but they needed a rope. They untied the rope holding a nearby cannon. The sailor yelled, "Hey, get away from that gun, you fools, don't take that rope off..." Screams enveloped the sailor's words as the cannon, loosed from its restraining ropes, rolled down the slanted deck. The cannon plunged through the Acadians like rag dolls. Smashing into the timbers on the lower side of the gundeck, it crushed several people. Screams and cries of anguish echoed through the dark decks. Others lay crying in agony.

An English officer appeared at the hatchway. Blood trickled down his face from a head wound. He spoke in halting French, "You people remain calm and stay below. We have run aground, but we are in shallow water and the ship cannot sink anymore. You are safer here than on deck. When we clear away the wreckage, we will take you ashore. Our doctor will see to your injured very soon."

The English sailors cleared away fallen rigging and set anchors seaward of the beached ship. Later, the ship's doctor and his helper made their way down the stairs. Wearing blood stained aprons, they examined the people under the light of lanterns held aloft. Atop, the surgeon made operating tables almost level on the canted deck. The doctor labored under the soft yellow glow of lanterns. With his scalpel, saw, and a tourniquet, he removed mangled legs and arms. Marie summoned her courage, rolled up her sleeves and helped hold the writhing patients. A young boy dashed up and down the stairs with bloody bandages and severed limbs, returning with pails of seawater.

It was almost noon when the French speaking officer again appeared at the hatch opening to say, "We will be coming soon to take you off the ship. We are lowering our boats into the water now."

But before anyone came for them, gunshots pierced the air. English officers shouted orders. Footsteps sounded from above, running across the deck. Acadians climbed to the open porthole to look outside but saw only the sky above. A British marine in his bright red jacket quickly descended the ladder, followed by several sailors. Roughly shoving the Acadians from their way, they waded the water to the arms locker where they removed weapons. They hurried toward the back of the deck, returning with an armload of weapons. They passed the weapons up through the hatch to eager hands. Sailors followed the weapons on deck and closed the hatch, barring it as they left. From the deck above blood curdling screams filled the air.

Henri cautiously made his way aft in the dim light but found a heavy padlock on the weapons locker. He returned forward, searching for a pry bar of some sort. It was then he heard the *Mi'kmaq's* war cry. Gunshots sounded loudly just at the top of the hatch. Henri heard the familiar shouting and cursing of battle. He climbed to the top of the ladder, pressing his shoulder against the hatch door. It was barred from the outside. He yelled loudly in the *Mi'kmaq* language and pounded on the door as smoke drifted through the lower deck. Fear of burning to death showed on every Acadian's face as smoke filled the gundeck.

A bar rattled on the other side of the hatch door. The door swung open. A British officer stumbled down the steps, an arrow in his back. Behind him, a warrior appeared at the opening, his tomahawk raised to strike. The Indian swung the tomahawk, crushing the officer's skull as the officer fell with wide, non-seeing eyes. Henri leaped to his feet and threw the dead officer aside. He forced his way up the steps. Shouting in the *Mi'kmaq* language, Henri raised his right hand in a gesture of peace. He lifted the crucifix hanging around his neck and held it for the Indian to see. He moved up the steps, speaking the *Mi'kmaq* language to the warrior. Several more warriors appeared, looking suspiciously down the smoke filled hatchway. Cautiously, the Indians moved away from the hatch. Ouilette moved quickly behind them, calling for the choking Acadians to follow.

Coughing and gasping, their eyes filled with tears, the weak, seasick Acadians climbed out of the hold. Mothers, children, and elderly men stumbled out of the smoking hold, their red, teary eyes wide in fright. They stared in horror at the carnage. Indians knelt busily over dead sailors, sawing away at their bloody scalps with skinning knives. Masses of tangled ropes and lines draped the deck, making movement difficult. Dead men hung lifelessly in the tangled maze. Everywhere there were bodies of sailors in pools of blood. Flames licked upward through the planks. A cold wind blew rain and salt spray across the carnage. Marie held back a scream; the sight of the warriors brought her back to the horrible night when LeLoutre burned their home. She looked away from the dead Englishmen. Henri, all too familiar with such mayhem, moved about the deck in search of weapons for himself, speaking to the Indians in their native tongue. All the while the English surgeon and his mate, still wearing their bloody aprons, stayed below and continued to minister to the wounded Acadians.

On the bloody, tangled spardeck, those Acadians who could do so, stood silently shivering in the cold. Soon, however, a brave came up the steps from the gun deck, shoving the surgeon and his mate ahead. Seeing the buckled shoes worn by the doctor, an Indian grabbed him by the throat, lifted his tomahawk and split the doctor's skull. In horror, Marie moved quickly in front of the doctor's helper, who crouched in fear behind her. The Indian stood looking angrily at Marie, pushing her aside as another Indian put his knife into the back of the doctor's helper. The angry Indian stood before Marie with his tomahawk raised until Henri approached the man and spoke to him in his language. Slowly, the Indian lowered his tomahawk and walked away. In tears, Marie knelt by the dying man, holding his hand and saying prayers.

The rain had stopped and skies begun to clear when a French officer stepped out of a boat and climbed on deck. The French Captain of infantry wore a blue military tunic and white trousers. He wore a black hat trimmed in gold lace and a richly gilded sword hung from his waist. A pair of pistols protruded from his belt. With a deep frown he silently surveyed the bedraggled Acadians, then ordered them into the English boats. Henri signaled to a brave to follow him and descended the steps to the gun deck. Breaking the lock on the English arms locker, he took a fine new musket for himself before calling the Indian's attention to this fortune in arms. As Indians rushed below to take weapons, Henri joined the other Acadians in the boat. He proudly carried a new rifle and, slung over his shoulder, a supply of shot and powder. A dirk protruded from the sash around his waist and another from the top of his mocassin.

As they rowed ashore, the women and children looked back sadly at the burning ship where flames turned the ship into a funeral pyre for many Acadians left behind. From his seat pulling at the oars, Henri looked around at the water and land. To Marie, he said, "This is Cape Chignecto. I remember being here in 'forty-four. There is a village of *Mi'kmaq*s just down the coastline of the Minas Channel."

The Acadians clumsily rowed the boats across the water and pulled them up on the rocky beach. *Mi'kmaq* warriors leaped from their canoes with much shouting and waving of their bloody souvenirs. Soon, however, they gathered in a throng of talking and trading. Neither blood nor bullet holes detracted from the value of the bright scarlet tunics of the marines.

Acadians gathered on the beach but there was little joy among them. Some had left loved ones on the burning ship and others writhed in pain. Most felt dread that they would never see their husbands and fathers again. Some were injured too badly to care; a few were dying. Some knelt in prayer while a few dropped to their knees and kissed the rocky earth.

Old Mr. Chiasson, an aging leader of the Acadians, rose to speak. "My brothers and sisters, let us rest here a few days. Then we can return to the boats and row back home. In a few days we can be back to our land at Beaubassin."

The tall French Captain rose from where he sat on a nearby rock. He left his Indian raiders to join the Acadians assembled around Mr. Chiasson. He held his hand aloft up as he spoke. "No, my fellow countrymen, do not think you can go back to Beaubassin. Remember what has occurred today on the English ship. The Englishmen will be very angry when they learn what has happened, and they will be quick to take revenge. Do you think they can take revenge on these Indian warriors here? No, our friends, the *Mi'kmaq*s, disappear in the forest like the wolf and the lynx. The Englishmen will take their revenge on you, who cannot disappear." He paused, looking over the Acadians. "You must take the boats and go quickly up the Minas Channel to the village of the *Mi'kmaq*s. It is not far and you should reach it before dark. They will feed you and take you into their lodges. Your sick and injured can rest there. When you are rested, you must set out for the safety of Fortress Louisbourg at Isle Royale. There is no other safe place to go."

Mrs. Levec, clutching her child against her breast, shouted, "The English have my husband. I will chance what the English will do to me; I want to go with my husband." Other Acadians agreed. They wanted to be reunited with loved ones, even in captivity in Boston.

The captain's eyes narrowed and he spat out his words, "You will do as I order in the name of the King. If you have no sense then I must have sense for you. You will enter the boats. I will send some warriors with you to protect you, and see that you follow my orders. You will take refuge in the *Mi'kmaq* village until you are able to travel. Then you will go to Louisbourg; there will be no more discussion."

From among the Acadians emerged the frail little figure of their parish priest, the man who settled their disputes and gave leadership in Beaubassin. Father Felix held both hands aloft. "My children, we must do as the officer tells us. But, before we go farther, let us give thanks to God for our deliverance and pray for the souls of our lost loved ones there in the burning ship." Almost reluctantly, one by one the Acadians knelt in silent prayer. Silently, the Indians knelt with the Acadians on the beach at Cape Chignecto. For a very long time they knelt, their priest praying to their God whose mercy some may have now questioned. There were Acadians who trembled and shuddered as their priest closed his prayer with a blessing. All knew they had looked into the face of death. Hungry, wet, cold, and afraid, they rose silently one by one and assembled around the boats. With each finding a place, the people set out in boats and canoes for the *Mi'kmaq* village. The procession of boats and birch bark canoes moved silently across the water, the silence broken only by a sob, the splash of an oar, or the call of a lonely loon.

Acadians looked back at the last resting place of their dead with tearful eyes. Wordlessly, boats and canoes followed their leader up the Minas Channel, often with tired, weak Acadian women straining at the oars. They were rounding a low headland with the ship now out of sight when the powder magazine on *Gladiator* exploded with a roar. Silence hung over the boats as the Acadians watched the billowing smoke rise suddenly above the tree line. The men paused at the oars and everyone watched silently as the smoke drifted into the sky.

Chapter Ten

It was the next morning with low, black clouds racing across white capped wave tops. Rain, whipped by a howling wind, stung the faces of men on deck. Showers of spray flew across the waves as *HMS Grenadier* thrashed through dark ocean swells. Everyone on deck looked anxiously for the other ships, but they were not to be seen. MacGregor whispered a prayer that their sister ship might suddenly appear. Had it been lost in the storm?

With a quartering wind filling her sails, the frigate raced down the Bay of Fundy. Mile after nautical mile slipped under her keel. Slowly, darkness swallowed the ship without sight of *Gladiator* or the troop ship. Throughout the night men climbed wet, slippery ratlines high above the ship to glass the darkness for sign of a riding light. Officers made precision tacks across the Bay of Fundy. Deck hands never rested as they wore ship, reefed sails, and sought to clear the rocky shoreline.

MacGregor sent word to Walshingham. "My compliments to the captain. Neither *Gladiator* nor the troop ship are in sight." Soon Captain Walshingham stomped angrily on deck and rattled a telescope from the binnacle. He searched the black horizon, swearing. "Turn back and search for the idiots." Walshingham paced the quarterdeck as MacGregor ordered a reverse of course. The captain fumed as sailors leaped into the ratlines, shortening sail. Slowly, the frigate beat back slowly over the ocean she had crossed so swiftly before. Sailors stripped off their heavy clothing under the clearing skies, and many who were cold a few hours before now found perspiration on their brows.

Throughout the long, hot day they searched the Bay of Fundy. Everyone kept a comfortable distance from the wrath of Walshingham as he paced the quarterdeck with eyes like fire. The winds blew lightly from the west, and the frigate resumed under full sails. As the tide turned to ebb, *Grenadier* made no progress forward but sailed just to hold her position. At midmorning, when the tide changed to flood, the ship moved slowly forward and the search resumed. Early in the afternoon, lookouts spotted the troop transport, now lumbering along the tide. A signal of brightly colored signal flags from slow transport revealed that smoke had been sighted from the east side of the straits.

The troop ship continued to lumber toward Boston but their news sent

Grenadier sailing away on a more easterly course. It was late afternoon before lookouts from the crow's nest saw the smoke. It curled lazily in the sky a few miles ahead on the east shore. Their telescopes soon revealed black, charred remains of a ship. As the frigate drew near the wreckage, all doubts disappeared. It was *Gladiator*. The frigate lay aground and heeled at a steep angle. Dismasted, its rigging lay in tangles on the deck. The ship was the slain *Gladiator*. Fire blackened sails slatted limply in tatters; the stumps of the mizzen mast projected impotently into the sky like a broken lance. Thin wisps of smoke rose from charred remains on the quarterdeck. An Indian arrow could be seen, imbedded in a stump of the mizzen mast. Lieutenant MacGregor's heart seemed to stop and squeezed the taffrail as if holding himself away from the horror ahead. *Oh, my God! Marie Gauthier was aboard that ship. Is she now dead?*

Captain Walshingham stomped across the quarterdeck, hands behind his back, his orders crisp. "Anchor in ten fathoms of water and put a boat over the side. MacGregor, take a boarding party to investigate! Take Sergeant O'Bannion and his six marines."

Doctor Abrams stood beside MacGregor, looking at the burning ship. He spoke softly, "It appears the ship was attacked by Indians. Take Seaman McCauley with you; he grew up with Indians in the Carolinas and knows their ways. Arm your sailors with pistols and cutlasses. I will go too. There may be survivors in the wreckage."

When the master at arms had distributed weapons, MacGregor took his place in the long boat. Sergeant O'Bannion sat in the bow, his rifle and bayonet held at the ready. With oars dipping silently in the littler strewn water, their boat covered the distance between *Grenadier* and *Gladiator*. Coming closer, MacGregor saw an object floating in the water. Warily, he turned the boat in that direction. Approaching more closely he recoiled. It was the body of a Royal Marine, stripped of his crimson jacket, and with a broken arrow shaft protruding from his neck. His scalp had been removed above the un-seeing eyes. With the boat moving slowly through the water they found several other bodies drifting in the flotsam.. *Will I find Marie's body the same way? What might the Indians have done to her if they found her alive?* MacGregor reached into the water and picked up the shaft of a floating arrow. Charred bodies hung in the tangled rigging of the partially submerged decks. Many deck guns were missing where gun ropes burned away and dropped the heavy cannons beneath the surface. Doctor Abrams said, "Any survivors in this cold water would only last a few minutes."

MacGregor's mind was already in despair. *How can I tell Mr. Gauthier that his only daughter has died aboard this wreckage?* He gripped the gunnels with tight fingers and steered the boat around the ship's stern. "Up oars," he called as they neared the shattered openings of the stern windows. Standing, he reached for the blackened window opening. Blue smoke still drifted through the empty windows. Inside, water sloshed back and forth with bodies swaying with the waves, their arms and legs moving in a grizzly dance of death. A kedge anchor could be seen on shore, its cable parted by the fire.

"We will look for survivors," MacGregor said. "Mr. Abrams, you can come with me if you like. Sergeant O'Bannion, take the boat around to the ship's quarterdeck. Put your marines aboard if it's safe and keep your guns ready. There could be hostile Indians hiding in the trees ashore. Coxson, after you drop us off on the wreckage, keep the boat away in case of attack."

The boat glided through the wreckage, bumping pieces of flotsam in its path. Where the ship's rail met the water, Sergeant O'Bannion held the boat to a charred section of taffrail. He climbed the steep angle of the quarterdeck. Taking a ready position with his rifle, he trained it on the rocky, evergreen-lined shore. O'Bannion signaled for his marines to join him. Without words, giving directions with his hands, O'Bannion assembled them in a skirmish line. The marines kneeled on the canted quarterdeck, their rifles aimed toward the trees on the shoreline.

The sailors in MacGregor's boat waited until he climbed onto the ship. Securing the boat, they followed him. MacGregor kicked at the black stairs leading down to the lower deck, testing their strength before descending. He cautiously stepped down the companionway, followed by Dr. Abrams.

MacGregor held to the railing, careful to avoid falling into the dark water below. He looked up toward the starboard gundeck where a cannon still hung precariously on its charred ropes. Gun ports had never opened, except one. A lone gun port on the starboard side stood strangely open, without cannon.

Several bodies floated on the surface, the waves moving their limbs in a macabre dance of death. One man's head was swathed in bandages and another showed white bandages on the stump of his leg. MacGregor recoiled at the sight of a woman floating face down in the dark water, her white apron and petticoat swirling on the sea. Beside her, he retrieved a fire blackened rag doll floating among the dismal debris. With nausea in his throat, he passed the doll back to Abrams in the boat and turned back to his gruesome work. Summoning his courage, he reached into the freezing water. Hesitantly, he touched the woman's body, holding to the folds of clothing that waved beneath the water. With reluctant fingers he touched the wet strands of her hair, moving them down to her cold body. Taking a firm grip on her lifeless shoulders, he turned her in the water. *Dear God, let this not be Marie. What clothing did she wear on the beach? The prisoners would have been held in the orlop deck. Would any who escaped that black hole of death have died in these freezing waters?* He turned her over, her lifeless limbs swaying lifelessly, until he looked into her open, unseeing eyes. When he breathed again, he realized the face was not that of Marie but of an older woman, perhaps a mother and someone's wife. *Where is the drowned child that hugged the rag doll against her fearfully beating heart? Thank God this mother has not been scalped as has most others! Had the Indians overlooked her, or had she drowned and not been seen? Who killed this woman? Was it Indians, or was it the British who forced her aboard this warship? Can I serve a King who orders such murder?*

He choked down the acrid bile forming in his throat. Forcing his mind back to the job at hand, MacGregor continued his examination. Smoke drifted through the gundeck, drifting from the still burning forecastle. Two anchor cables ran off the stern, disappearing into the murky water. "Likely, the fire in the stern was extinguished by the explosion of the magazine," he said to Dr. Abrams. "Aside from some smoking charcoal, only the forecastle burns now. *Gladiator* ran aground. Indians massacred the crew while they were trying to kedge themselves off the shore."

As Dr. Abrams examined the dead, MacGregor made his way up the slippery, canted steps to the quarterdeck. "Sergeant O'Bannion, keep good watch from here with your rifles. I'm taking the boat ashore." MacGregor signaled to be picked up by the boat. Stepping into the stern as the boat drew near, he stood, directing the crew to row toward a clearing in the shoreline. He said, "Ready with your pistols men." As the boat neared the rocky shoreline, MacGregor ordered, "Coxson, you and Elston remain with the boat. Keep just offshore. Smith and McCoy, take cover behind those rocks and keep your pistols ready." MacGregor spoke to McCauley, who looked not at all as one would expect from his name. His skin was dark, hair straight and black. MacCauley's large, dark eyes surveyed the dark forest impassively. MacGregor called softly, "McCauley, you come with me."

With his sword drawn, MacGregor leaped from the boat into the cold, thigh-deep water. Struggling for good footing on the slippery rocks, he kept his sight fixed on the dark shadows of the tree line. MacGregor made his way slowly over the mossy rocks in the shallow water. They splashed through the shallow water and walked up the rocky, pebble-strewn beach. McCauley hurried across the open interval to the tree line. Lieutenant MacGregor followed close behind. Carefully, slowly, they looked around into the dark forest. They examined the clutter on the ground where discarded clothing and broken utensils littered the open interval of the beach.

McCauley knelt and pointed to a track. "Many people have walked here," he said softly. "There are many moccasins, many wooden shoes, like those worn by the French peasants, and a few boot tracks." McCauley stood up and walked back to the water's edge. "They beached canoes and boats here. Indians have taken people away in canoes and boats."

MacGregor moved into the shadows of the forest. Standing motionless, he listened. Above the sound of his own breathing, birds chirped and wind rustled the branches. In the distance a crow called raucously. McCauley backed slowly toward the beach, still straining his eyes toward the forest.

MacGregor turned his attention to the litter on the beach. Most of the clothing was the worn and tattered slops of English sailors. There were a few dishes from the ship's mess and a few empty wine bottles. McCauley picked up the handle of a British officer's sword, bloody and broken at the hilt. Neither man could speak as they made their way back to the boat. Returning to the ship, MacGregor heard the retching of a marine being sick as he made another search for Marie Gauthier. Hope was but a tiny, flickering flame in his heart as he failed to find her among the dead.

Returning to *Grenadier*, the men found Captain Walshingham waiting at the spardeck, his hands behind his back, his feet wide apart, his brow furrowed in thought. MacGregor reported, "Sir, *Gladiator* ran aground. Some of the crew and many of the Acadian prisoners were drowned or killed as the ship ran aground. While the crew tried to kedge themselves off the rocks, Indians boarded her and massacred the crew. It appears the entire crew was slaughtered and the surviving prisoners carried away. They never brought a cannon to bear, with the port guns all under water."

Walshingham stepped toward the landward taffrail, his eyes bulging, his face red. He slammed his fist on the oak as he looked out upon the wreck of *Gladiator*. He wheeled suddenly and shouted, "Make sail for Boston. There's nothing more to be done here."

MacGregor stood squeezing the hilt of his sword as he looked at Walshingham. "Sir, think of our French prisoners. We should hold a Christian burial for the dead."

Walshingham's face reddened. "Would ye instigate a riot on my ship? Not by your life, Mister! The Acadians will stay below, and no word of this will be spoken to them. Now make sail as I ordered."

* * *

With the setting sun bright on her vast spread of canvas, H.M.S. *Grenadier* sailed southward. On the morrow she should dock in Boston. Lieutenant MacGregor turned to his dreaded task and descended the steps to the gun deck. He walked across the gun deck and stood above the locked hatch leading down to the orlop deck. *I must tell Gaston Gauthier that the ship that carried his daughter was lost... and perhaps she is dead. Dead at the hands of the British... dead at my hands, perhaps, since I serve the British. Mr. Gauthier was not the only one who lost loved ones aboard the sunken frigate; many others held as prisoners in our orlop did as well. What do they know already? Surely, they suspect something is wrong.*

A marine removed the lock and the hatch creaked open as the man lifted the cover. Lieutenant MacGregor took a gulp of fresh air and reluctantly descended the steps into the smelly, dark hold of the orlop deck. He stood for a moment wondering, hesitating with only the creaking sound of the ship and sporadic coughing. He looked for Gaston Gauthier, wondering if he would recognize him. With hesitation MacGregor began, "Some of you may have loved ones aboard our sister ship. I regret to tell you it ran aground on Cape Chignecto. Indians killed the crew and took the surviving Acadians away." MacGregor waited for the comments and cries of alarm to subside before continuing. "Some Acadians died, but I believe most survived. Where they have been taken, we do not know. Perhaps you know better than I, the Indians are your allies. We can only make inquiries through the French government about your loved ones. It appears all the English were killed.

"Tomorrow we arrive in Boston. There, the French officers will be ransomed to France. You and Acadians may book passage to France, if you have sufficient means. Those who have no money will be resettled in English colonies. If I can help you, ask for me. I'm Lieutenant Charles MacGregor. Send a message to me by the guards. I will come to you again when my duty allows."

Gaston Gauthier stood up slowly. "Pardon! Marie... was she? Did she survive?"

MacGregor stood almost unable to speak. His mouth was dry. "Sir... I'm sorry, I do not know who survived or who was killed. I looked for Marie and, thankfully, did not find her. I pray she survived." He watched as Gaston Gauthier stood with tears in his eyes. The old man's hand trembled as he put it to his eyes and his voice broke as he asked, "If you did not find her body, I choose to believe she is still alive. Thank God that Henri Ouilette was with her. If anyone can look after her, Henri can. I will believe she survived unless I see... different." The old man lowered his head and turned away.

MacGregor put a hand on the man's shoulder and said, "As soon as possible I will make inquiries for you... for all of you. Please do not lose hope, for many Acadians survived, I think. Now I must find some food for you, and drink too, whatever. I'll be back to see you later." MacGregor turned and ascended the steps, pushing open the hatch which was slammed shut and locked immediately by the marine.

Chapter Eleven

The long procession of boats and canoes reached the *Mi'kmaq* village on the north shore of the Minas Channel. As the boats drew near, Marie Gauthier saw many lodges, some with white smoke curling skyward. Fish cured in the open air around the lodges. Dogs barked noisily at Indian children playing in the village. One by one the birchbark canoes slipped ashore with warriors leaping into the water, shouting, and displaying trophies of war. Happy *Mi'kmaq* women and children ran eagerly to meet them and looked with awe at the Acadian visitors.

The Indians gradually warmed to the Acadians, proudly showing off the crosses they wore around their necks, displaying with pride that they were Christians. Some offered them food and those refugees who had not eaten for so long consumed the strange fare. Henri recognized an elderly warrior, speaking to him in the *Mi'kmaq* tongue. They embraced and spoke excitedly for several minutes before Henri brought Marie forward, speaking to him of her. A smiling *Mi'kmaq* women engulfed Marie, hugging her tightly against her ample bosom and led her away toward her lodge. Indian children hung merrily to Marie's hands as they walked to the lodge while a mangy dog barked at her feet.

A portly Indian sat in front of the lodge making snowshoes from willows and sinew. Smiling, the woman pointed to herself and lifted her crucifix. She pointed to the man, and then to herself again. The woman wanted Marie to know they, too, were married Christians. She pointed to a drawing of a running bear on the side of their birch bark lodge. The woman set Marie on a deer hide. She dipped soup from an iron kettle simmering over the fire, placing it in Marie's hands. Marie wolfed down the soup and held out her bowl for a second helping. This was followed by a bowl of dried berries covered with maple syrup. With her hunger satisfied, Marie sat nodding on the deer skin.

Overcoming an urge to enter the lodge and sleep in her filthy clothing, Marie forced herself onto her weary feet. Finally communicating the desire to her friendly hosts to bathe, the woman led Marie to the nearby creek.

Relieved to find no one else around, Marie stripped off her soiled clothing. She waded into the water with her soiled clothing over her arm, the cold, fresh water biting at her naked flesh. Her bare feet slipping on slick rocks, Marie waded into a shallow area, kneeling to pick up a handful of sand. Laying her wet clothing on a boulder, she rubbed the sand into her soiled clothing. Piece by piece she scrubbed and rinsed, hoping to remove not only the stains of confinements but the memory of their horror as well. Satisfied with her washing, she hung her clothing over nearby branches and settled down to scrubbing herself. That night Marie slept nude, wrapped snugly in a caribou robe on a bed of pine boughs. Children slept on either side of her; across the lodge, Running Bear and his wife snored loudly.

Throughout the next day the Acadians rested and recovered from their journey. That evening the Indians provided a feast for the Acadians, with laughing and dancing around the council fires. An elderly Acadian produced his treasured violin which he had rescued of all his belongings and began to play the familiar Acadian tunes. As the sun set and the people sat in darkness, their faces lighted only by the red glow of the campfire, the tunes turned to melancholy, with moistened faces singing sad songs of their lost homeland.

The next day another French military officer arrived from Cape Breton. With a group of Indian warriors, he walked through the Indian village, speaking to the Acadians. He called the Acadians to a council. Before them the officer stood with two *Mi'kmaq* chieftains and Henri Ouilette. He addressed the Acadians. "I have conferred with our *Mi'kmaq* friends. We have decided that the English may attempt retaliation by shelling this village. Tomorrow morning the chief will move his entire village inland, into the forest, out of range of English cannons. It will make life harder for the village and any who stay. We have decided you, Acadians, will continue to the safety of Fortress Louisbourg. It is a long journey overland and it will be dangerous, but *Mi'kmaq* warriors will escort you as far as Canceau Bay. You can go by boat to the Truro village, but from there you must walk to Louisbourg. You must walk over rocks, tundra, and dense forests. There will be mosquito filled swamps. You may encounter barbarous Englishmen who will try to kill you. A few warriors from the Truro Village will escort you the remainder of the long walk to Louisbourg and help you hunt for food. This village will be short of food as they leave the sea, and you will have only that provided by our *Mi'kmaq* friends along the way. It will be a long and difficult journey for the young children and elderly, but there is no other safe place. Winter must not find you in the wilderness. Mr. Ouilette will be in command of the group. You will leave early tomorrow, and may God preserve you on your journey."

Early the next morning the little priest of Beaubassin, Father Felix, held a service for one of their number who had died of his wounds. As the rays of the morning sun filtered through the tall evergreens, the Acadians buried the old man in a nameless grave in the forest. Later, they set out on the long journey to Fortress Louisbourg.

Settling down to the even rhythm at the oars, their boats moved steadily over the waters. Over the sparkling water, past rocky headlands and towering firs that swayed in the breeze, passing kingfishers that plunged into the water to emerge with silvery fish, the procession of boats plowed in their journey. Pelicans, cormorants, and herons observed these strange beings in their passage through the lonely vigil of their wilderness. Hour after hour they rowed, out of the Minas Channel into the mouth of Cobequid Bay. The elderly Acadians were not strangers to hard work and songs took their minds from lost loved ones and homeland.

Marie sat in with Henri rowing on one side and another gray haired man rowing on the other. She watched the eagles soaring in the blue sky. She listened to the gulls and the mournful cry of loons. At other times there was only the chunking of oars and hushed voices sounding louder across the quiet water.

Fingering the crucifix hanging from her neck, she thought of her brother. It had been his. *LeLoutre had returned it to her mother on his last visit to their cabin, saying, "You must be proud of your son; he died fighting the heretics. Any man who shall lose his life in My name, sayeth the Lord, shall find it."*

Pierre had been only a boy. He was afraid when that mad priest, LeLoutre, took him away with the warriors. Her mother had given him a woolen cap. At her father's request, Henri Ouilette had come to their cabin to talk to Pierre. He gave him a pair of tall, knee length moccasins. Henri showed him how to carry his bedroll across his shoulder, wrapping his belongings so that he could walk quietly and effortlessly. Henri had tried to tell Pierre about living in the forest and how to survive in a battle. But Pierre would never be a soldier, Marie and her mother had known that.

Her mother's heart had broken that day; it was more than she could bear. She had endured all the hardships with courage until the day LeLoutre returned Pierre's crucifix. From that day she sat silently in the cabin, hardly eating, withering away. She died less than a year later.

The children in Marie's boat grew restless, bringing her back to reality. Marie remembered the songs she sang as a child. Smiling at the children she began to sing. Soon people in other boats lifted their voices in song. "Bells are ringing, bells are ringing, dee, daw, dee. Dee, daw, dee," they sang in a happy broadside melody.

That evening, arriving at the *Mi'kmaq* village just before dark, many farmers slumped over their oars and slept where they sat. Children yelled gaily at being liberated from the boats; they dashed happily about the Indian village in play, chased by barking dogs and Indian children wherever they went. Marie enjoyed a meal of shellfish and roasted roots, eaten from her hands like her hosts. With an ancient *Mi'kmaq* man and his frail, coughing wife, Marie settled down on a warm caribou robe for the night. Food, fresh air, and exhaustion helped Marie forget her father as sleep overcame her. Like the other Acadians, Marie slept warmly in a dry lodge while a light rain fell outside.

Early the next morning, laden with every morsel of spare food in the village, the Acadians set out walking. A difficult journey lay ahead. Walking through the dense forests of spruce, pine, and maple, over rocks and boulders, through bogs with mosquitoes and flies, they toiled toward a destination so far away that it was difficult to imagine. When the soft, cold rain began to fall during the night, there was no *Mi'kmaq* lodge to protect them. They lay uncomfortably in their damp clothing. The next morning they arose, wet and cold. The Indians provided a breakfast of dried berries and jerked meat, served with spruce bark tea. Acadians shivered in the cold until midmorning, when the sun burst forth. Then heat and perspiration added to their discomfort. Wooden shoes slipped on the wet grass of the forest. Hands and knees bled from falls. As wooden shoes were removed and stuffed in their bags, bare feet treaded the rocks and stones, their feet now cut and bleeding. Acadian spirits fell.

Arising on a cool, grey morning, the Acadians found old Mr. Chiasson lying under his damp blanket, dead. Henri Ouilette allowed the little priest a very brief service over the old man's grave. Sooner than they were ready, Father Felix had hardly finished the burial, Henri lead the Acadians down the forest trail. Marie walked beside Mrs. Chiasson, her arm around the little gray haired lady as they talked of Mr. Chiasson and Beaubassin.

One morning a young mother, thin and pale, lay at the base of a maple tree as the Acadians prepared to set out on their day's journey. Holding her baby at her breast, covered by a baby blanket, she looked up at Marie with her dark, hollow eyes and announced that she would go no farther. "I'm staying here in the forest," she said.

"You can't stay here," Marie answered patiently. "The winter will come soon and you will freeze. You must think of your baby." She extended her hands to her. "Come, give me the baby; I will carry him for you."

"No," she exclaimed. "My baby and I are staying here." She pulled it tightly against her breast and rocked it back and forth, humming a lullaby.

Marie knelt beside the woman and put her hand beside her thin face. She brushed the young woman's hair away from her face and put her arm around the woman, hugging her close.

As Marie embraced the young woman, she put her face against Marie's breast and began to cry. Marie placed her hand tenderly on the cold baby at Mrs. Gaudreaux's breast. Looking up at Henri, she lifted the dead baby from the thin, flat breast. On her knees, Marie gently closed Mrs. Gaudreaux's dress and held the dead baby in her arms.

"Please," called Mrs. Gaudreaux in a weak, trembling voice, "give me back my baby."

"We will take care of your baby," answered Marie, "but we must take care of you too. You are sick and need rest."

Marie looked at Henri Ouilette. "We must rest here today; our people are too tired to travel."

Swearing under his breath, Henri looked up at the sun and kicked dust with the toe of his moccasin. "The snow must not find us in the wilderness, or everyone will be dead." With a sigh he turned to two Indian warriors standing nearby, giving instructions in the *Mi'kmaq* tongue. The two warriors walked back down the trail a short distance and began to dig.

The Acadians rested and dried their damp clothing in the sunshine. That evening, at sundown, they buried the baby with a crude wooden cross at its head. Day after weary day they trudged through thickets and marshes, slowly inching their way closer to Fortress Louisbourg. In sight of breathtaking beauty, Indian canoes carried the Acadians across the sparkling, placid waters of Lac Bras d' Or. At Soldier's Cove, the Acadians again set out on foot.

Chapter Twelve

On an autumn day of 1755, citizens in Boston thronged the waterfront and children hailed the brave victors of Beausejour. Colorful signal flags flapped merrily, sounding like clapping hands in the afternoon breeze. Aboard *Grenadier*, sailors in their Sunday best stood in every yard and their stations on deck.

Red-coated soldiers marched to meet His Majesty's Ship, *Grenadier*, their fifes and drums echoing through the streets on this beautiful day. But to insults and derision of Boston's citizens, French officers marched off *Grenadier*, heads held high. They were followed by Acadians, old men and young boys. They clopped down the gangplank in wooden shoes, clutching a few precious possessions under their sunburned and sinewy arms. The last such prisoner to exit *Grenadier* was Gaston Gauthier. He stopped to look around at the city he had sometimes visited as a trader. But on this visit a rifle butt shoved Gaston in the back, pushing him forward. He stumbled after his fellow Acadians. From the quarterdeck MacGregor saw him. He hurried down the gang plank, interceding at Gaston's side, directing the soldier to step aside. "I will try to learn more about Marie," he told him. "You will be confined in the town prison. I'll find you as soon as possible."

On the ship Captain Walshingham beamed and doffed his hat to the cheers. He bowed deeply. Drums rolled and pipes squealed as the admiral stepped aboard *Grenadier*, followed by the commodore and his staff.

Captain Walshingham shook hands with everyone. The admiral showered Walshingham with compliments, seemingly unaware of the commodore's dark look. This man stood glowering at Walshingham. At last, with the congratulations at an end, the commodore approached Captain Walshingham. With eyes burning he asked, "And where is your sister ship, *Gladiator*?"

Captain Walshingham turned slowly to face his commodore. "I regret to inform you, Sir, *Gladiator* is lost with all hands. They ran aground on Cape Chignecto. Indians massacred the crew and freed their prisoners... those that survived."

The commodore stood in silence, stunned by Walshingham's offhand report of tragedy. "And the *Gladiator*'s crew, Captain Walshingham, what of them? And where, may I ask, was the gallant captain of H.M.S. *Grenadier*?"

Walshingham looked condescendingly at the commodore, as a teacher might address a dull student. "It's too bad ye don't know the treacherous Bay of Fundy tides. I anchored at Ft. Lawrence and transferred cargo and prisoners on a ten-fathom tide with gale force winds blowing on shore. I completed the loading of my human cargo in an expeditious manner then clawed offshore against the wind, watching rocks beneath my keel. *Gladiator*, however, was tardy in completing her exchange. Her captain was, as usual, slow in executing his departure.

"Confident that ye, Sir, would not have me risk two ships for the sake of one, I proceeded without her. I departed before the falling tide and an onshore storm might overcome me. I held some hope *Gladiator*'s captain might, through luck, bring his ship to safety. But in the darkness and foul weather that followed, his ship could not be seen. I did not see *Gladiator* again until my vigilant search found him wrecked on Cape Chignecto. He had run aground, a victim of the treacherous tides and fogs, as well as his own negligence. While trying to kedge themselves off-shore, they were attacked by hostile Indians who massacred the crew and freed the prisoners."

The commodore stood stiff and silent, his eyes like steel. "Captain Walshingham, I want your documented report on my desk in two days. There will be an inquiry. Let us hope the board finds no negligence on your part. I would not like to see you shot on the poop of your ship." With those words the two officers strode down the gangplank followed by their staff.

Captain Walshingham's ebullient mood melted. With an impotent look he turned his back to the cheering crowds. "Listen to the cheers of my admirers. Why can't the commodore respect my accomplishments? My critics never rest. While I destroy the King's enemies, my peers assault my reputation." He paced the quarterdeck, his chin on his chest, his lower lip out thrust, his hands behind his back. A few minutes later he called out to the boatswain, "Secure the ship and assemble all officers in the wardroom. No one shall leave this ship until I give the order."

In the wardroom Walshingham waved and pointed with a dagger as he spoke. "Gentlemen, ye know how everyone covets my seamanship and brilliant tactics in warfare. Ye can be sure my peers will be dropping their poisoned words into the ear of the commodore. Therefore, we must mount our defense. Lieutenant MacGregor, ye will do a complete report. Describe the weather and tides in the Bay of Fundy at the time of *Gladiator*'s grounding. Ye will write a detailed report of the conditions surrounding *Gladiator*. An analysis of her angle of repose must prove she ran aground, of her own negligence. Let yer evidence show Indians attacked and carried away her prisoners.

"And I shall make a courtesy call on the Governor, with a gift of French wine. I will remind him of the large sum of prize money I contribute to his purse. If ye care to recite my bravery and genius to influential ears, I shall not be embarrassed. Be certain yer kindness will not go unrewarded.

"Mr. Farwell, Mr. MacGregor, the two of ye shall see that my reports are polished to perfection. Remember, those who would tarnish my reputation paint with a wide brush. Yer reputation is also at stake. Do a good job and yer stars will soar with mine. Thank ye, gentlemen." Walshingham walked from the wardroom, his chin on his chest, his hands behind his back.

It was two days before MacGregor completed his report to Walshingham's satisfaction. Free to leave the ship, he made his way along the dark, empty streets to the old stone prison. He identified himself to the bearded jailer. "I'm an officer of the King's Navy. I want to interview a prisoner we delivered from Canada."

The jailer looked at MacGregor suspiciously before leading him down the dark hallway. At the Acadian's cell the jailer fumbled with his keys while MacGregor held the lantern. The jailer rattled a key into the door and pulled the squeaking door. The prisoners inside stirred, talking excitedly among themselves. Some stood. MacGregor walked inside, holding the lantern high and shading his eyes. Prisoners observed MacGregor with white eyes contrasting against their dark, bearded faces as they looked up into the light. "*Monsieur* Gauthier," MacGregor called.

Gaston sat on the stone floor with other captured Acadians, his head in his hands. He lifted himself slowly to his feet. "Yes, yes, who calls? I'm Gaston Gauthier."

"Mr. Gauthier, it's Charles MacGregor. I came as soon as I could."

Gaston stood, taking MacGregor's hand in his. "My daughter, what have you heard?" His hand swept the dark dungeon. "All of these men had loved ones on the ship. Like me, they are desperate to know of their loved ones. Please, you must help us." A loud crescendo of assent arose from the other prisoners. Gaston Gauthier continued, "The guards ignore us and tell us to be quiet. They want money, but we have no money, eh? We are broken men; everything we have is gone. Without money we will be sold into bondage and sent to some English colony, only God knows where. From there we may never find our loved ones.

"God be merciful! Do with us what you will but at least tell us of our loved ones." The other prisoners agreed loudly. Gaston spread his hands, exposing his trembling fingers and ran them through his gray hair. With pleading eyes he continued, "I know a trader here that knows me… a man named Edward Brumley. He owes me a considerable sum of money. I sold him farm produce some six years ago on consignment. I left my goods with him for his resale, as I had done with other Boston merchants, and he was to pay me later. But the French Government prevented my returning to get my money. I have no receipts. No Boston merchant would offer a French trader a receipt. It's against both French and English law for us to trade with each other. I have no written record. There is only my good word, that of Mr. Brumley, and an honest handshake. He surely will acknowledge that he owes me a debt, one I have been unable to collect since France and England began fighting. Please see this Edward Brumley. The man can pay me the money he owes, and I will pay for my freedom and perhaps that of my friends here. I can buy the freedom of my daughter if I can find her, and I think I might know where to find her. We have had much time here in this cell to talk about our lost loved ones. We think they will have gone to Louisbourg on *Isle Royale*. That would be the most secure French stronghold they could reach. Perhaps they would have help from the Indians." Gaston Gauthier, looked at MacGregor with moist, pleading eyes. "Please, help me get out of here so I can find Marie."

MacGregor looked stunned, his mind racing. Then he stiffened and spoke between clinched teeth, "I have met Edward Brumley. He's an upstanding citizen here. Would he trade with you in violation of the Navigation Acts? Likely! But then, what successful American merchant does not? No ship sails without a manifest, accurate or not, and every ship's sailing is documented in port records. There must be some record to help your claim. If there is, we'll find it, and I will see Brumley for you. Surely he will pay his debt." MacGregor looked into Gauthier's red, moist eyes. "I will go to Brumley; I will do all I can to help you and perhaps you can help the others. I doubt you can get to Louisbourg to find Marie, but I may. My frigate will soon be blockading Louisbourg. If I find a way to get ashore there, I might find her, whatever." His thoughts turning to the actions he must take, he continued, "Mr. Gauthier, I will come to you again… soon!" MacGregor turned and rattled the door to call the jailer. Saying not a word, his mind deep in thought, MacGregor left the cell and walked out of the prison.

It required only a few inquiries that afternoon to learn the location of Brumley's office, and it was still early afternoon when MacGregor stood before that imposing building. A large sign read, *Edward Brumley Trading,*

Ltd. Both sides of the sign bore a picture of a lone oak tree and a loan oak flag hung above the door. Without hesitation he opened the front door and stepped inside. The office hummed with activity. Clerks worked busily at high standing desks as others carried books and papers between the desks, glancing up to see the strange face in their office. Behind a closed door and visible through the glass in the door, Edward Brumley sat. From his private office he looked up to see MacGregor. Brumley registered surprise then hurried from his chair, rattled the door open, and walked out into the main office with a wide smile. He pumped his hand, saying, "Lieutenant MacGregor, first officer of *HMS Grenadier*." Brumley's exclamation was made loudly as an explanation to the office staff. While viewing MacGregor with wary eyes he asked, "And how is my friend Captain Walshingham?"

"Walshingham's fine, Sir," he replied politely. "Mr. Brumley, could we go inside your office and talk?"

"Of course, my good man. Please pardon my manners but you caught me by complete surprise. Please step inside." Brumley bowed slightly as he held the door open for him.

In Brumley's office MacGregor began. "We just returned from Canada with Acadian prisoners. They are men who have allegedly violated their oath of neutrality and joined the French Army against their oath. There is one man, a trader named Gaston Gauthier from the French settlement of Beaubassin, who knows you and says he has traded with you. He claims you owe him money, and it would be generous if you paid that now. Unless he can raise money for his release, Mr. Gauthier will be indentured to some English colony."

Edward Brumley shifted his stare from MacGregor to the ceiling. "Well, this is unusual. I do not keep records beyond five years. Does your Mister… Gauthier have records of the alleged transaction? Does he say when it is supposed to have occurred?" Brumley stroked his chin and smiled as he continued, "This man's misfortune is indeed distressing to me, this Mr. Gauthier, but I cannot for the life of me recall the man or such a transaction. It must be that he has mistaken me for some other English trader. I certainly do not violate the Navigation Acts and trade with France, but I hear there are those who do."

Brumley rose from his chair and opened the door, smiling. "Mr. MacGregor, please give my respects to Captain Walshingham."

MacGregor continued, looking intently at Edward Brumley. He put on his hat while walking to the door. "I thank you for your time, Mr. Brumley, whatever."

MacGregor walked slowly along the busy docks, not hearing the gulls nor the hucksters. He thought, *I must help Mr. Gauthier, even if I never see my beautiful Marie again. No! My God! I must see Marie again. I will begin tomorrow for Mr. Gauthier and I will find Marie... whatever.*

The next morning MacGregor awakened to a knock on his cabin. "Beggin' yer pardon, Sir, Mr. MacGregor, but Captain Walshingham wants to see you in his cabin. Right away, Sir!"

MacGregor rose and dressed, trying to imagine what urgency lay behind Walshingham's summons. By the time he arrived at the cabin, he thought he knew the answer. His knock at Captain Walshingham's cabin was punctual as ordered. He hesitated, then knocked again at Walshingham's cabin door, almost unaware of the marine guard's salute as he considered his problem with Gaston Gauthier and Walshingham's friend, Brumley. MacGregor entered Walshingham's cabin of gleaming oak, art, and books. The captain wore a crooked smile, but his demeanor changed rapidly. He jumped from his Louis XIV chair and strode across the cabin, standing behind his desk as MacGregor approached. Walshingham leaned over his desk as he faced MacGregor, saying, "A Royal Navy lieutenant must be highly motivated to risk his career for some French peasant. I find it difficult to believe that even you would be so stupid, MacGregor. However, others report to the contrary. Therefore, I'm persuaded accordingly. I endured your Jacobite ancestry and your colonial illiteracy. But now you are into something I can no longer ignore." Walshingham's frown changed to a demonic sneer. "Bring any, I say *any* discredit upon me or my ship, and you will rather be dead!" Walshingham sighed and his crooked smile returned. "Personally, I don't give a damn about this Acadian. But I am concerned for the good name of Edward Brumley, a colonial like yourself, a man you should cultivate, not castigate. Please, do not let me hear your name mentioned again in this matter." The scowl returned. "You can be replaced... or worse." Walshingham's wicked sneer slowly disappeared to be replaced by a smile. His eyes softened and he looked at Lieutenant MacGregor as a wayward son. "Ah, you are young, my boy. A young man is entitled to a mistake. But nothing makes a poor man more responsible than wealth, and I remind you, you are on your way to wealth." Walshingham's hand moved to his desk drawer. Slowly pulling the drawer open, the captain looked intently into MacGregor's eyes. He lifted a bundle of Stirling Pound notes tied in a red ribbon. He lifted the bundle, slowly laying it on the desk in front of MacGregor. Still looking into MacGregor's eyes, he said with a smile, "This is yours, all yours! More money, I'm sure, than you have ever had in your life! It is your one-eighth share of a little prize money, a sample of much more to come. It is yours to spend as you will and be confident there will me more, much more." As MacGregor stood with his hands at his sides and looked at the bundle, Walshingham picked it up, placing it in MacGregor's hands and opened the door to the cabin. With a hand guiding his lieutenant out the door, Walshingham said, "No need to thank me, MacGregor; you have earned this money. Go out on the town and see what pleasures a little money will buy. You will come back in a lighter mood and ready to serve this ship like a good officer should."

Dejectedly, MacGregor returned to his cabin. He placed the money in his trunk and sat looking at it. *What must I do with this money? Walshingham has warned me to stay out of Brumley's affairs, or I might lose my commission. How would I get to Louisbourg if I'm discharged? I don't know how, but somehow I will. And who will help Mr. Gauthier if I do not?*

Chapter Thirteen

Meanwhile, a motley column of weary Acadians emerged from the forest where leaves of birch and maple were turning to gold. After their long and arduous journey, the refugees stood in tattered and soiled clothing, looking in awe at the mighty fortress of Louisbourg. They had never seen the likes in their village of Beaubassin. The imposing stone battlements rose above a wide harbor with the tall bell tower of the King's Bastion rising above all. Great stone ramparts bristled with cannons, and soldiers could be seen walking the battlements. A great citadel towered above the ramparts with great cannons protecting the lesser ramparts and their smaller guns. Hundreds of chimneys sent thin strands of smoke into the gray sky, promising warmth against the coming winter. Within the massive walls stood a small city reflecting the culture of its European settlers. Many of the homes were built on two levels. Louisbourg seemed a beehive of activity. The masts of many ships rose from the harbor. Fishermen dried cod and mended nets near the wharf where numerous palisade log buildings stored their wares. Dozens of boats were careened on the beach with men from all over Europe tending them. There was a hospital run by Catholic Brothers of Saint-Jean de Dieu. It too had a tall spire rivaling that of the King's Bastion. A convent and school housed the Sisters of Notre-Dame and educated the children. Few citizens of Beaubassin had ever seen a city so large nor one whose appearance promised so much safety. Many Acadians fell to their knees in thanksgiving for their deliverance. At the sight Marie also paused. She swung her heavy seedbag off her neck and laid it on the ground. Acadians laughed and hugged each other at the sight. Marie wiped tears of joy from her eyes.

Fortress Louisbourg's massive walls towered above the Acadians as they drew closer. Uniformed soldiers with long rifles and glistening bayonets, clad in blue jackets and white trousers, stood beside the gate. With a look of impatience, an officer admitted the long column of happy Acadians. Walking in awe, they wandered through the high, arched gate while soldiers hurried them along with sharp words and gestures.

Henri Ouilette, still dressed in fringed buckskin, his gray hair flowing from beneath a blue toque, his rifle cradled in the crook of his arm, led the column through the gate. A *Mi'kmaq* warriors walked on either side. Walking slowly, they too looked in awe of the massive stone walls. Inside the city, doors opened and heads popped out windows. Citizens gathered to see them entering their city, and again the country people looked in wonder at the city people's strange dress. Cooking smells promised food, warm meals and comfort against the cold nights. Joy showed on the faces of the Acadians, but that joy was not matched by Louisbourg's inhabitants. A citizen was heard to complain loudly, "Now we have even more mouths to feed." Marie, walking slowly on weary legs, handed the baby she carried to its mother. She tried to brush the trail dust from her threadbare dress and raised her chin, aware of the hostility in people's eyes.

The Governor, the Chevalier, Augustin de Drucour, met them inside the gates. This former commander of the French naval war college inspired confidence. Madame Drucour, descended from a family of French admirals, men whose service to King and country was legend, was present as usual to welcome these refugees. Other officials responded to the call of the guards and now arrived at the Dauphin Gate. Unlike the common citizens of Louisbourg, they greeted the Acadians warmly. Governor Drucour took Henri Ouilette's hand and led him aside. After a short, whispered interrogation of Henri, the Governor turned to the Acadians. "Welcome to Louisbourg, where you are now in the safety and protection of His Christian Majesty, Louis XV. Here you will be given food and shelter as is available to us, although the British blockade of our port has hindered the arrival of supplies. Like all citizens here, in exchange for your upkeep and well-being, you will be expected to work for the good of Louisbourg and defend it with your life if necessary."

Madame Drucour made her way among the women. With moist eyes she ran her hand over the hair of a young girl and whispered encouragement to the adults. When the other officials had left, Madame Drucour stayed with the Acadians, leading them to a military kitchen. Holding hands with the children, Madame Drucour approached the cooks, saying, "Quickly, prepare hot soup; feed these children and our hungry countrymen."

Madame Drucour turned to a thin young girl with hollow cheeks and dark eyes. "Look at you, my little darling! Bless your heart, you need food and rest." Calling for a servant she said, "Quickly, let us have some fresh milk for the children."

Marie found a shady area beside the building where she sat on her heavy knapsack. Leaning her head against the brick building, she wearily closed her eyes. While the Acadians ate hungrily, Madame Drucour busily hovered from one group to another, like a humming bird. She asked questions of the people. She offered encouragement when the people showed signs of despair and answered their questions. After the Acadians had eaten, Madame Drucour put them in the custody of a beefy woman wearing a white peasant's cap and wooden shoes. The woman led them to the horse stables. As Madame Drucour watched, the weary Acadians pitched into the arduous task of cleaning the stables, their new temporary home. It would be a castle compared to sleeping in the open as they had on the journey. Marie dropped her knapsack and flew to the task. Acadians were not strangers to this work; they impressed the noblewoman with their industry. Soon the barn was almost as clean as a home.

Placed in a stable with a widow and her two young children, Marie threw aside her heavy knapsack and crawled into the clean hay. She had only a few moments to worry about her lost father. Her heavy eyelids closed and her tired, aching muscles relaxed. Marie was fast asleep.

Early the next morning Madame Drucour reappeared with men pulling a cart of donated clothing. The lady pulled clothes from the cart and looked over the Acadians until she found someone to match the clothing she had in hand. Reluctantly, she turned the chore over to local women. The governor's lady organized baths for the Acadians and, with the surgeon in tow, tended their medical needs. Marie emerged from the bath with her hair in braids, covered by a clean, white Norman cap. A threadbare dress covered her new wooden shoes, now clicking across the paving stones as Marie assembled in the courtyard with the other women.

Madame Drucour again stood before the group. "Cleanliness," said Madame Drucour, "and hard work are virtues we all appreciate. While you are my guest here in Louisbourg, I will expect you to acquiesce to those tenets. I will also expect you to attend mass regularly. Do those three things and do not become drunk or promiscuous. Then shall we be good citizens and friends. Now, you elderly men and boys will labor in the fields to feed the growing population of Louisbourg. Mr. Garcin, here," said Madame Drucour, pointing to a tall man with a sun tanned face, "will show you to your work. You will work every day except Sunday, from daylight until dark. There are still a few crops to be harvested; we must glean the fields of every morsel of food for people and animals.

"And the women will report to Mrs. Wallez," continued Madame Drucour, pointing to the same beefy lady from yesterday. "She will assign as many of you as possible to house chores, but some of you must help look after the soldiers and some must assist in the fields. Your children will be looked after while you work, and you will be treated well in Louisbourg. We will move you out of the stables soon. Do not despair. Be happy in serving His Christian Majesty, King Louis XV. Remember, you are now in his care and all will be well."

As Madame Drucour concluded, two young women walked by in long colorful dresses adorned in silk and lace. Above their fine coiffures the young women wore large hats covered by dainty ribbons and lace. They carried colorful parasols to shade their painted faces from the sun. Silk gloves covered their mouths as they whispered about the peasants standing before them. Marie looked away in embarrassment while hiding her suntanned hands behind her frayed brown dress.

Madame Wallez called out the domestic jobs for women from a long scroll. "Madame La Valliere needs a woman to clean chamber pots and do general house cleaning... she may look after her own children in the lady's home. Madame Denis needs a woman who sews well and is not afraid to work... the bakery needs a woman who knows baking. The single officer's quarters require a woman to clean and mend. In the officer's quarters, Madame La Lalonde needs a woman to clean chamber pots and do general house cleaning. Madame Denis needs a wet-nurse."

Madame Wallez continued to call out jobs to the end of her list, but there were fewer domestic jobs than women. With two girls and a young widow, Marie marched to the fields with the men. For the first time in her life, Marie would harvest hay from the fields. She stood in a large meadow of yellowing grass as the gentle breeze sent undulating waves through the field like an ocean. In the heavy dress, patched and sewn, Marie turned to the task with a sickle in hand. Bending low, she slashed the standing grass. Her sickle swished through the grass as her mind turned to past events. Anger welled within her and she slashed faster. Tears welled in her eyes and rolled down her cheeks. Her sickle slashed wildly. When sobs broke from her lips, she stopped and dropped her sickle. "Damn the English! Damn the French," she shouted. "Why couldn't they leave us alone?" At last Marie wiped her eyes with her apron and looked upward. A prayer fell from her lips and determination replaced despair. She picked up the tool. With the sickle she slashed rhythmically, cutting the hay and assembling it into shocks. Her sickle made a rhythmic slashing sound in the tall grass while ravens called in the distance. The cold surrendered to hard labor and sweat rolled down her brow. Mud streaked her face as dust found the perspiration. Aching muscles protested the strain of bending low to slash the hay and blisters formed on tired hands. Like other Acadians, Marie tied the bundles with strands of grass. When the sun turned golden in the west, shocks of hay soon stood like hundreds of tents across the fields. It was after sunset and twilight lingered gold and green when the Acadians laid aside their chores to file back into the massive stone walls. With crickets chirping in the darkness and stars twinkling overhead, Marie ate a paltry dinner and fell asleep in her bed of musty hay.

Days passed and callouses replaced blisters on Marie's hands. Rising before daylight, Marie ate a Spartan breakfast and marched to the fields. Grain that was missed in the first harvest was in the second and third gleaning until hungry birds could find not a grain. At sunset she marched wearily back to the fort for another dinner of bread and cod fish cooked in many different ways. Exhausted, she quickly fell asleep in her straw bed. Long days and uncomfortable nights passed before Marie found new quarters. As colder weather covered the ripe yellow straw in the fields with a glistening white frost, Madame Wallez moved Marie out of the stables. She placed her in a small room with two beds, shared by a widow and two children.

Chapter Fourteen

In Boston at that time, Captain Walshingham lubricated the squeaking wheels of politics with prize money, and Lieutenant MacGregor made a decision with what should be done with his. Soon it was said they would sail for Louisbourg, despite the approaching cold weather. Feeling pressed for time, MacGregor walked down the business streets of Boston, looking up at the signs. Feeling the unusual bulge of bank notes in his pocket, he stopped before a sign that read, *Samuel Steinbach, Barrister*. MacGregor thought, *One is as good as another, whatever.* He walked inside. A pale and thin man with bushy black eyebrows looked up over his eye glasses. He removed his hat and asked, "Would you be a lawyer?"

The lawyer's lip curled and his eyes narrowed as he spoke. "I'm a *barrister*, Sir, the best in the colony. Have you the need of the best barrister in Boston, Sir?"

MacGregor's eyes narrowed and he ignored the question as he asked, "Is Edward Brumley a client of yours?" He stood with one eyebrow arched as he waited for an answer.

The lawyer rose from his chair and removed his glasses. "My only associations with Edward Brumley have been adversarial, Sir." The lawyer pointed to a chair, continuing, "If you plan a lawsuit against Edward Brumley then sit down. We can certainly do business."

MacGregor removed an envelope from his pocket. "I have here a certificate for one hundred pounds." He handed the envelope to the attorney. "Edward Brumley owes a large sum of money to my… friend from French Canada. His name is Gaston Gauthier, and he is being held in the old jail after being, er… taken from his home in Beaubassin. If he can't raise enough money to buy his passage to France, he will be sold as a bond servant in an English colony. I would like you to find Mr. Gauthier and recover his money from Edward Brumley." He fumbled in his coat pocket until he found a hand written card. He handed it to the lawyer. "This is the card of my banker here in Boston. He has my agreement to disburse additional funds to you as you make progress on this case. Say, one thousand pounds when you free Mr. Gauthier and ten percent of the money you recover from Brumley."

The lawyer's narrow eyes widened just a bit and his lips turned up slightly at the corners as he pulled out his silver snuff box. "Twenty percent *when* I win the suit from Brumley and I believe we can do business." The barrister sniffed his tobacco and smiled. Mr. Steinbach put away his snuff box and leaned across the desk. "You take care of King George's business, young man, and leave this problem to the best barrister in Boston."

H. M. S. Grenadier sailed the next morning before daylight. She resumed her station in the blockade of Louisbourg, and First Lieutenant MacGregor fretted over Marie Gauthier.

On this cool day of 1755, a carriage rattled to a stop outside the Boston courthouse. A thin little man dressed in black stepped out of the carriage and lifted his coat collar against the cold. Mr. Steinbach stood on the cobblestones of the street and withdrew a silver snuff box from his pocket, helping himself to a pinch of tobacco as he approached the old jail in Boston. At the door he stopped and took his cane from beneath his arm. With the brass head of the cane, Mr. Steinbach rapped loudly on the heavy wooden door. Presently, the door creaked open and the bearded jailer's droopy eyelids opened wider as he beheld the well dressed gentleman at his door.

The little lawyer reached inside his pocket and withdrew a document wrapped in red tape and sealed with the familiar crown of government. "Sir," Steinbach said, "I have here a writ issued in my name for the purchase of my new bond servant, one Gaston Gauthier of French Canada. I am a busy man with much for my new bond servant to do and require that you deliver him to me immediately."

A few weeks later another carriage rattled down the front street of Boston. Stopping in front of a trading company, the coach door flew open and Mr. Steinbach stepped out. With his cane under his arm, the little lawyer stood on the paving stones and looked around. Gaston Gauthier, his newly purchased bond servant, slowly stepped out of the coach behind him. Steinbach's cane rapped upon the rough stones impatiently until he sighted another man, a younger man, approaching at a fast gait. The impatient man asked, continuing to tap the cobblestones with his cane, "Have you the documents?"

The young man seemed hurt by the question and raised a leather case, saying, "They are all here, of course."

Steinbach snapped his snuff box shut. "Are they all in order?"

"They are all perfectly in order," the younger man answered, displaying a sense of injured pride.

"Then let's stop wasting time," said Steinbach who wheeled around and tapped his way across the paving stones and threw open the doors of *Edward*

Brumley Trading. In smaller letters beneath the main sign it read, *Boston Prize Commissioner.* This thin little man put his cane under his arm and pinched his eye glasses to his nose. He stopped before a long counter. Taking his cane from under his arm, he rapped loudly on the counter. Ink wells and letter openers rattled on the polished wood. Several clerks looked up from their desks. One moved quickly to the counter, saying, "Oh, good day Mr. Steinbach, what can we do for you today, Mr. Steinbach?"

Samuel Steinbach raised his bushy eyebrows and lowered his head, looking at the clerk over the top of his glasses. Wordlessly, the lawyer stood. With his eyes on the clerk he extended a hand to his assistant. The assistant withdrew the documents from his brief case and laid them in the extended hand. Mr. Steinbach glanced over the papers quickly and laid them on the counter. He looked up at the clerk again, saying, "There is naught you can do for me, Sir! But there is a grave error to be corrected, and corrected quickly it must be." Steinbach lifted his cane and guided the clerk aside as he walked toward Brumley's office. Stopping briefly, he placed his cane under his arm, tugged at his vest, and opened the door widely. Holding the door open, he turned to look at the gray-haired man behind him. "Let us go in, Mr. Gauthier, time is of the essence!"

Without so much as a knock on the door, Steinbach threw the door open and motioned the other two men in after him. Brumley looked up quickly from his desk as the men filed into his office. "Oh, it's you, Steinbach. Please excuse me, but I'm too busy to see you today. Come back tomorrow," he said with a rising inflection that bordered on a shout.

Without a greeting, the lawyer began, "Mr. Brumley, contrary to common law and decency, you have subjected my client, Gaston Gauthier, an upstanding businessman of French descent, to the humiliation of labor in bondage. You are denying him his just reward for trade. You have thereby maliciously done him injury. This gentleman is now *my* bond servant and in my safe care and custody. But the travesty of justice that placed him there must be corrected immediately or I shall seek redress from a higher authority!" The barrister slapped the papers on the counter. "Mr. Brumley, I'll be brief and take very little of your personal time, nor give you an undue amount of my own," said the lawyer. He hastily opened his leather case, laying a sheaf of papers on Brumley's desk. "His Majesty King George, through his court in Boston, has issued a subpoena for certain of your papers."

Edward Brumley looked up at the lawyer. "What do these papers mean, Steinbach?"

The little man's cane thumped on the floor. "They mean, Sir, I will examine all of your books and papers. You are in breech of contract with Gaston Gauthier, formerly of Beaubassin, lately of Boston, whom you see standing here. As you know, he sold you a shipload of produce for an agreed price which was never paid. He seeks, Sir, just compensation for the produce, a fair interest on the money long since owed him, redress for said injury, and reimbursement for solicitations made in his behalf."

Brumley sat looking at the lawyer, slowly turning his gaze to Gaston Gauthier who stood with his hat in hand. "And what the hell does that mean, Steinbach?"

"It means, Sir, you pay Mr. Gauthier the money you owe him… his lawyer's fees, interest and an agreed amount of damage. It means we endeavor to keep this quiet among ourselves to avoid your going to jail for violating the Navigation Acts, which would make it more difficult for me to collect the sums demanded. Let us not make this matter more complicated than it already is, Sir!"

Brumley stood up with fists clinched, swollen neck, eyes wide and bulging. His mouth opened but no sound came out. Silently, Brumley sat loudly in his chair, his entire body limp.

Steinbach pointed a bony finger at an empty signature line, saying, "Sign your name right there, Brumley, to acknowledge the time and date of their presentation. Let us hope this miscarriage of justice can be overturned out of court before I am forced to disclose all in a court of law before the public and higher authorities! I have a subpoena for the papers of The Edward Brumley Trading Company, Limited. My assistant will conduct a search of your office on my behalf. Therefore, it is the Crown that wishes to examine your books and justice shall not be deterred. Penalty for resistance is five years in jail or five hundred pounds, or both."

Steinbach turned to his assistant. "Young man, let's stop wasting time. You know your business, so go about it diligently. If anyone interferes in your mission, carefully note his name for proper punishment by the authorities."

Casually, the lawyer strolled out of Brumley's office. In the middle of the main office he stopped and rapped the wooden floor with the tip of his cane. In a loud voice he announced to Brumley's many clerks at their tall desks, "Gentlemen, no papers shall leave this room until I say they may leave. No one will leave this room without my permission, and you can expect to work quite late this evening. Your cooperation will be expected and appreciated by the Crown. Mr. Brumley shall adequately compensate you for your extra work,

I am sure. Now gather around while my assistant acquaints you with the work you will be doing this evening."

* * *

As the winter of 1755 blew across the frothing waves, *Grenadier* sailed her blockade course with the mighty French fortress just visible on the horizon. Back and forth they sailed, wore ship, beat to windward, wore ship, and sailed back to repeat the process day after day. Fresh new winds of winter blew down from the icy north. Those cold winds blew over the warm northerly setting current, generating dense fog with the dangers of collision and running aground. *Soon*, thought Lieutenant MacGregor, *we will return to Boston for the winter, and I can learn what has happened with Mr. Gauthier... and maybe his daughter, Marie.*

But in a surprise to everyone in the fleet, a long string of signal flags, whipping in the cold north wind from the signal halyard of the command ship, relayed orders from the Admiralty. "British ships would continue to blockade Louisbourg this year, even into winter. There would not be the usual return to Boston to wait for spring."

So as the days turned darker and colder, the ship beat miserably against the north wind and then, with a little respite, ran downwind before Louisbourg again. Sailors on watch felt the downwind run to be downright balmy compared to the freezing run to the north. They sailed the same boring and miserable tack repeatedly, day and night, week after week. Those northwest winds that filled *Grenadier*'s sails often brought sleet and snow that froze those sails into solid sheets of ice. Picture a man standing ten stories above a tossing ship trying to handle a stiff, solid sail with frozen fingers. The wind whipped tall waves over the men on deck and soaked them with freezing saltwater. Every item of clothing was either wet or frozen solid. A frost bitten toe could be smashed against a timber but hardly noticed until warmed over a lamp. On watch, fingers numbed by cold lost their grip on the ratlines high above the deck. More than one man fell to his death that year.

When off watch, men lay in damp blankets on the gundeck, trying to sleep. They shivered, coughed, and walked the decks without rest. Dr. Abrams amputated a number of fingers and toes that became gangrenous. The weeks of boredom were interrupted by brief interludes of panic. The invisible tide could set a ship two miles off course in the darkness, dashing them on the rocks. An iceberg, unseen in the fog and darkness, could drift down upon them, taking them all to a cold, watery grave. Even if a man could swim, as most could not, a fall overboard into the icy water would bring instant death from exposure. In those waters that winter, the enemy was seldom French. Fresh fruit and vegetables disappeared from the daily rations, with the main fare being salted beef, beer, and stale bread. The symptoms of scurvy appeared in men's teeth and gums.

Chapter Fifteen

Unknown to Lieutenant MacGregor or her father, Marie stood at Government House in the French fortress of Louisbourg on this day in 1755. Madame Drucour, wife of the governor, stood looking down at the rough wooden shoes on Marie's feet. The young woman hid her rough, red, and calloused hands behind the folds of her coarse brown dress. Marie asked, "You called for me, Madame?"

"Yes," answered Madame Drucour. "You have worked well in the fields and barns. Madame Wallez recommends you as a willing worker, one who is polite, and speaks well. She says you read and write. Is that true?"

"Yes, Madame, it is true that I read and write. Before the Abbe LeLoutre ordered them burned, we had schools in my village of Beaubassin."

Madame Drucour shook her head, saying, "War is a terrible thing and I wish the English had left your people in peace. But that is out of our hands, my dear. We must serve our king as best we can. Now, I need another chamber maid, especially one who reads and writes. If you would like, I am willing to give you a chance at the job. Our winters are hard here in Louisbourg. You will find it warmer and the food better here than with the commoners. I demand perfection and I am not easy to please, but the work will not be nearly so hard as that in the barns."

"I will do my best, Madame," Marie replied.

"Good. If you are assiduous in your duties, you can have a good life here, Marie. Do your work faithfully, be courteous and attentive, and we will all do very well. I will often send you written instructions, and you will carry them out exactly as I have ordered."

Madame Drucour led Marie up the stairs to the bed chamber. "This," said Madame Drucour, "is my bed chamber. This will be your primary responsibility, but you will also be my messenger to the chefs and other servants. You will make my bed and help me in dressing. Since I bathe almost every day, you will help me with my bath. When you are not attending me personally, you will help clean Government House. Your job will include helping the kitchen staff when we entertain, and serving guests if needed. Six and one-half days each week will you work, with a half day off on Sunday. You will attend church during that half-day and any other time services are held.

I expect you to obey the commandments and not be tempted to take anyone's belongings."

Marie's mind struggled to hear the words of Madame Drucour as her eyes beheld the splendor of the lady's bed chamber. Marie had never seen anything like it in her life. An enormous canopy bed with more lace than she could have imagined stood against one wall. Lavender silk from China covered the bed. The ornate bed posts towered above the bed with a high, lace canopy. Tapestries and paintings from Europe adorned the walls. Gold, silver, and crystal dazzled her eyes. The luxury of the Governor's mansion was more than a girl from Beaubassin could imagine.

"The bed linen you will change weekly," Madame Drucour continued, "and no dust shall ever be found on the window sills or furniture. You will help me in my toilet and keep my clothing neat and tidy. You will keep the chamber pots clean—very, very clean.

"Cleanliness is next to Godliness, you know, my dear. And we who live in Louisbourg need, of all things, cleanliness and Godliness. After all, we are many people in a small area, besieged by the English on one side and the wilderness on the other. There is not enough food, not enough clothing, not enough culture, not enough music... not enough of anything, but that is not your problem. We will get by in service to our King. It is your problem to help keep this place clean so that I can spend my time looking after the needs of our citizens.

"In payment for your work, we will keep you in lodging and feed you. Everyone in Louisbourg must work, and I can tell that you are one who is not afraid of work. You and I shall grow to be good friends, I am sure of it."

Marie replied, "I will try very hard, Madame."

"I know you will," replied Madame Drucour. "I can tell you are of good stock, and I hope to know you better through time. Ah, time," reflected Madame Drucour, "time is all that's plentiful here in Louisbourg, time, the cold, and the long, dark winter. But, we must make the best of it. If you really try, my dear, you can find something good in this place. You will learn the good things about our seasons here. You already know about the beautiful summers here; they must be very much like your Beaubassin. But there are some pleasures of the cold, dark winter. In wintertime, the English ships retreat to their ports in Halifax and Boston. Then our brave sailors fight their way into Louisbourg, braving the cold and the icebergs to bring us supplies. In the winter our brave sailors bring food while the English flee the stormy ocean for the safety of their ports. We have no mosquitoes or flies in winter. Snow covers the ugly mud and dirt while the sky radiates the beauty of the northern lights, lights you can almost hear. And the stars are so close, you can almost reach out and touch them. At Christmas we celebrate the birth of Christ with beautiful music and lights. English pirates fear the winter storms at sea. They stay by their firesides and allow us to celebrate Christmas in peace. You will come to like it here, Marie, especially in winter. I will help you."

Madame Drucour gave Marie a black dress of fine material to replace her course brown one. She gave her a little white apron to match her white cap. The lady gave her white stockings, darned and threadbare, but clean and white. She also gave Marie leather shoes. Thus Marie became Madame Drucour's third chamber maid in Government House. Berthe and Agnes had worked as chambermaids since the deaths of their soldier husbands. The two women came from neighboring villages in France and became close friends while working for Madame Drucour. Berthe was tall and broad shouldered. An unruly mop of red hair surmounted her round, freckled face. With her muscular arms and thick hands, Berthe could work like a draft horse. But the gentle and simple heart of a little girl beat within her rugged body. Agnes was thin and frail, with angular chin and brown eyes that looked from the depths of dark sockets. Given to fits of coughing, her every move seemed made with effort.

Marie set her mind to the task of pleasing Madame Drucour. If her lot was to be a chamber maid, she would be the best chamber maid possible. She found the work helped pass the time and took her mind off her lost father. Not satisfied with cleaning, Marie polished to perfection everything she cleaned. But she did not work mindlessly. Late one evening Madame Drucour rushed into Government House exclaiming, "I was reviewing the soldiers at the parade grounds and completely lost track of the time! I completely forgot that I had guests coming for dinner this evening. I have not told the kitchen to prepare food for our guests and now it is too late."

"No, Madame. You told me to have your blue dress ready to entertain your dinner guests this evening," Marie answered. "When I went to the kitchen for lunch today, I learned that no food was prepared for tonight. I informed the chef you were having guests for dinner. He has prepared the food already."

"Oh, bless you, my dear," answered Madame Drucour. "I don't know how I managed without you."

"You have many things to remember, Madame. Few could do as well," replied Marie. "I have your clothing laid out, and Berthe has drawn your bath."

Madame Drucour said, "Oh, thank you so much, Marie. But I have a dreadful headache. I'm going to my bed chamber. Bring me a glass of brandy."

Madame Drucour rushed upstairs, followed by Marie. As Marie undressed her, Madame Drucour removed her jewelry. With a pail of hot water in each hand, Berthe clopped into the room, her big feet pounding on the floor. Steam rose above the bath tub as she emptied the pails into the tub.

As Madame Drucour stepped into her bath tub, Agnes appeared with a glass of brandy. "Thank you, my dear," said Madame Drucour as she quaffed the brandy. The lady hurried through her bath, and with the assistance of the maids, dressed and went downstairs to greet her guests.

Through the cold, dreary days of winter Marie Gauthier went about her chores in Government House. She often cleaned in the drawing room and looked longingly at the harpsichord sitting idly in the corner. Sometimes she let her mind wander the keys and play from memory the songs she played so long ago. In her imagination her fingers deftly leaped across the keys to play the music that she read from her memory.

Marie's mind drifted back to those happy days with her family in Beaubassin when they gathered around the harpsichord to sing. Her happy thoughts always turned dark, however, with an unpleasant ending.

The Christmas season brought much more work to Madame Drucour's charges. There would be endless rounds of entertaining Louisbourg's *aristocrate,* for they must be kept in good morale. This demanded long hours of work from the maids. Marie worked hard, and often inspected her work after completion to insure that nothing was left undone.

It was two days before Christmas and a fresh blanket of new snow had fallen over the brown Cape Breton landscape. Fresh vegetables had long since disappeared from the tables of Louisbourg commoners. Rare was the dinner that included salted beef or pork in the common homes. Acadians in Louisbourg drank spruce bark tea and French commoners drank water. Cod was the staple of all. Pickled, baked, boiled, or fried, cod was the everyday fare of Louisbourg's commoners. It was at this time that Henri Ouilette came again to call on Marie. Although the hour was early, darkness had already descended through the grey December sky when Henri knocked at the servants entrance.

Henri's knock was not the gentle little rap which had become the custom, popularized by King Louis XIV who demanded that servants scratch at his door to avoid the harsh noise of a knock. Henri knocked at the door like the rough woodsman that he was, almost shaking the door on its hinges.

When the cook opened the door, prepared to admonish the rude intruder, the fire in his bosom was diminished somewhat at the sight of the big woodsman leaning against his long rifle.

"Yes, yes," said the cook with apprehension, "what do you want at Government House? This is the governor's house, and we don't admit drifters."

Henri removed his blue toque and attempted to smooth his grey hair with his hand. "Uh, I have come to see Marie Gauthier, eh?"

The cook found his courage at the sight of Henri's humility. "You wait outside the door. I will send someone after her." The door slammed in Henri's face. Ouilette found himself standing in the cold, looking at the door. Henri put his toque back on, sat on a small cask and filled his pipe. He was enjoying his smoke when Marie opened the door. Marie threw her arms around Henri's neck. "Henri!"

"Hello, little one," Henri answered with chest thrust out and his chin lifted high. "I'm here to introduce to you the chief hunter and scout for Fortress Louisbourg. Me, one Henri Ouilette, eh?"

Marie led Henri to the warmth of her quarters as he told her of his experiences. "I lead the hunting parties. We shoot moose and trap hares for the soldiers to eat, eh? We scout for the soldiers and I lead the Indian scouts. I now have a warm place to sleep. Like before, I go and come as I please. And I'm cared for by His Royal Highness, the King." Henri's booming voice dropped to a whisper. "You see, our King provided these birds for you. Perhaps he thought they would go on the table of his officers, but even kings are mistaken once in a while, eh? There is more than enough for you and the big ones who live in this mansion. And, a Christmas present from the English at Halifax… a little bag of sugar."

"Henri, it's wonderful that you think of me, but I will not eat the grouse nor the sugar. I'll serve the grouse at Madame Drucour's dinner and bake a cake for her guests. She's worried there won't be enough food. Now we'll have a banquet. Perhaps I can win the favor of the Governor. If anyone can help me find my father, it must be the governor. Your gifts may help."

From deeper in his knapsack Henri produced a loaf of bread and a bottle of wine. "And the English king," he whispered, "donated these treats from Halifax. I know he would be happy for us to have them. And our King Louis would want us to toast his health!" Reaching into his knapsack, Henri withdrew two wine glasses and filled them from the bottle. He handed one to Marie. "I give you the King!"

"To the King," Marie responded gaily. "Long live the King."

Henri drew his hunting knife and carved a slice of bread. "I have already had my dinner of suckling pig, roasted in honey," he said. "A bit overdone it was, but then, it's difficult to get good domestic help these days, eh?"

They ate bread and drank wine. Marie and Henri talked and laughed. Afterward they walked through the snow as a panoply of stars twinkled from the black sky. Marie lifted her woolen shawl to fend off the cool night air. "Henri, I pray every night that I can find my father someday. Do you think we will ever see him again?"

Henri was quiet for a long time before answering. "The other ship probably went to Boston like the soldiers said it would. I think maybe Gaston went to Boston with the French marines. Maybe they will be sent to France, I think. Your father will be a successful businessman again maybe. He will get rich in France and come to find you."

Marie squeezed the still strong arm of her aging friend. "Henri, I know you are saying that to comfort me. Maybe Father is safe somewhere. I tell myself he is. I can't bear to think anything else."

"Your father is maybe not a good soldier or farmer, Marie, but he is a smart businessman. He will look after himself in the city and will find you someday, for sure," Henri said.

With her arm in his, they walked through the cold night talking quietly of Beaubassin. From the ramparts of the wall they looked at the golden moonlight reflected on the ocean. Many ships, like black silhouettes on a mirror, lay to their anchor in the calm bay.

"If they took Father to France then I must find a way to France. Perhaps a ship like one of those would take me," said Marie looking over the parapet. "Someway I will go to France and find my father."

Henri led Marie down the parapet stairs as he replied, "Many doors will open for a smart girl like you, Marie. You will find a way."

Henri walked Marie back to her little room. Outside the door she kissed him on the cheek. "You are my uncle Henri; I have decided. Come to see me when you can. And take care of yourself in the forest. You are my only relative here."

Henri laughed loudly. "Worry only for the English when I'm in the woods, my child." He thumped his chest with his fist. "I'm getting old, but I can shoot better than the old warriors and track better than the young ones. I can outfox any American in the woods and whip two Englishmen with my bare hands. Don't worry about Henri. You just take care of my little Marie, eh? When your father comes, you must be ready to wear beautiful clothes and ride in his fine carriage." Marie's mind turned rapidly as Henri walked away in the moonlight.

Hunger, Marie's good sense told her, would be a problem until spring if the supply ships could not come, as many said they could not. *I could put the grouse on the roof outside my window in the snow. Hidden there, they would remain frozen all winter until I needed them. But then I could not live with my conscience.*

In preparation for her party, Madame Drucour admired the grouse, served golden brown and stuffed with a bread and berry pudding. "You are a magician, Marie. Some of our most influential guests are coming for dinner, and they will by now abhor cod fish. Cod they will have eaten in every possible form and fashion. I will not ask how you came by these birds, I will only show you my gratitude. The Governor has exhausted his government allowance for food and now spends our personal money on our guests. I have the feeling there will be no savings left for our old age."

Marie was given the honor of serving the grouse to the lady's guests. Served on a silver platter of wild rice, they won unending praise from Madame Drucour's guests. Louisbourg's elite drank the best wine from the governor's cellar and ended the meal with sweet cake, an unusual treat for blockaded Louisbourg. It was a feast the commoners of Louisbourg could not imagine as they sat down to their own meager rations.

Out on the gray, tossing ocean, ice-encrusted ships of the British Navy continued their blockade. Unlike previous winters, they did not retreat to Halifax or Boston. French ships had much trouble running the blockade and many were captured by the enemy. Short rations continued for Louisbourg for the remainder of 1755 and well into 1756, and even guests of Government House found the fare to be sparse at times.

Chapter Sixteen

On this cold February day in 1756, MacGregor's enemy again appeared to be fog. *Grenadiers* sailed silently over the cod fishing banks, now covered by an early morning fog. Lookouts strained their eyes to penetrate that fog shrouding their world. At any moment a ship might appear beneath the bow, for this was a favorite haunt of cod fishermen. Here the fishing ships of Portugal and many other nations disgorged a multitude of little one-man boats, the dory, to cast their long lines into the freezing water for cod fish. Beneath the busy waters, the Labrador Current swirls over the Grand Banks to meet the warm water of the Gulf Stream, producing fogs that blind this busy activity. Above the swish and swash of the ocean waves, the soft moan of conch shells could be heard, the traditional fog horn of Portugese fishing dories. Occasionally they were answered by the clang of a ship's bell. Ships sailing in this fog played a dangerous game of blind men's bluff.

Lieutenant MacGregor lifted the collar of his oil cloth coat around his neck to shut out the cold, damp, morning air. He thrust his right hand under his coat to restore warmth to his cold fingers. Maintaining his perch on the horse block step required a grip on the port taffrail exposed to the frigid sea spray. The fingers of his steadying hand turned a bright red to match that of his legs exposed between his tall stockings and the lower edge of his woolen trousers. He squinted into the dense gray fog to no avail. His legs ached from his uncomfortable perch on the tossing horse block step. Lieutenant MacGregor looked quickly over his shoulder at young Collingwood standing pensively beside the helmsman. The midshipman's three-cornered hat dwarfed his small face and pressed over his large ears. "Mr. Collingwood, we need keen eyes today, double the lookouts aloft and send a couple of good men to the head to watch at water level." Then, over his shoulder, MacGregor called to the sailing master, "Mr. Sethford, bring our bow a point closer to the wind; let's reduce speed. We don't want to run over some luckless Frenchman and deny our gunners their share of glory."

Mr. Sethford did not look at Lieutenant MacGregor, instead his eyes lifted upward, scanning the set of the sails. He wore a well-oiled hat with a few drops of water condensed on the brim, dripping off the back. His rheumy eyes displayed no emotion. "Aye, Sir, up a point."

"Sound the bell," ordered MacGregor, as he had at the turn of every half-hour glass, and immediately the big brass ship's bell rang out an ear splitting *clang*.

Clung came a new sound, echoing faintly out of the fog. Every sailor stood stiffly. The miserable cold was quickly forgotten. "Mind your watch," ordered MacGregor. To Sethford he asked, "What do you make of that bell?"

"That is a big-throated bell," Sethford replied. "Likely a big ship to support such a big bell," he continued.

"Answer the bell," ordered Lieutenant MacGregor. *Clang* the bell on the *Grenadier* replied to the sound from out of the gray fog. Pensive men strained their eyes for form and ears for sounds.

It seemed an eternity of waiting but no sound came other than the waves washing against the bow, the creak of oak, and the low sporadic moan of the conch shells from the little fishing boats. A light gray mist obscured everything above the water and blended with a dark ocean below. Could it be a French ship trying to slip into Ft. Louisbourg through the fog? MacGregor ordered, "My compliments to the Captain and would he join me on deck."

"You may extend your compliments personally, Lieutenant MacGregor," replied Captain Walshingham as the portly captain stamped up the stairs to the quarterdeck. Walshingham's long black cape drifted in the breeze behind him. A woolen scarf tied his hat to his head, covered his ears, and formed a long flowing knot at his throat. Very quietly, Walshingham spoke to MacGregor. "Clear the decks and beat to quarters." But Walshingham could not have whispered the words quietly enough that they would not be heard by all ears listening intently on the quarterdeck.

MacGregor ordered, "Beat to quarters!" A ship that had seemed lifeless, crewed by frozen statues, suddenly burst into activity. Pounding hearts sent warm blood to cold hands and feet, and men rushed into action. The boatswain's whistle sounded shrill across the deck. A drummer ran to the quarterdeck with MacGregor's call and began the rat-tat-tat staccato of drumming. Midshipmen ran off the quarterdeck to their stations. Lieutenant Black took up the cacophony, barking orders through a speaking trumpet. A flurry of activity erupted throughout *Grenadier*. Running feet pounded across the decks. Officers barked orders punctuated with curses in haste to clear the decks for action. Pipes twittered their call to action stations as the boatswain's men ran up into the ratlines, securing the lower courses being raised on their halyards. Blocks and tackle rattled on the cannons, gun doors pounded up and the crews prepared for firing. Men carrying pails of water to swab the guns and douse fire dodged men carrying pails of sand to secure their footing on bloody, slippery decks. Men no longer bored and cold rushed to their action stations. Young boys, powder monkeys, dashed to the guns with their charges of gunpowder. Red jacketed marines climbed the ratlines, their long rifles slung from their backs, and took their marksmen positions in the fighting tops while their less proficient comrades formed a red barrier at the perimeter of the quarterdeck and forecastle.

Walshingham stood watching the hour glass on the binnacle. Every officer knew there would be hell to pay if the cannons were not manned and ready to fire before the sand ran out. "Hoist the colors," he ordered, and the signalman who stood waiting ran the Jack up the mainmast, bringing a cheer from the throats of men who had time to observe the event.

Idlers unrolled the top row of hammocks stored above each side of the main deck to form a barrier against boarders. Servants found hand weapons and rushed to the sides of their masters. One hundred seventy-two men soon stood ready for action. As every man found his place, the frigate again became deathly quiet, a wooden fortress slipping across a leaden sea, filled with motionless statues.

Onward they sailed until Captain Walshingham broke the silence by saying, "Mr. MacGregor, bring the ship about on the starboard tack, course south by east."

Again Lieutenant MacGregor lifted the speaking trumpet and barked orders. Again feet pounded the decks and eager sailors ran to brace 'round the yards. The helmsman spun the wheel. Slowly, the ship turned around on a new course, sails flapping noisily until the wind caught the canvas and made it rigid boards.

Grenadier's decks shifted slightly as the easterly breeze heeled them to the new tack. "Set the top gallants and flying jib," ordered Walshingham. "That's a Frenchman making for Louisbourg, I'll wager. The hound is on the fox, and we'll soon have him in our teeth. There's a double tot of rum for the lookout who first locates the enemy."

Grenadier charged through the tossing waves, riding up over the Atlantic swells. They sailed in a gray envelope, with only the leaden sea brushing the ship's sides. Onward they sailed, wave after wave, seeing nothing, saying nothing, as the cold wind chilled their bones.

Sethford, the old sailing master, walked from lee rail to weather rail and back again, time after time, peering down into the waves. He watched the water surface for signs of another ship's wake, but nothing appeared. The long minutes ran into one hour and then another while the men stood to battle stations with the cold again creeping into their bones. The sand seemed frozen in the hourglass on the binnacle. Each minute seemed to pass more slowly than the one before as the men blew on their hands and stamped their feet to fight the cold.

Walshingham ordered, "Down helm, steer south by west." Spinning the ship's wheel, the helmsman laid *Grenadier* on a new course, filling the sails with the easterly breeze. Blowing abaft the beam, the wind sent the ship speeding over the swells. Waves beat faster against the ship's bow. A change, any change, relieved boredom, and the men would be warmer with the wind behind them.

Mr. Sethford leaned far over the weather rail watching the waves. The sea gulls seemed to sense that this was no fishing boat from which they could beg food. One by one, the gulls dropped away from the stern, leaving only the sound of the waves breaking across the bow and the creaks and groans of the rigging. This routine continued until midmorning when Mr. Sethford, examining the waves in front of the ship declared, "Crossing a ship's wake to starboard, course southeast."

"Up helm," called out Captain Walshingham, "course southeast." Again *Grenadier* turned to the chase. Now every man's heart began pumping warm blood once more. It was early afternoon when the dark gray fog turned a lighter shade of gray. The wind freshened and glimpses of sunlight penetrated the fog.

From above the lookout shouted, "Sail ho, bearing two points off the larboard bow, course southeast! Only his sails are visible above the fog."

"Down helm a point and close the distance, a double tot of rum for that man," ordered Walshingham. "Mr. Collingwood," he continued, "climb to the top with a telescope and give me a report on the type of ship we have found."

Midshipman Collingwood took a telescope from the nearby rack and thrust it under his belt. With his hair falling loosely from his hat, young Collingwood dashed down the steps to the spar deck. He ran to the mainmast ratlines and began the long ascent to the mast top. All eyes on the quarterdeck turned toward the top of the main mast where Collingwood disappeared in the fog. All ears waited for his report. At last his young voice sang out, "Man-o-war, half a league off the port bow, course east by sou'east."

"Hah! By damn, now I know it is a Frenchman," exclaimed Captain Walshingham in ecstasy. "If we have seen him, he has seen us. He hoists no colors. That tells me he is French and doesn't want a fight. It is a French ship all right. Yes, by damn I have him!"

At half past one in the afternoon, the golden sun blazed down from a clear, blue sky. Brilliant flashes of sunlight danced on the ultramarine sea, reflecting the blues of the sky amid a symphony of flashing waves, topped by white foam. Sailing through this lovely picture appeared the French warship, all sails set and drawing. The ship's black hull swept aft to reveal a high poop glistening in gold leaf. A stripe of white in three tiers marked the gun decks. A blue and white flag of France fluttered from the gilded stern.

As MacGregor watched, the gun ports fell open with the angry snouts of cannons easing out of the dark ports. Soon the sunlight reflected off two rows of cannons protruding from the starboard side. Two more cannons projected from the gilded stern. The bottom row of gun-ports remained closed as a white band above the water line.

Slapping his hand on the taffrail, the captain ordered, "Mr. MacGregor, assemble all hands on the spar deck; I have a few words to say to these lucky fellows who sail on *Grenadier*."

The first lieutenant's command through the speaking trumpet brought a crowd of eager sailors waiting for words from their captain. Walshingham strode to the taffrail and looked down on the men, a bright smile on his face. He threw the down scarf from around his ears and lifted his hat above his head as he spoke into his megaphone, "Boys, there goes a fat Frenchman. He will be *en flûte*, carrying cargo, with few of his cannons manned. He is hauling supplies to Louisbourg I wager. He does not want a fight, even with our little frigate; because he has few fighting men aboard. I am going to take that big ship as a prize and make us all rich. How many of you are with me?"

A loud cheer erupted from the men on the main deck, to be taken up by the men on the gun deck and soon the entire ship's compliment reverberated their affirmation. Cannon rammers and rifle butts thumped on the deck and a few hats flew in the air. Men whistled and clapped. Walshingham looked around at the drummer who began drumming his roll. The noise sounded across the waves. "Hurrah! Hurrah! Hurrah!"

"God save Captain Walshingham! Hurrah! Hurrah! Hurrah!"

Walshingham lifted his hat in the air, acknowledging their cheers. Presently, he raised a palm and motioned for silence, waiting patiently, smiling benevolently, before saying, "Go back to your guns, and when I give the order, pour the shot into them. Show them no mercy, the scalp buying papists! Send them all to hell!" Sunlight flashed and dimmed in rays through the ragged clouds above.

Eager sailors rushed to their guns, bare feet pounding. Pipes twittered.

Officers shouted. Sailors swore. Water tubs thumped on the decks and chains rattled on the guns. Young powder monkeys added their tenor voices to the cacophony. Gun commanders sought targets and barked orders to aim the guns, then stood waiting for the word to fire.

Captain Walshingham tilted his head back and returned his hat to his head. With chin out thrust and hand on the hilt of his sword, he sauntered back to his position on the quarterdeck. "Crowd on all sail," yelled Walshingham, standing with feet wide apart and hands on his hips. A fresh breeze blew across the water.

Grenadier settled down on a starboard tack, slicing through wave after wave, gaining on their quarry. Crewmen stood by their guns. They laughed and slapped each other on the back. Lieutenant Black made the rounds of the cannons, checking each gun. Sergeant O'Bannion, in his scarlet uniform, stood with his hands on his hips and his head tilted back, surveying his Royal Marines in the fighting tops. He then made his rounds of fighting men on the forecastle and down below deck to check his guards at the stairs to insure no sailor retreated below. "Colors," yelled the lookout above. "He's breakin' out his Lilies! French, he is!"

Again, cheers rang across the water. Captain Walshingham was close to dancing as he ran to the lee bulwark. Lieutenant MacGregor jumped down from the step, just in time to avoid being knocked over by Walshingham who was already mounting the lee step. Walshingham looked through the telescope for a moment and slapped the bulwark in joy. "By God I have you," he shouted at the image through the fog. Turning to MacGregor he said, "Do you see that? I have a lovely prize, and soon we will sail her to Boston, flying the King's 'X' on her topmast. And richer men we shall all be!"

MacGregor's heart beat faster. He wondered at Captain Walshingham's wisdom. *Should this small frigate attack a second-rater? We pit Grenadier's twenty-four guns against perhaps ninety or more guns on a second-rater. We have 172 men aboard our ship while a second-rater might have six hundred. But Walshingham will not hesitate. This frigate attacks the battleship, whatever.*

Captain Walshingham yelled, "Hove to! Ready a boat over the side quickly! Hoist the white flag of truce. Boson' blast you, get my musicians on deck, quickly. I want their instruments and my valuables brought with them. And don't forget my silver tea service, chandelier, and King Louis chair." Walshingham paced impatiently back and forth across the quarterdeck while the sails were backed until the ship moved neither forward nor backward any great distance. He watched as his musicians and servants loaded their instruments and his valuables in the boat. Lastly, the boatswain thrust a large white flag into the hands of a violinist. The cello player held a big lantern amidship along with his cello. One of Walshingham's servants held the King Louis chair, and another held his chandelier. With instruments and valuables between them, the other musicians and singers took their places at the oars, and the coxson commanded from his place in the stern. The boatswain blew a call on his pipe. Ropes squeaked through the davits, and the boat with its cargo of captain's servants, musicians, instruments and Walshingham's valuables splashed down into the waves. After grind and crashing between boat and ship, the men rowed clumsily away. Captain Walshingham watched with taunt knuckles on the bulwark while the men pulled away at the oars. Their boat drew slowly away over the wave tops, the white flag flapping in the breeze. Satisfied that the boat was a safe distance away, he hurried to the spardeck, drew his sword and waved it aloft. He pointed at the French ship and bellowed loudly, "Ready the port bow chase. Lower the white truce flag. Fire a shot over his bow as the truce flag comes down."

His gun crew anticipated Walshingham's order. They stood by their guns, tense and ready. A midshipman leaned over, checked the gunner's bearing, stood, and ordered, "Fire!" The cannon crashed out an explosion of fire and smoke followed by a geyser of white water erupting off the French ship's bow. The signalman quickly recovered the truce flag.

But the French were ready to do battle. Fire and smoke erupted from the battleship's stern. The sea exploded in a shower of salt water off *Grenadier*'s port bow while a cannon ball tore through the rigging of the foretop mast.

Captain Walshingham waved his sword, yelling, "Hurrah!" He turned to the other men on the quarterdeck, stabbing the air with his sword as they dutifully returned his hurrah. Men on the spar deck took up the cheer. Soon *Grenadier*'s decks rang again with cheers. "Bow-chasers, fire as you bear," Walshingham shouted.

Sailors echoed the order and the port bow-chase discharged fire and smoke. A shower of flying debris flew from the stern of the man-o-war. Another wild cheer rang out through *Grenadier*. "Ready the starboard broadside," ordered Captain Walshingham. Fire, smoke, and the explosion of the big stern guns of the French second-rater punctuated Walshingham's order. A geyser erupted beside the quarterdeck, dousing the officers with seawater.

"Hah! He is trying to douse our anger," said Walshingham as he removed his hat and shook the water from it. He withdrew a lace handkerchief from his sleeve, dabbing at the water on his face as another ball sang between the stays of the mizzen mast. One of Walshingham's servants, with seawater dripping from his nose, withdrew a handkerchief from his own pocket and brushed at the water on Captain Walshingham's back. The big battleship, heavily laden and low in the water, lumbered slowly. The distance between the two ships diminished as the little frigate sailed faster in the light breeze.

MacGregor watched and waited for Walshingham to give the order to tack. On his order, the little frigate would cut across the French ship's stern and rake them with a broadside. The big battleship would turn to bring its bigger guns to bear but would be much slower in turning.

Walshingham stood staring at the enemy. "What say you, MacGregor? Are we ready to lay a broadside into her?"

MacGregor did not think about the question at all. He measured the distance and calculated the positions in his subconsciousness, utilizing a library of experience gained over ten years at sea. "Not yet, sir, we should be closer and lay every ball down his spine."

"Aye, you are indeed right," said Walshingham. The two ships ran along their course while *Grenadier*'s port bow cannon dueled with the two big guns in the stern of the French ship. Occasionally, the howitzer arched a shell at the enemy.

Walshingham ran to the binnacle, rattled the speaking trumpet from its cage, and lifted it to his mouth. "All hands except the port bow gun crews lay flat on the deck! Be quick about it!" Questioning eyes lifted toward Walshingham and then slowly, a few at a time, the sailors reluctantly lay down beside their guns. Only the officers remained standing, seemingly oblivious to the enemy's shells tearing past them. The enemy shells cut the rigging, dropping ropes and pulleys to the deck. A big French ball burst into the forward bulwark, scattering a deadly shower of wood and steel across the deck. The lee helmsman standing beside MacGregor dropped to the deck, his hands gripping a flow of blood streaming from his throat.

The ships exchanged volleys of cannon fire. After several exchanges, *Grenadier*'s bow chase put another ball into the stern, disabling a gun in there. A cheer went up from the British sailors on the forward gun. A voice from somewhere out of the distance said, "Now, captain." MacGregor, without thinking, heard himself say the words.

"Aye, now," replied Captain Walshingham. "Starboard gun crews up! Man your guns! Ready the starboard broadside, fire as you bear, down helm!"

The bow of *Grenadier* swung down wind as the helmsman spun the wheel. Men jumped to their tasks, bare feet pounding across the spar deck, readjusting the yards. Unintelligible commands echoed from the gun deck. The yards swung around on the French vessel as the enemy attempted to turn with *Grenadier*, but the ship was late. *Grenadier*'s starboard bow chase, long deprived of its target, fired a ball into the stern of the battleship as the bow swung down wind. Walshingham dashed to the starboard bulwark as fast as his fat legs would carry him and hopped on the horse block. Suddenly, ten guns along *Grenadier*'s starboard side erupted in a volley that shook the entire ship and completely hid the enemy in a cloud of smoke.

As the smoke cleared, the enemy ship reappeared, laboriously trying to turn with the little frigate. Rigging rained down on the Frenchman's decks and smoke trailed from the stern windows. The volley had indeed raked him from stem to stern. Again, it seemed every shell found a mark on the enemy.

"Hah! Pour it on, lads," yelled Captain Walshingham. "Like shooting ducks in a barrel.

"Why haven't the guns fired again? I want faster volleys. See to it, Mr. Collingwood. Get your ass down to the gun deck and tell them I want faster volleys. Faster volleys, or by God they will spend the next two weeks in gun drills, I say!"

Another discharge of the starboard guns drowned Walshingham's words. "Ah, that's better," shouted Walshingham. "Up helm, lively now, ready the port broadside." The second broadside tore through the battleship's rigging and his mizzen mast toppled down, entangling the enemy quarterdeck in sails and rigging. But now the big guns along the side of the French ship fired for the first time in the battle. A ragged volley erupted as guns fired a staccato eruption of shells at *Grenadier*. Smoke boiled out of the battleship's side. One of its balls crashed into a starboard gun of *Grenadier*'s just as the crew had returned to ready their gun. The explosion ignited their powder and sent a secondary explosion of loose balls, splinters, and bodies across the gun deck. Other gun crews fell to the first explosion. Amidship became a writing, tangled mess of bodies. They screamed, cursed, and yelled as idlers rushed about spreading more sand. Two enemy cannon balls struck the high bulwark of the spar deck, showering the ship with deadly splinters.

Grenadier swung up into the wind. For what seemed to MacGregor an eternity, *Grenadier* sat waiting for the wind to fill the sails. MacGregor watched the big guns along the waist of the French ship and waited for their second volley. At last, the wind snapped the sails rigid and the frigate again began its course across the battleship's stern. A ragged volley from the man-o-war discharged, with most of the shot falling harmlessly astern of *Grenadier*. The frigate raced for the stern of the French second-rater. *Grenadier*'s guns fired a rolling volley into the port quarter of the battleship. Flames licked out of the cannons and smoke trailed downwind. The volley thundered into the stern of the French ship, raking the length of the hull. It caught the French crew as they attempted to free themselves of the tangle of rigging and sails. MacGregor's telescope revealed the massacre on the French deck. "Ready about," MacGregor heard himself yell and listened as the sailing master and weather helmsman repeated the order. *Grenadier*'s gunners swabbed their guns and reloaded as top men and landsmen brought the ship into irons. With thundering sails the ship again caught the wind on the other side and began its slow turn. Loudly flapping sails grew rigid in the breeze and propelled the ship forward again. It was a splendid ballet of seamanship that set the frigate on a new course with minimum delay. *Grenadier* once more raced across the stern of the enemy vessel. At the precise moment their ship crossed the French ship's stern, Lieutenant Black gave the order to fire. Walshingham's gunners released another salvo. Red-yellow flames and white smoke again erupted from the guns of *Grenadier*. In a cloud of smoke the enemy ship disappeared, reappearing so close that MacGregor easily saw the sailors struggling on the French ship's poop. *Grenadier*'s deadly volley raked the battleship again. A thunderous explosion, followed by long yellow flames and smoke, rocked the stern of the French vessel. A topmast fell in a tangled heap across the enemy main deck.

Onward, *Grenadier* raced past the stern of the Frenchman. "Ready about on a port tack, ready the starboard broadside, load the port guns with chain-shot. Hold the fire of the howitzers," ordered Captain Walshingham in a steady stream of orders. "Watch as the sparrow out flies the crow," he continued.

MacGregor judged the distance. "Down helm!" His words were repeated as the helmsman spun the wheel. Men rushed across the deck pulling round the yards. Again sails thundered and slatted. *Grenadier* again ceased the headlong charge and, hanging motionless for a brief instant, waited for the wind to cross the stern. At that instant the English gunners fired a third salvo into the stern of the French ship. Ten twenty-four pound guns fired in unison from the portside of *Grenadier*. Every gun found its mark. Death and carnage rained down on the decks of the French ship. Slow in responding to the helm, its officers disorganized on the quarterdeck, its masts and rigging a tangled mess; the French ship foundered.

Walshingham pounded the taffrail. "Hah! Did you see that? Three volleys, not two, but three volleys from my guns, those sweet sons-of-bitches," yelled Captain Walshingham. But the look of delight on Walshingham's face turned instantly into rage. "Chain-shot, chain-shot," he yelled again. "Switch from ball to chain-shot! By God, I have captured a prize ship, and I don't want the lovely bastard sunk! Gunners! Load every gun with chain-shot, and I don't want any howitzer shells through my ship's decks. DeWitt! Where is Midshipman DeWitt? Mr. DeWitt, get down to the gun deck and tell the gun crews to load every gun with chain-shot. If they sink my ship, I will keelhaul them! Why doesn't that damn frog strike his colors; doesn't he know he's beaten?" Midshipman DeWitt touched his hand to his hat and ran across the deck, leaping bodies and fallen rigging.

In answer to Captain Walshingham's question, the French battleship fired a shell into the starboard bulwark amidship of *Grenadier*. The explosion sent splinters of wood and bodies flying across the spar deck. Midshipman DeWitt, running across the deck, fell backwards with blood flowing from his chest. He raised himself to his knees, looking down at the blood flowing over his hands and pooling on the deck. With ashen face he turned to look up at the officers on the quarterdeck. He summoned his entire strength to raise himself to his feet, turned, took several staggering steps in the direction of gun crews and fell to the deck. On hands and knees, DeWitt crawled along the deck. As his life's blood drained away, he rolled over and lay on his back. With his arms outstretched, unseeing eyes wide open, one leg cocked crazily over the other, he died.

Again *Grenadier*'s cannons fired a broadside of cannon balls into the French ship, punching gaping holes in the Frenchman's hull. Captain Walshingham turned to Lieutenant MacGregor. "Where the hell is Midshipman DeWitt? I sent him to tell the gunners to fire only chain shot, by God!"

Lieutenant MacGregor looked at Captain Walshingham with disgust as he answered, "Midshipman DeWitt is dead, Sir."

"Well, MacGregor, would you have me stop the fight because that little bastard has got himself killed?" Walshingham turned to a nearby sailor. "Go down and tell the gunners to fire only chain-shot before I thrash them. Cannon balls do too much damage to my prize. It won't be worth a farthing."

MacGregor lifted a telescope from the rack, aiming it at the French vessel. "He has raised a flag of truce, Sir."

"What? A flag of truce? Give me that damned telescope," blurted

Walshingham as he snatched the telescope from MacGregor's hand. He placed it to his eye. Captain Walshingham snapped the telescope shut with a grin spreading over his face.

"Hold your fire! Cease firing men," Walshingham yelled through a speaking trumpet. "Make sail and approach the beggar, Mr. Sethford." Walshingham turned to Lieutenant MacGregor with a sly smile on his face. "His truce will give us a chance to get closer where our smaller cannons can give a better account of themselves."

Slowly, little *Grenadier* approached the big French battleship, looking like a terrier beside a great draft horse. Smoke streamed from the Frenchman's stern and trailed downwind. Through the telescope a flurry of activity could be seen as men hurried around the decks, tending to the wounded.

Aboard *Grenadier*, the surgeon and his mate hurried about the blood-covered deck. They tended the men lying on the deck, pausing only to glance at the dead. Men roughly carried the wounded below while others rushed powder and shot to the guns.

As *Grenadier* came within hailing distance of the French ship, an officer on the enemy quarterdeck called out through his speaking trumpet in a fine French tenor that echoed the refined language of the court of King Louis.

Lieutenant MacGregor interpreted, "Sir, he thanks you for the opportunity to clear his decks of wounded. He will be ready to resume the fight very soon unless you are ready to yield."

Walshingham kicked the binnacle. "That miserable son of a bitch! Is he so crazy he doesn't know he's beaten? And why does he speak to us in French? How does he know anyone on board speaks French?"

MacGregor replied, "He speaks French, Sir, because in his eyes, all cultured gentlemen speak French."

Captain Walshingham turned slowly to MacGregor, his face red, his anger visibly rising. "Well, then, Mr. MacGregor, would you give the cultured son of a bitch his cultured French reply?"

MacGregor seemed not to notice Walshingham's anger as he replied, "Aye, Sir, do you wish to continue the battle?"

Captain Walshingham threw his telescope to the deck in anger. "Aye, by God, tell him that in one turn of the glass I will begin firing. If that son of a bitch does not surrender, I will sink him all the way to hell!"

MacGregor replied, "I'll try, Sir." Whereon he lifted the speaking trumpet and replied to the French officer. After his translation, MacGregor replaced the speaking trumpet in its rack and touched his hat to Captain Walshingham

Walshingham, his eyes bulging and his neck red, turned his attention to the sand glass on the binnacle, waiting patiently for the thirty minutes to pass. At last he shouted, "I have him where I want him, at close range. Resume firing round shot! Haul down the truce flag."

Immediately, *Grenadier* rocked to a broadside from the blast of their own guns. But soon a broadside from the Frenchman answered. At close quarters the two ships hammered each other as smoke engulfed both ships. Again rigging rained down on the deck and lethal splinters flew like deadly missiles across *Grenadier*. Two red clad bodies fell from *Grenadier*'s fighting top as French marksmen took their toll. A musket ball dropped the helmsman beside Walshingham, a shot probably intended for the captain. Walshingham's hat flew off from another ball as Sethford rushed to replace the fallen helmsman. Grenades crossed the distance between the ships, exploding on deck in a shower of shrapnel. Cannon balls crashed into *Grenadier*'s bulwarks. Deadly splinters flew through the air. Flesh and blood fell to the carnage. Yardarms, topmasts, and great lengths of oak fell to the deck, crushing men and guns beneath their mass. Rigging lay all over the ship, ensnaring everything like a giant spider's web and trailing away into the ocean. MacGregor fought back the urge to hide behind the bulwark. He walked upright about the quarterdeck, careful not to stand for more than a few seconds in one spot as French rifle bullets spattered the decks around him. Walshingham too moved about quickly, his wig askew, while only Sethford must stand fixed at the wheel. For half an hour the fighting raged but success favored the smaller ship. *Grenadier*'s cannons fired twice or maybe three times for every one of the French. The English sailors hauled their short cannons and re-loaded the muzzles much more quickly than their enemy while their enemy hauled the longer barrel. French gunners had trouble depressing their guns to fire on the lower ship, and the bottom row of cannons remained idle behind closed ports. Gunfire lagged further from the French cannons on deck as O'Bannion's marksmen cut down their gunners. With sail and rigging cut to pieces, the enemy ship lay dead in the water. As the enemy cannons fired with less frequency, Lieutenant MacGregor turned to Captain Walshingham. "Side arms, Sir?"

"Aye, side arms, Lieutenant," replied Captain Walshingham. "Signals! Hoist the signal for parley," he continued. *Grenadier*'s guns roared another broadside of round shot into the French ship, sending the hail of deadly shot across the mangled decks of the ship. Dead and wounded lay bleeding on the spar deck of *Grenadier*, but it was much worse on the deck of the French battleship.

Smoke and flames poured from the stern of the French man-o-war and drifted off downwind, laying a line of smoke across the surface of the water. Both stern guns of the battleship hung silently. Its mizzen mast floated near the stern where the crew had thrown it to clear the quarterdeck. Only a stump marked the enemy topmast, shot away by one of *Grenadier*'s balls. Her foremast was shot away, and the mizzen floated behind the ship, towed by its remaining shrouds. A secondary explosion sent a shower of sparks and flames out of the French stern. The big ship lay helplessly, yet its fleur-de-lis flew proudly. MacGregor watched a signal run up the enemy main mast. "Parley, acknowledged," MacGregor called.

"Very well, cease firing. Lieutenant," Walshingham said, "Take Sergeant O'Bannion, two marines and six well armed sailors in the cutter. Take Midshipman Thomas; he needs the experience.

"Take a signal flag with you. Hoist it when you are ready for the remainder of the boarding party. You will return with the French officers and marines in the boats of the boarding party and provide me a report on the prize. Oh, yes, and you may tell those cousins of Louis and his Royal Court that I will have no hesitation in sinking their ship and sailing away if they should refuse surrender. If they accept my generous offer, the officers may keep their side arms. They like that, hah, the cultured bastards," Captain Walshingham continued gaily. "Bosun, away the cutter and six good men, all well armed."

MacGregor tucked a pistol under his leather belt. He felt for the dirk strapped to his waist. He stepped forward and picked his way through tangled cordage to the spar deck, now littered with wreckage. The decks of *Grenadier* were strangely quiet. Wind moaned in the torn rigging while dying men moaned on the damaged decks. There Dr. Abrams walked slowly amid the torn bodies, bending to look into a face or touch a throat. The surgeon stood, wiped his bloody hands on his white apron, pushed up his glasses, and moved on to another man. He pointed to a man with a leg askew. The surgeon's assistants moved quickly to the man, lifted him onto their litter and carried him away. The doctor continued to walk the deck, separating the wounded from the dying. Like the angel of death, he dispensed judgments of death and hopes of life. MacGregor saw that a row of feet protruded from beneath a shot shattered sail spread on the bloody deck. *There must be dozen or more dead beneath that sail already. I expect there will be twice as many before the decks are clean.*

MacGregor stepped over the body of young Midshipman DeWitt, trying not to look down at the corpse as he asked the surgeon, "Doctor, what insanity brings us to this slaughter? Is it prize money, patriotism, or the work of the devil?"

Dr. Abrams did not look up as he answered, "Gold! Such is their answer if you ask them. But don't believe it, MacGregor. Men die for a few moments admiration in the eyes of their demented shipmates; they die because everyone else does; men die because it's expected of them; they die as the price of killing." The surgeon dropped a limp, bloody arm he had held and hurried away beside two of his helpers, lifting a moaning sailor to a stretcher. "Put him down you fools! Don't waste your time on him; he'll be dead before you get him below. Find a man I can save!" He turned back to MacGregor. "Lieutenant Black is dead on the gun deck below. Killed by an exploding cannon."

MacGregor continued across the carnage. MacGregor stepped over more dead as he reviewed his boarding party at the waist of the ship. These were King George's men, stout marines in smart red tunics with muskets and bayonets, street fighting sailors from the slums of London, but every man was strong and tough as nails. Every sailor wore a cutlass with a pistol in his belt. Some held boarding pikes. Daggers glistened in their belts. MacGregor looked them in their eyes. *I'd lead these men into any fight.* Without saying a word, he conveyed to all that he found them more than satisfactory. He turned to young midshipman Collingwood, whose wide eyes betrayed his fear, and motioned for him to lead the men into the boat. The young midshipman hurried over the side, followed by eager sailors. They climbed down into the tossing cutter as it slammed against the stout sides of *Grenadier*.

Six strong sailors rowed MacGregor's cutter across the ocean waves, now littered with wreckage. The short distance closed quickly between *Grenadier* and the enemy ship. MacGregor looked into the wide, fearful eyes of Midshipman Collingwood, who looked back like a spanked dog. Sitting nearby, a seasoned sailor, a man named Murphy from County Antrim in Ireland, worked at the oars with an empty clay pipe in his mouth. Murphy was a hot tempered and vituperous man, whose sharp words often earned him the displeasure of the boatswain. MacGregor reached across, withdrawing the clay pipe from the mouth of the Murphy. He thrust it into the mouth of young Midshipman Collingwood. "Keep that pipe in your mouth, Mister Collingwood. Anytime you feel like saying something, just bite down on the stem of the pipe. And you, Mr. Murphy, if you feel like saying anything, just bite down on your tongue. The wrong words to the boatswain earned you this opportunity to die for King George. Be wise and deny King George your service."

Murphy looked for a moment as if he would explode then glanced over his shoulder at the angry Frenchmen and their rifles trained on his back. He addressed MacGregor, saying, "I'll no mind sharin' me pipe with officers, Sir, if it will help me keep me hide in one piece. But, Sir, could ye make things aboard our ship a bit more fair? Could ye not distribute the enemy cannon balls to the officers in the same proportion as prize money?"

Lieutenant MacGregor smiled, then burst out laughing, loudly. Another man or two took up the laughter and soon the entire boat rocked with laughter while men close enough to do so slapped Murphy on the back. "At's right, Lad, give 'em the rights 'o it, Murph," they shouted. What the French may have thought of this crazy boatload of laughing Englishmen could never be known.

Turning his attention to the enemy, MacGregor surveyed the great ship as it wallowed almost helpless in the swells. A column of white smoke poured from the once beautifully gilded poop, blowing away downwind in little whisps floating over the wreckage on the waves. As the cutter drew along side, MacGregor read the name on the stern of the battleship: *Chasseur. The hunter, a second-rater, a battleship with more than four times as many guns as Grenadier. A hunter that became the hunted, hunted by a little frigate, a little puppy dog.*

The battleship towered above the men in the cutter. Blue-black snouts of cahnons protruded from their gun ports. Tangled rigging lay strewn across the sides of the ship and dangled into the water. Chunks of floating oak bumped against the side of the cutter. The French crew lined the weather rail and looked down on their enemies with sullen, smoke-blackened faces. Every French sailor held a musket, cutlass or pike. French muskets traced the progress of the cutter through the water. MacGregor mustered another grin as he said, "Steady, lads, don't let 'em in on our little joke. They may be mad as *hornet*s, but we beat them. I will convince them. Look smart and ready in all you do, whatever."

The cutter drew alongside *Chasseur's* lee. "Ship oars," MacGregor called as the British cutter brushed the side of the enemy ship. The boat crew raised their oars as one man. In unison they laid them inside the boat. MacGregor leaped to the boarding ladder as the cutter coasted past and pulled himself up the ship's side. Taking a deep breath to calm himself, he climbed over the taffrail. He stood on deck, his hat in his hand, one hand on his claymore and the other gripping the brass crest at his belt. Lieutenant MacGregor looked levelly into a host of hostile faces. Behind the angry crowd he saw a scene of carnage eclipsing that of *Grenadier*. He turned to an extravagantly dressed young officer standing in front of him. Addressing the officer in fluent French, he said, "Thank you for allowing me to come on board to parley. I'm Lieutenant MacGregor of His Majesty's frigate, *Grenadier*. May I speak to your captain, please?"

The young French officer looked not much older than Midshipman Collingwood, certainly younger than MacGregor. His curly golden locks fell from beneath his plumed hat. Elegantly clad in a royal blue coat, the young man wore gold epaulets on his narrow shoulders. A bunch of lace gathered at the throat of his white shirt. Blood spattered his white breeches and stockings. The young officer's blue eyes narrowed at MacGregor's question. With a confidence spawned by noble birth, he replied in a high pitched voice, "I am the captain, the Chevalier Marcel De la Court. And you, I presume, are an English pirate, since there is no war declared between France and England. This is piracy."

MacGregor concealed his anger at the young man's assertiveness; a cool head was needed. He replied, "The King of England proclaimed a quarantine of ships entering Fortress Louisbourg. Having attempted to violate that quarantine, your only recourse is to surrender honorably and avoid further loss of life."

"My dear lieutenant," replied the young Captain De la Court, as a teacher would reply to a student, "by your excellent French I determine you must have some intelligence, if not breeding. Perhaps I detect the trace of an accent of Scotland... no doubt you are Scottish. The English have stolen your throne as they would steal the throne of France if we let them. How can you serve Scotland's tormentors, the English? What Scotsman follows the edicts of German George?" The young Frenchman did not wait for a reply; it was apparent his question was rhetorical. "You are a toady, servile, lackey of the English. England has no king, merely a Godless German puppet of the *bourgeois* rabble. By what authority does this rabble impose their will on Scotland? Who gives them the right to impose a quarantine on Louisbourg? And who says my destination is Louisbourg? We are on the high seas, the dominion of God in Heaven. Surely the English do not usurp the dominion of God? My destination might well be Quebec, the West Indies, or London for that matter. Clearly, lieutenant, you are engaged in an act of piracy on behalf of your English oppressors."

MacGregor's face grew red. He considered some form of rebuttal, decided against it and said, "Captain, more to the point, you have a fire burning dangerously close to your powder magazine, I judge." He paused for effect and looked slowly around at the French crewmen standing nearby. Speaking in their direction he continued, "We must extinguish that fire, or the magazine will explode, killing everyone on board." MacGregor decided he was as eloquent as the young Frenchman. "Look at the dead and wounded who litter your decks already. Further bloodshed is pointless. Let's sail safely away and live to see our loved ones another day."

"France doesn't recognize your so-called king," replied De la Court, "nor do we recognize your quarantine. I am a Chevalier, and I do not intend to surrender my sword to a commoner. We shall fight to the death instead."

MacGregor eyes burned brightly and his jaw tightened noticeably. Through clinched teeth MacGregor replied, "Sir, I'm a MacGregor, and my race is royal! I'm a descendent of King Alpin, of the royal blood. We trace our lineage for almost a thousand years of royalty… while you Frenchmen still ate toads! Mighty saints of Christendom walked the glens of Scotland while your ancestors worshiped pagan clay. Do not call me a commoner, Sir… my blood is more royal than that of your King Louis! You will find no one more deserving to take your surrender." MacGregor's jaw muscle loosened noticeably with the release of his invective. When he spoke again, it was with his head, and not his heart. When again he spoke, his words were to Captain De la Court, but his question was directed to the Frenchmen standing nearby, at whom he looked. "Would you ask all these men to die for your vanity? Too many men have died today already. Captain, you may keep your sword, as may all your officers. As a gentleman, you need only swear an oath of neutrality for the duration of your capture. If you have any doubts that you have not lost this battle, I tell you this: You see here only a little frigate, but you are surrounded by British warships, a mighty fleet. So you do not surrender to this frigate alone, you surrender to the British fleet, which will soon be here in answer to our gunfire. You have fought bravely and will have lost honorably. You will have acted with compassion for your men. Now, let's act quickly to prevent further bloodshed. Let's extinguish the fire below before this ship explodes and kills everyone aboard." MacGregor looked back at the French captain. The look in the young Frenchman's eyes told him the nobleman had little interest in further fighting.

De la Court asked, "Have I not met you before, at the court of King Louis? I think I remember a haughty kid who claimed to be more royal than our king. By your speech I know you have been raised a French gentleman; it must be you I met when we were children."

MacGregor answered, "It was indeed me, and I remember you. My family was as royal as the Stuart they followed into exile in France. My mother was a French noblewoman. But there is no time to discuss such things. We must put out the fires."

De la Court stood tall and lifted his chin as he removed the ornate sword from its sheath. Handing it to MacGregor he said, "Perhaps I can surrender my sword to a gentleman from the French court... even though he has become a pirate."

Lieutenant MacGregor replied, "Keep your sword. There are more important things." He turned to the French crew and said, "Men, extinguish the fire burning below before this ship explodes and we are all killed."

Looking around the deck, MacGregor surveyed the French seamen. *There were fewer men on this battleship than on the little frigate, I think. A British ship this size would carry nearly 600 men while our frigate has 172. There can't have been more than 300 men here, if that. And they have suffered badly. There must be fifty dead on this deck alone.* Many cannons lay idle and had never been fired. They were neither run out nor loaded. Those cannons served by a crew were only half manned, and the long guns required more men to serve them than the shorter, English cannon. It was little wonder this battleship offered so little resistance.

MacGregor addressed the French crew. "Men, stack your arms here near me and get below quickly. Put the bilge pumps to work and a hause pipe on the fire." Ignoring the young French captain, MacGregor turned his back to his own crew. He called for the English boarding party, knowing this was a crucial moment. *I pray I judged correctly. There will be a slaughter if I erred.* Big sergeant O'Bannion, his red face matching his scarlet tunic, climbed first over the rail. His crossed white belts made his broad shoulders look broader. His big boots sounded loudly as they crashed to the deck. With a quickness uncommon for a big man, he suddenly stood at MacGregor's side with his musket and fixed bayonet. Two marines looking just as fierce as O'Bannion followed. Young Midshipman Collingwood, whose jaunty clay pipe gave him some air of self-confidence, clambered over. As the other crewmen scampered aboard, MacGregor ordered, "Sergeant, collect the weapons of the crew. Stack them on the quarterdeck and place a guard on the swivel gun there." He pointed to a swivel gun pointed their way on the quarterdeck. "Only British sailors will be allowed on the quarterdeck."

MacGregor glanced at the French marine aiming the swivel gun in his direction. The gun was capable of killing them all in one shot. MacGregor ignored the gun and continued, "Men, the officers will be allowed to retain their side arms and are to be treated as gentlemen."

Switching adroitly from English to French, MacGregor continued to issue orders at a rapid pace. "Man the bilge pumps; extinguish the fire; stop the leaks; repair the rigging." *A busy crew will have little time for mischief.* One by one, the French crewmen reluctantly laid down their weapons and hurried below to fight the fire. Young Captain De la Court stood dangling his hat and plume as he looked away into the sky, disinterestedly. Only a handful of French marines stood defiantly holding their weapons at the ready.

An officer of the French marines looked at the young French Captain in disgust, his sword hand almost trembling. It seemed he might use it against his own officer. In a bold move, MacGregor stepped toward the marine officer and held out his hand, palm up. "May I have your pistol, Sir? You may sheath your sword and retain it. Order your men to stack their arms at the quarterdeck. Too many men have died today already." The two men looked each other directly in the eye without movement.

At last, Captain De la Court said, "I demand the privilege of deck freedom for all officers and gentlemen, and you may raise your bloody pirate banner over the decks of our ship.

The sword shook rigidly in the hand of the marine as he glowered at his commander. French marines standing nearby raised their weapons. Hammers clicked loudly as British and French prepared to shoot each other. MacGregor's thoughts of defending De la Court from his own officers turned quickly to his own peril. In a calculated risk, MacGregor took the sword from the trembling hand of the marine officer. He sheathed it in the officer's scabbard as he said, "Officers and gentlemen will be granted deck privileges and may keep their side arms." MacGregor removed the officer's pistol from his belt and tucked it in his own. He ordered his men to disarm the French marines. Three English marines went about disarming a dozen or more French marines. Sailors carried French weapons under the glowering eye of a French marine at the swivel gun. Sergeant O'Bannion carried an armful of muskets up the steps and dropped them to the deck in a rattling heap. He replaced the reluctant French marine at the swivel gun with a British marine. Other Englishmen continued to carry arm loads of weapons to the quarterdeck. Then O'Bannion led his little band back to disarm the French crew on the gun deck.

MacGregor checked the priming on his pistol. "Let's go below, Sergeant O'Bannion, and finish our job. While we disarm the men on the gundeck, you send two marines down to the orlop deck. We must guard the powder magazine." He drew his cutlass and descended the smoky companion way leading to the gun deck. With eyes burning and smoke filling his lungs,

MacGregor set Sergeant O'Bannion's men to stacking captured weapons near the stairs. In the smoke French sailors labored at the bilge pumps. A double row of sailors sweated, seesawing the big pumps. The pumps clanked, rattled, and spewed a flood of seawater onto the fire. MacGregor watched his men disarm the French marines. He directed the fire fighting effort until satisfied all was well. Then he hurried aft into the blinding, choking smoke where French sailors hosed the searing flames.

The aft deck was like the bowels of an angry furnace. With his arm lifted in front of his face to shield against the heat, MacGregor searched for the hatch leading down to the orlop deck. Threading his way through the maze of cargo and unused cannons, MacGregor found the hatch leading to the orlop deck and powder magazine. He descended the ladder. He stood at the bottom of the ladder and waited as his eyes adjusted to the darkness, breathing easier in the better air. Down he stepped into the cooler, darker recesses of the orlop deck, almost free of smoke. Clanking sounds of the bilge pumps echoed loudly in the orlop deck. Cold, black water swirled around MacGregor's thighs as his feet found the floor of the deck.

Strange, he thought, *the marine guards I had sent to the orlop deck are not to be found.* Turning toward the stern of the ship, he felt his way through the darkness of cargo and water. *The powder magazine should be just below the burning stern*, he thought. *If the fire reaches the magazine, the ship will be blown out of the water and all of us with it.*

MacGregor followed the narrow isle between the cargo as the stinking bilge water rose almost to his waist. An erratic movement against MacGregor's body sent a shudder through him. He recognized a rat swimming past him. He continued to feel his way along the narrow corridor until he stumbled on an object beneath the water. Losing his balance, MacGregor almost fell into the murky water. His hands felt the object over which he had tripped. A body!

MacGregor stepped back in shock, looking down at his hands. Even in the poor light he recognized blood. Fresh blood! He put his hands beneath the surface, under the arms of the man, and lifted him. Open, unseeing eyes looked at MacGregor from a head with wet hair dripping water over the face. He lifted the shoulders out of the water to reveal the body of the English marine from his boarding party. Several stab wounds still oozed blood.

MacGregor pressed his fingers to the marine's neck in search of a ripple of pulse. None came. Slowly, he released the body to the dark water, knowing there was nothing he could do.

Moving cautiously, he tugged at the wet pistol in his belt, changed his mind and drew his cutlass. Except the rasp of the cutlass as he withdrew it, only the sound of the bilge pumps clanking and his own heartbeat filled his ears. Coming closer to the powder magazine, MacGregor saw a ray of light from the open door where a shaft connected the magazine to the upper deck and a prism. No lantern flame could be tolerated here, for this was the powder magazine. At the sound of splintering wood MacGregor moved faster toward the open door, the water sucking at his waist. From the open door, a shadow moved across the light.

Chapter Seventeen

Lieutenant Charles MacGregor sloshed through the pungent bilge water of the French battleship, coughing and eyes burning from the smoke. It was almost impossible to see in the smoky darkness, but his senses guided him ever to the stern. He was confident the powder magazine would be aft. As in all warships, a prism would admit light into the ammunition magazine, and if it were not locked, he should see light. Sure enough, after pushing a floating sail and a box or two out of his way, he saw a dim shaft of light farther down the orlop. From the magazine he heard a noise! MacGregor quickened his pace. Reaching the open door of the ship's ammunition magazine, he found powder kegs and cartridges floating amid the debris. There, a French officer of marines stood emptying a broken powder keg over the piles of explosives. Seeing MacGregor, he threw the empty powder keg in his direction. As MacGregor dodged the flying keg, the officer withdrew a small pistol from his waist. He pointed the pistol at a nearby broken powder keg.

MacGregor's thoughts raced as he realized that the entire ship would be destroyed with all its men. As bilge water sucked at his legs, he sloshed awkwardly toward the officer, watching as the man cocked the pistol. MacGregor's legs seemed immobile, as in a dream. The officer moved his cocked pistol toward the powder. He leaped, stretching his hands forward toward the pistol, expecting a flash at any moment. The pistol hammer began its fall. If flint touched steel, it would ignite a spark that would blow the ship to pieces. MacGregor's fingers touched the pistol. His thumb slipped under the hammer. It snapped painfully on the web of MacGregor's thumb. His body crashed into the officer and both men fell hard against the powder kegs, sliding down into the dark bilge water. With a bleeding hand, MacGregor pulled at the pistol. He must force it below the surface of the water to end the threat of an explosion. MacGregor pulled with all his might while his adversary countered valiantly. He added his body weight against the man's arm. The pistol sank beneath the water and came away in his hand.

MacGregor dropped the pistol and engaged the desperate adversary as the French officer's strong hands squeezed his throat. The man's body weight forced MacGregor's head down, toward the dark water. Gasping desperately for air, he sank beneath the surface. He struggled to free himself from the strong hands around his throat. His adversary moved astride him, holding him down... drowning him. MacGregor twisted at the hands around his throat. He writhed and squirmed with his body. A single finger yielded to his pressure, torn away from his throat. MacGregor heard and felt the snap of the finger as it broke under his pressure, but the weight holding him down never faltered. Bubbles rose from his mouth. His lungs ached for air; his heart pounded in his chest. MacGregor kicked. He clawed at the face of the officer above him, but to no avail. An urge to relax and inhale water swept over him. It would be so easy to relax, relax... and die. It would be comfortable. No! He must not quit; he must live. MacGregor struggled with his brain. Feeling sluggish, like a cloud of fog crossing the ocean of his mind, he felt death. *It's not fair to die so soon. Many MacGregors have died at the hands of their enemies! My race is royal... I am one of the few... we must claim our heritage.* Anger welled within him. MacGregor twisted his body and moved his free hand to the hilt of his dirk below his knee. MacGregor raged. With his arm feeling heavy like a tree trunk, he pulled the dirk from its sheath. Unconsciousness would soon overtake him. He heard the scrape of metal as the dirk came out of its sheath. In a desperate struggle for his life, he thrust the seemingly heavy, ponderous dirk upward. It seemed weighted with a thousand anchors, the heaviest weight he had ever lifted in his life. His lungs screamed for air as he lifted the dirk up and out of the water toward the enemy taking his life. He could not see but thrust the sharp blade blindly. He felt the point of the dirk slice through heavy cloth and slip into soft flesh, then strike solid bone. He summoned more strength, shoving harder. The dirk slipped off the bone and eased farther into flesh. *If I must die, I will take an enemy with me,* he thought. As the fog enveloped him, he summoned his last bit of energy. He shoved the dirk deeper still. Through soft and hard flesh he shoved until the hilt was tight against the man's body. Then he twisted the blade. As the strength in his arm faded, a fog descended over his brain. The muscles locking air in his pounding chest relaxed as the fog covered his brain. With a roar, the water exploded from his lungs and almost as quickly began to suck water in its place.

    Lieutenant MacGregor found himself rising in the water as his lungs inhaled the foul, tepid bilge water. He thrashed and flailed in his dizzying fog, coughing and choking. Trying to inhale air into his burning lungs, he wrapped his arms around a floating keg and lost consciousness. Slowly, the fog in his brain lifted as MacGregor found himself sitting in the water, gasping, hugging the keg against his chest. His enemy lay half submerged beside him with the dirk protruding from his abdomen. The man lifted his head and looked down with wide eyes at the instrument of his death. The French officer hurled an angry growl toward him and slowly sank below the water, wide, unseeing eyes slipping last into the foul water. MacGregor struggled to his feet, still coughing and gasping for air. With water streaming down his face, MacGregor staggered against the powder kegs. He stumbled out of the powder magazine, forcing the door closed against the weight of bilge water. He found the padlock hanging nearby on its chain and snapped it shut. As his brain cleared, he again heard the sound of bilge pumps clanking in his ears. MacGregor weakly waded through the sloshing bilge water, supporting himself with his trembling hand on nearby cargo. At the stairs he shoved aside a body and climbed slowly, shakily to the gun deck.

The fire now yielded to the streams of water pumped from the bilge. Now only smoke filled the deck as sailors stumbled and dragged their mates into the fresh air on the upper deck. Lieutenant MacGregor examined the cargo stored in the holds, prying loose boards and chopping into barrels with an axe, as he peered into the containers. Gaining the upper deck with shaky legs, he found Sergeant O'Bannion rushing toward him, alarmed at his disheveled appearance. "Let me help you, Sir," urged a concerned O'Bannion.

"I'll be all right," replied MacGregor. "Send another man to guard the magazine. Your marine is dead, and I came close to the same fate."

"Aye, Sir," returned O'Bannion, "McGrath! Down to the orlop deck and guard the powder magazine. Keep your back to the wall and your bayonet ready." In response, a red-coated marine trotted away at the command.

On the quarterdeck, Midshipman Collingwood approached MacGregor with a sense of urgency. "Mr. MacGregor, the quarterdeck is secure, Sir. Oh, you look frightful, Sir."

MacGregor removed his wet jacket. "I look much better than my opponent intended. We are all fortunate, considering he was about to blow up the powder magazine."

"I beg your pardon, Sir? The powder magazine?" Midshipman Collingwood questioned.

"Yes, Mr. Collingwood, we had a close call. But let's not tarry, there's more work to be done. Signal for carpenters and sail makers. Get new sails aloft and the hull planked." MacGregor inhaled deeply of the fresh sea air and looked across the water at the little frigate, riding so confidently with its sails aback.

A cable length apart, both warships lay hove-to under a warm afternoon sun as MacGregor loaded the French officers in a long boat. With a fresh breeze blowing through his wet hair, the disheveled MacGregor took his place in the back of the long boat. Exhausted, he waited for his return to *Grenadier*. Sullen French officers, many wounded, some with their heads in their hands, took to the boat for their journey to captivity. With French sailors at the oars, MacGregor gave the order to row. As their boat lifted on the ocean swells, other boats passed in the opposite direction, carrying English sailors to the captured ship. Men cheered as they passed. Soon MacGregor saw and heard the jubilant rows of English tars lining the rail of *Grenadier*. They cheered victoriously as the boat approached. Hoots and catcalls greeted the French officers as they climbed aboard. Amid insults and taunts from the sailors of *Grenadier*, the French officers, injured in both body and pride, assembled on the spar deck.

The decks of *Grenadier* had been cleaned spotlessly. The blood, shattered wood, tangled rigging, shards of canvas, and mutilated bodies had already yielded to hard-working sailors. Yet the canvas-covered piles on the deck with dozens of pale, stiff feet sticking out gave mute evidence to the cannonading suffered by the men. Lieutenant MacGregor, his clothing disheveled and wet hair streaming down his face, was the last officer over the bulwarks. Captain Walshingham stood before the French officers, holding his paunch and rocking back and forth on heel and toe with a satisfied smile on his face. Scrawny old yeoman Farwell stood behind him, his wrinkled face looking apprehensively around Walshingham's shoulder, his slate under his arm. Captain Walshingham took a bottle of wine from one of his batsman and moved among the French captives, followed closely by a retinue of servants carrying wine bottles and glasses. As fast as his servants uncorked the wine, Walshingham poured for the French officers, welcoming them like long lost friends. He examined Captain De la Court carefully. Walshingham poured this guest an extra measure of wine. MacGregor, too, found a wine glass in his hand. They toasted King George, King Frederick, King Louis, chivalry, seamanship, and anything that came to Walshingham's mind, MacGregor translating.

Captain Walshingham lifted his hand to stop the merriment and turned to MacGregor. "Lieutenant, inform these gentlemen they will be my guests for the next few days and will be permitted deck privileges with their oath of neutrality. However, it will first be necessary to conduct a body search." The faces of the English sailors, which had fallen in dismay as they watched the toasting and drinking of wine, rose in happiness once more.

"Explain to them that devious captives have oft tried to hide valuables from me in the past. Explain that I am an honorable man but I detest such unscrupulous practices. The gentlemen will immediately disrobe. I will conduct a body search to insure they are not depriving me of my just dues. If anyone has hidden jewels in their privy parts, I shall find them." Walshingham held his lapels and looked placidly at MacGregor as he waited the translation.

Captain Walshingham repeated his order. "Order these Frenchmen to remove all their clothing and bend over. I will search them to insure they are not trying to deceive me."

MacGregor's face grew a scowl. His reddened neck swelled. He gripped his sword, tugging as if to withdraw it, than slammed it back in its scabbard. "I gave my word to these officers… they may keep their side arms… in exchange for their surrender. Without their sidearms these gentlemen will be at the mercy of your boatswain and his thieves!"

Walshingham's narrow eyes slowly relaxed and smiled. "They may keep their sidearm then. Now, translate the rest of my order, Mr. MacGregor," he shouted.

MacGregor translated for Captain Walshingham. A murmur of indignation swept through the group of French officers. Young Captain De la Court, with hand on the hilt of his jeweled sword, stepped angrily toward Walshingham, an oath squeezed between his clinched teeth. With wide, wild eyes, De la Court put his face into Walshingham's. He shouted in good English, "Thieving pirate!"

Walshingham nodded at his boatswain's mate. With a wicked grin, the boatswain swung his belaying pin. It struck De la Court's skull with a terrible crack. De la Court pitched forward. With a stream of blood running from his scalp, he fell to the deck. English sailors cheered. Like a herd of squealing pigs, they pounced on the unconscious young nobleman. They stripped him of his jewelry, his coins, and his clothing. The jewelry and coins they dutifully handed to Walshingham. Sailors stripped clothing from the unconscious man and ran away with their prize, waving the clothing in the air. The boatswain proudly handed the jeweled sword to Captain Walshingham while his shipmates continued stripping De la Court of his last remnants of clothing. Naked and bleeding, De la Court lay unconscious on the deck.

Captain Walshingham took the sword with a triumphant shout. "Hah! Look at this beautiful sword." He turned to Lieutenant MacGregor, his smile fading. "Next time, ye shall not promise our captives a side arm. This is a beautiful sword, and it is a shame to disfigure it. However, I am an honorable man, I will honor your promise." Walshingham took a dirk from inside his coat and pried a large jewel from the hilt. Putting the jewel in his pocket, he tossed the sword on the naked form of De la Court.

Walshingham turned his attention to the other officers, pointing at their shoes and trousers. To prods and shoves from derisive sailors, the French officers reluctantly removed their clothing. They stood in naked ranks before Walshingham. Those not totally naked wore only bloodstained bandages. As Walshingham went from man to man, he removed rings and jewelry. The boatswain searched the piles of clothing, removing valuables, knives, trinkets, and anything of interest, handing them to Walshingham. Anything of little value Walshingham threw back to the waiting sailors around the boatswain.

Then, like a plantation owner buying slaves, Captain Walshingham passed down the ranks of officers, pulling down their chins and peering into their mouths. After looking in each man's mouth, Walshingham bent them over and put a hand on either hip. Leaning over with his nose near each man's anus, he poked and prodded, carefully examining his private parts for hidden valuables.

Satisfied at last that he had extracted every valuable, Captain Walshingham motioned the officers to don their clothing. All except poor Captain De la Court, who still lay unconscious on the deck. "Find the captain some sailor's clothing from our slops," ordered Walshingham as a grin spread across his face. "He's a gentleman. Ye must treat such captives as their station deserves. Show him yer respect!"

Captain Walshingham stood before the French officers with hands on his hips and a friendly smile on his face. "Tell them, MacGregor, I compliment their integrity in not trying to hide valuables from me. Now, I suggest they avail themselves of a hot bath. I will put servants at their disposal to attend to their personal needs. Anything at all that they might need to make their visit with us more comfortable, they should not hesitate to ask. I will expect all the gentlemen to dine with me in my cabin this evening. Mr. MacGregor, I want yer report immediately on my prize."

Looking as worn as his captives, Lieutenant MacGregor followed the French officers as far as his cabin. He ordered water and quickly bathed, packed his personal belongings and stood before Captain Walshingham in a clean uniform. Walshingham's yeoman stood with his slate, ready to record MacGregor's report. "It's a second rater, Sir, by the name of *Chasseur* loaded with rifles, uniforms, and other supplies for Louisbourg. We are fishing the mizzen mast and installing new main yards. Much of the rigging must be replaced, but Mr. Collingwood will soon have the essentials in place. I judge there are over one hundred shot between wind and water. We destroyed the poop; it's shot to pieces and burned out. There's three feet of water in the well, but the bilge pumps are keeping up with the flow and carpenters will soon have it seaworthy," MacGregor concluded.

Walshingham beamed as he listened to MacGregor's report. Leaning back in his desk chair, he pointed at his yeoman saying, "Read our report, Mr. Farwell."

Farwell adjusted his glasses while holding the journal at an arm's length, reading. With his Adam's apple bobbing on his skinny neck he read, "Twenty-one shot twixt' wind and water. We lost only fourteen dead and twenty-six wounded, of which no more than three-fourths are expected to die."

Captain Walshingham looked back at MacGregor with a smile. "Aye, 'twas a fine day for King and country. A fine day also for the good Lord, for we saved many riches from the hands of the Papists, some of which may even return to his hands in English tithes." With a wicked twinkle in his eye Walshingham added, "As for me, I intend to offer the Lord a share of my tithe. I will toss it into the air and what he wants, he may keep; what comes down I will keep." Captain Walshingham roared in laughter. Mr. Farwell grinned broadly, displaying his missing teeth. Walshingham's smile disappeared as quickly as it had come as he continued, "Mr. MacGregor, take my prize ship safely to Boston. Remember that it is now His Majesty's ship under my care. Every gun, every sail, every rope, every chain, and every piece of cargo shall ye deliver safely to Boston, or die trying. I am entrusting ye with a small fortune. If through yer negligence it diminishes one farthing, I shall have ye keelhauled and yer remains fed to the sharks. Do I make yer orders perfectly clear, Mr. MacGregor?"

Lieutenant MacGregor picked up a chart from Walshingham's desk and studied it. Without looking up he replied, "Aye, Sir, God willing your ship will be in Boston within three days."

Walshingham walked close to MacGregor. He whispered, "Ye shall speak to no one about the cargo aboard my prize ship, MacGregor. Neither ye nor the midshipman nor any sailor. Is that perfectly clear, Mr. MacGregor?"

MacGregor looked puzzled but pulled his hat on, answering, "Aye, Sir, I will do as you order, whatever."

Half an hour later Lieutenant MacGregor stood on the French warship's deck. He found the French crew assembled on the spar deck watched by Sergeant O'Bannion, his marines, and a swivel gun. O'Bannion reported as MacGregor stood overlooking the prisoners. "Except for a few French marines working off their anger on the bilge pumps, all the enemy stands before you. Our men killed a few marines while you were gone, but they insist it was self defense."

MacGregor stood looking at O'Bannion before replying, "Our prisoners will be treated with civility. Anyone abusing a prisoner will wish he had been killed on boarding. Be certain everyone knows that, Mr. O'Bannion." He addressed the dispirited French captives before him in their own language. "Prisoners will be confined to the orlop deck, except those volunteering to work the ship. Volunteers will be treated with courtesy and will serve the ship just as one of our Englishmen. You will be free to go anywhere on the ship except the magazine and arms lockers. Volunteers will take an oath of loyalty to the English officers of this ship until it reaches its destination. You do not have to swear loyalty to King George nor anyone else; you are loyal to King Louis and so you shall remain. But any man breaking his oath may be shot, summarily. When we reach Boston, we will begin making plans for your return to France. When your feet reach terra firma once more, you will be freed of your oath.

"Now, let us make sail for Boston. All those not volunteering to man the ship will immediately go below to the orlop deck, others will man the braces and leeward haul. Set the jibs and shake out the fore sail." The English sailors stood dumfounded until MacGregor ordered, "Set a two-man guard, around the clock, on both the magazine and arms locker."

A gray-haired French sailor with a bloody bandage on his arm approached the quarterdeck. Holding his cap in his hands he volunteered, "I'm a quartermaster, Sir."

Lieutenant MacGregor turned to Midshipman Collingwood. "This man will take the helm." Sergeant O'Bannion watched with puzzled eyes as the former enemy took the ship's wheel. The man looked up at the set of the sails. Reaching across the shattered binnacle he lifted a damaged speaking trumpet. He called out orders to the sailors on deck. French sailors hesitated, stood looking as few experienced sailors began to follow the quartermaster's orders, then rushed to his commands. Slowly, others drifted to their stations with only a handful standing motionless. These O'Bannion motioned below.

Chasseur sailed for Boston. With jury rigged masts and a leaking hull, they limped away over the rough seas. French sailors made ingenious repairs to keep the ship afloat and moving. That evening, as a golden sun dropped below the clouds, MacGregor called the men on deck. French sailors stood in a long, loose line. In front of them lay their dead in a long row, their bare feet protruding from beneath bloody shards of sailcloth. It was quiet. Only creaks and groans of the ship and sounds of wind and wave broke the silence. English marines stood at attention as the French sailors buried their dead.

Chapter Eighteen

A few days later, with white clouds drifting slowly across the blue sky, MacGregor stood on the quarterdeck, sailing the flood tide into Boston Harbor. *Chasseur*'s black hull reflected in the azure water. From the main mast top a Union Jack fluttered in the breeze. Passing in the opposite direction, a schooner beating out to sea against wind and tide dipped her colors in salute. Sailors lining the rail of anchored warships cheered at the sight of a captured French battleship flying the King's Crosses. But war was undeclared and few civilians in Boston thought about war this winter day nor would they know a French ship from any other.

Lieutenant MacGregor unbuttoned his heavy cloak, lifted a telescope, and scanned the ships in the harbor. "Mr. Collingwood, Captain Walshingham has arrived before us. His frigate is anchored just inside the harbor. Ready the anchor party, prepare a cannon salute." MacGregor turned to Sergeant O'Bannion. "Sergeant, ready a side party to receive Captain Walshingham. I assure you he will be waiting to inspect the prize."

The cannon broke the silence of Boston's harbor with a loud crash that resounded across the water and echoed across the town. Sea gulls shrilled in protest at this intrusion, rising in white waves to circle above the harbor. White smoke drifted away from the cannon on *Chasseur*'s port rail. Presently, a canon from Grenadier answered the salute with a soft explosion that echoed across the roadstead.

"Ready to bring the bow up," MacGregor ordered to the helmsman as *Chasseur* reached a spot about a cable length from *Grenadier*. He judged the exact distance carefully before he called out, "Hard over." Picking up a speaking trumpet he called, "Mainsail haul, ready the main anchor." *Chasseur* eased slowly around in the harbor, her bow pointing upwind. With the big ship's jibs slatting and flapping noisily in the wind, *Chasseur* coasted to a stop. "Let go the anchor," MacGregor ordered. With a splash and rattle of chain the big anchor hit the water. High above the deck, sailors hurried nimbly over the foot ropes, tying the sails on the yards. MacGregor assembled the French crew below the quarterdeck, addressing them in fluent French, "You are good sailors who would make any king proud. You have fought a good fight and surrendered honorably. When our officers come aboard, stand in ranks with your heads high as befitting the proud seamen you are. You have earned my respect and you deserve theirs as well. Now go below and make a small bundle of the things you most treasure to take away with you. Then come topside and form ranks to await your boat ashore."

A few minutes later Captain Walshingham's gig approached *Chasseur*. It was followed by *Grenadier*'s long boat and a crew to take charge of the prisoners. The French crew watched as Captain Walshingham climbed quickly aboard with an agility surprising for a man of his portly stature. Walshingham's purser followed with a journal and slate under his arm. Walshingham's absent-minded nods acknowledged the colors. He threw back his cape, patted his fat belly with both hands, and looked around the ship, nodding briefly at the ranks of French sailors. With feet planted wide apart, his body leaning far back, he looked up at the ship's topmast. A smile spread across his face as his beaming eyes inventoried the big prize ship. Presently he turned to MacGregor, saying absently, "Order the crew into our long boat which shall ferry them ashore." Eagerness sounded in his voice again as he said to MacGregor, "Let's go below and see how rich a prize she is, and I hope ye have lost nothing of value."

Captain Walshingham's hurried through the decks. His inspection missed nothing. All morning, with lantern in hand and perspiration glistening on his face, he inspected the cargo. Mr. Farwell followed close behind, entering the inventory into his journal while beads of sweat dripped off his nose. Walshingham fondled the rifles as though they were a cache of diamonds and rubies.

It was almost noon before Walshingham led the way on deck. He was preparing to leave *Chasseur* when a long boat appeared, making its way toward the captured battleship. A dark look crossed Walshingham's face as he observed that the boat carried no less than the Governor of Boston and the commodore, accompanied by other high ranking officers of the Boston garrison. Walshingham looked with interest upon his old friend, Edward Brumley, now in the company of the governor.

"Mr. Farwell, hide yer journal lest some busy body asks to inspect it," Walshingham whispered. "I will do the talking and the two of ye will smile and nod."

Pipes twittered as the Commodore and his aid, the Governor in his black woolen suit with French lace, and the Army officers in their red tunics made their way up the boarding ladder. The Governor strode across the deck with his hand outstretched, his eyes alight, and a wide smile on his face.

Walshingham twisted his face into a smile and swept off his hat with a bow. The governor pumped Walshingham's hand as he spoke. "Congratulations, Captain Walshingham, what a gallant accomplishment. I understand from Mr. Brumley that you have previously met our new prize commissioner?"

Walshingham bowed again to Brumley, saying, "Of course, everyone knows of Edward Brumley's broad knowledge of shipping and marketing. I am indeed honored to know him." Walshingham shook Brumley's hand.

"And you, of course, know the Commodore and his staff," continued the governor. "To think, a French battleship captured by your little frigate!"

The smile on Walshingham's face broadened as he replied, "Twas' a vicious fight. But the French captain was no match for my cunning and seamanship." Captain Walshingham grasped his coat lapels with both hands, now rocking confidently on his heels as he spoke. "Yes, just think of all the carnage I have wrought on the enemy. Why, if a poor captain's share of the prize money where just a little more, I might sweep the sea clean of the enemy." Walshingham's arm shot out to sweep the air as the officers jerked backwards, avoiding Walshingham's gestures.

Rearranging his hat after dodging Walshingham's gesture, the governor offered, "Perhaps, Commodore, Captain Walshingham should be given command of this battleship. As successful as he seems to be in a little frigate, how much better could he do with a big battleship?"

Walshingham's face fell. His eyes blazed as he replied, "Governor, ye do me too much honor." A smile reappeared on Walshingham's face as he continued, "I must not take too much credit for this capture. I must recognize the contribution made by my young Scotsman here, Lieutenant MacGregor. He led the fight in fierce hand to hand fighting. Such vicious fighting the Navy has never before seen. It is he who should be given command of this battleship, not I."

With a puzzled look on his face, the Governor shifted his gaze to look over Walshingham's shoulder, searching for the lieutenant that Walshingham described. The governor's eyebrows raised when he saw MacGregor standing behind the captain, his long Scottish sword dangling from his belt. Clearing his throat, a thin smile appeared on his face. "Well, congratulations, young man. A splendid job you have done. I'm sure the Admiralty will find a deserving captain for this ship if you are not so lucky."

Walshingham resumed, "I estimate the value of this prize to be no less than sixteen thousand pounds. Its cargo of food and uniforms will bring some nine thousand pounds additional. Mr. MacGregor, our young first officer, receives one-eighth as his share. I make that to be worth some three thousand, one hundred, and twenty-five pounds. A prince's ransom for a young colonial, what say?"

MacGregor wondered, *Walshingham did not mention the rifles. Why? They are worth far more than uniforms and food.*

The commodore turned to Captain Walshingham. "Mr. Walshingham, did the French Captain survive the engagement?"

Walshingham nodded. "Yes, he is a prisoner aboard my vessel, along with his subordinates. The enlisted prisoners have already been ferried ashore."

The commodore ordered Captain Walshingham, "Mr. Walshingham, send the French officers ashore and put them in custody of the Port Captain. However, I want the French Captain brought to my flagship where I shall interview him myself. Does he speak English?"

Walshingham turned his burning eyes and a frown upon Lieutenant MacGregor. "Does he speak English?"

Lieutenant MacGregor replied, "He either does not or will not speak English, but I would be glad to accompany him as translator if you like."

Walshingham hurriedly interjected, "I don't think I could spare ye here, MacGregor. There are others who could translate just as well."

"Nonsense!" interrupted the commodore. "I will take but a little of your lieutenant's time, and I would also like to hear his comments on the actions taken by the French in combat. That information can be useful to our fleet." He turned to MacGregor. "Young man, if there is a water tight boat aboard this ship, get it in the water and go for the French captain. Bring him quickly to my flag ship. I will see you both there."

"Aye, aye, Sir," replied MacGregor. He turned to the ranks of French seamen and barked out a series of orders in French. As the British dignitaries departed, French sailors hurried to launch one of the few surviving boats on *Chasseur*.

MacGregor readied to followed a group of his chosen sailors aboard it when Walshingham said, "MacGregor! Say nothing of the rifles aboard this ship." MacGregor looked at his captain levelly then turned slowly and followed the boat's crew over the side.

Arriving at *Grenadier,* it was a reluctant and disgruntled Marcel De la Court who rode across to the flag ship with MacGregor. The young French nobleman brightened, however, when he saw the commodore with a resplendent retinue of marines drawn up to salute his arrival. A cannon boomed and pipes twittered as De la Court made his way up the boarding ladder. The commodore welcomed him aboard in passable French, removing his hat and bowing low to the young nobleman. With pipes and drums playing, the commodore led both MacGregor and De la Court to his great cabin. In halting but passable French the commodore said, "I have been told of the valiant fight you made to defend your ship. It is indeed an honor to be in the presence of such a... brave knight. I saw with my own eyes that you had little with which to fight. Few cannons could be operated you were, what is the word? Oh, yes, *en flûte,* and loaded with cargo." The commodore stopped before entering his cabin and turned to De la Court to ask, "What was your cargo?"

De la Court's countenance, which had brightened slightly, turned sour as he replied, "I would not tell you pirates what is in my cargo nor anything else of use to you in the rape and pillage of our vessels on the high seas! But if you do not know already, there were uniforms and rifles, many rifles, for the many volunteers in Canada who would fight you heretics."

The commodore smiled and opened the door to his cabin, saying, "Your answer is of little importance. My prize agent will soon be conducting an inventory of all your cargo, and we shall know every detail."

Inside the cabin MacGregor saw a yeoman writing furiously at a side desk while an English officer dictated to him. The commodore stood a moment looking over the shoulder of the yeoman at the document being written then offered both MacGregor and De la Court a chair. The commodore rang a small bell beside his own chair and a boy appeared beside the commodore. "Kindly pour us a glass of my finest port, Boy," ordered the commodore.

When each man held a glass of wine in his hand, the commodore offered a toast. "Let us drink a toast to peace. Let us hope that soon the powers in Europe will end this nonsense of hostility between our two great nations."

With a toast to peace, the commodore again resumed questioning De la Court. De la Court's refusal to answer the commodore's questions did not upset the commodore at all, however. The older man seemed to be enjoying himself, and his smile was interrupted only when the officer standing at the yeoman's desk lifted the document from in front of the yeoman and walked across the cabin. The officer handed the paper to the commodore and said, "This document will stand the test of any judge in England or France, I assure you, Sir. It sets out all the provisions you requested, Sir."

The commodore looked over the document and handed it to MacGregor, saying, "Mr. MacGregor, as one who made this capture, you are entitled to know everything that is written here and be assured you will receive your one-eighth portion of anything returned. Do you read French as well, Lieutenant?"

MacGregor took the letter and saw immediately it was written in French. Absent mindedly MacGregor, answered, "Yes, Sir." He then quickly read the document aloud and was surprised to read that it was a parole with promise to pay a ransom. At the bottom of the letter Marcel De la Court's name and title was carefully printed below a line for his signature. Aside from the space for De la Court's signature, only the amount of the ransom was left blank. Finishing the reading, he quickly looked up at De la Court and then shifted his gaze to the commodore.

MacGregor handed the document to De la Court as the commodore said, "There remains only to fix the amount of the ransom, and you can be on your way to Louisbourg. There you may be put ashore by one of our ships under a flag of truce, and you will soon be on your way back to France. Now, I suggest the amount should read ten thousand pounds, Stirling. And what do you say to that, Captain De la Court?"

De la Court jumped to his feet, shouting, "I should not pay you English pirates an ounce! This is nothing but thievery." He lifted the hilt of his sword, minus the expensive jewel, and rattled it home in its metal hanger. Then, through clinched teeth, he said slowly, "My father would not pay more than five thousand pounds, ever!"

The commodore stood and bowed slightly to De la Court with a smile and turned to the British officer standing nearby. "Then let the yeoman make the amount for seventy-five hundred then." He looked at De la Court pleasantly. "The amount is seventy-five hundred pounds Stirling and the choice is yours, Chevalier. You may be our guest in jail here or sail to Louisbourg and freedom. What is your answer, Sir?"

De la Court's answer was only a whisper that no one in the cabin could understand, but his actions spoke volumes. With document in hand he walked across the cabin and laid the paper in front of the yeoman. He watched with interest as the yeoman wrote in the agreed amount, after which the French nobleman took the quill from the yeoman's hand and wrote his name across the bottom with a flourish. He watched as the yeoman sanded the ink then shook off the sand and handed the document to the commodore, saying, "Here is my signature. Be kind enough to make your seal on my copy."

The commodore bowed and nodded to the British officer who quickly affixed the seal to a copy which the yeoman had already prepared. When the wax had set, the commodore handed the copy to De la Court, saying to the British officer, "Please show Captain de la Court to our best cabin and arrange his immediate transfer to Louisbourg." He turned to MacGregor, still speaking

French, "Lieutenant, tarry a moment. I would like a word with you."

Captain de la Court turned to MacGregor; still speaking French, he said, "Lieutenant, I honor your bravery in boarding my ship with so few men as you did, but I will never understand how you can serve your English pirate masters." He then turned to the commodore, saying, "I surrendered my ship to this man only when I learned he was a gentleman, educated at the court of King Louis. Otherwise, I would have fought to the death." De la Court nodded at the British officer and stalked out of the room, slamming the door behind him.

Smiling, the commodore looked for a moment at the door then turned to MacGregor. "You do speak French very well, Mr. MacGregor. Is De la Court correct in saying that you learned your French at the court of King Louis XV?"

"When I was a child living at the court, De la Court insisted I bow to him because of his noble birth. I did not recognize him aboard *Chasseur,* but he later remembered me."

Again the commodore smiled. "I take it your father took refuge in France with their so-called Bonnie Prince Charlie?"

MacGregor nodded. "My father *and* my grandfather were both exiled in France. There was a bounty on MacGregor males in Scotland, dead or alive."

"I take it your mother was a French noblewoman?" the commodore quarried. "And you were educated at the King's court?"

"Yes," replied MacGregor. "But I would never have been considered French any more than I would be thought of as English. I'm neither, but like many men in the Royal Navy, I have sworn my loyalty to King George and will die by that oath if I must."

The commodore stood and held out his hand. "Indeed, I believe you *would* die for your oath, Mr. MacGregor, and I pledge the loyalty of the Royal Navy to you in return. But now, I want you to tell me every detail of the action taken against *Chasseur* and especially the reaction made by the French. That information may be useful to other English ships encountering them in action."

Lieutenant MacGregor related every detail he could recall to the commodore, interrupted many times by the commodore's detailed questions. At last, the commodore stood, saying, "Good luck to you, Mr. MacGregor. I will see that you get your one-eighth share of all that is coming to you, and more if I can justify it. You are fortunate to serve under Captain Walshingham as I'm sure you know. You will earn far more prize money aboard that frigate than will any post captain aboard one of our big battleships." With a casual wave of dismissal, the commodore returned to his desk and sat down at the papers before him.

Before he walked out, however, MacGregor stopped to say, "Commodore, remember that I'm fluent in French and know the ways of French gentlemen. If you ever need an emissary to the French, I can serve you well." Without waiting for a reply, he walked out and shut the door behind him. He felt uneasy as he walked on deck and descended the boarding ladder to the waiting gig. *Did I overreach in asking to be an emissary? Will the commodore trust me?*

Chapter Nineteen

The long, dark nights that shrouded Louisbourg through winter abated with the spring of 1756. Warm weather burst upon Isle Royale. Morning's golden sunshine melted snow on the red tile roofs. Overnight, the dripping water froze into long icicles to sparkle like jewels in the sunshine. People no longer wore their heavy coats out of doors. Where they had silently trudged through the snow with scarfs over their faces, they now greeted each other with smiles and pleasant words. People stood on the parapets of the great stone bastion, enjoying the warm sun and perhaps thinking of the food that would come with the supply ships.

This morning Marie paused in her cleaning to run her fingers lovingly over the hard, polished wood of the harpsichord. Silently, she spread her fingers across the keys. She did not hear the approach of Madame Drucour. "My dear, wouldn't it be wonderful to play the harpsichord?"

Marie turned quickly to her master. "Please excuse me, Madame. I can't help touching the instrument; playing the harpsichord is something I miss very much."

Madame Drucour's eyes suddenly glowed. "Did you have a harpsichord in your own home?"

Marie looked down at the keys to hide tears forming in her eyes. "Yes, Madame, we did. My mother taught me to play; we passed the long winter nights with music of the harpsichord. That was before the Abbe' LeLoutre came and burned our home."

Madame Drucour asked, "Are you telling me you play the harpsichord?"

"Yes, Madame," Marie replied. "I once played the harpsichord, but I have not played for some time. I think I can still play, yes."

Madame Drucour looked at Marie with arms folded across her chest. "My child, maybe you have been sent by heaven. My harpsichord is idle while I long for music. Let's see if you can play something for me."

Marie looked into Madame Drucour's face, smiling in anticipation and disbelief. Madame Drucour took the dust cloth from Marie's hands. "Go ahead, Marie, let's see if you can play the harpsichord. Play something, Marie."

Marie hesitantly ran her fingers lovingly over the keys. She smiled at

Madame Drucour as she sat. Looking at the harpsichord, she adjusted the bench. At night Marie often imagined the notes and pretended to move her fingers on the keys; it would surely come to her. Marie placed her fingers on the keys, closed her eyes, and began to play from her favorite French composer, Rameau. Haltingly at first, and then with feeling, she played and smiled at Madame Drucour. Marie completed the passage of Rameau, looking up at Madame Drucour. "Do you have music I could play?"

"Don't tell me you also read music," Madame Drucour exclaimed.

"Yes," Marie answered, "although I'll need practice; I haven't played for a long time."

The governor's wife walked quickly across the room. She lifted a heavy leather folder from the bureau. The lady rummaged through the music and returned with a concerto by Bach. Madame Drucour placed the music on the lyre of the harpsichord and stood back as Marie's eyes moved over the notes. Soon Marie placed her hands on the keys. Haltingly at first, she began to play the concerto.

Madame Drucour stood with her arms folded while intense concentration furrowed her brow. The halting notes flowed into a smooth melody. A broad smile formed on Madame Drucour's face as Marie continued with the music. At the conclusion, Madame Drucour lifted Marie from the harpsichord. Facing Marie with her hands on Marie's shoulders she said, "Marie, you will be my musician and entertain my guests. My dear, you shall practice every day."

A few days later Marie arrived in the drawing room to find Madame Drucour waiting. "I have a surprise for you, my dear. You may follow me." Madame Drucour led the way to her bed chamber. There in her bed chamber stood an open trunk with many lovely dresses draped across the bed and furniture.

"I have some gifts for you. All these lovely dresses are wasted in my trunk. They fit me perfectly when I was young and now I think they will fit you much better. Now they are only reminders of a happy youth. They should be worn and not be rotting away in the bottom of a trunk. Come, my dear, let's see how you look in these dresses. I think they will fit you perfectly."

Marie's head was in a whirl as the governor's wife helped her out of her simple peasant dress and into the elegant dress of a French lady. Wrinkled and musty, the dress still looked like new. Looking in the mirror at an image that revealed the soft cleavage of her breasts, Marie felt like a queen. She could not help herself; she smiled and whirled around as she imagined dancing in a ballroom with a handsome young man.

"Beautiful, absolutely beautiful, my dear," exclaimed Madame Drucour. "But, we can't stop here. We have more dresses for you to try on and then we must find you shoes to wear. Tomorrow I will have my hairdresser work on those lovely tresses. And then one evening very soon, you may entertain my guests on the harpsichord. Are you agreeable?"

"I will do my best, Madame." Marie's heart leaped with joy.

Madame Drucour smiled at Marie's image in the mirror. "I'm jealous, Marie. I never looked quite so good in that dress. The young men in Louisbourg will see no one but you. Let's try on these other dresses."

At long last, after several cruel teasing hints of spring that brought only snow storms, winter finally loosed its grip on Louisbourg. Summer flowers dotted the pastures and green sprouts appeared in all the gardens. Citizens of the city where happy as food once more appeared in the larders. But Louisbourg citizens so far removed from home could not know of the important news brought by a warship from France. Madame Drucour already knew the contents of the important message delivered by the frigate. But she often toured the military facilities and decided to visit this ship and meet its captain. As a descendent of French naval heros herself, she wanted to meet this man who was making a name for himself. Her military guards led her to the boat docks, paying particular attention to the attractive young lady accompanying her.

Brightly colored signal flags whipped loudly in the blue sky as the ladies came aboard the warship. Ranks of sailors, marines, and officers lined the deck, resplendent in their fine uniforms. Drums rolled and a band played as Madame Drucour came aboard the frigate, *Pélerine*. Marie Gauthier followed Madame Drucour, and the eyes of the sailors followed Marie. "Welcome aboard His Majesty's Ship *Pélerine*, Madame," spoke the captain of the frigate. "I'm Jean Renau, brevet[3] captain of His Majesty's Frigate, *Pélerine*."

Madame Drucour lifted her hand to the Captain. "I know you through your reputation, Captain Renau. My husband speaks of you often. I'm delighted at your frequent petitions to fight the British. Your exploits at sea delight everyone, Captain."

"You honor me, Madame," replied Captain Renau. "But I must tell you, I'm only a brevet captain. I'm not a regular captain in the Navy; I'm but a merchant seaman, temporarily commanding a warship. However, one need not be regular Navy to know what is to be done at sea. If I could sail as I pleased, my exploits would indeed be worthy of your praise. But our leaders are timid and reluctant to risk our ships in battle."

Madame Drucour replied, "If it were within my power, you would have it, Captain, and I shall call you *captain,* even when it is difficult for me to apply the title to some others I know. A dozen ships would be under your command if I but had my way. You see, Captain Renau, I come from a long line of naval officers. My father and his father before him were admirals in the King's Navy. You have heard of the Courseracs, I'm sure. I recognize a fighter when I see one. And I am confident you could teach the British a lesson on naval warfare, as well as most of our French naval officers." Madame Drucour looked away as if hiding the contempt in her eyes. "Ah, but the King will not listen to any woman, except perhaps that whore, Madame Pompadour. His court followers tell him only what he wants to hear." She turned quickly to Marie as she remembered her presence. "Oh, yes, this is *Mademoiselle* Marie Gauthier. She is my musician and my *protégée.* I have brought her to your ship today that she may remind your brave young men of their girls back home."

Marie blushed as Jean Renau took her hand and brushed her wrist with his lips. "I'm honored, *Mademoiselle*," he said. Captain Renau spoke to Madame Drucour but his eyes met Marie's. He said, "Seeing Marie, the men will not be so anxious to go home. We must show her to them and then you must come below deck, Madame. I have a gift for you."

True to Madame Drucour's forecast, Marie's smile won the hearts of the sailors aboard the frigate and watched longingly as their captain led his guests below deck. In the captain's cabin, Renau lifted a bottle of wine from the rack along the wall. "Madame, may I present you with a gift of this bottle of fine wine? It comes from the Island of Madeira in the eastern Atlantic, off the coast of Africa. I took it from an English frigate that attacked me off the port of Brest. I'm glad to say the Englishman was in for the surprise of his life. We outsailed him so badly, he was hardly able to get a shot into us. We raked him from stem to stern three times before he fired a broadside with those wicked English cannons. You see, Madame, our French cannons are too long. Much time is wasted reloading the long barrels; if they were shorter, we could cut in half the time it takes to reload. The English can reload and fire their shorter cannons much faster than we. Had I not been able to outsail the Englishman and stay away from his broadside, he would have sunk *Pélerine* as he had many another.

"And like most British captains I have encountered, he was brave and determined man. His ship was barely afloat when at last he surrendered to save his wounded. He told me he had captured six French ships before he met our warship. They made the mistake of trying to outshoot the British rather than outsail him as I did. I have tried to explain this to my commanding officer, but he will have none of it; he will not believe that we cannot outshoot the English.

"You know the English sail wherever they like on the oceans of the world, the oceans that I would sail if but given the opportunity. In the last year the English have sunk or captured some five hundred French ships. Without a declaration of war they do this. Madame, the holds of English merchant ships are bulging with fine wine and many things that we badly need here in Louisbourg. Forgive my impertinence, Madame, but allow me to take my ship out of this harbor. I will return with badly needed supplies for Louisbourg and restore honor to our King."

Madame Drucour held the bottle of wine against the light of a porthole. "This wine withstands the light of scrutiny; I hope your commander's theories do as well, but I am not convinced. I'll share this wine with the governor, and when the time is right, perhaps the strings attached to it. Don't despair, brave Captain. There is no one more anxious than I to see our idle warships in action against the enemy. I'm angered that our ships lay in our harbor when we are desperate for supplies. You may be sure I shall not be idle on that problem. But you must also know military matters are not the governor's purview alone. Least of all should the governor's lady give such directions. The matter requires much diplomacy."

Madame Drucour gripped the wine bottle until her knuckles grew white and her brow furrowed. She turned again to Captain Renau, her mind seemingly far away. "Thank you for your hospitality, Captain. I must return now to Government House. You will be my guest for dinner at an appropriate time. Perhaps we can persuade our leaders to use your talents."

Marie lifted her skirts to ascend the stairs, stopped, and turned to Captain Renau. "I'm a commoner, Captain, an Acadian. I think, Sir, I may know how you feel in dealing with your superiors, and I want you to know you have an ally in Government House. You can be sure I will do anything I can to aid your cause." Together they walked on deck.

"*Mademoiselle* Gauthier," Renau said, "now that I know you are at Government House, I shall visit at every opportunity."

It was a few weeks later as Governor the Chevalier Augustine Drucour and Madame Drucour greeted their guests at the door of Government House. A long receiving line extended beyond the front door. Officers in gold braid and jeweled swords, ladies in silk and taffeta of blue, purple, and red and servants in black and white uniforms filled the hall with a din of talk and laughter. Only a scarcity of food and shallow wine glasses dampened the enthusiasm of the evening, but the chefs prepared the game and fish to perfection. Ice, cut and stored in the winter, provided cool drinks and cold deserts. Excitement filled the air; some already knew the announcement that the Governor would make.

With the guests seated, the Governor stood before them, his usually impassive face looking radiant. "War! It is war at last. On May ninth last, the year of our Lord, seventeen fifty-six, our King declared war on the British. Our long suffering shall soon be ended as our King makes the English pay for the indiscretions committed against us. Our great fleet will soon clear these English pirates from Isle Royale." Citizens cheered. Ladies and Gentlemen toasted their soldiers as conquering heros. Soldiers hailed their King and each other. "Soon the English heretics shall feel our cold steel in their guts," they said.

Later, Madame Drucour held a tiny brass bell aloft, ringing softly to gain the attention of her guests. "Ladies and gentlemen," she said, "I take pleasure in introducing a wonderful musician whom I found living *en secret*, right here in Louisbourg. Unknown to us all, this lovely young lady plays the harpsichord most beautifully. Her music rivals that heard in the Court of Versailles." Madame Drucour took Marie's hand. Borrowed jewelry, sparkling in the candlelight, fell across Marie's cleavage as she walked to the harpsichord. Her elegant gown whisked across a floor so polished, her reflection seemed to follow her to the instrument. As Marie lifted her skirts and moved to the harpsichord, she remembered to smile through her nervousness. With a curtsy to her audience, she sat on the gleaming bench. Marie felt her pounding heart and fast breathing as she turned to the music of Jean-Philippe Rameau. The dancing light of twenty candles reflected on the polished wood of the harpsichord.

With nervous fingers Marie opened the sheets of music. She closed her mind to the throng of important people and focused on the rhythm of notes as she placed her fingers to the keys. With Herculean effort, Marie's mind registered the notes before her and sent a clear message to her nimble fingers. All nervousness disappeared. The notes flowed clearly and effortlessly as her hands moved over the keyboard. As always, music tranquilized her. She drifted into a world far removed from embattled Louisbourg, a world before war came to Beaubassin, before homes were burned and family killed. Guests listened intently as Marie played Bach and Handel. With the music flowing from her fingers, Marie found she could look up and smile at her audience. Their eyes reflected her own warm feelings. The officers and their wives sat in chairs listening attentively as Marie played, her melodious chords ringing throughout the ornate room. Her eye caught that of Madame Drucour, who stood nearby beaming proudly. Marie wished the music would never end as she played the closing notes with reluctance.

Applause rang in Marie's ears as she laid her hands in her lap. She had never known such happiness as she rose and bowed to her audience. As the applause continued, Marie saw a nod of assent from Madame Drucour. With a calm and light heart Marie sat back down at the harpsichord, playing the beloved music of Europe.

Afterward, Marie found the guests thronging around her in waves, all eager to compliment her playing. Unfamiliar faces that had seemed distant and unfriendly now displayed warmth and friendship. A young nobleman, resplendent in a powdered wig, tailored uniform and silk hose, approached Marie. "My dear, your music was lovely, almost as lovely as you. How on Earth could a creature so lovely as you allow yourself to be taken to such an unhappy place as this?"

Marie's polite smile faded slightly, but her smile quickly returned as she remembered this man was the guest of honor. "Captain, I was born here in Acadia, in a place called Beaubassin. It was a happy place before the English came and started a war with France. The English captured us. But we escaped with the help of Indians and came to Louisbourg. I disagree that Louisbourg is an unhappy place. If you but knew our people, you would find this a wonderful place."

The nobleman bowed slightly. "God protect me from such a fate as knowing these people, ah, but *you* I would like to know... intimately. Maybe even in Paris?"

Marie's eyes flashed but they quickly softened again and a smile crossed her face. "I hope I can visit Paris some day, Captain, and I hope some day you learn the strength and goodness of the people of Louisbourg. Please excuse me," she said as she moved away toward Governor Drucour.

The governor's eyes sparkled as he saw Marie approaching. "*Mademoiselle*," he said as he lifted her hand, "you are more lovely than I first remembered, and I had no idea you played so beautifully." He lifted his hand toward a man standing nearby in a naval uniform. "*Mademoiselle*, you have met Captain Renau I believe, a Captain of the Blue, recently arrived from Brest in command of our warship, *Pélerine*."

"Yes, Governor," replied Marie, "I have had the honor of touring his ship."

Governor Drucour smiled proudly at Renau. "He has distinguished himself in our Navy beyond compare. Captain Renau sank or captured five British ships while other captains are surrendering their ships beyond number. This man is a special guest, Marie. Please play a request for him if he asks."

As the governor left them to join another conversation nearby, Captain Renau's eyes softened and a relaxed smile crossed his face. "Forgive me, *Mademoiselle*, but my knowledge of music is limited. I should rather use this opportunity to tell you how beautifully you play."

Marie was captivated by his clear, sparkling eyes. Renau's black hair was tied neatly at the back of his neck in a small bow. She heard herself say, "I'm pleased you think so." Marie wanted to ask if he were married but such a question would be unthinkable. Suddenly, Captain Renau's attention turned across the room.

He seemed to have forgotten Marie completely when he said, "Please excuse me." With determination in his eye, he strode across the room to Madame Drucour. With difficulty he finally gained the attention of the Governor's lady. After some delay, the lady came to him. He spoke to her in rapid conversation Marie could not hear. In a few moments Madame Drucour led him across the room. They approached the military commander.

Madame Drucour approached the general. "My dear General, this is Captain Renau, commander of the frigate, *Pélerine*, whom we have heard so much about. He's most anxious to talk to you and has some ideas I think you will want to hear."

The general looked sharply at Madame Drucour and forced a smile as he looked down his nose at Renau. "Ah, yes, a brevet captain, you have something you wish to say to me?" The general looked distractedly around the room as he awaited Renau's reply.

"Yes, Sir," Renau, answered firmly. "Now that we are officially at war with England, I propose we sail. I'm concerned that our ships lay idle in the harbor. We are wrong, Sir, to leave them inactive. Ships must be sailed and men must sail them, or the ships rot and men loose their discipline. We spend too much time in harbor. The place for our ships is at sea. There are ample opportunities to evade the English blockade and disappear in the wide ocean. It is a very big ocean, General. The ocean is too big for English ships to be everywhere at once. Our warships should be at sea, taking English prizes and picking our time and place to fight. While my ship lies idle in port, it is matched by a single English frigate. At sea, the English will need a dozen warships to seek out my little frigate, ships that can no longer blockade Louisbourg. One French ship at sea is worth a dozen in the harbor of Louisbourg."

The general smiled at a passing lady and nodded to a gentleman as Captain Renau completed his statement. "I appreciate your enthusiasm, Brevet captain. But you must leave complicated military strategy to professionals. Your time may better be spent in learning to fight your ship as your commander may require. When the King gives his command, we will seek out the English in battle. We will all be quite happy, but until then we will all do as we are told. Good day, Mr. Renau."

"I hope," replied Renau, "you will encourage the King to take the offensive. It is the only way to prevent Louisbourg's strangulation. The English can't spare sufficient ships to blockade Louisbourg and search for a dozen French warships in the open sea. Although the British ships are better armed, ours are faster and better manned. We can out sail them and the better sailors can win. As it is now, we grow weaker every day as English warships sink and capture our ships. Unless we take action soon, we will have no warships with which to fight."

"Very well, er, Brevet captain. You are to be commended for your enthusiasm," said the General as he bowed to a lady. "Now, may I suggest you have a glass of wine and allow me to listen to our lovely musician playing the harpsichord." The general put a hand on Renau's elbow and led him to a servant holding a tray of wine glasses. The general took a glass for Renau and one for himself. The general smiled in Renau's direction and swept away through the crowd with his sights set on a group of ladies. Renau stood near the door holding his untasted wine. He attempted a conversation with a young artillery officer standing transfixed by either Marie's music or her beauty. The man's attention could not be swayed so Renau handed his glass to a servant and returned to his ship.

Chapter Twenty

Returning from his meeting with the commodore, MacGregor was unsure if he had made an error in judgement. *Will the commodore accept my offer to act as emissary to Louisbourg? How long must I wait? Could it be this year, or must I wait until 1757? I will find a way, whatever.* His thoughts were interrupted when he arrived at *Chasseur*. There he found one of *Grenadier's* boats tied to the boarding ladder of the French prize. He climbed the icy boarding ladder with cold hands to find Sergeant O'Bannion's marines, red tunics and crossed white belts, diligently guarding the French prize, *Chasseur*. *What was Grenadier's boat doing tied by the boarding ladder?* Seeking answers, he went below. In Captain De la Court's cabin he found the purser, Mr. Farwell, dictating to Walshingham's yeoman. The yeoman's quill scratched paper as he dipped the quill in ink and wrote. The boatswain and his mates seemed to be hurrying back and forth from the cargo in the orlop deck. As MacGregor entered the cabin, Farwell looked up to say, "Ah, MacGregor, we are inventorying the cargo, and I have a message for you. Captain Walshingham directs that you return immediately aboard *Grenadier* and take charge of repairs. He wants the frigate ready to sail in the shortest time and feels you are the best man for the job."

Leaping to the task, MacGregor soon saw set the shipwrights to hammering and sawing. The blacksmith's forges belched black smoke and sparks into the cold, gray air while their hammer rang on the anvil. Lieutenant MacGregor pushed and prodded the repairs with a mission of his own. *I must get back to Louisbourg.*

With much organization to do in repairing his ship, it was another two days before MacGregor could find time for his personal mission. Then he made his way to the office of Samuel Steinbach as a cold wind blew down the street. At the direction of a clerk, MacGregor reluctantly took a chair near the blazing fireplace, and there he sat, re-arranging his long sword at his side which thumped and rattled on the floor. The law clerk walked across the squeaky wooden floor and disappeared into the lawyer's office behind the rattling door. Presently, the clerk returned, informing MacGregor, "Mr. Steinbach is a busy man. He hopes you do not mind to wait a few minutes while he tends to important matters that will not wait." For the next hour MacGregor watched the law clerk standing at his tall desk. *This man, Steinbach, has my money now. What service will he have done for me? Does he keep everyone waiting? Maybe I should rattle my sword on his blooming door.* Gritting his teeth, he stood and squeezed the hilt of the big claymore. He took two steps toward Steinbach's office before the door was thrown open and Samuel Steinbach appeared.

Steinbach did not look at MacGregor, but with his eyes fixed on a piece of paper, he said, "Come in, young man, I have here a letter which will interest you."

Lieutenant MacGregor snorted, "Perhaps, whatever. But I'm interested in the whereabouts of Mr. Gaston Gauthier. Let us speak first of that."

Steinbach lowered the paper to his side and looked at MacGregor in surprise. "Why, of course! Yes! You would be most interested in that. Well... let me tell you. Having legally and irrevocably purchased the debt owed the Crown by Mr. Gaston Gauthier, I found I could no longer afford the services of a bond servant. I therefore subordinated his services to a competitor of Edward Brumley and a former colleague of Mr. Gauthier, one Timothy McQuade, trader. I'm speaking of *the* Mr. McQuade of McQuade Trading Company Limited. Mr. McQuade was quite happy to have the services of a man so well versed in trading from Canada to the West Indies. Mr. McQuade is so fond of his services, he hired a bodyguard to protect him. That bodyguard has already earned his keep by injuring some highwaymen who sought to kidnap Mr. Gauthier. I will not conjecture who might have employed such ruffians, but I sent a message to Brumley, apprizing him of their lack of success. I further informed him that next we shall capture anyone attempting to repeat the attempt so that the Crown might learn who hired them." Samuel Steinbach sniffed impatiently. "Now, if you will permit me, I will acquaint you with Brumley's response." The lawyer lifted the letter in his hand, holding it up as he continued, "In this letter, Brumley states that he has never had any business relations with Gaston Gauthier, but he is so sympathetic to his plight, he is willing to donate five hundred pounds Stirling to his cause, with certain reservations to be clarified later." The attorney laid the letter on his desk and opened a silver snuff box. Pinching the tobacco between thumb and forefinger, he snorted the brown powder into his nostrils. Motioning MacGregor toward a chair, Steinbach sat down behind his oak desk and looked absently at the ceiling. "I intend to settle with Brumley for say... five *thousand* pounds. That figure satisfies Mr. Gauthier and includes the fee for my humble services. Will that amount satisfy you, Lieutenant?"

MacGregor ignored the offered chair as he replied, "If Mr. Gauthier is happy, whatever. Now, kindly tell me where to find Mr. Gauthier."

Samuel Steinbach hurriedly stood. "Just walk down the wharf and look for McQuade Trading and Chandlery. Ask for Mr. McQuade himself and he can direct you to Gauthier."

McQuade's business was as impressive as that of Edward Brumley but larger, for in addition to the trading office, there was a large marine chandlery. The chandlery sold every item that could ever possibly be needed aboard a ship. There were sails, anchors, cable, and every kind of fishing net and device. There were oarlocks, fids, needles, shackles, catheads, clews, and cleats in gleaming brass and polished oak all neatly piled from floor to ceiling in every nook and cranny. A smiling clerk approached MacGregor as he made his way past the merchandise. The man seemed impressed with his officer's uniform as the clerk asked, "Aye, Sir, and might you be needin' top quality fittin's for the King's ship?"

Better play my cards close to my vest, MacGregor thought. He replied, "Aye, I might be. But first, I would like to speak to Mr. McQuade, personally."

With a little bow the clerk said, "Of course, Sir. I know Mr. McQuade would want to look after any need of the King's Navy himself. Just follow me, if you please, Sir." He led MacGregor through a maze of tables, shelves, and merchandise, coming at last to a door with white-painted glass bearing the name: *Timothy McQuade, proprietor.* There the man knocked quietly on the door and rattled it open to a command within. To the proprietor inside he announced, loudly, "An officer of the King's Navy to see you, Sir". Holding the door wide, the clerk stepped aside and bowed slightly as MacGregor entered.

McQuade was a short, portly man with red face, balding head, and a wide smile. He extended his hand to MacGregor, saying, "And what might I do for you, Sir, or the Kings Navy? I'm anxious to serve as did my ancestors in County Antrim of Ireland for three generations."

Lieutenant MacGregor took the man's hand in a firm grasp, replying, "Perhaps we could have a word or two in your office, privately?"

With a sparkle in his eye, McQuade gave MacGregor's hand another shake and motioned him to a chair as he closed the office door. "Please sit down, Sir, and tell me how I may help you. Most pursers take their needs from the Admiralty stores, but I would be pleased to supply anything you might need."

MacGregor held his hat in hand and rattled his sword clear of the chair as he sat. "Mr. McQuade," he began, "a number of years ago my ship rescued the crew and master aboard a sinking ship bound for Boston with a cargo from French Canada. That cargo belonged to a man named Gaston Gauthier." He saw McQuade's eyes widen at the mention of Gauthier's name. "I came to know Mr. Gauthier... as well as his daughter, Marie... during the time they were aboard our ship." MacGregor thought, *How much should I tell this man of my involvement? But McQuade is also involved with Gauthier, and I believe I can trust this Irishman.* "God... put my frigate in the Cumberland Basin when Acadians were being resettled from Beaubassin. As you may know, Mr. Gauthier was taken aboard my ship as a prisoner. You may also know I hired Mr. Steinbach to pursue his claim against Brumley and free him from bondage."

"Bless you, young man," replied McQuade as he again grasped MacGregor's hand. "Gaston was an old friend and trading partner of mine until he was wooed away by Brumley... to everyone's harm. Thanks to you, he is safe from that harm. He does not leave this office, and I have armed men around him day and night. Come, I will take him to you." McQuade opened the door to a closet in his office and stepped inside, leaving the door open. Inside the closet he pushed back coats and cloaks to reveal a hidden panel. He pushed gently on the panel which opened to the pressure. Bending low, McQuade stepped through the small door and held it open to MacGregor.

Lieutenant MacGregor carefully crawled through the opening to find himself inside a window-less room filled with books and journals. Gaston Gauthier had left a standing desk and stood with arms wide, and MacGregor stood straight again. Overcome with emotion, Gaston embraced MacGregor, saying, "My friend, I can never repay the debt I owe you. Surely you were sent from Heaven."

With a smile MacGregor asked, "Has Mr. McQuade locked you away in this den of bookkeeping to work you day and night?" It was only then that he saw a muscular man standing in the corner, a pistol and dagger in his belt. In his sinewy hands he held a dangerous looking club. His appearance would scare a grizzly bear.

The happy look on Gaston's face disappeared as he asked plaintively, "Marie... have you any word on Marie? Is she at Louisbourg?"

MacGregor looked away. "I have not been able to go ashore at Louisbourg. I expect my ship will return to Louisbourg, and I will do all in my power to go ashore and look for her. I have... strong feelings for your daughter, Mr. Gauthier. If she is alive, I intend to ask you... for her hand in marriage."

Again Gaston embraced him, saying, "Charles MacGregor, that makes me a happy man. I pray that she is safe and God will bless your efforts to find her. I think maybe she likes you pretty good too, eh?"

MacGregor looked away again. "I must return to my ship before I'm missed. Are you comfortable here? Is there more I can do?"

Gaston waved his hand around the room. "Here I have work to do that a man of my experience can do and have no dikes to mend or fields to tend." He pointed to a low bed on one side of the small room. "I have a bed that is better than the one in my cabin at Ft. Beausejour and a room that's little smaller." Pointing to the body guard he continued, "My friend here sleeps outside my door every night so I rest in peace. The work takes my mind off my worries of Marie, so I'm well, eh?"

MacGregor turned to Mr. McQuade. "We are both in your debt, Sir."

"Nonsense," smiled the rotund Irishman, "it is I who is indebted to you both. My friend Gaston Gauthier has many friends from French Canada to the West Indies. If… and I say *if* I were inclined to violate the British Navigation Acts and trade with such people, his contacts would be invaluable. Who knows, there may come a day when it is legal for colonials to trade with each other. If that day comes, my friend and I will do well." He placed a hand on Gaston's shoulder and smiled broadly. "Isn't that so, my friend?"

"I live for that day when my daughter is safely with me, and I can provide for her as I did before with the help of friends like Timothy McQuade."

MacGregor replied, "I must return to my ship before someone asks questions. If I have any news of Marie, I will get word to you somehow." He ducked beneath the small door and left the little cubicle. McQuade followed behind. He escorted MacGregor through the office and out to the front door, saying loudly as they passed the working clerks, "Lieutenant, you may be assured I will provide a very competitive bid for your needs and will deliver it personally myself. You can be sure I will not delegate so important a bid as that to the Royal Navy." As he walked back to his ship, MacGregor did not notice a carriage that passed carrying his smug and smiling captain.

The carriage stopped at the office of another Boston trader to discharge Walshingham. An ebullient captain entered the office of Edward Brumley, trader, and prize agent of Boston. For over an hour the captain conferred with Mr. Brumley in somber tones. Later, another carriage came for the captain, who now no longer smiled. Walshingham sat brooding in the back seat of the carriage, his hands clasped on the gold-plated head of his cane, his eyes narrow and filled with vehemence.

MacGregor returned aboard *Grenadier* and pursued repairs with new vigor, assured that every inch of progress brought him closer to Louisbourg and perhaps, Marie Gauthier. Late one afternoon, he looked across the anchorage toward his French prize, *Chasseur*. Laying along side of the French prize, he saw a schooner flying the lone oak flag of Edward Brumley Trading Co. The next morning the schooner was gone, and he felt sure the French prize ship rode higher in the water as if some of her cargo had been removed. *Walshingham ordered me not to mention the existence of the rifles aboard Chasseur. Were the rifles aboard Chasseur reported to the Admiralty? Have Walshingham and Brumley taken the rifles for themselves? To whom could they sell them? It could only be to the French. What shall I do about the matter?*

MacGregor spent a long, sleepless night in his cabin aft of the gun deck. When daylight finally penetrated the frost on the tiny stern window, he rose and collected the many thoughts running through his head. He had long ago made his decision; he had now only to deliver his message to his captain. He waited, however, on the cold, icy deck until Walshingham's servant had returned with the captain's chamber pot and the empty pewter vessel in which he had delivered hot water. MacGregor walked slowly to the quarterdeck and watched the midshipman turn the half-hour glass. He walked down to the wardroom and sat down for a cup of tea. Confident that the glass would be turned again, he stood up and walked to Walshingham's cabin. He nodded at the marine guard and stood aside, waiting. When the captain's servant appeared carrying a tray of food, he quickly followed the man inside the cabin. Walshingham stood looking out the stern window, his back turned to the door. The servant noticed MacGregor following him inside and spoke, "I beg your pardon, Sir! I did not know ye were here! Captain, Mr. MacGregor is here!"

Walshingham wheeled around quickly with fire in his eyes. "MacGregor! I did not send for ye. What do ye want? Can ye not see I'm having my breakfast?"

MacGregor spoke calmly, "Captain, there is a matter I must discuss with you, privately. It can't wait. I must know the truth from you, now."

With dark, brooding eyes Captain Walshingham looked at the servant. He nodded toward the door in a signal the man could not fail to read. He bowed and walked backwards toward the door, holding his bow as he exited. Walshingham's blazing eyes were fixed on MacGregor, but he was silent, waiting.

Lieutenant MacGregor's jaw muscles quivered as he spoke. "Captain, if

I'm right, and I must hear it from you, the rifles from *Chasseur* were not listed on the prize manifest. I have reason to believe they were loaded aboard Brumley's schooner that sailed last night. If you have made such a deal with Brumley, I can't serve you any longer in good conscience. I must leave this ship and find another or resign my commission. I will take your silence as an admission that what I suspect is true."

Walshingham's eyes blazed but his mouth turned upward in a crooked smile. "Ye would leave my ship? Ye would resign yer commission? No, Mr. MacGregor, ye will not leave my ship nor resign yer commission. Ye will continue to serve me as my first lieutenant or as a prisoner in our brig, the choice is yers; but that is yer only choice." Walshingham's smile disappeared and his face grew contorted and red. "Ye will not leave this ship nor communicate with anyone. Ye are, as of this moment, confined to yer cabin under guard until this ship leaves port." Walshingham stormed to the door, throwing it open to say, "Marine! Take the lieutenant to his cabin and guard his door until ye are relieved. If he tries to leave this ship, shoot him!"

It was early on a cool gray morning of 1756 when repairs were nearly finished and new cannons filled the blank spaces on *Grenadier*'s deck that MacGregor reported to the Captain's cabin. Grimly, he greeted the marine guard in front of Walshingham's door and rapped loudly. He waited for a few moments, listening at the heavy oak door. The sound of retching came from within. MacGregor knocked again, more loudly. A reply from Walshingham's cabin almost shook the cabin door. "Yes, by God! Who's there?"

Lieutenant MacGregor, who stood with his fist poised before the door to knock again, slowly lowered his hand and replied, "It's Lieutenant MacGregor. You sent for me."

"I did?" the reply came from within, followed by the sound of more retching. As the vomiting ended, Walshingham spoke with a gravelly voice, "Oh yes, I did. Get the hell in here, MacGregor!"

MacGregor glanced into the eyes of the marine guard standing nearby and reached for the knob. There was the sound of more retching. Lieutenant MacGregor opened the door but chose not to remove his hat. Inside, Captain Walshingham's white legs shown almost to his bare buttocks beneath his nightshirt as he leaned over a chamber pot. With a hand on his hip, he slowly stood erect and turned to face MacGregor. Walshingham stood swaying in his soiled, white linen nightshirt, wiping his mouth on the back of a lace-trimmed sleeve. His nightshirt hung in fullness over his rotund abdomen while his thin, white legs poked from beneath, looking like the legs of a plump, white chicken.

Walshingham's red rimmed eyes looked sadly from an ashen face with a black stubble of beard. The room smelled of vomit and stale whiskey and looked as though a party of French marines had torn through. Lifting his feet as though walking on broken glass, Walshingham hobbled to his desk. He lifted some women's undergarments from his desk and tossed them on the floor. He picked up a whiskey bottle. Lifting the bottle against the light, he saw it was empty and tossed it angrily on the floor. He rummaged around his desk for another bottle. Picking up a large bottle filled with amber liquid, he removed the cork with his teeth and held the bottle to the light, mumbling his approval. He lifted the whiskey to his lips and drank heavily. With his last pull on the bottle, he swirled the liquor inside his mouth before swallowing. Exhaling loudly, Walshingham made a face of excruciating pain. With trembling hands he coughed and returned the whiskey bottle to the desk. There he leaned over with both hands on the desk and stood breathing in short gasps as a shudder ran through his body. Slowly, Walshingham stood erect, hand on hip, a grimace on his face. Lifting the bottle and tilting his head back, he took another long drink from the whiskey bottle. Sighing loudly, he took the bottle from his mouth and corked it, grimacing and shaking from head to foot. Slowly, he turned to MacGregor, asking, "Ye wanted to talk to me?"

"No, Sir," replied MacGregor. "You sent for me."

Walshingham walked over to a wash stand and poured a pan of water from a brass pitcher to splash water in his face. He looked up at MacGregor as he dried his face and hands on a linen towel. Walshingham looked back at MacGregor and replied, "Of course I did. Our repairs are finished. We have our new cannons mounted, the ship is refitted, and there's no reason to remain in port. I want new replacements for our lost crewmen before those battleship captains take the best. We'll need new sailors, and I think the best way to get them is with a training cruise to Barbados." Walshingham looked up wistfully. "Yes, a cruise through the tropics for their training, and perhaps press a few replacements there as well if still needed. In the West Indies we may even take a few prizes before sailing to Louisbourg. With such experience our crew will be richer, experienced, and ready for action against Louisbourg." Walshingham's eyes lost their focus as he looked over MacGregor's head, smiling. "Barbados! It will be an excellent place to train our crew and have them ready for action." He cocked his head to one side and smiled at the ceiling. "By God, Walshingham, ye are a genius! His Majesty's Ship *Grenadier* will sail from this freezing Boston with the most eager crew of new recruits that ever climbed the ratlines. We shall bathe in tropical sunshine and feast on pineapple and coconut. Every man shall have his own lovely concubine from under the swaying palms. We will have the happiest crew in the Navy. Ye, MacGregor, will see that recruiting posters are made with the picture of a half naked woman dancing beneath a palm tree. Say that H.M.S. *Grenadier* sails for the warm sun and sand of Barbados in ten days. I want pictures of swaying palm trees and bare breasted women in every tavern in town," he ordered. Walshingham's eyes turned to the ceiling as he mused, "Barbados, where the blue ocean rushes on soft, yellow sands, and palm trees spread their fronds in the warm sun, with rum flowing like water, and girls who never heard of the ten commandments. And rich, French prizes filled with treasure await us all.

"MacGregor, get those recruiting posters made and sent ashore, dozens of them. Ye are still confined aboard the ship but have Sergeant O'Bannion and his marines put them in every pub in town. With drums and pipes playing, our marines shall put up recruiting posters. Every man in this city will want to join our crew." Captain Walshingham whistled a little tune as he disrobed. He looked for his pants, tossing women's clothing in all directions as he searched.

MacGregor plotted how he might slip away and ship out to Louisbourg aboard another vessel, but he noted that the master at arms and armed marines watched his every move. There was naught to do but work as ordered. A few days later, the beat of drums and music of pipes echoed through the streets of Boston. Sunshine bathed the scarlet clad marines in glowing colors as they led a procession through the crowded streets. Drummers sent their staccato beat reverberating through the alleys and byways while pipes wailed their high pitched call across the town. Under the colorful Union Flag, flapping and snapping gallantly in the breeze, they marched. Sergeant O'Bannion had his chin tucked into his neck, his back as stiff as a ramrod and his arm with gold stripes swinging back and forth like a pendulum while his other held a stack of recruiting posters.

The next week a similar parade processed through Boston. Sunshine glistened on the bayonets of the marching marines who looked straight ahead as they marched, their boots crashed loudly in unison on the paving stones. Behind the marching marines today, a motley crew of men walked, swaggered, shuffled, staggered, and trotted; they were a mixed assortment of drunken, chattering men. Some wore buff and buckskin while others wore the rough homespun of the working man. A few wore dark tailored suits and hats while an oriental recruit wore his black hair in a pigtail, speaking no English. Young boys laughed and waved with the glint of adventure shining in their eyes. They all smiled and waved at the bystanders. Children and dogs ran laughing and barking after the group. Girlfriends, camp followers, and tearful mothers trotted along the sidewalks, waving and blowing kisses at their departing heroes. Around corners, down streets, gaining additions as they marched, the pipes and drums filling the air with music, the procession came to a stop opposite the frigate, *Grenadier*.

To the cheers of women, children and well-wishers, and winks between salty old sailors, the new recruits filed up the gangplank. The volunteers laughed and shouted happily, waving goodbye to the women ashore.

Captain Walshingham watched the new recruits with a look of smug satisfaction. "Lieutenant MacGregor," he said, "one should never be caught with a stable full of race horses when there are fields to plow! But we can tolerate a race horse now and then. And that's what we have here, a lovely bunch of frisky young colts. I shall enjoy breaking them to the plow."

Captain Walshingham called out, "Bosun, where are your manners? Our new shipmates should not think us inhospitable. They may be uncomfortable out here on deck. Take them below and tickle their innards with a tot of rum, several tots if ye please."

As a murmur of approval passed through the new recruits, the boatswain replied smugly, "Aye, Captain, and may me' name be struck from the Blue Book if ever I'm so impolite again."

The Royal Navy's press gang then appeared at the wharf with a meager supply of draftees. Wild looking misfits, hollow faced malingerers, and grubby jail house fugitives struggled up the long gang plank and stood under the tall masts of the warship. A wary jailor released the leg irons on a string of grave looking, bearded prisoners while the master-at-arms and six burly sailors stood man to man with heavy oak belaying pins.

Walshingham surveyed these men carefully, saying, "These work horses are likely already broken to the plow. Take them to the brig. Issue them a double ration of rum and lock the door." When the last recruit had disappeared below, Captain Walshingham turned to the sailing master. "Mister Sethford, take this ship to sea."

"Aye, Sir." Sethford picked up a speaking trumpet and placed it to his mouth. "Cast off all lines," he yelled. Walking to the starboard side, he again raised the speaking trumpet. "Long boat, haul!"

From behind the ship a long boat coursed forward as twenty sailors pulled at their oars. Their boat slowly towed the frigate away from the pier. Captain Walshingham waved gaily at the women still standing near the pier. The music of fifes and drums drifted over the water as *Greandier*'s musicians played on deck.

In the open harbor *Grenadier* caught the ebb tide, moving more quickly down the harbor. Men scrambled out up into the masts high above the decks. Sails blossomed on the yards and a fresh northerly breeze turned the flaxen sails rigid, driving the frigate out to sea as the sailors hurried to recover the long boat.

Most of the new recruits tasted their first ocean swells at dinner time, spoiling their appetite for the next few weeks. Those who could spent their time vomiting and coughing over the ocean from the beak's head; those who could not lay in their vomit-soiled bunks. When the ship was well out of sight of land, Walshingham turned to a his first lieutenant, ordering, "Mr. MacGregor, lay a course for Louisbourg."

MacGregor's eyes widened and his hopes fell. "I thought we were sailing to Barbados."

Walshingham looked away with dullness in his eyes. "Healthy landsmen are hard to find, MacGregor, and have them we must."

The wind freshened and brought cold during the night. Under full sails, *Grenadier* rushed east-northeast at a globe girdling pace. The next morning, when told that the landsmen were seasick, Walshingham said, "They need something to take their minds off their sickness. Send them up the ratlines. A man has no time for seasickness while balancing on a foot rope a hundred feet above the deck." When a mutinous delegation of the volunteers approached Walshingham to complain about the change in destination, they were met by a party of experienced crewmen. With three men dressed as women dancers, the ratings put on such a show for the new recruits that they retreated to the gun deck where copious quantities of rum and beer were served.

Nearing Louisbourg, lookouts stood aloft, anxiously looking for icebergs and their quarry, enemy ships. Sleet stung the faces of men on deck. They shivered in their bunks as cold made sleeping uncomfortable. Worried officers dreaded the crash of an iceberg. A few days later, when snow began to fall, heavy ice coated the ship. Its shrouds, decks, ratlines, and anchors were all encased in ice which threatened to sink them under its weight. As the frozen recruits came down the ice-encrusted ratlines, relieved to be out of reach of the boatswain's rattan, officers stood waiting. "All right, let's man the cannons for gun drills!"

With the coming of spring, many men suffered from scurvy and lost teeth. Some had lost toes and fingers to frostbite. A few had died of exposure and many suffered disease. But by the spring of 1756, most were seasoned sailors, tough and convinced they would soon be rich with prize money. Those working topside lined the rail to watch as *Grenadier* hove to alongside the flag ship. Many men were happy seeing the bag of mail being delivered aboard their ship while others knew that no one knew their whereabouts. Along with the mail came an important message for Captain Walshingham. Soon the little boat returned to the flag ship and both ships fell off to leeward, picking up speed as they sailed away from each other.

That night, as the frigate plowed through tossing seas off the coast of Louisbourg, Walshingham joined his officers at dinner in the wardroom. His little followed and played *Rule Britannia* as Walshingham took his seat. All officers stood as their ebullient Captain took his place at the table. Walshingham moved his empty wine glass half an inch across the linen table cloth, eliciting an immediate movement of the steward to fill the glass. Without looking at the glass, Walshingham lifted it aloft, beaming. The officers lifted their glasses in anticipation of the toast. An imperceptible nod from Walshingham brought the little orchestra to a finish as smoothly as if Handel himself had written it there. Captain Walshingham lifted his glass an inch higher. "Gentlemen, this is a grand day for England and her empire. Today we take the banner of the realm from the hands of those snuff sneezing politicians and place it in the steady hands of the Royal Navy. War! Yes, sweet war, gentlemen." Walshingham gloated as the officers looked at each other in wonder. "Yesterday I learned that England officially declared war against France, on May eighteenth, seventeen hundred and fifty-six.

"In America, Africa, India, the Mediterranean, and the Indies, the Royal Navy shall replace the French flag with that of Britain." Walshingham bowed his head momentarily. "The wretched inhabitants of those places shall be enlightened by Englishmen, we who stand ready to shed our blood that others may know our glory. And the symbol of our glory, gentlemen, is the King. God save the King!"

"God save the King!" responded the officers, except one. MacGregor's mind was lost in a whirl. *I'm being drawn deeper into a war I do not want. Should I resign my commission? How then would I get back to Louisbourg to find Marie? Without money, what could I do if I found her? I know nothing but the Navy. God, help me.*

That night a morose Lieutenant MacGregor lay in his swaying bed, looking up at the deck beams. *It would be impossible to swim ashore in these freezing waters. There must be a way, whatever.*

Chapter Twenty-One

Cannons boomed and thundered across Louisbourg this summer day of July 26, 1756. High on the walls above the Dauphin Gate, Marie stood watching with excited citizens. Captain Renau hurried up the steps and stood beside Marie. "Can you see our fleet, *Mademoiselle?*"

"Yes," she replied. "Why are the cannons firing? Are our warships practicing fighting the British?"

Renau pointed to the many white sails on the blue ocean. "No, they *are* fighting the British. Look! Do you see those sails? Those are French sails, not English. And there, that is an English sail, running in retreat! Our ships are those of Admiral Beaussier's fleet from Quebec. His cannons scattered the British blockaders. He is sailing into Louisbourg now. At last, we fight. Now that our King has declared war on England, we will surely fight the English. Our ships will no longer sit idly."

Marie's thoughts raced to unknown fears. "Can we defeat the British?"

With a smile Renau replied, "Of course we can defeat the British. But not by acting as we have in the past. We must go out and fight."

Marie looked at Renau. "I fear a declaration of war changes nothing; the English have been at war with us for years."

"Yes, Marie, they have seized over three hundred of our ships in the last three years. But our Navy has been bridled." With a bow to Marie, Renau hurried down the steps and pushed his way through the crowd until he stood by the water at the wharf. He hurried to the warship, *Le Heros,* sailing into the harbor with all her colorful signal flags flapping in the breeze. Following *Le Heros*, three other war ships anchored in the harbor.

Captain Renau pushed his way through the happy crowd where a ship's boat discharged officers from *Le Heros*. A throng of military men stood around the distinguished Beaussier, congratulating him on scattering the English ships. As Renau arrived on the dock, he heard Beaussier say, "Now that war has been declared, Louisbourg must have supplies. I have brought you food, clothing, ammunition, and arms. Now the British will learn we too can fight."

As Commodore Beaussier turned toward Government House, Captain Renau stopped him. "Sir, I'm Captain Renau, brevet commander of the frigate, *Pélerine.*"

"Oh, yes, Captain Renau, I've heard of you. Your daring capture of the British frigate off Brest is told by every mariner coming to Quebec. I'm delighted to meet you personally," Beaussier replied.

"Sir, we beat the British that day because we outsailed them. We can outsail them again today. I'm only a reserve officer, and our frigate is small; however, I want you to know our ship is ready to put to sea against the British immediately. *Pélerine* is in excellent condition, and the men are anxious to sail. We met the English off Louisbourg before and gave a good account of ourselves, but we have unfinished business with the enemy. Beside your seventy-four guns, Sir, we would do a fine job of whipping them."

Commodore Beaussier leveled his gaze at Captain Renau. Softly he replied, "Captain, Le Heros is *en flûte*. She does not carry seventy-four guns. We have had to strip her of many guns to carry cargo for Louisbourg. She has only forty-six guns mounted and not enough men to serve even those. Nevertheless, I will discharge cargo and take on soldiers, artillery men to man the guns we have, and infantrymen to fight on deck. What we lack in firepower, we will make up in man power. We will sail against the British at first light tomorrow. You know the local waters and tides. Your frigate will lead the van in our attack on the British. We have but four ships with which to attack them, but we can make up for our lack of cannons with superior manpower.

"At first light, Captain Renau, load your ship with volunteers willing to fight. You will outsail the enemy as you did at Brest. You must stay at their bow or stern and avoid their broadside. Load your cannons with chain shot to disable their sails. When they can no longer sail, engage closely and grapple to board them. Rush your volunteers aboard the English ships and overcome them with your superior numbers of men. That will be the strategy for all our ships. Go make your ship ready, Captain. Tell your men our army has captured the British bastion of Minorca. Our fleet controls the Mediterranean and will soon control America."

Captain Renau hurried to ready his ship. As news of the impending battle spread through the fortress of Louisbourg, the garrison celebrated. The excitement spread to every man of the fort. Hats flew in the air and cheers rang in the air while many men set to the task grimly. As a dog trained to hunt the hare but who has lived his life without the sight of his quarry, so the soldiers of Louisbourg had trained and drilled. Year after dreary year they trained to fight but never fired a shot in anger.

"Come, my dear," said Madame Drucour to Marie as she hurried toward Government House. "You and I cannot fight the English; I would to God that

I could, but we can serve our country. Put on your loveliest dress, one that shows where our young soldiers would lay their heads, and you can indeed fire a shot for France. Our Commonwealth needs brave men today. Look your prettiest, smile, and remind our young men for whom they fight."

Marie Gauthier, with curls falling on her bare shoulders, slipped into a soft satin gown. A single crucifix hung from Marie's slim neck, over the cleavage of her soft white breasts. With Madame Drucour giving orders, her maids worked feverishly to prepare Marie for the mission. The Lady left no detail untouched and at last, pleased with her results, stated, "Marie, you are beautiful indeed! Now, come, we have work to do for the Realm."

Marie quickly fell in step behind the hurrying Madame Drucour. From regiment to regiment, they walked throughout Fortress Louisbourg. At every regiment Madame Drucour spoke to the men, asking for volunteers to fight the English. And as she spoke, the men listened to Madame Drucour but most young eyes were on Marie. Everywhere they went, at the conclusion of Madame Drucour's speech, every man stepped forward.

Throughout the evening Captain Renau and his lieutenant readied the frigate *Pélerine* for the long sought battle against the English. Soldiers readied their muskets and spoke of the upcoming battle. Commanders huddled under lamplight to review signals and plan strategy. Preparations for battle made the short summer night even shorter.

Captain Renau, reluctant to leave the preparations for battle, lay in his bunk reviewing their readiness. It seemed he had hardly slept when the rattling of muskets and murmur of men's voices woke him. Arising in the early morning darkness, he found what seemed to be the entire garrison waiting to volunteer for the impending battle. Row on row of soldiers stood on the pier, talking excitedly, their rifles and bayonets glistening in the morning light. Artillerymen dragged carts of powder and chain shot and all showed their eagerness for the coming fight.

The naval officers lowered their boats into the water and began shuttling artillery men aboard. They quickly learned naval orders and how to sight the guns on tossing decks. Then companies of riflemen climbed aboard. With rifles and bayonets they worked their way aboard. So many men climbed aboard the ships that some thought they were in danger of foundering.

On the flagship *Le Heros*, the commodore's white pennant fluttered lazily from the masthead in the early morning breeze. On the deck Beaussier reviewed strategy and prepared signals. "Sail down on the enemy, grapple, and board."

Captain Renau hurried up the boarding net and vaulted the rail to the deck. "Stop, stop," he yelled at the boats pulling along side *Pélerine*. "We can't take any more men! We may sink here in the harbor. There will be no room to work our cannons." But determined soldiers kept coming. There was hardly enough room on deck for the gunners to operate their cannons. Captain Renau drew his sword, waving it at the soldiers climbing aboard. "Go back, we can't take another man. Go back or I will use my sword on you." Reluctantly, the men stopped climbing, hanging to the side, disappointment in their faces. Renau watched with his sword drawn as the soldiers slowly climbed down into the boats.

The golden glow of sunrise on the masts of the French fleet illuminated row on row of faces, some radiating the confidence of victory, a few the fear of death, and others a mask that hid the owner's true thoughts on this twenty-sixth day of July in seventeen hundred fifty-six. *Pélerine*, its twenty-six cannons filled with chain shot, its rails lined by soldiers with fixed bayonets, eased out of the anchorage. Boat crews, sweating and straining at their oars, towed the heavily laden frigate out into the expanse of the harbor. In the harbor mouth the wind found the great flaxen sails. The sails rattled and thundered as they stiffened to the breeze. Slowly, to the cheers of the soldiers, *Pélerine* moved away into the harbor channel, its bow lifting to the Atlantic swells, eager to meet the enemy.

With pride, Captain Renau noted that his ship led the fleet into battle. Behind *Pélerine* and the frigate *L'Alicrone*, thirty guns eased out of the anchorage. "Top gallants and studding sails," shouted Captain Renau. "We have an appointment with the Englishmen today!" With waves and a warm smile for their captain, sailors rushed up the high masts to add more sail, hastening their ship to their encounter with the English.

As *Pélerine* rushed along under full sail, the big flag ship, *Le Heros*, emerged from Louisbourg Harbor. *L'Illustre*, sixty-four guns, followed the flag ship. Captain Renau smiled and excitedly clapped his hands as he watched the other ships of their fleet falling behind *Le Heros*. Slowly, the ships sailed out of the harbor as *Pélerine* circled, waiting to form the van.

"Form line of battle," burst the message in a string of colorful signal flags flapping from the halyard of *Le Heros*. Slowly, with great skill in overcoming the contrary winds and shifting tides, the captains maneuvered their ships into a line of battle and sailed into the bright void created by a blazing sunrise.

Captain Renau stood before his young lookouts. He smeared coal soot below their eyes. "I expect the English will come from out of the sun," he said.

"You will need every advantage to see them from the mast tops. Look carefully into the sun."

His young lieutenant bounded up the steps from the gun decks. "Captain, the soldiers are seasick. I fear that many of them will be too sick to fight."

Captain Renau turned slowly and stood looking down on the sick soldiers before replying, "No, Lieutenant, when the shells are flying and the blood is flowing, the soldiers will forget their seasickness. But until then, their sickness will be unpleasant for our sailors." He lifted a telescope from the rack and placed it at his eye, looking back at the big battleship, *Le Heros*. Even with many empty gun ports, she was an inspiring sight. Acres of canvas spread across the sky above the ship. The commodore's white pennant trailed from its mizzen top as the white and blue ensign of France flew proudly from the main. Off *Pélerine*'s port quarter sailed *L'Alicrone*, thirty guns, eager to meet the foe. *Pélerine* rushed ahead to scout for the fleet. Renau was determined to find the English before they found him. But soon a young lookout in the mast top called, "Deck there! Sails ho, bearing east north east, in the sun!" First a small sloop loomed in view, then quickly other ships appeared.

Captain Renau called for the signal officer. "Send this message: Enemy squadron sighted bearing to the east north east, sloop and two second raters." Soon the message burst in colored signal flags flapping from the halyard of *Pélerine*. More signal flags relayed the message down the line of French ships.

On *Pélerine*, Captain Renau turned his telescope to the signal halyard of *Le Heros* for the Commodore's reply. Their commander's message snapped into the wind. "Frigates engage and board enemy sloop. *Le Heros* and *L'Illustre* will engage enemy battleships." Captain Renau stepped forward, overlooking the spar deck where rows of French soldiers crouched between the cannons. Many were sick, holding their heads in their hands. Sailors laughed and joked with their sick compatriots but a hush fell over the deck as Renau called to them, "Run out and shot the guns," he ordered, and men sprang into action. A cacophony of orders filled the gun deck as the gun commanders gave their orders. Sailors spread sand on the wooden decks. He lifted a speaking trumpet and said, "Men, today we show the enemy that we are not afraid to fight. Your anger, restrained for many years, you may vent today on our enemy. Today the enemy will know our wrath. Long live the King. Long live France!"

Every man on the spar deck leaped to his feet, cheering and shouting, "Long live the King! Long live France!" With the men still cheering, Renau turned to the next task. He raised his telescope to watch the distance closing between the opposing forces. The two fleets approached each other from the wide legs of a V and would meet in battle at the point of the V.

"Ready the bow chase," he ordered. Renau turned toward the approaching enemy. "Fire at their sails the moment the enemy is in range."

The deck officer waited impatiently as the English sloop loomed larger off the port bow. At last he turned to the gunner and took his slow match. The officer stooped to sight over the gun again and satisfied that the aim was right, touched the slow match to the cannon. The cannon bucked and roared. White smoke engulfed the bow of *Pélerine* as the cannon discharged its chain shot at the English sloop. Captain Renau watched a hole appear in the enemy sloop's foresail. An instant later, a puff of white smoke appeared on the enemy's bow. There followed the sound of a cannon and the splash of a cannon ball in the water a cable length ahead of *Pélerine*. "You have his distance, now blast his sails to pieces," shouted Renau. The gun crews on the bow cannons hurried their pace while the other crewmen and soldiers cheered. Aware that their's were the only cannon able to fire on the enemy, the sailors on the bow worked feverishly to load and fire. But the English bow cannon also fired and its expert gunners fired one and one-half times for every shot from the French. The English fired round shot, some of which hit *L'Alicrone* and *Pélerine*. A ball hit Renau's frigate just above the waterline, smashing a hole.

The English sloop opened fire with a howitzer as the distance closed, the balls falling closer to *Pélerine* in towering splashes of water. An English ball from the sloop's bow chase ripped through *Pélerine*'s poop, whereon the English captain ordered his ship about. Knowing that he now had his enemy's range, he would tack and give them a broadside. But the wind that had blown fresh from the northwest in the early morning now fell to a soft breeze. The English sloop failed to answer its helm and its captain could not bring his broadside to bear.

Captain Renau too ordered his helm over, hoping to bring the entire line of portside cannons to fire on the English. But the wind had died and his sails hung limply like laundry on a line. Captain Renau heard the slatting of his sails as the wind diminished. He slammed his fist hard on the taffrail. "Damn, the wind subsides just when we need it most. The old sailors say cannon fire stills the wind. It's damnably true today." He placed his telescope to his eye, shouting, "Ready to come about when there is a breeze... our broadside will reach them now." Captain Renau watched a faint breeze fill his sails. But the wind also filled his enemy's sails, and the bow of the small enemy sloop swung slowly around faster than his frigate. Quickly, he shouted, "Hard a'starboard!

Mainsail haul, ready the port broadside, fire as you bear!" Fire and smoke clouded the English ship, followed by rattling explosions of its cannons. The sloop blasted its eight-gun broadside of nine-pound balls at *Pélerine*. Geysers of white water rose in the ocean around *Pélerine*. A swishing and ripping sounded in the rigging as cannon balls tore through sails badly needed for speed. Splinters of wood exploded over the deck as a ball crashed into the bulwarks, felling men where it struck. The men aboard *Pélerine* hardly heard the English cannons as the roar of their own twelve cannons shook the ship. French soldiers cheered as they saw their shots tearing through the sloop's sails and rigging. Cannon smoke drifted slowly away downwind, toward the sloop, hanging in cloudy wisps above the waves. The French line of battle now formed one leg of a V, terminating at *Pélerine*. The English fleet approached the French, forming the other side of the V.

Le Heros, its sails a spreading tower of white, floundered in the seas with those sails slatting emptily. The frigate moved very slowly over the blue sea, sailing toward the English battleships at the wide part of the V, the rear of the column of French ships. Returning his attention to the enemy sloop, Renau stood with his telescope on the English sloop as enemy shells tore through *Pélerine*'s rigging and bits of wreckage fell to the deck. He turned to his lieutenant. "We hold the weather gauge and I intend to keep it. Stay at the extreme range of the enemy's guns; we will batter his sails and rigging until he can no longer sail. Then we will approach and board the sloop with our soldiers. Ready our boats. We'll put them in the water and tow our ship to him if we must."

In a few quick strides Renau reached the binnacle. He lifted the speaking trumpet to his mouth and leaned across the taffrail, shouting at the troops on deck, "Men, British ships are loaded with rum, and by God's grace, you'll be drinking it tonight!" A load cheer returned from the deck below as jubilant men waved rifles and boarding pikes.

But the vagaries of the wind were beyond Renau's control. The breeze that filled the sails and drove the ship now trailed off to a whisper. The French ensign hung limply from the mizzen top. In the dying breeze, the smaller, lighter sloop of the British widened the distance between the ships. Cannons boomed and thundered but Renau watched his shot falling harmlessly in the ocean. The old sailor's axiom that cannon fire stilled the wind seemed a truth today. Captain Renau looked astern; his flagship sailed slowly toward the English, its bow cannons now striking the enemy. Between the thunder of his broadsides, he heard the ragged firing of the battleships. He steered the sluggish bow of his ship toward the enemy sloop, reducing the distance. But sailing toward the enemy took his broadside cannons out of action. "Port the helm, fire the bow chase as you bear," he ordered. "We must catch him before he escapes! Ready the boats and launch them if she does not answer the helm."

It seemed an eternity before *Pélerine*'s bow swung slowly toward the enemy sloop. The broadside guns of *Pélerine* fell silent. The enemy disappeared from their view. Now only shells from the bow cannons reached the English ship. As *Pélerine*'s bow swung toward the enemy, British cannon balls raked the ship from stem to stern. Men fell injured or dying from splinters and shrapnel. Renau lifted his gaze to the sails and rigging above. He must have every ounce of energy from those sails to reach the enemy. "Aloft! Let's have new sails and shrouds before the English escape our guns." Brave sailors hurried up the damaged masts to set new sails and some fell as English shot tore through the rigging. With courage they spread new canvas across the sky, and the French frigate moved toward the enemy. Slowly, so very slowly, the distance between the ships closed. "Pound for pound, I can sail faster than any English ship, but the enemy sloop is longer and lighter. However, I'm out sailing him and will soon have him in my grasps," he muttered. He lifted a telescope out of its cage by the binnacle and turned away to glass the big battleships.

Away to the north, *Le Heros*, and the English battleship, *Nottingham*, raged against each other, their big cannons volleying and thundering. A maelstrom of fire and smoke obscured the opposing battleships. Close behind *Nottingham,* the English battleship *Grafton* worked its way into position to squeeze *Le Heros* in a pinchers movement between two English ships. Captain Renau's concern mounted as he saw *L'Illustre* and the other French vessel becalmed far off on the northern horizon, offering little assistance to the flagship. The ships were too far away to help Commodore Beaussier on *Le Heros*. As he watched the flagship, the recall flags fluttered from the signal halyard of *Le Heros*. "Damn," he lamented, "our flagship flies the recall flag! Beaussier orders us to come immediately to his assistance. We must help him in his battle against the two English battleships."

Renau turned his telescope back to the enemy sloop. "The Commodore signals recall just as the enemy is in our grasps. Victory slips through our fingers, but we must go to the assistance of our Commodore. There sits *L'Illustre* with its sixty-four guns silent, tossing helplessly in the swells. What a poor showing our fleet provides to the English. Our line of battle has not brought our manpower against them. Damn!"

Captain Renau looked longingly at the British sloop, sailing slowly to the south, a hare slipping from the grasp of the fox. "Wear ship—we must go to the aid of the Commodore, but let's give our enemy sloop a parting broadside before we depart. Load with round shot, and fire at will. Put the helm over!"

Sailors ran to the yards and the helmsman spun the wheel of the frigate. The deck canted, and high aloft, the sails slatted and thundered, joining the sound of cannons. As the frigate turned slowly with the wind, a row of cannons facing the English sloop erupted in a ragged volley. Debris and wreckage leaped into the sky as their shots struck the English sloop. When the smoke of the cannons cleared, the French soldiers cheered, raising their muskets in the air and waving their hats. Sailors hurried to reload and fire again. The faster gun crews fired first while the slower guns followed in a staccato of thunder that sent balls flying harmlessly into the sea.

"Disengage from the sloop and sail to the flag ship," shouted Captain Renau. Smoke blackened faces turned toward the quarterdeck in disappointment as the order ran the gauntlet down the deck. A murmur of disappointment spread over the soldiers and sailors. Slowly, the frigate turned around to beat laboriously upwind in the light breeze, sailing as best she could to the rescue of their flag ship. Captain Renau trained his telescope on the English sloop. He watched longingly as the sloop limped slowly away to the south, its masts and rigging in shambles, smoke boiling from its stern windows. "We had him," he lamented as he watched the distance grow with the enemy. He turned his telescope in the opposite direction toward *Le Heros*. There the flag ship, in imminent danger and unwilling to wait for the frigates, hauled its wind. As the thunder of their cannons drifted across the water, Renau watched *Le Heros* with his telescope. "Beaussier worries that his reinforcements cannot sail upwind to him so he sails downwind to his reinforcements."

The French flagship moved slowly southward, pounding with its cannons at the two pursuing English battleships, who returned their cannon fire with even greater fury. The raging battle drifted slowly toward *Pélerine*. Renau watched with a sense of helplessness as the enemy hammered his flagship with their cannons.

Every man on *Pélerine* strained to see the battle taking place across the water. Deck officers climbed the ratlines with drawn swords, turning back men looking for a higher vantage point for observing the battle. There was nothing that any man could do to help their embattled flagship; they could only watch and wait.

With the battle still far out of range of his guns, Renau watched the lee helmsman turn the sand glass, frustration burning within him. He paced the deck and slammed his fist against the taffrail as sailors hurried to step out of his way. Renau paced back again, grabbing a telescope from one of his midshipmen as he passed. Stopping abruptly, he pulled the telescope open and placed it to his eye. It was then he noted the distance growing between his flagship and the enemy. As he watched, the British battleship sailed away. "The English fail to make chase!" Renau watched the English battleship veer away.

Captain Renau stood with his telescope on the ships. "They have no stomach for a fight with four French warships. We must alter our course and prevent their escape. Perhaps we can delay them until our battleships come to our assistance. We will launch our boats and tow the ship to the enemy if we must."

But a string of colorful signal flags unfurled from the French flagship. He read their message immediately. Captain Renau snapped his telescope shut and rattled it into its rack. "Damn, look at the signals from the flag ship. Our Commodore orders us to join his movements. He is turning toward Louisbourg. He allows the English to escape."

The cannon fire that rolled like a drum died away to random booms as the enemy ships parted. Plumes of water shot skyward as cannon balls fell short of their mark while the smoke from the earlier broadsides drifted slowly down on *Pélerine*. Soon, no more cannon shots could be heard, only the creak and moan of the ship as it wallowed in the ocean swells, and cries of the wounded filled the air.

Slowly, the English ships receded on the horizon while *Pélerine* dutifully followed the flagship, sailing slowly back into Louisbourg Harbor and an ignominious conclusion to their long anticipated battle. Disappointment lay heavy on Captain Renau as their ship anchored in the harbor. So close they had come to the long sought victory, only to be recalled.

With loud cheering, every citizen in Louisbourg turned out to welcome the fleet home from their victory, not knowing that victory had slipped from their grasp. Marie Gauthier, standing in a throng of people, strained to catch a glimpse of the valiant ships returning from battle.

Also, the great news had now reached all the citizens of Louisbourg regarding the capture by valiant French forces of the British bastion of Minorca. Now that Mediterranean fortress was in Christian hands and the tide of the war was turning. The people of Louisbourg celebrated in dance and song. But the celebrations, like Louisbourg summers, were short lived. In October of 1756, a cold wind blew out of the north, raising wavelets on

Louisbourg Harbor. Dense, gray fog chilled the spirits of Louisbourg's citizens as well as their bodies. Marie, with a woolen shawl drawn tightly around her neck, stood on the wharf among other citizens of Louisbourg. Despair reflected in their eyes as they watched the ships sailing slowly out of Louisbourg Harbor. One by one, like shimmering, white ghosts, they disappeared in the gray fog. "De la Mott's ships are sailing for France." Those desperate words were on every lip. French ships, the umbilical cord from mother France, were leaving.

Small boats plied the waters, rowing back and forth with men and supplies. Other boats carried food from De la Mott's ships, unloading it on the docks. Boats unloaded every item not essential to the homeward voyage, and some which were. Departing seamen bade goodbye to their friends and loved ones. The sailors knew by the large piles of food on the docks they faced starvation en route to France. Citizens of Louisbourg knew by the paltry piles of food on the docks they faced starvation in the coming winter. Meanwhile, the ships would sail with barely enough food for the ocean passage.

A Navy boat eased past the wharf where Marie stood, the sailors rowing together with smooth strokes. Renau sat in the back of the boat. Seeing Marie on the wharf, Renau put the tiller over. The boat turned quickly in Marie's direction. At his order, all oars lifted into the air, shining, wet with water. The boat glided to stop in front of Marie and a young sailor leaped from the front. He held the cutter steady as Renau stepped easily on the dock.

Renau tossed his cloak back over his shoulder as he approached Marie. The officer reached out, taking both of her hands in his. Looking down at Marie he said, "Our fleet sails for France tonight. We will slip out in the fog, unseen by British blockade ships. Come with us, Marie; sail to France, and safety."

Holding his hands, Marie answered, "I can't go." She looked up with misty eyes. "I would go if times were different... and fate kinder. But God brought me to Louisbourg and has bound my heart to the people here. I can't leave, not now, not with the hardship to be endured by my people."

"Marie," he said, "this winter will be worse than last as more ships are needed for fighting. Your leaving will be one less mouth to feed; you can think of yourself as helping in that way. Come to France aboard my ship. I personally guarantee you will arrive safely in France." The look in Marie's eyes told him she would not leave. "I'll be back. I will not rest until I'm granted permission to sail again to Louisbourg. I will come to fight the last battle, until victory or defeat. Goodbye, Marie, until I return." Marie put her arms around him. With a warm embrace Marie kissed his cheek. Renau turned and walked slowly across the wharf, looking back over his shoulder. He looked once more as he joined the men in his boat. With ease he directed his boat to the navy pier. As darkness descended, the citizens of Louisbourg watched silently while the last ships weighed anchor. Under a westerly wind and an ebbing tide, the ships drifted out of the harbor, one by one, swallowed by the gray, swirling fog. Out into the void they sailed, taking the hopes of Louisbourg with them, swallowed by the vast, empty ocean, unseen by British warships blockading the harbor.

With the departure of De la Motte's fleet, a mood of gloom descended over the people, a feeling they stood alone to their fate. Madame Drucour increased her already busy social life. Determined to lift the morale of the beleaguered city, she visited the soldiers more often, and was seen everywhere, even among the common people. The greatest challenge for the Drucours were the aristocrats, for unlike the commoners, the military officers and their dependents were at Louisbourg in service of their King. The commoners, however, were in Louisbourg to seek better opportunities than they would have found in France and were more accustomed to depravation. As food became scarce that winter, despite the rumored full stores of food, costs increased and Governor Drucour expended large sums of his personal money to entertain Louisbourg's *aristocrate*.

The hearty people who survived that awful winter of 1756 at last saw hope in June of 1757. As spring flowers blossomed on Cape Breton, badly needed supplies from France arrived. Commodore De Beauffremont eluded the British blockade to lead four ships into Louisbourg. Laughing and shouting, citizens of Louisbourg ran into the streets to welcome them. Hunger would be ended by salted beef, ham, flour, lard, and even wine. Renau was the first captain ashore. Marie saw Renau's boat approaching the wharf. When Renau stepped ashore, she ran to him, dropping her shawl on the ground, throwing her arms around him and kissing him on the cheek. Renau hugged her tightly, and laughing, held her away from him. He looked her up and down saying, "Marie, you are a lovely sight. I worried that you might not survive the winter. It is wonderful to see you alive, even though thin and pale. Our ships have food, perhaps not enough, but Louisbourg's people will eat again, for a while."

Marie grew serious. "Yes, I've grown thin, but I survived. Some were not so lucky. Among the commoners, the young, the old, and the sick died. I shared my rations at Government House with my fellow Acadians from Beaubassin." She looked down.

Chapter Twenty-Two

This spring day of 1757, Lieutenant MacGregor trained his telescope on the spires of Louisbourg, still hoping and searching for some way to get ashore. All through the previous winter they had suffered the cold and storms off Louisbourg. Many men had lost toes or fingers. All had signs of scurvy. Some died of exposure. But with summer, provisioning ships arrived with fruit and fresh vegetables from colonies in Virginia and the Caribbean. Their health was restored and their spirits rose. Fine weather also brought the British flagship along side *Grenadier*. She was a grand sight with all sails drawing and her bow parting the waves in puffs of white spray. She flew the Union Jack form her foremast top, the noble crosses of the patron saints of England, Scotland, and Ireland. At her main top flew the white ensign of the Royal Navy, crossed by the red emblem of St. George. The blue flag of the fleet flew at the mizzen top. A long string of colored signal flags on the signal halyard spelled out, "Prepare to take aboard passenger." The commodore's vessel hove to a cable length away.

From his quarterdeck, Lieutenant MacGregor sent a messenger for Walshingham and watched as a boat approached from the flagship. A French officer sat prominently in the boat. When the boat plowed through the waves and MacGregor saw the Count, Marcel de la Court, former captain of *Chasseur*. De la Court climbed the boarding ladder, and looking into MacGregor's face, said in surprise, "Alas, the same Scottish pirate who took my ship must now deliver me to Louisbourg!" He climbed aboard and stood with hands on hips as he looked about the ship. "Well, I see you have rebuilt this tub from the pounding my cannons gave it."

As Walshingham appeared on the quarterdeck, Lieutenant MacGregor asked, "Is it indeed the same Captain de la Court whom I captured last winter? I see you have paid your ransom and are now free. Are we to take you to Louisbourg?"

De la Court withdrew a folded paper from his pocket and held it out to MacGregor, its red tape blowing in the breeze. MacGregor unfolded the letter, glanced at its contents, and handed it to Walshingham. Captain Walshingham bowed and asked sweetly, "Would ye join me in my cabin for a glass of sherry?"

De la Court lifted his chin and said to MacGregor, "I have nothing to say to vile ruffians who rob me. Take me below to my cabin before I am forced to look into the eyes of such a base animal as your captain."

Walshingham snorted a raucous laugh and replied, "MacGregor, ye will take *Monsieur* fancy pants to Louisbourg in our long boat. But first, take him down to the brig. That shall be his quarters until we reach Louisbourg Harbor." He turned to Mr. Sethford. "Sailing Master! Lay a course for Louisbourg Harbor as straight as she will bear and lose no time in getting this frog off my ship."

MacGregor led him below and aft on the gun deck. He opened the door to his own cabin and said, "This is my own cabin and the best I can offer. Make yourself comfortable while I go topside and make haste for Louisbourg." He continued, "Count, I suggest you stay here for now, and keep your door locked. I will come for you as we near the harbor." Lieutenant MacGregor then hurried forward to the cabin of Dr. Abrams. "Quickly," he said, "I need a pen and paper."

As he replied, Abrams closed the book he was reading and cleared the papers from his writing desk, knocking over a bottle of whiskey in the process. "Has it now reached the point with our captain that you are writing your will?"

"No," answered MacGregor, watching Abrams wipe up the spilled whiskey on the tail of his shirt. "I'm going to take our prisoner to Louisbourg. The young lady I spoke to you about may be there. I'll write a letter in hope she will get it." He quickly sat down, taking the offered paper and dipped the quill in the ink. MacGregor looked up absent mindedly and then began to write. Abrams stood by the door and waited quietly while MacGregor wrote. Lieutenant MacGregor sanded the wet ink and blew on the page. With a happy smile he folded the paper and wrote Marie's name on the outside. Sanding that too and again waving it for drying, he secreted it in his coat pocket and nodded at Abrams, saying, "I thank you, good friend. Let us hope you are Cupid, bringing good luck, as well as a friend."

When MacGregor reached the quarterdeck, he found Walshingham saying to the coxson, "Hang two lead lines from the stern of yer boat, Coxson. One at a depth of three fathoms and the other at one fathom." He looked up at MacGregor to continue, "Pick triangulation points and remember them at each location the lead lines are ripped off. Be able to mark them on a map. Take a lead line hidden in yer boat and take readings every cable length on yer way back to the ship." He turned to Midshipman Thomas, saying, "Ye go along also, mister. Make a mental note of every warship in the harbor and their harbor defenses. Take a very good look at the entrance of the harbor and be able to draw a fair representation of the entry on the map when ye return."

A white flag of truce fluttered from *Grenadier*'s mast top as she neared Lóuisbourg Harbor. The white ensign at her stern identified her as British. Sailors had changed to their Sunday best and lined the deck and yards of the frigate. Under the watchful eyes of French gunners, she hove to a league outside the harbor mouth and prepared a boat for launching. Sailors fed off the lines, the ship's davits whirred, and the boat splashed into the water. Mr. Thomas quickly slid down the rope and stood in the bow of the boat. Six smartly dressed sailors took their places at the oars while a yeoman with slates squeezed between. Followed by Marcel De la Court, Lieutenant MacGregor took his place in the stern sheets. When he had taken his seat, MacGregor spoke to the count in French. "If you find a young lady at Louisbourg named Marie Gauthier, please tell her that her father is safe in Boston." With some hesitation he added, "And you may tell her that Charles MacGregor will come as soon as I may and take her to her father."

Marcel De la Court smiled wryly. "Ah, the Scottish pirate courts a French lassie in Louisbourg? I wonder if she is attractive? Yes, she must be to hold the Scotsman's interest, so I shall find her if she is there. Perhaps I might give her the thrill of a French count. Then what would she have left for a landless Scotsman?" De la Court laughed loudly. "But first I must see just how unwashed she is!" He looked around in wonder as the coxson called out landscape features to the yeomen seated near him.

MacGregor answered, "Whatever... but if you find her, tell her that her father is safe. I will tell her other things much better one day myself." MacGregor sat glumly in the stern sheets looking up at the French soldiers lining the wharf as they approached.

English sailors held their wet oars aloft, glistening like two rows of glistening lances as the boat bumped softly against the pilings. Mr. Thomas leaped lightly to the dock with bow line in his hand. Marcel De la Court lifted his hat to the crowd gathering at the wharf and stepped ashore, losing his balance and almost falling into the water.

MacGregor followed De la Court ashore and found a young French army officer approaching. Speaking in French, MacGregor hurriedly explained that he was returning the Count from captivity, then reached into his pocket for his letter. He handed the letter to the officer, saying, "I have a letter here for a young lady named Marie Gauthier, from the French colony of Beaubassin. I don't know if she is in Louisbourg, but if she is, kindly give her this letter. She will be anxious to know about her father." He looked up to see a well dressed gentleman approaching in the company of two senior military officers.

De la Court pushed his way through the crown and approached the gentleman and the two older officers. "You must be the Chevalier, Governor Drucour. I am Chevalier the Count Marcel De la Court. I was captain of the late ship, *Chasseur*, a wretched ship, poorly armed, unseaworthy, unable to defend itself, and crewed by the dregs of humanity. Otherwise, I would not have fallen into the hands of English pirates. I protest the poor resources given me to defend myself and the barbaric treatment received at the hands of these English ruffians. You may be sure the King shall hear of it as soon as I return to France."

Governor Drucour listened to De la Court's tirade until the nobleman paused for breath. He interrupted the discourse by addressing Lieutenant MacGregor. "Please let us not keep you from your duties, Captain and be about your quick exit from our Harbor." MacGregor thought, *Should I speak to this governor about Marie? Would it cause problems for her? No, I will trust that the young officer will give her the letter if she is here or maybe De la Court will give her my message.*

MacGregor now turned his mind to his orders from Walshingham and tried to remember everything in the harbor as the boat coasted back through the harbor with oars dipping gently. The coxson busily dropped the lead line and called out water depths and landscape features to a yeoman who busily wrote on slates.

With their passenger offloaded and boat recovered, the sailors aboard *Grenadier* raised their anchor. Working slowly, taking more than two hours to get under way, the sailing master sketched the harbor and the midshipmen described in detail every French warship in the estuary visible from a league offshore. Walshingham stood surveying the harbor with his telescope. Then slowly they sailed out to sea, casting a lead line and charting depths as they sailed. Reaching the open sea, MacGregor looked back wistfully toward Louisbourg.

MacGregor's mind was much on Marie Gauthier as he cruised off the coast of Louisbourg. The exceedingly fine weather that summer continued through August and well into September of 1757, with blue skies in the day and bright stars at night. But men who travel the seas are always suspicious of long intervals of fine weather, knowing that nature often changes direction with a fury. Apprehension increased this day when the northwesterly winds, which had blown so steadily for weeks on end, disappeared without a trace.

Such seafaring men plot their position by the sun. They are attentive to its travel across the sky and mark its crossing of the equator as an occurrence of importance. Therefore, on this day when the sun deserted the northern hemisphere to seek the south, sailors watched the skies apprehensively, wondering what strange weather change might be wrought by the autumnal equinox. Misgivings multiplied when the wind fell from force three to a baby's breath. On the ocean off Louisbourg, ships foundered helplessly in the calm.

The sun heated the placid stillness like a burning ball of fire. Captain Walshingham stood in the sweltering stillness of the quarterdeck with beads of perspiration glistening on his forehead. He held an empty wine bottle in his hand. Across the mirrored stillness of the ocean, low swells lumbered slowly, traveling without interruption to the harbor entrance at Louisbourg. There, the ghostly spires reflected the shimmering afternoon heat amid the dry countryside. Turning back toward the open sea, he counted the ships of the British squadron, all wallowing helplessly without wind in their sails. *Grenadier* rolled uncomfortably in the swells as her empty sails slatted and slapped noisily. Sailors worked with bare chests, their flesh turning red, perspiration running down their bodies in the stillness.

But weather can change quickly. On the first day of autumn, September 24, 1757, the English squadron found a strong breeze blowing across their decks. As they sailed, more anxious eyes turned upward to watch the weather. Every old salt on an English warship knew a celestial event such as the autumnal equinox has a profound effect on the weather. While some describe its wayward effect on the weather superstitiously, others give lengthy scientific dissertations on how this event produces climatic calamity.

Such were the discussions in the wardroom of *Grenadier* during breakfast. Later, on the quarterdeck, officers stood with hats in hand, facing the freshening southeast wind.

Walshingham paced the weather rail, his eyes on the southeast horizon. The Admiralty's orders were explicit: stay within sight of the harbor entrance, prevent the entry or exit of any shipping, and record events within sight of Louisbourg. Yet the Admiralty would not condone the loss of a ship. It is foolish to sail on a weather shore with a storm brewing. He labored with his decision to quit the station.

The old sailing master approached the windward side of the quarterdeck. "The glass is falling, Sir, and the swells are coming the wrong way for the wind. I make the wind to be at least force five. I think we should take the top gallants off her."

"Aye," replied Captain Walshingham. "The air has a warm, wet smell. I don't like it. Do what ye thing best, Mister Sethford." Captain Walshingham pulled his hat down tightly and took refuge in his cabin.

Just before sundown MacGregor joined Sethford on deck and sent the boatswain up into the masts with orders for removal of the fore and main topgallant masts and yards. It was dangerous work on a ship tossing on a rough sea. The yards being lowered to the deck by strong ropes, swayed with the pitch of the ships and crashed into men and masts on their way down. By eight o'clock the officers found it necessary to hold their hats and lean into the wind to walk on deck. By nine o'clock they leaned into the wind and held the life lines to move. Lieutenant MacGregor held to the binnacle, shouting, "Take her out to sea, Mr. Sethford, as directly as you can."

"Aye, Sir, with pleasure," replied the sailing master as he picked up his speaking trumpet and began shouting orders. Men scurried across the decks and into the rigging, sensing the urgency of their situation. The frigate clawed desperately in an attempt to move away from the rocky shoals where surf exploded in violent showers of salt spray.

Sails, hauled back so far that the slightest variation in wind direction sent them shuddering into uselessness, strained to pull the ship forward. At times the ship moved forward until an unusually large wave crashed over the bow and stopped progress. Recovering from the impact of the wave, *Grenadier* again gathered headway, only to be stopped by another wave.

At MacGregor's orders, Midshipman Thomas led crews through the ship, securing cannons with extra lashings. At noon Mr. Sethford kneeled on deck and used his hand compass to fix their position by triangulation. Lieutenant MacGregor looked over his shoulder, asking, "What progress have we made?"

Sethford looked up to report, "The ship has not moved more than one hundred yards since ten o'clock this morning."

Lieutenant MacGregor reacted immediately to his calculations. He turned to a midshipman, ordering, "Hang the bower anchors on light rope and stationed men on the bow with sharp axes. Watch for a signal from the bridge and be ready to chop the ropes if the ship begins drifting back on the rocks."

Around two o'clock in the afternoon, when it appeared the anchors might have to be dropped, the wind veered. It came around to the east by southeast and the ship began making a little headway. But as the wind veered toward the east, it freshened. By sundown it blew a full gale. Waves crashed over the bow, sending a stinging salt spray into the men's faces while the pitching deck and waves washing across made it difficult to walk.

A wave lifted the stern of the ship. Leaning into the wind as he walked along the slippery deck, Lieutenant MacGregor found himself slammed into the scuppers. He pulled himself up, continuing to walk over the tossing deck, holding himself erect with an aching wrist.

Just after sundown, as darkness made every move more dangerous, Lieutenant MacGregor looked at the boatswain whose sleeves were ripped, his arms bloody, and hand bandaged. His wet hair streamed down over his bruised face. MacGregor had to look away as he reluctantly ordered, "Into the masts, Bosun. Reef the topsails. Let's go, look lively now." The boatswain ran for the ratlines, blowing his tin pipe, and top men hurried to his call. Soon anxious landmen joined them in the masts and those not moving quickly enough felt the sting of the boatswain's rattan.

MacGregor watched as the ship's bow turned away from the wind. The helmsman fought the wheel. "Our helm is too difficult to handle," he yelled.

MacGregor knew the ship was in danger of being pitch-poled as he yelled above the wind, "Cut the jibs loose!"

Sailors scrambled to the bow as it began to speed through the water. With even more water pouring over them, they chopped away the sheets holding the jibs. Soon the wind caught the flapping, flailing sails and tore them away. With shattered sails disappearing into the stormy night, the ship slowly turned back to a safer course. All jib sails had disappeared except one. A single jib stay did not tear away but blew back into the main mast when the bow turned. The wind tossed cable struck the boatswain's men on the fore yard like a whip lashing out of the storm. Tired hands lost their grip on the wet shrouds. The blow of the heavy cordage knocked one man unconscious and broke another's leg. Both fell to their death as their mates scrambled to hold the shred of their own. The boatswain, who now had been in the tops longer than any man, found his muscles failing him. He recognized the knotted feeling that comes before the spasm begins. Quickly throwing a line around his own waist, he began to tie a bowline with one hand as all experienced seaman learned to do. But the spasm came quick and sharp. The muscles would no longer move the fingers in the dexterous movements required. His bowline became a slip knot. The exhausted muscles gave way and the boatswain fell from the yard. At the end of his tether he was jerked to a stop by the slip knot which squeezed tightly at his body weight. Now the boatswain dangled like a rag doll in the gale with the rope cutting off his breath. His mates on the fore yard, already seeing two of their fellow falling to their death, could not be moved from their precarious perch.

Men on deck looked up to see the boatswain being bashed against the yards with his breath squeezed from him. But the boatswain was not a popular man. His ratan had raised whelps on many backs while his dice game had taken the earnings of many more. No man would risk his life in the yards for an unpopular boatswain.

MacGregor watched from the deck and knew the boatswain would soon be dead, one way or another if not rescued. He dashed to the ratlines and lifted the belaying pin of an empty halyard. Yelling against the howl of the wind, he ordered the men to wrap the tail around the cathead. Gripping the distal end in his teeth, MacGregor threw himself in the ratlines and began the perilous climb to the fore yard. Every step upward seemed to find a stronger wind blowing against his body. Buttons were ripped from his coat. When the wind threw his body outward from the ratlines, he forced his way around to the bottom side and continued to climb, now hanging from the ropes. He clung desperately with fingers unaccustomed to climbing tarred ropes. Upward he climbed until he reached a position on the ratlines level with the swinging boatswain. There MacGregor waited until the man swung near him. He reached a strong hand out as far as he could and took the weak hand extended by the desperate and nearly unconscious boatswain. Feet locked in the ratlines, one hand holding his own weight, another gripping the rain-slicked wrist of the boatswain, MacGregor thought desperately, *the boatswain is the most experienced man aboard when it comes to working the tops. If he can think at all, he will be thinking what to do. His arms will not hold, so he must use his legs.* MacGregor knew his muscles would tire quickly so he must make his move at once. With all his might he pulled the boatswain closer. Taking a desperate gamble, he let one foot slide down in the ratlines and then the other, locking his knees about the ropes. He now turned loose the ratlines with his one free arm and grabbed the rope around the boatswain's waist. *If I have erred in my assessment of the boatswain's knowledge or if he can't think properly, we will both fall to our death.* Pulling for all his worth, MacGregor inched the boatswain closer to the ratlines. His assessment was correct. Weakly, but surely, the boatswain extended a leg into the ratlines and began to pull himself against them. With MacGregor's legs slipping on the ropes, the boatswain found the ratlines with his other foot and now they both hung by their feet. Seeing the boatswain's legs locked in the ratlines, MacGregor loosened one hand from the man and reached wildly, seeking the ratlines. Now hanging upside down, he found the ropes with his other hand and righted himself, swinging to the topside of the ratlines. Quickly, he moved upward and took the halyard from his teeth. With one hand MacGregor made the deft moves known by all experienced sailors. He put the halyard under the boatswain's armpit and took the bitter end again in his teeth. With the free hand he quickly tied a bowline around the man. The boatswain looked at the knot with approval. The man could not speak, but his eyes shouted his gratitude. MacGregor lifted the standing end of the halyard as a signal to the men below and watched as the line grew tight. With the leverage of the cathead below, the men on deck pulled the boatswain away from the ratlines and slowly lowered him to the deck. Climbing down himself, MacGregor found a shaken and exhausted boatswain resting on his hands and knees, his hand hanging down near the deck. "Take him below to Dr. Abrams," he ordered.

The boatswain looked up to say, "No, Lieutenant, Sir. You will need me on deck. Let someone help me to my bunk where I can wrap my hands in bandages and rest a moment. I'll be back soon to help you." Wet sailors climbed into the masts, supervised by the boatswain. They worked aloft for almost an hour before they dragged themselves below where they ate a cold meal and climbed, still wet and cold, into the relative peace of their tossing bunks.

But at ten p.m. the wind veered to east-southeast with even greater fury. Midshipmen made their way between the sleeping men's bunks. "Back on deck, men. Lower the main and fore topmast and yards!" Men moving too slowly felt the sting of a rattan on their damp blankets.

With torn and bleeding hands, the sailors climbed back up the ratlines and lowered more heavy spars to the deck. Swinging and swaying with the pitch and roll of the ship, the spars would become lethal battering rams if loosed of their restraints. As it was, another man was seriously injured when a yard smashed his legs and almost sent him crashing to his death on the decks below.

With the topmasts and yards securely stowed, the exhausted men again climbed into the masts to reef the main and fore sails. Descending to the wave-washed deck, sailors held tightly to any solid object, waiting for their next orders. The odd big wave washed over the bulwarks and flooded the sailors on deck in torrents of green water rushing past the men in depth up to their waists. Any man caught in such a torrent without a good hand hold would be swept out to sea. As the storm raged and the ship resisted its wrath, MacGregor dismissed the double watch. The men, with sighs of relief, fell into their bunks, too tired to remove their salty, wet clothing. Even with saltwater stinging their bleeding wounds, the men fell instantly asleep.

At midnight the full force of the wind struck; a full-blown hurricane lashed them with all its fury. On deck, Lieutenant MacGregor tightly hugged the mizzen mast. He sensed a strange, silent calm. MacGregor shouted, "Everyone hold on! We may go under!"

Chapter Twenty-Three

Earlier that evening, with the wind buffeting shutters outside, Marie Gauthier smiled at her audience from the harpsichord, glancing occasionally at the keys as she played. Soft candlelight bathed Marie's bare shoulders in its warm glow. Her white gown reflected the gold and brown of the drawing room in Government House. With the conclusion of her sonata, applause erupted from the Louisbourg guests. Madame Drucour beamed proudly, sharing the glory in her discovery of Marie's talents. General Du Bois De la Motte smiled broadly as he clapped his hands. Captain Renau stood looking out the window, his back to Marie as he watched the gusting wind with apprehension.

Marie's slim fingers danced over the harpsichord. The stirring chords thrilled ears starved for music, music not heard since leaving France. No musician ever played before a more attentive audience. When Marie bowed her head and again sat with her hands in her lap, the applause almost drowned out the thunder outside.

Marie looked up to see a young man standing beside her, clapping loudly. Jeweled rings flashed on his fingers. It was a young nobleman, immaculately dressed in a military uniform. His long, hair fell across his shoulders. "Wonderful, my dear young lady." He bowed slightly. "Why have I never met you at the court of my cousin, King Louis?"

Marie smiled. "Because I have never been to France, much less Versailles. And the King has never had the pleasure of hearing me play."

The young officer laughed. "It would be one of the few pleasures he has not had. If he took one look at you, I'm sure other pleasures would come to mind before your music."

Marie's eyes flashed briefly but an easy smile returned. "I'm not prepared to serve as queen of France, and I doubt your cousin is prepared to pay my price."

"Well, he seems to pay Madame Pompadour's price," laughed the young man. "She's queen in all but title."

"And she, too, pays a price, in loss of reputation if nothing else," replied Marie.

The officer laid his hand on Marie's bare shoulder. "Allow me to introduce myself. I am the Chevalier, Count Marcel De la Court. I'll be sailing to France soon. I could take you with me."

Marie removed his hand from her shoulder, saying, "Your price, too, is more than I'm willing to pay, my Lord. But there must certainly be brothels in Paris to cater to your needs."

He laughed loudly. "There are maidens more fair than you by far, eager to serve my needs. It's too bad you will never know the real world, the art, culture, and... love of Paris. This land is a pigsty by comparison. We in France are more liberal and cultured than you colonials. You people took the culture and morals of our grandfathers, implanting them in this God forsaken land. Here, time stopped a century ago, with all the silly ideas of those times. But I am not here to lecture, young lady. I have told you my name, now tell me yours," he commanded.

She hesitated ,then answered, "I'm Marie Gauthier, a war refugee from Beaubassin and now musician to the lady, Madame Drucour."

De la Court stood back in surprise. "*You* are Marie Gauthier?" He laughed loudly. "A queen pursued by a knave then!" Again he laughed.

Marie now reacted with surprise. "You act as though you know my name, my Lord. How would you know my name? We have never met."

De la Court smiled. "No, we have never met, to my regret. But I do have some news for you and might provide even more to interest you if you could show me the proper appreciation. Young lady, I have news of your father. He is well and living in Boston. Now, what do you think of that?"

Marie looked ashen. She could hardly speak. "You have seen my father? Where is he and is he well? Is he a prisoner of the English?"

De la Court held the palm of his hand as if to halt Marie's rush of speech. "Now don't get too excited, my dear! Let us not have a scene here in Government House. I have not seen the man and would not know him if I did. I do not know if he is a prisoner or not; I only know a pirate told me he is in Boston. Do you know a Scotsman named MacGregor?" He did not wait for an answer. "It seems the Scottish pirate has eyes for you, my dear. He sent you the message when he brought me here to Louisbourg and said something about taking you away." De la Court laughed. "I think he will not be back. Your governor gave him a cool reception, and our soldiers would love to have shot him." The young nobleman stepped in front of a passing servant and took two wine glasses from the man's tray. He placed a glass in Marie's hand and lifted his in a toast. "I drink to the day you see the wonders of Paris yourself... with me as your guide. You can be sure that with my help, you can find your father and rescue him, wherever he is." He tossed the wine down his throat and laughed. Marie set the full wine glass on the harpsichord as a painted young woman joined the nobleman.

Wearing a huge wig, with dazzling jewels bouncing on her bare bosom, she planted a kiss on his cheek. "Chevalier," she said, "you have not introduced me to the court minstrel who keeps you from my company."

"Good evening, *Mademoiselle* Verville," he said. "The musician is one of our colonists, a native of this land. She is Marie Gauthier of some place called Beaubassin."

"Oh, yes, the colonial musician. I hardly recognized you, my dear, without your wooden shoes and cute little peasant cap." Her lips smiled with the sweetness of honey but her eyes drew blood. "Madame Drucour is fortunate to have a servant who plays." *Mademoiselle* Verville smilingly twirled her lace handkerchief toward the young nobleman as she turned to walk away, saying, "I must be careful of men unable to resist sexy servants, you devil."

Marie watched the full-hipped dress moving away across the room as the young nobleman laughed loudly. "Marie Gauthier, you were paid the finest compliment known to the company of such young ladies as *Mademoiselle* Verville. You threaten her sovereignty in this kingdom of hers. She is a goddess of this desolate, despicable outpost. But in Paris or Versailles, she would be a head in the crowd, obstructing the view of a marriageable young nobleman looking for a bride."

A group of chattering young army officers swept around the nobleman. "De la Court, where have you been? We've been looking for you. We're going to have another game of cards when this affair is over. Did you bring money?" With laughing and back slapping, they carried the young nobleman away, casting glances appreciatively at Marie as they departed.

Governor Drucour walked up to the harpsichord. "You played beautifully, my dear," exclaimed Governor Drucour. "Your music makes our life here more tolerable and too seldom do we adequately thank you."

In the quiet that followed, people turned to listen to the thunder and roar of wind. A crash sounded as some object, caught by the wind, slammed against the wall. The governor stood silently listening for a moment. "It sounds as though we are in for a storm. Let us go into the dining room; I believe the food is ready."

Marie rose to follow Madame Drucour as the other guests filed into the dining room. As she stood near the harpsichord, another young officer approached her. "You play beautifully, *Mademoiselle*. Unfortunately, I was forced to listen from the doorway since I'm not a guest. But I wanted to bring you this letter personally from an English officer. I was afraid to give it to someone else lest you be suspect. It was given to me by the officer who delivered the Chevalier. I hope you are happy with the message it brings." The young man bowed and hurriedly walked away.

Marie stood looking down at the letter as Captain Renau hurried over. "I hope you will express my apologies to Madame Drucour, but I've been uneasy all day about the change in our weather. The noise outside tells me the wind is blowing near gale force. I must return to my frigate. Your music was beautiful, *Mademoiselle*." Captain Renau hurried away. Marie quickly unfolded the letter and read, holding her hand over mouth with a gasp as she read of her father. With tears of joy in her eyes Marie held the letter over her heart, smiled and crossed herself.

Captain Renau, holding his hat and leaning heavily into the gale, struggled to the wharf. There the crew of his gig fought to keep the boat from smashing against the dock. "We must get back to the ship," he said. "We will need more anchors." With difficulty they launched the boat. Waves, unusually high for inside the harbor, smashed at the bow of the boat. The wind blew against the crew as they struggled with the oars. Wave after wave covered the gunwales. Saltwater threatened to swamp the boat. Renau's sailors pulled desperately at the oars, stroking as fast as they could. But the boat moved almost imperceptibly. With water rising around his ankles, Captain Renau removed his dress hat and baled water from the boat. Great curtains of driving rain spread across the harbor. Like sharp pellets, the wind drove the rain drops against their faces. Reaching the lee of their ship, the crew collapsed breathlessly over their oars while the rain beat down upon them.

Renau, however, quickly climbed to the quarterdeck of the frigate. His hair streamed down in his face and water poured from his chin. To the midshipman in charge Renau shouted, "Send a fresh crew into the boat. We will row another anchor out to the southeast and set it tightly. Launch another boat, it will require at least two boats."

Renau climbed back down into the boat, helping the exhausted crewman climb aboard *Pélerine* while arranging the new crew in the boat. Flashes of lighting illuminated the men's faces in a ghostly gray-green cast as rain poured over them. Captain Renau took his place in the sternsheets and directed the crew to the bow of the ship.

At the bow of the ship, the two row boats converged on the anchor lowered down to them, secured it between the boats and began rowing into the wind as crewmen on *Pélerine* paid out the line. The progress was painfully slow. Several times the men slumped breathlessly at the oars, and Captain Renau shouted, "Row, damn you! If you stop rowing, you will drown; row for your life."

As Renau cursed and prodded, the men continued to strain against the oars. When an elderly sailor slumped unconscious at the oars, Captain Renau pulled the man aside. He lurched across the tossing boat and took his place at the oar. The heavy anchor and chain dragged beneath the surface of the water, slowing the boat. Only with great difficulty did the boat gain the far end of the anchorage.

Renau lifted his hand into the air, shouting to the other boat, "Now! Drop the anchor here." With the weight of anchor and chain no longer slowing them, and the gale at their back, the boat raced back to the ship.

Captain Renau was the first man up the ladder on *Pélerine*. "Sailors aloft," he yelled. "Take down the top masts and yards."

Reluctant sailors, dripping wet and struggling to stand erect, climbed into the rain slicked spars, taking them down and lowering them to the deck. After the grueling, exhausting work, the rain-soaked men lay listening to the howl of the wind. They gave thanks for the shelter of the harbor and smiled at the thought of the English sailors out on the wave-tossed sea.

Later, the wind veered to the east and grew in intensity. Renau was convinced that a hurricane churned toward them. Elsewhere, other ships followed *Pélerine*'s actions, but in some cases, too late. Screams in the stormy night told them a boat had upset and men drowned.

On the nearby battleship *Hercules*, Captain DuTiel led his men into a boat, also rowing out another anchor. With its stern dragged too low in the water by the heavy anchor, the boat began taking on water faster than the men could bail. Sailors found their boat sinking and the black waves engulfing them. Howling wind engulfed their screams and black water engulfed their bodies.

The hurricane howled and screamed as the water depth increased in the harbor and waves, of a size expected in mid-ocean, crashed over the many ships huddled in Louisbourg Harbor. Soldiers manning the shore batteries deserted their positions, retreating to higher ground at risk of being drowned.

Pélerine, now swinging to two anchors and with reduced resistance aloft, settled down with her nose into the wind. Captain Renau paced the foredeck, watching the anchor cables for signs of chafe that could snap them under the strain. Minutes that seemed like hours, and hours that seemed an eternity dragged past as wind and wave thrashed the ships and men of Louisbourg.

When it seemed the wind could reach no greater velocity, it intensified.

Then, from out of the darkness a short distance away, a cannon sounded short and hollow as the hurricane quickly blew the sound away. "It's *Le Dauphin Royale* firing a distress signal," shouted a sailor on deck. "I saw the muzzle flash when she fired."

Lightning flashed, exposing the entire harbor scene. "There! *Le Dauphin Royale* is drifting down upon *Le Tonnant*."

As the men watched the big battleship *Le Dauphin Royale* in the flashes of lightning, it reeled backwards under the hurricane pushed it toward a line of ships anchored behind her. As the battleship reached the next ship, the bowsprit of *Le Tonnant* tore through her stern. *Le Tonnant's* anchor cable parted under the impact and she drifted down upon the rocky shore. Every flash of lightning revealed more carnage as ships and boats washed in splintered wreckage along the rocky shore. The frigate, *L'Abenaquise*, her anchor cable parted, drifted ashore and foundered.

As men struggled outside in the hurricane, Marie closed the door to her room. She rushed to the lamp beside her bed and took the folded letter from her bosom. Over and over she read the brief missive.

Chapter Twenty-Four

The hurricane of 1757 raged at the men and their only link to life, *Grenadier*. MacGregor felt the ocean close over him. As if he had dived from a great height, he plunged downward in the swirling ocean. Down, down they plunged as the water lifted him off the deck, tethered by the frayed piece of halyard wrapped around his wrist.

Inky blackness engulfed him. MacGregor's head felt as though it might explode. Then the deck slammed into his body as the bow rose from beneath the sea. Tons of seawater cascaded down the deck, sucking sailors into its all powerful grasp and crushing them against wood and steel. The powerful, cascading river of water tore at MacGregor's grip on the rope. Muscles ached in his shoulder and pain radiated through his torso. His wet fingers slipped on the rope; the rope cut into his wrist. MacGregor used his last ounce of energy as the water began to subside. His head rose above the water and his lungs inhaled air, precious air. His mind cleared. Again the sea rose around him, tearing at his grip on the bulwark, sucking at his body, and buffeting him with loose boards and flotsam. When the quarterdeck rose again from beneath the sea, he struggled up. Higher, with the seawater now swirling beneath him, MacGregor found his clothing ripped and arms bleeding. Pain radiated from every limb. His lungs pumped rapidly and his heart thundered in his chest. From the ship's wheel Midshipman Thomas shouted, "There's six feet of water in the well."

"Do you have men on the bilge pumps?" he asked.

Thomas shouted over the tumult, "Aye, Sir. We're taking on water from the anchor damage, but the bilge pumps are keeping up."

"Bend on a storm jib and stay sail! Let's hope they will keep us off the rocks," yelled MacGregor to the boatswain. "We may survive this storm yet."

With a respect he had not shown before, the boatswain answered, "Aye, Sir, with you at the helm we will." Quickly, the boatswain rushed away and up into the yards.

"The wind has veered a point to our bow," shouted Sethford over the roar of the storm. "That's a good sign; we may be on the lee of the hurricane."

Throughout the night they fought to keep the ship afloat. As the storm railed at them, they slowly clawed away from the dangers of being dashed against the rocks. After perilous hours of bone breaking work, they saw the dawn. Daylight's first gray glow illuminated the monsters that had roamed the darkness. Mountainous waves rolled across the ocean with froths of foam filling the air like a wind-whipped fog.

When three bells rang in the forenoon watch, a pale and somber Lieutenant MacGregor still paced the windward side of the quarterdeck. Bareheaded, with a stubble of beard, and wearing a soiled shirt, he stood silently in awe of the storm. "The ship's riding better," he said.

MacGregor sent a lookout aloft. The man laboriously climbed the tossing foremast and came back with a report. "Several ships are in view, some driving northward in the storm in various states of damage, one without masts drifting toward shore, another without masts hanging by her anchors just offshore; another is wrecked on the beach."

At noon, with still no sign of Captain Walshingham on deck and the ship still wallowing in heavy seas, MacGregor went below. He heard the clanking of the bilge pumps as he walked down the narrow corridor inspecting damage in the orlop deck. At times losing his balance and stumbling, MacGregor made his way back to the water-filled powder magazine. The ship was defenseless against an enemy. MacGregor made his way topside again, and with waves attempting to pull him overboard, he waded the torrents back to Walshingham's cabin. A seasick marine tried to stand at attention as he reached his cabin door. He turned the knob and entered. He found much of Walshingham's priceless furniture a smashed pile of splinters, but the captain lay restrained in his tossing bed with a whiskey bottled cradled in his arms. MacGregor shut the door on the carnage and went back on deck. There he found the ship's officers on the quarterdeck. "Alright, give me a damage report," he ordered.

Mr. Sethford reported, "We've lost our foremast; our bows are stove in; we have no bower anchors."

Midshipman Thomas added, "And there's still two feet of water in the bilge."

Dr. Abrams, who had now come to the quarterdeck, added, "We've lost twelve men overboard and fourteen injured, six may not recover."

Sethford added, "Our lookout saw several of our ships, most without masts. At least one was wrecked on the beach. Most are severely disabled."

MacGregor ordered, "There's work to do. Double the lookouts; raise every sail this ship will carry. Order the gunners to man and ready every cannon we have left; pass out small arms; hang the boarding nets; put marksmen in the mast tops; we must be ready for the French when they come, as come they will. They'll sink our ships one by one. Wear ship and stand off to the southeast. Lay a course for Halifax, Mr. Sethford. Watch for signals from our commodore, if his ship is still afloat, but waste no time here. Surely, any British ship in these waters will be sunk by the French warships coming out of their snug harbor."

Chapter Twenty-Five

Morning of September 25, 1757, found Captain Renau standing at the rail of his ship in Louisbourg Harbor. The winds had shifted to the south. Raindrops like pellets still stung his face. With squinting eyes and water dripping from his nose, he ordered, "Roust the men from below. Get the topmasts and yards back on *Pélerine*."

"But, Captain," replied the midshipman, "the men are exhausted. They worked like slaves all night. Is there a need for the masts now?"

Captain Renau's grimace would have been answer enough. "Be quick about it! Now is the time to defeat the English." Renau pointed at the wreck-littered shore. "Look at the damage the hurricane did inside the safety of our harbor. Can you imagine what has happened to the British fleet on the open sea? If any ships survived, they will be badly damaged and unable to defend themselves. If we are to save Louisbourg, we must sink the English fleet today. The time is now; our Lord has given us a victory. Get the ship ready to sail."

Renau strode down to the spar deck. To the deck officer he ordered, "I want a boat and crew in the water immediately. See what assistance we can offer the damaged ships. I'm taking the gig to Government House. If ever there was a time to sail against the English, it is today. I want this ship battle-ready when I return."

Rowing ashore, Renau found wreckage littering the shoreline. Bodies floated face down in the water. His boat approached the big battleship, *Tonnant*. Climbing to the deck, he found the officers discussing their plight. He joined the anxious, gesturing officers on the ship. He listened briefly, studied the situation, then formulated a plan in his mind. "The tide is beginning to rise. Let's row anchors out into the harbor. With the wind blowing from the south and a rising tide, I believe we can kedge her off. Put a crew on your windlass and have them ready to work. If she holds out the water, we must sail her against the English immediately."

Other officers, some senior to Renau, accepted his plan. Sailors hurried to their orders. Soon the big windlass clanked and clattered, pulling against the anchors as men strained against the oak. Mainsail and jib caught the wind, pulling the ship off the rocks. The ship floated off the rocks, damaged and leaking badly, but saved. Satisfied that he could do little more, Renau went to shore. The wharf was littered with bodies of drowned sailors.

Young officers stood waiting along the wharf as Renau approached in his boat. They asked, "Is *Pélerine* safe?"

"*Pélerine* is safe and ready to fight the British survivors of this hurricane, if there are any," Renau answered. "Let's go to Government House. Perhaps the governor will see us. Surely he will convince Du Bois De la Motte to sail against the English. An act of God put the British fleet at our mercy. We can't lose this opportunity."

The officers, all junior in rank, set off for Government House.

Walking along the wharf they encountered a throng of people looking at a body. The group of officers pushed their way through the crowd and looked down. Someone asked, "Who is it?"

A young lieutenant answered, "It is Captain DuTeil, commander of *Hercules*."

Renau stood with hat removed. "God rest his soul; there's nothing we can do for him now except win a victory in his name. Let's talk to the governor."

One of the officers said, "Perhaps we should wait and assess the damage from the storm before venturing outside the harbor."

Another asked, "Can we be sure the storm is really over?"

Renau put on his hat. "The storm is indeed over for us, but not for the English, if we have the courage to fight them. You may all do as you please, but I'm going to Government House and speak to the governor."

At Government House Renau found several senior officers gathered around the governor and General Du Bois De la Motte, who turned to him and asked, "How is the little frigate *Pélerine*?"

"*Pélerine* survived the hurricane well, Sir, with two anchors out and her topmasts down," Renau replied. "But now her topmasts are up and she's ready to sail. We are ready to seek out and destroy the British fleet."

De la Motte's eyes widened and his mouth opened. Presently, his face softened and he said, "Perhaps you don't know, Captain, but we have had several ships badly damaged, and *Le Tonnant* is driven hopelessly upon the rocks."

"I have just come from that ship," replied Captain Renau. "She's now off the rocks and floating at anchor, although leaking badly. She's not ready to sail but we have others which are. We now have many more ships, in better condition, than the English, I'll wager. If any of ours are damaged, theirs will be many times more so. It's time to go out and do battle. God has given us a victory."

With sad eyes De la Motte looked Renau. "My orders are to defend Louisbourg and protect our fleet, not seek a battle with the English fleet."

Renau answered, "We can best defend Louisbourg by destroying the English fleet, Sir. You can defend our fleet and hundreds of other defenseless ships by destroying this enemy fleet. Our time has come; let us seize the moment, General."

"I appreciate your fighting spirit, Captain Renau," replied General De la Motte, his patronizing smile fading to a grimace. "All of us applaud your bravery. But I must insure the defense of Louisbourg while preserving the fleet entrusted to me. I cannot accomplish my mission by rushing our fleet into a hurricane with enemy ships lurking nearby."

Madame Drucour had quietly approached the officers. She said, "Gentlemen, perhaps as a woman I shouldn't intrude upon your discussions of war. Women are not supposed to discuss such things, but we are allowed to discuss literature, and I would like to quote words from the English playwright, William Shakespeare. His words, written two hundred years ago, are most appropriate today. He wrote, *There is a tide in the affairs of men which taken at the flood leads onto fortune; Omitted, all the voyages of their life are bound in shallows and in miseries. On such a full sea are we now afloat, and we must take the current when it serves, or ever lose our ventures.*"[4] Madame Drucour looked at the men with fire in her eyes. "And so we are now on such a tide of fortune, Gentlemen. Seize the moment! Strike now!"

De la Motte replied, "Madame, I defer to your greater knowledge of literature, but it is war we discuss here, a much more serious matter. Our Captain Renau might be right in that the hurricane destroyed the English fleet. And if it has, that will be good news to all of us. But we do not know that nor do we know if the hurricane is over. For all we know this may be a lull in the storm. Its full fury may be just outside our harbor."

"General," argued Captain Renau, "those of us who have spent our lives at sea know winds revolve counterclockwise in a hurricane. Therefore, knowing what the winds have done, and with the winds now coming from the south, we know the hurricane has gone ashore and will now break up and disappear. The hurricane is over, done, past, forgotten!

"I'll eagerly take my frigate to sea. Let me sail out with *Pélerine* and see exactly what has happened to the English fleet. The English fleet will be in such a sorry state that my frigate alone can equal a battleship of the English. I'll sink any I find and come back and report to you the condition of the English. You can make your decision with the exact knowledge of the enemy's forces and sea conditions. Send a trusted observer with me, if you will."

The general's eyes narrowed. He slapped his gloves against his side. "Are my decisions being questioned by a merchant marine? No! I won't sacrifice a single frigate. You may risk your own life, but you shall not risk the lives of your crew nor a King's ship. If I intended to send the fleet out to meet the English, I would do so with every ship at my disposal, not a mere frigate. That, my young man, is the first rule of war.

"We considered sending out the fleet; we were discussing the question when you so rudely interrupted. But the storm has left our ships in very poor condition. They are unready to engage the English in battle and it is our judgment they remain in port. I have the concurrence of these distinguished officers in that decision." Waving his hand in the direction of his colleagues, De la Mott put his hands behind his back and paced slowly across the room, his head hanging with chin on his chest. "The king has entrusted me with a very great responsibility. This weighs heavily on my mind. In my orders he instructed that I take good care of his fleet. The life of the realm depends upon it." De la Mott stopped and looked at the men around the room. "As you all know, we have far too few ships for the needs of the Commonwealth. Our King has instructed me to husband our fleet most carefully. He does not expect me to go cruising about in a hurricane nor venture into unknown waters perhaps filled with English warships just waiting for such an opportunity.

"No, the fleet will remain safely anchored in Louisbourg Harbor. Here it can be used in the defense of this fortress. This is the King's most precious foothold in North America, and I'm willing to defend it with my life."

Throughout the next few weeks, men of Louisbourg worked feverishly, repairing their ships. After weeks of work, *Tonnant,* the last of the damaged ships, slipped away from the work barge. With coat collars turned up against the cold winds, her crew waited impatiently for orders. The cold weather brought fogs that grew more dense as winter approached. When lookouts on the hills above Louisbourg could no longer see the horizon, General the Count Du Bois De la Motte announced his intentions to return to France.

As departure time drew near, Madame Drucour gave a party for the departing officers. All officers and every civilian of note came to the party. As musicians from the fleet played, the guests arrived at Government House dressed in their finest clothing. The scene might have been Paris or Marseilles as the women in their beautiful gowns paid their respects at Government House.

Marie Gauthier entered on the arm of the handsome Captain Renau, turning the heads of several young officers standing in a group nearby. Her satin gown accented her thin waist. Marie felt the admiring glances of many men and the jealous glare of a number of younger women.

After dinner General Du Bois De la Motte proposed a toast, "To the brave people of Louisbourg. Your courage at this remote outpost of the Commonwealth is an example to us all. I regret to be leaving you; however, the war now rages in Europe. That is where we are now needed.

"I am removing every morsel of food from my ships, leaving only enough food for the sail home to France. All of my extra powder and shot I leave with you so that you may continue the fight against the English. You are well prepared for the winter ahead. Long live the King! Long live France," continued the General as the guests joined in the toast.

General Du Bois De la Motte continued, "Also at this time, I wish to recognize our newest battleship commander. A man much loved by the King and by all of us here. To command our battleship, *Hercules*, we have selected the Count, Captain Marcel De la Court, recently released as a prisoner by the English. His ship, *Chasseur*, was captured after a valiant fight against a mighty English fleet." The general held his hand in the direction of the young nobleman as everyone applauded.

Marcel De la Court stood, plumed hat in hand. He wore a powdered wig; his clothing was magnificent, and gold rings glistened on his hands. He waved and smiled. Suddenly offering a look of sadness, he said, "I'm honored to succeed the late Captain DuTeil, God rest his poor soul." The count whipped a lace handkerchief from his sleeve and dabbed at his eyes. His expression suddenly changed. "And I am much honored to serve under the great General Du Bois De la Motte." Everyone applauded.

A mischievous look appeared in the eye of the young Count as he continued, "And I am much honored to serve under the King... but perhaps not as honored to serve under the King as Madame Pompadour." De la Court burst out laughing in loud, high-pitched strings of laughter, clapping as he bowed. Women turned to look at each other in embarrassment, hiding their mouths with their hands or fans. Men guffawed. Scattered applause from the guests joined De la Court's. Bowing and waving, Marcel De la Court sat dangling his hat and plume.

The fleet sailed back to France, and the winter of 1757 proved to be terribly cruel to the citizens of Louisbourg. It was one of the worst winters ever. Firewood had become scarce as the forests were denuded in previous winters.

Armed guards used force to protect the rationed firewood inside the fortress. Coal had been shipped to Louisbourg due to the earlier scarcity of firewood but now that precious commodity could be found in the apartment of the governor but few others. Commoners huddled in one small room of their homes and cooked their food when the temperature fell so low as to force them to burn their precious ration of wood.

Marie had been freed from most of the household choirs, but she more and more assisted Agnes. The frail maid's cough had grown worse and her sallow skin barely concealed the bones beneath. Every step seemed a drudgery for Agnes.

In early December Madame Drucour called the physician to Agnes' bedside. Madame Drucour hovered near as the doctor laid his hand on Agnes' clammy brow. He felt her thready pulse and unbuttoned her nightgown to lay a bamboo tube on her bony chest. Putting his ear to the tube, he listened to her labored breathing. With sad eyes the man laid the tube aside and buttoned her nightgown again. Slowly, he stood and looked sadly into Madame Drucour's knowing eyes. Marie took Agnes' hand and pressed it to her cheek. Berthe added another log to take the chill off the room.

A week later a freezing wind cut Marie's cheek like the blade of a knife as she walked in the streets of Louisbourg. She pulled the folds of her hood over face, leaving only her nose and eyes exposed to the biting cold. The cold air burnt her lungs as she laboriously lifted one foot after the other, struggling in the deep snow to keep pace with Madame Drucour. The bag over her shoulder, light when she first lifted it, now pounded her back and upset her balance. Although the sky was clear and blue overhead, a brisk wind blew snow from the drifts, stinging their faces. Madame Drucour's scarlet cloak trailed over the snow as she leaned into the wind and pressed forward. "Hurry, Marie," she said, "we must get to the Dauphin Gate before a mob assembles. Our citizens are in a bad mood. I can't say what they might do."

Marie did not answer. She saved her already exhausted breath in trying to keep pace with the governor's wife. Walking close to the houses brought respite from the biting wind, but there the snow was deeper and walking was more difficult. Marie avoided the deep drifts and tried to step in Madame Drucour's tracks. In words that seemed to trail away in the wind she heard Madame Drucour say, "We are too late, Marie; a crowd has already gathered."

Marie tried desperately to quicken her pace. Peeking out through the folds of her hood, she saw people gathered around the gate. A soldier pushed an angry citizen backward with his rifle. Angry shouts came from the citizens as more people poured out of their houses to join the mob.

"Savages!"

"Beggars!"

"Get out of here. Go back into the forest where you belong!"

Madame Drucour reached the mob and pushed people aside. "Out of my way," she shouted. She took Marie's bag, thrusting it into the arms of a startled soldier. She said, "Follow me, young man."

Pushing and shoving, Madame Drucour forced her way through the crowd. With Marie bumping and jostling along behind, they reached the center of attention. There a motley, emaciated band of Indians, men, women, and children, cowered from the shouts and fists of the crowd. Hollow cheeks and sunken eyes told of their starved condition. Soldiers tried desperately to protect them from the blows of the people. "Go back to the forest," someone shouted.

"We work for our food, as little as it is," yelled another.

"We don't have enough food for ourselves, and we don't intend to share it with savages!"

Madame Drucour threw her hands up, yelling, "Silence! These people are our friends and wards of the Crown. Our King will provide for them just as he does for you. Now go back to your homes! Go back I say, in the name of the King! I so order you!"

A vicious looking woman standing nearby began to utter a rebuttal when Madame Drucour drew herself to her full height and stepped in front of the woman. Silently, she stood with her face a few inches away. The woman's courage melted. She stepped backward and hastily retreated to her home, uttering unintelligible words under her breath.

Madame Drucour took the bag from the soldier, opened it and passed out the hard loaves of bread to the Indians. Eagerly, they snatched the bread from her hands. The Indians gnawed savagely at the hard bread while Indian children fought for crumbs.

That night, Berthe called Marie to Agnes' room. The first thing Marie noticed was Agnes' rattling breathing. Her eyes were wide and her gasps prolonged. Marie sat down beside her and took her hand which felt so cool and lifeless. Agnes turned her head to look at Marie and seemed to be trying to speak but no words came. Marie squeezed her hand and held it close to her breast. She bowed her head and whispered a prayer. Later, Madame Drucour arrived with Father Falchion who administered last rites. Shortly before daylight, Agnes' suffering ended with a gasp and long exhalation. Marie closed her eyes and drew the sheet over her head. Berthe began to cry and moan loudly as Marie stood and put her arm around Berthe's big shoulders.

The next afternoon Father Falchion conducted a burial service for Agnes, and her body was placed outside in a log enclosure with the many other bodies of those who had died that winter. The ground was frozen too hard for digging. The bodies would be buried in spring or committed to the deep.

Weeks later, during a clear, cold night, Marie Gauthier walked alone on the dark ramparts of Fortress Louisbourg. Overhead, millions of stars twinkled in the clear, black sky. She took her hands from her muffler and ran her fingers across the cold, rough stones as she looked out across the stormy ocean. In a wide avenue of gold pulsations, the sea reflected moonlight. Marie pulled the folds of her cloak tighter around her neck and thrust her hand back in the muffler. The cold wind moaned in the ramparts as Marie stood looking at the dark, pulsating ocean.

"There are no supply ships coming for Louisbourg, *Mademoiselle* Gauthier." Startled and surprised to hear her name, Marie turned quickly to see a soldier behind her. The young man wore a scarf over his hat and tied beneath his chin. With several layers of clothing he seemed large. His long, dark cape covered his hands, with only the butt of his rifle and point of the bayonet glistening in the moonlight. "I've been watching all evening. Do you think they will bring food?"

Marie caught her breath but her heart still raced. "Governor Drucour says food will be sent. I believe him."

The soldier wiped his nose on the back of his sleeve. "I hope so; we're near starvation in our barracks. All we have to eat is codfish and not much of that."

"Food will come. Soon you will see our ships and there will be feasting for everyone. If the ships do not come, the governor will open the emergency storehouse. The governor says there will be no starvation," Marie replied. She smiled at the soldier and hoped she looked confident of her reply. She walked on along the ramparts, thinking, *My father is somewhere across that dark ocean. Perhaps he's ill, waiting for his only daughter, his only loved one in the world. I hope he knows I'm alive. Perhaps he needs me more than anyone in Louisbourg; I wish I knew.* She walked along the ramparts with snow squeaking and crunching under her feet.

A dark shape loomed in front of Marie. Startled, she stopped abruptly, colliding with the soldier on the narrow walkway. The young man reached out to support her as she reeled backwards from the collision. When he spoke, his voice sounded as lonely as the moaning of the wind. "Good evening, *Mademoiselle* Gauthier."

With her heart again racing, Marie asked, "You, too, know my name?" The young man stood silently on the rampart in the darkness, his dark cape blending with the night, only his pale face and white trousers illuminated by the moonlight. His long rifle clicked against the fortress stones as he turned. Marie balanced unsteadily on the icy stones. The young soldier moved to protect Marie from falling off the rampart.

"Yes, *Mademoiselle*, of course. Every soldier in Louisbourg knows your name." He spoke proudly, with emphasis on your. "We see you often inspecting the defenses with Madame Drucour. If we are lucky enough to have you inspect our regiment, we all try to see you. If you speak to one of us, we often boast of this to our comrades."

Marie, standing very close to the young man, stepped back, again momentarily losing her balance. The young man reached out quickly, taking her arm. Marie clutched his hand as she looked down into the dark chasm below.

She regained her balance and the soldier removed his hand. He smiled again, saying, "I will be the most envied man in my barracks when I tell my comrades I have spoken with you. I will not tell them you touched my hand; they would only think I lied."

Marie's eyes softened. "I had no idea I was so popular as you say. Surely, you are making a joke of me."

The young man grew serious. "Oh, no," he said in an urgent voice, "I do not jest. When you walk past with the governor's lady, your eyes meet our's. To you we are real people. You are not like the other ladies of Louisbourg. They behave as if they cannot see us. We are beneath them. No, *Mademoiselle*, when the English come, we will fight, not for those women, but for you, *Mademoiselle* Gauthier, and your kind of women. We fight for our kind of women. We know the fleet sailed home for France without us. Soldiers know supplies are running out, and there will be starvation before the English attack. Perhaps we are left here to die. But we are not afraid, *Mademoiselle*. We show no fear because you show no fear. We know you can sail away anytime you please, but you choose to stay with us. How could any man lack courage when he sees yours? *Mademoiselle* Gauthier, my comrades and I are willing to die for you. No vile Englishman shall lay a hand on you."

Marie reached out. She took his cold, rough hand in hers and pressed it against her cheek. The young man felt her wet tears as she kissed his hand. Wordlessly, Marie hurried across the rampart, her long cloak flowing behind her. Quickly, she hurried down the steps, wiping tears from her eyes. Marie disappeared into the dark shadows below the wall.

On this cold day, Marie Gauthier found she must almost run to keep up with Madame Drucour. With her hands buried in a fur muff in front of her, the lady walked swiftly toward Government House. Her long, black cape trailed in the snow while her rapid breathing made a contrail of fog in the freezing air. Madame Drucour muttered to herself as they walked. This was truly the most angry Marie had ever seen the wife of the governor. The cold air burned Marie's lungs as she struggled to keep up; the hood of her cape fell from her head as she half ran, half walked. Hesitantly, she took one thin hand from the fur muff in front of her to pull the hood back over her head. A startled soldier stepped out of the snow path to allow Madame Drucour and Marie to pass. Madame Drucour did not look at the soldier. She continued with head down while Marie smiled as she passed. Madame Drucour threw open the door of Government House, marching straight to the office of the governor. Without acknowledging the greeting of the elderly servant at the door, Madame Drucour marched inside her husband's office. Marie followed, stopping just inside the door. Governor Drucour rose from his desk with a look of concern as he saw Madame Drucour's anger.

"This is enough," Madame Drucour said loudly. "Marie and I have just come from the hospital. Sick children there cry for food. Even doctors and nurses are hungry. Soldiers are starving. Several poor people are said to have died of starvation. No family in Louisbourg has a sack of flour. Everyone is hungry yet we have two year's supply of food in the storehouse. It is nonsense! Your storekeeper should open the storehouse. What's the use of keeping food after everyone has starved to death?"

Governor Drucour hung his head briefly and looked up with compassion in his eye. He walked around to Madame Drucour and placed his arm around her shoulder, leading her over to the fireplace where a fire cracked in the logs. "Marie, come here and warm yourself," he called.

The governor placed the two women in front of the fireplace, then stood in front of them. He rubbed his hands together and looked at the women with a furrowed brow. "Heavy hangs the head that wears a crown," he said. "This is not a good time to be governor of Louisbourg, just as it is not a good time to be a soldier or citizen here. But fate has dealt us our hand, and we must play it out as best we know how. We are at war," the governor continued, "and war is not kind. It is the life we officials have chosen, but the civilians of Louisbourg are different. My heart aches for them… for you, my dear, and you, Marie."

The governor looked at the women with sadness in his eyes. "I wish to God I could spare you from the suffering."

Madame Drucour looked at her husband in astonishment. "Don't tell me the storehouse of food was a lie." She watched the governor closely. His silence spoke loudly in the room as only the fire hissed and crackled. "It was a lie, wasn't it? Your storekeeper refuses anyone entry into the storehouse because it is empty. There is no food!"

Governor Drucour turned slowly away, saying, "General De la Motte promised to send more supply ships."

"But, how?" Madame Drucour asked. "The ships cannot reach us. The sea is frozen for miles around. You have said yourself ships would be crushed in the ice."

Governor Drucour lifted his hands. "They must try. I know they will try."

Madame Drucour's eyes narrowed. "Why did you not send the civilians back to France with De la Motte?"

"The crown has ordered our colony of Louisbourg not be abandoned," replied Governor Drucour.

"The crown! The crown," cried Madame Drucour. "What is the crown? A King who agrees with the last person to seek his ear? And the last to seek his ear is usually that whore, Pompadour." Madame Drucour turned her head to hide the tears in her eyes. Governor Drucour stood silently looking out the frosted window, his hands clasped behind his back. With furrowed brow and ashen face he turned to look at Madame Drucour. On a fine linen handkerchief Madame Drucour wiped her eyes and blew her nose. When she lifted her head, a smile crossed her face. Her red, swollen eyes glistened and sparkled. "Death is always certain... but it is equally certain that I am not dead yet! I am a Courserac. Until they throw the dirt in my face they shall know that a Courserac is still alive and fighting for our motherland. As long as I have a morsel of energy, my face will be seen and my voice heard. Louisbourg's citizens will know they are not alone in their suffering, for everywhere they look I will be there. I can neither shoot Englishmen nor sink their ships, but I can still be their bitter adversary." She walked across the room to embrace her husband and then stood holding his hands. "You did what you must to serve the Crown and I will support you. Let us go out and show the people that our stomachs are as flat as theirs."

In that terrible winters, snow blanketed Louisbourg throughout the spring. On May 12, 1758, eighteen inches of snow remained on the ground and not a family had an ounce of flour remaining.

Chapter Twenty-Six

On May 19, 1758, British headquarters hummed with activity as they prepared to invade Louisbourg. Hundreds of British ships lay off Louisbourg. Captain Walshingham stood aboard *Grenadier*, patting his abdomen and rocking on his heels. Lieutenant MacGregor directed the frigate into Gabarus Bay. On the spar deck, men stood by their guns. Sand covered the deck to absorb blood. Cannons stood shotted and ready. Deep in the bay now, the ship sailed leisurely across the placid waters. MacGregor lifted his telescope to watch French gunners on shore, leveling their cannon. He lowered his telescope and saw the flash. Smoke blossomed from the gun before the explosion reached his ears. A geyser of water rose a cable distance off the bow.

"Tack closer to the point of that explosion," ordered Walshingham. The helmsman spun the wheel. Cannons fired at the ship from both opposing points of land. Other cannons joined them from trenches in the center of the bay. *Grenadier* sailed slowly through the bay, closer to the geysers of water rising from the French shells until droplets fell on deck. Walshingham ordered a reverse in course. When water from the enemy balls no longer splashed on the ship, Captain Walshingham ordered, "Wear ship and ready the anchor." He measured the distance, the frigate sailing well out of range of the enemy guns. "Hand the sails! Let go the anchor," he yelled. Chain rumbled through the hawse pipe and the big anchor splashed in the bay while cannons thundered on shore. *Grenadier* lay at anchor, peacefully outside the range of French guns.

Walshingham rocked back on his heels, holding the lapels of his coat with his hands, saying, "Mr. Sethford, get Mr. MacGregor a lead line. We must chart depths in this bay." He turned to the boatswain. "Pick twelve men, Bosun! Put a boat over the side." As MacGregor stood at the waist with a lead line in his hand, Walshingham looked at him with a wicked smile on his face. He said, "Ye will chart to a depth of eight fathoms. Ye must chart the depths from point to point around the bay, all under fire of the enemy gunners."

MacGregor stood looking at his boat crew, whose unlucky names were called by the boatswain. They were all landsmen whom the boatswain considered of little use or someone who had incurred the boatswain's wrath for reasons unknown. A few looked angry but most looked helpless with nervous, shifting eyes. His chin set grimly, he hefted the lead line and climbed over the bulwark. Carefully, he let himself down the rope ladder and took his place in the boat as it filled with a crew of wide-eyed, tense sailors. "Let go the boat," he ordered, and repeated the order when a sailor, his hand trembling, hesitated to turn loose the rope. When he continued to hold the rope, the coxson tossed it into the boat from above. It slapped the water hard, almost throwing the occupants into the ocean as the lines ran free. With effort MacGregor righted the boat and fished a lost oar from the water. He handed it to a nearby sailor and ordered, "We have work to do, men. Let us be quick about it and we can return more quickly to safety. A fast boat is harder to hit, so let us not stay in any spot long enough for them to find our range. If any man falters at the oars, I will toss him overboard as he endangers everyone here. If I fall, the closest man will take the lead line, except the yeomen. They will continue to write the depths and positions on their slates."

MacGregor pushed the boat away from *Grenadier* and ordered his men to row toward shore, toward the French cannons. Reluctantly the men took up their oars but remained motionlessly sitting in the boat. MacGregor said, "Let's get this job done, men. The longer you sit here the better targets we make for the French!"

Reluctantly, the men took up the oars, pulling toward shore. The French cannons renewed their chorus as they neared their range. Cannon balls splashed geysers high above them as water fell in cascades on men and boat. "Keep the boat moving, men," shouted MacGregor over the din. "If you stop, we're dead! Yeomen, keep your slates covered under the oilcloth."

With renewed vigor the sailors rowed around the bay while cannons volleyed and thundered around them. An air burst rained hot metal on them from above; the hot metal was quickly quenched by cascading salt water from other falling cannon balls. A sailor jumped erect in the boat, looking down at a widening circle of blood on his shirt, and screaming. The man continued to scream as he fell overboard where the water muffled his cries. "There is no time to stop for rescue... for anyone. Keep this boat moving!" With the struggling man left behind, MacGregor dropped the lead line into the water. Stretching the line tight, he called out depths to a man sitting nearby who wrote the depths with a shaky hand. Another air burst sent a piece of hot shrapnel into the skull of another sailor, killing him instantly. The man's eyes widened, his mouth opened, and blood ran down his face before he toppled over the side with a splash. The sailor floated face down in the water, motionlessly, as his shipmates rowed away, looking anxiously over their shoulders.

MacGregor struggled to put the incident out of his mind, continuing to chart the depths of the bay. They repeated the process of dropping the lead weight and writing the numbers as they rowed around the bay with cannon balls falling around them. Slowly, in spite of all odds, MacGregor and his anxious crew circled the bay, recording depths. Enthusiastically, they rowed out of the hell and returned to their ship. The wet, shaky, ashen-faced survivors crawled silently out of the boat. They went aboard without a word where MacGregor handed the slates to Mister Sethford. Walshingham looked at MacGregor, saying, "Ye must have a lucky star, MacGregor, but it will not last forever." MacGregor turned and silently walked to his cabin. Later in the afternoon, after an artist sketched the shoreline, *Grenadier* weighed anchor and sailed away from Gabarus Bay to make their report to the commodore.

* * *

The day before had been sunny with the promise of spring. But now on May 24th a cold north wind blew over the ocean in the predawn darkness. As MacGregor left his warm cabin to answer a summons from Midshipman Thomas, he noted snow flurries. Turning up his collar against the howling wind, he heard Mr. Thomas say, "Sir, the lookouts think they saw sails to windward through a break in the weather."

Buttoning his cloak MacGregor asked, "How many sails did they see?"

Thomas turned his back to the wind and tilted his head to one side in an attempt to keep the cold from his body. "They could not be sure. Several, they think. I tacked in the direction they seemed to be traveling, and now I'm closing to windward as best I can. Waves are getting higher; I think we are approaching shallow water."

MacGregor asked, leaning over the bulwark, looking down into the inky water, "Have you a leads man in the chains?"

"Aye, Sir," replied Thomas. "I have two men in the chains and doubled the lookouts. Should I beat to quarters?"

MacGregor looked aloft where snowflakes blew between the masts. He walked to the windward bulwark, resting his bare red hands on the freezing oak. MacGregor lifted a telescope, looking across a dark, empty, snow swept ocean. Lowering his telescope he stood with the cold stinging his face. Snowflakes caked his eyelashes. He wiped his eyes on the back of his hand and strained to see into the gray-black void. "No, let the men sleep, Mr. Thomas. It will be daylight soon. Then we will know if an enemy is nearby. If there's fighting to be done, better the men be fresh and rested."

The two officers strained their eyes into the dark void and listened for calls from the lookouts. MacGregor stamped his feet to drive out the cold and blew on his numb fingers. Tears obscured his vision as the cold wind blew in his face. He thought of the lookouts in the masttop. How much colder must it be aloft? MacGregor thought of the sailors hanging in the chains just above the ocean waves, swinging a lead line with frozen fingers.

"Three fathoms on the line," shouted a sailor on deck, relaying the message from a sailor in the chains.

"Ready about," ordered MacGregor. "We'll not run aground chasing the enemy into Louisbourg." He gripped the ice encrusted bulwark and stood looking into the grey-black void, his cloak blowing in the wind. "Send a message to Captain Walshingham. Tell him we observed unknown ships, thought to be French, chasing them into Louisbourg, and we are turning back in shoal water. We will hove to in a safe depth of ten fathoms."

Later that same day at Louisbourg, cannons boomed. Awakening to happy voices in the street below, Marie hurriedly dressed and went outside. Throwing her cloak over her shoulders as she ran, Marie felt joy and excitement. Other people ran through the streets, too, yelling, "Ships! Our ships are here."

She ran to the wharf where a throng of excited citizens gathered. "It's the fleet! Our supplies have come! Food! Now we will have food; there will be no more hunger," they shouted.

Marie watched as one by one the ships tacked into Louisbourg Harbor. Pulling up her hood against the cold wind, Marie watched them hand their sails. The big ships dropped their anchors and began unloading supplies into lighters plying between the ships and shore. *Our Navy again foiled the English fleet, slipping our ships through the blockade, undetected.* There are six warships in total. There are three armed, while four are *en flûte*, carrying supplies. Marie whispered a thankful prayer as she looked at the food being unloaded. She also watched for a familiar face among the officers arriving. With disappointment she turned away. Lifting her cloak around her cold, ruddy face, she walked back toward town when she heard her name called. "Marie! Marie!"

She turned to see Captain Renau hurrying toward her. Joy surged through her as she ran toward him. Marie threw her arms around him and kissed him on the cheek. *Why am I so happy to see this man? Am I falling in love with him?*

"Marie! Thank God you are well," he said. "I worried about you all winter."

He held her away from him with a hand on either shoulder, saying, "Let me look at you. You are even more beautiful than I remembered. A little thin perhaps, but the food we bring will ease your hunger."

Marie wiped tears of joy from her eyes. Laughing, she threw her arms around him again. Holding herself close against him, Marie laughed through her tears. *I must not let myself fall in love with this man. I don't know if he is married or loves another woman. What of Charles MacGregor? Will I ever see him again? He is the enemy of my people, and must he now be my enemy too?*

Later, at Government House, Henri Valentin Jacques D'Anthonay took his plan of defense to Governor Drucour. "Sir, I propose we not wait within these walls for the English. If they establish a toe hold on Isle Royale, they will invest this fortress. The English fleet will blockade as they did in 1745, and I fear our cause will be lost. We must prevent their establishing a beachhead, Sir." He spread his map before the Governor. "We must establish a defense on all the high ground overlooking any feasible landing site for the British." Pointing to the map, D'Anthonay said, "We need guns brought round and set up at the points I have marked on the map. We need flanking infantry who can protect the guns and defend the positions with musket and bayonet. I have inspected the area and marked on the map every defensible point I can find."

The governor was pleased. "We will need all these defenses. Indians report a large English fleet gathering at Halifax. They will invade soon. I pray our supplies arrive before the English."

Work on the trenches at Gabarus Bay now moved forward. Governor Drucour visited the site often. D'Anthonay unrolled a map of the bay. "Here," he said, pointing to White Point, "we will place a large cannon. And here, another, on this point. The English landing in this bay will find themselves in a crossfire."

Captain Renau, at Gabarus Bay with several Basque fishermen, pulled a heavy nine pound cannon. Behind them a dozen sailors dragged heavy swivel guns. They dragged, pushed, pulled, and carried their heavy guns across the rocky, marshy, wooded ground. Arriving where the land falls off toward Gabarus Bay, Captain Renau conferred with D'Anthonay regarding the defense. "Where," asked Renau, "do you expect the English attack?"

The officer withdrew a map from a leather case, spread it out upon the ground as the men held the corners down with their feet, and pointed. "Here," he said. "In 1745 they landed here in Gabarus Bay, between Flat Point and

White Point. There is not such a good beach for miles. And we have shown them very little defense here."

Renau studied the map a few moments. "Yes, I think you are right that this is a good beach. But if I were English, I would seek the sheltered waters here, at Coromandiére Cove," he said pointing at the map. "Let's take swivel guns from our ship and put three in this area. The nine pounder brought by the Basque fishermen, let us set here," he pointed. "The other swivel guns we will put here, here, and here," added Renau, pointing to the map. A group of Acadians joined the French sailors at Gabarus Bay and soon the forest rang with the sound of their axes. They cut poles for the swivel guns and cleared the field of fire.

Henri Ouilette watched as Captain Renau stood behind the gun and swung it from side to side, aiming down the barrel. "This is perfect. We can cover the most likely landing area with a murderous field of fire." Henri Ouilette picked up his rifle and walked over to Captain Renau.

He humbly removed the toque from his head. "Sir, pardon me, but I would make a suggestion, eh? I have fought the English before."

Renau looked up at Henri quickly. "Of course," he answered. "We need all the help we can get, my friend."

Henri answered, "The English can't see us setting up our cannons in the fog. They must not know of their existence. We can cut nice green boughs from the spruce trees to hide them. Acadians will work every night and keep the boughs always green and pretty, eh? When the English come close enough to count the buttons on their coats, we can throw aside the spruce boughs and surprise the English with gunfire. They will fall like flax to the scythe."

Renau smiled. "An excellent idea."

"I do not agree," interjected D'Anthonay. "That is not an honorable way to fight a war."

Captain Renau clamped his hand on Henri's shoulder. "Be about your work, and take as many sailors as you like to help; let us have a nice surprise waiting for the Englishmen when they arrive. We are not knights jousting for the hand of a lady; we are fighting for our survival against a cunning and ruthless enemy."

The next day Captain Renau appeared at the city gate leading a contingent of sailors who dragged a twenty-four pound cannon. All day they labored, and far into the night, until at last the gun stood near Gabarus Point. Here, Colonel St. Julhien commanded four six-pounders in addition to the twenty-four.

Early the next morning, when the twilight revealed the black silhouettes of frigates sleeping quietly on the water, Renau said, "This big cannon we need not hide. We will let the English taste its metal. That will keep them far enough from the land that we can see them when they come."

Renau's cannon exploded across the bay. French shells exploded among the English warships. Startled English seamen quickly realized the French had moved big guns to Gabarus Bay, guns capable of reaching their ships.

Chapter Twenty-Seven

In late May *Grenadier* sailed into Halifax. There, amid a vast flotilla, she took aboard supplies and thousands of soldiers. Scottish Highlanders, clad in black kilts, wearing red jackets and carrying bayoneted rifles, climbed aboard MacGregor's frigate. Under the command of Lieutenant Hopkins, a young English officer, a contingent of Highlanders filled every vacant space aboard the frigate *Grenadier*. Men were even housed in temporary shelters built on deck. On June 1, 1758, they reached Louisbourg. Hundreds of ships from Halifax met Admiral Boscawen's armada from England in Gabarus Bay. The mighty armada filled the ocean as far as the eye could see. One hundred and twenty-seven troop transports escorted by more than thirty big ships-of-the-line and countless smaller ships and tenders spread across Gabarus Bay. Methodically, the big ships dropped anchor in their assigned places while frigates continued to orbit the fleet, ready to fire at any target on shore.

As *Grenadier* threaded through the fleet, MacGregor took another telescope from the rack and handed it to Lieutenant Hopkins standing beside him. He pointed out landmarks on shore and told the soldier of his survey of the bay. Making a long circuit seaward before returning to sweep again around Gabarus Bay, *Grenadier* fired at French batteries on White and Flat Points. Twelve times that afternoon *Grenadier* weaved and ducked through transports and battleships, firing broadsides at shore. Later, they anchored a little more than a mile offshore, just out of range of the French twenty-four pounders. Other frigates anchored in a long arc out of range of the French guns, their bowsprits pointed westward by the gentle westerly breeze. Just beyond the frigates, battleships dropped their anchors in a second line of defense some two miles farther out from the head of the bay. Inside this protective arc, troop transports anchored. In open sea, beyond the ships anchored in Gabarus Bay, a protective screen of frigates and second raters patrolled a dark blue ocean, guarding England's invasion fleet, their tall mountains of canvas stacked against the light blue sky. Slowly, as the day wore on, the white canvas turned golden, and the sun sank below a band of western clouds. With nightfall, gentle westerly winds breathed more softly. Later the winds died completely; Gabarus Bay was dead calm. Stillness hung over the dark ocean, making even whispered voices seem like shouts across the water. Every bump and rattle echoed across the bay, and there were thousands of bumps and rattles. Long after most officers had retired for the night, Lieutenant MacGregor lay in bed, looking at the low ceiling. *Is Marie in Louisbourg? Will De la Court have given her my message? Maybe he did not tell her the message was from me, if he told her all, whatever.* MacGregor felt a wave lift the stern of the ship and wash toward the bow. He felt the ship turning and now the bow raised to the waves before the stern. Dressing in the darkness, he walked on deck and sniffed the air. The bow now faced out to sea. Walshingham paced the quarterdeck, his hands folded behind his back, a scowl on his face. The captain shifted his glare from the clouds now obscuring the stars to the nearness of hostile land to the west. When a heavy, damp, easterly breeze lifted the ensign, he grew more agitated. He ordered, "Top men aloft! Coxson and landmen to the boats!" Pipes twittered and midshipmen yelled on the gundeck. Men poured from their hammocks, some without shirts and others with bare buttocks. Walshingham yelled, "Away the long boat. Row the bower anchor seaward; run out every foot of cable. Aloft, top men, and lower the top yards!" Slowly at first, and then quickly to the prods of rattans, sailors hurried up the ratlines. In the quiet dark night, with only gentle gusts of wind cooling their nakedness, men labored to loosen the heavy yards and lower them to the deck. Struggling in the darkness, sweat forming in spite of the breeze, some men cursed their officers. At two in the morning with now a stiff breeze out of the east turning bare flesh blue, Walshingham dismissed the off-watch crew. Shivering men hurried below to crawl between warm blankets. All the ships in the bay had now moved on their anchors, closer to the hostile shore. With the easterly wind came a heavy fog. Within the fog it was impossible to sail out of the crowded anchorage lest they collide with other ships. Walshingham ordered, "Quickly, Coxsun on deck and row another anchor upwind to the length of its cable. Bosun, get the men in the ratlines! Be ready to hand the sails, if needed." The bosun's whistle sounded sharp and long over the deck, followed again by shouts of men and pounding of feet. Again sailors labored to row the heavy anchor and cable into the now breaking waves. The heavy anchor threatened to sink the boat, pulling the back of the boat so low that waves lapped over the gunnels. Desperately, the sailors pulled at the oars, inching slowly against the now freshening wind. Behind them the long anchor cable stretched from their ship. In deeper water they cut the rope, dropping the anchor to the bottom of the bay. Exhausted men returned to their ship where they took positions at the big windlass. Slowly the men pushed the windlass, tightening the cable until their new anchor sank its flukes into the muddy bottom. The cable pulled tautly. As the wind howled, the grunting, groaning men kedged the ship farther into deeper water. Throughout the night, ship's officers stood anxiously as Captain Walshingham paced the deck. By sunrise a gale flapped *Grenadier*'s ensign loudly, tearing it into shreds. The ship lay helpless in the wind, barely visible through the fog. *Grenadier* strained and lurched at her anchors. A crash and splintering of wood from out of the fog told the officers that a nearby ship had dragged her anchor and crashed into another ship across the bay.

Meanwhile, at Louisbourg, Captain Renau trotted over the cobblestones toward Government House. He pounded at the door until a servant opened. The gale immediately caught the door, throwing it wide open, and the startled servant staggered backward. Renau stepped past the servant to walk briskly toward Governor Drucour's office as the servant closed the door against the wind. A surprised Governor Drucour opened the door of his office, rushing out to investigate the noise as a shower of papers fluttered off his desk and around the room. General Des Gouttes followed, looking angrily at Captain Renau.

Renau spoke, "General, so I have found you. I was told you were here at Government House. The English fleet anchored in Gabarus Bay will be desperately hanging on their anchors in this gale. If we hurry, General, we can take our fleet out unseen in the fog and sail into the English troop transports. We can destroy their invasion fleet at will."

General Des Gouttes replied dourly, "I was just explaining to the governor how difficult it is to protect the fleet in this harbor, Captain Renau. We can use the fog to sail out of Louisbourg and return to France."

Tartly Renau replied, "We would better use our fleet to destroy the English invasion fleet! There is little good it can do Louisbourg at Brest."

The general ignored Renau's remarks to ask, "And just how will we avoid collisions in this fog? And how do you propose to withdraw our fleet to safety after you have destroyed the English transports? How will you avoid running aground with our own ships?"

Captain Renau looked incredulously at the general and then at the governor. "General, we have an opportunity for a French victory that will delay the English invasion by a year at least. If we lose every one of our ships, we can take ten English ships down with every one of ours and force the enemy to abandon their plans. Failing that, the English will continue victoriously with their invasion and destroy our fleet here in the harbor."

Des Gouttes shrugged his shoulders as he spoke. "I will not have the fleet destroyed; that is why I recommend we return to France. My orders from the King are to husband our fleet as France is desperately short of ships."

Captain Renau returned, "I hope your orders also direct you to wage war against the British."

"That is exactly what I intend to do, Captain, at a time and place of my own choosing, when it is most advantageous to France. But I do not intend to risk my fleet blindly thrashing about in the fog where they may be driven up on the rocks in the gale or trapped by the English."

Renau looked patiently at Des Gouttes. "General, it is the English who are trapped. They are trapped in Gabarus Bay in fog with a gale blowing them onto the rocks. We who know these waters better than anyone will have the wind and fog to our advantage. The fog conceals our movement yet we know exactly where the English are; they can't move. We can sink fifty of their ships before they know we are in their midst."

General Des Gouttes rolled his eyes upward and spread his arms as in an appeal to heaven. "Lord grant me such a simple viewpoint. But, no, I must consider all aspects of this decision. I must consider the safe keeping of the King's ships and the welfare of the men who sail them. I cannot protect Louisbourg with this fleet if I throw it carelessly against the first Englishmen who appear before us. No, I will not be so foolhardy as to send my handful of ships against an English fleet of hundreds."

"General," replied Captain Renau, "most English ships are unarmed transports. It is those unarmed transports I propose to attack, while their escort ships are busy trying to avoid being blown upon the rocks. But, if you will not send the fleet to fight the English, then at least allow me to take my frigate against them. I will sink a dozen troop transports and drown a thousand enemy soldiers. We can save the lives of thousands of our own."

General Des Gouttes gestured with his palms upward as he turned toward the Governor, saying, "Captain Renau, your courage is admirable, but your wisdom is lacking. I do not have so many frigates that I would sacrifice one to sail into an English fleet of hundreds. Please excuse me now while I resume my discussion with the Governor." General Des Gouttes slowly walked alone into the Governor's office as Captain Renau watched incredulously. Governor Drucour stood for a moment with his head bowed before following the General. Upon reaching the office Governor Drucour turned and quietly closed the door, stopping briefly to look up at Captain Renau without speaking.

Chapter Twenty-Eight

Later that morning, with the fog still hanging over the surface of the sea, Captain Walshingham stood on the quarterdeck. A boat rowed out of the fog and came alongside the ship. A young lieutenant stood in the stern sheets, shouting, "Commodore's orders, Sir: All captains repair to the flagship at once."

Captain Walshingham replied, "My compliments to the commodore, Mister, and convey that Captain Walshingham will repair to the flagship as soon as I have had my breakfast."

Eventually Walshingham did arrive at the flagship, late as usual. The commodore spoke before an assembly of post captains and naval staff. To the consternation of the commodore, Walshingham walked in, smiling and nodding greetings to other captains, oblivious to his commodore's speech.

At this point the commodore was saying they would land some 13,000 soldiers in the invasion, and they could be supported by over 14,000 sailors aboard British ships. He went on to say that the Navy must send experienced officers ashore with the soldiers to insure they found the correct landing sites. Walshingham interjected, "An excellent idea, Sir. I suggest my Lieutenant MacGregor lead the invasion. He has sounded and mapped the most promising landing area on Cape Breton, and that is Gabarus Bay. My man charted and mapped those waters. Not only does he know the bay better than any other, he is a Highlander and everyone knows of their courage and fighting skill. I will send signal flags with him, and he can even direct naval gunfire on the beach. He will be invaluable to yer plans and ye would be remiss in not utilizing him."

So, Captain Walshingham's persuasive recommendation resulted in Lieutenant MacGregor's selection to go ashore in the invasion. Not only that, but he was selected to join those special forces under General Wolfe to spearhead the attack. MacGregor reported to the commodore and soon found himself with those being prepared. With the invasion scheduled for early July, he imparted his knowledge of Gabarus Bay and learned General Amherst's plans for the invasion. Every officer must know every facet that could be known about enemy locations and anticipated strengths. Their intelligence indicated there were just over 3000 French soldiers, irregulars, and Indians opposing their invasion. The enemy would have the advantage of terrain, erection of barricades and perhaps fortifications. The French force could draw on an additional 5000 men if they used every sailor of their navy. Most of the area around Gabarus Bay is rocky. Landing boats will be difficult, even in good weather. Likely landing areas will be heavily defended. The land rises away from the beach, offering the enemy splendid high ground covered in trees and scrub, good ground for defense and a good view of British boats. Every officer must know exactly where he is to lead his men.

There were days of planning, learning, and training. Then it was into the boats and train the soldiers that must fight their way to the beaches. After weeks of training MacGregor and his compatriots were ready to go ashore. Supplies were issued, knives sharpened, and nerves honed to a fine, sharp edge. Men sat anxiously awaiting the order to go ashore. Church services were popular. They knew that many would die on those beaches when French cannons began to fire.

On the night of July fifth, 1758, the British invasion force lay in the darkness off Louisbourg, a fleet of black silhouettes. General Amherst's signal blinked from a flashing lantern across the darkness of the ocean. Other lanterns relayed the code from ship to darkened ship. "Proceed with the invasion!"

At three in the morning of the sixth of July, Lieutenant Charles MacGregor quickly dressed as planned and strapped on his claymore. He assembled with the frigate's marines and their passengers, the Scots Highlanders. Landing boats were soon in the water and rowing to the assembly point, just as they had rehearsed. MacGregor felt some comfort at the fog blowing in off the ocean. *Hopefully, the fog will conceal us from French cannons as we approach the beach.* MacGregor knew how dangerous cannons can be when loaded with grape shot.

Now the little boats tossed in the heavy swell rolling in from the Atlantic Ocean. The stiff breeze buffeted the boats, waves splashed over the gunnels, and water sloshed in the bottoms. Many men were sick. Before any boats actually reached the beach, rain began to pepper down. Men in the open boats shivered and sought vainly to keep their powder dry. They would be lucky if a single rifle would fire. Scouts sent ahead of the invasion force reported that the surf was so high, they might be unable to land. So it was back to the ships with the wet men to wait once more.

The next day a gale blew in off the ocean so there would be no invasion on this day. Action was postponed until tomorrow. There would be another day of waiting and anxiety for men who must storm the beaches. Long before daylight the word went out; Lieutenant MacGregor again responded to a knock on his door. A voice called, "Begin yer' pardon, Sir, but its six bells of the watch, Sir."

MacGregor sat up on his bunk and peered through the small porthole above him. There was only darkness outside. Standing, he pulled the black out curtains over the porthole, removed the hood of the lamp, and turned up the wick. A soft, warm glow illuminated the tiny compartment. MacGregor put on his shirt. His feeling was strong that there might be no need of these clothes after today. He donned his white trousers and blue service jacket with its gleaming brass buttons. He strapped on his grandfather's old claymore, now brightly polished, and fastened the black leather at his waste. He lifted his father's dirk, viewing the thin blade. Placing its sheath in his right stocking as his father might have, he tied the leather thong. His pistol, with oil cloth cover, he tucked in his belt and swung a horn of powder over his shoulder along with his ammunition pouch full of lead balls and wad. From a cord around his neck hung a brass telescope. MacGregor reviewed his orders in his mind. *The invasion force would be composed of three divisions. General Whitmore's force would attack White Point to the east of Gabarus Bay. Another division under General Lawrence would attack Flat Point on the west. The smallest division, that commanded by General Wolfe and composed of a number of elite and special forces, would lead the attack. Wolfe would have the Scottish Highlanders and American Rangers, reinforced with a few marines, but his body would be composed of a quickly assembled force of sharpshooters formed from the other divisions and elite forces. Rangers and Highlanders would spearhead Wolfe's force, followed by the Irregulars and Light Infantry. Next would come the 63rd Fraser's Regiment and Companies of the Grenadiers. These would be followed by the 2nd and 3rd Battalions of the 60th and 48th Regiments. Wolfe would lead a feint, leading between the other two divisions, as if his division would attack in the center of the bay. However, Wolfe's division would make an abrupt left turn at a point in the bay where an imaginary line joined White Point and Flat Point. There the division would turn to the west and land in the little cove of Coromondiére. The frigate Kennington and Halifax snow, deep inside the bay, would support Wolfe's landing with their cannons. After Wolfe's spearhead lands, the other two divisions will bear off, one to White Point and the other to Flat Point.*

MacGregor would direct the leading contingent of Wolfe's force to their landing site where he would direct gunfire from the nearby ships. He tied a white cape around his neck and picked up his hat, polishing the brass strawberry leaves. *Is this for luck or to appease my father and grandfather? It is my fate I'm fighting their enemy, whatever! My boat will be the first ashore, if I'm lucky; I'll die in the bay if I'm not.* He propped his will against the pillow, prominently visible on his bunk. His belongings were packed carefully in his duffle with his personal security knot tied thereon. Ready to go on deck, he stood quietly in the flickering light of the oil lamp with his head bowed. Quickly, he made the sign of the cross, put on his hat, and throwing back the white cape, stepped out the door.

On deck MacGregor took note that the wind was up, again a stiff breeze blowing across the deck. He distributed tall flags to his three signal men, keeping one for himself. Lieutenant Hopkins came on deck and joined him in glassing the enemy shoreline. There was nothing to be seen but black trees and white surf breaking on the beach. *The landing will not be easy. By now, Commodore Durell will have personally taken a boat ashore to assess the danger. If he finds the surf too high to land our men, we will be told.* Sergeant O'Bannion led his thirty-nine marines while Hopkins' eighty-five Scottish Highlanders assembled on deck. All carried Brown Bess muskets with bayonets. Their black-dyed kilts flapping in the cool wind, the Highlanders checked each other's equipment. MacGregor looked across the deck at these men. *Fellow Highlanders, they are, from a land I never knew. Many will have ancestors who fought the English. No doubt some were enemies of my people, Campbells perhaps, who loved the English and stole our land. Today we are all brothers, all of us serving German George of England.*

The galley crew came on deck, issuing sufficient rations of bread and cheese to last the men two days ashore. All the soldiers carried flasks of water tied to their belts. Most soldiers eagerly accepted a cup of rum, strong and undiluted, also offered by the stewards. The men sighed in appreciation as the burning liquid chased the cold from their bones and bolstered their courage. It was a heartier group of men who now stood waiting. Lieutenant MacGregor walked among them, his white cape billowing in the wind. He said, "Men, the success of this day may well depend on each of you. Every man must do his utmost. You will lead the van in taking the beach from the enemy. Others will follow under Brigadier Wolfe, but *you* must take and hold the invasion beach. Lieutenant Hopkins will lead the first wave ashore. Do not bunch up. Keep your distance from each other and don't give the French an easy target. I believe the worst danger will be on the water in the open boats. Get ashore as quickly as possible where there will be rocks and trees for cover against French guns. Let's give a good account of ourselves today, and God be with you." MacGregor nodded silently, pointing to the boarding ladders. The men moved quietly to the rail. The coxswain's crew moved around the deck with rope and squeaking blocks, lowering their boats into the water. Lieutenant MacGregor stood, a silhouette in the darkness, watching young Lieutenant Hopkins, the Highlanders, his marines and signalmen take to the boats. Three signalmen holding their tall flags joined the Highlanders in separate boats. It was now three o'clock in the morning darkness, and several boats from other ships had arrived to take the excess men, as *Grenadier* had not nearly enough boats to take them all. Pipe smokers coughed and the occasional musket rattled despite their best effort. MacGregor climbed over the rail and took his place in the dew-dampened stern sheets of his boat. Sergeant O'Bannion waited with *Grenadier*'s contingent of marines. Whispering quietly, O'Bannion directed the men from the bow as they worked their way into the boat. The marines were silent as the boat rocked under the weight of their movement, with only the squeak of oars and muffled voices carried across the dampness. Overlooking the boats, MacGregor stood and ordered the boats away. "Row out to sea," he ordered. "Keep your eyes on the white cape and follow us."

Most men said little but a man with a Welsh accent suggested, "It's a hard row ahead, boys; the Scotsman is leading us back home to England." There were a few nervous guffaws as they bent to the oars and rowed eastward into the darkness, toward the open sea. Lieutenant Hopkins' Highlanders followed closely behind. They skirted several darkened vessels at a safe distance. A chilling wind swept over the men as they left the shelter of the bay and lifted on the open ocean waves. They rowed past the outer most line of ships and MacGregor saw the single dim lantern tied on the ocean side of a ship. He ordered the sailors to row toward the light. He knew men of another division would be rowing toward a ship with two lanterns while three lanterns would guide the last division to their assembly point.

It was three-thirty in the morning and a pale haze of gray-green light glowed dimly in the northeastern sky when Lieutenant MacGregor's boat stood a few yards off the assembly ship. The single lantern swung just above the water's surface, illuminating the stern of the big transport, *Neptune*. American Rangers, in rowboats as well as a few in canoes, joined MacGregor's contingent of Highlanders and marines. The Rangers were an undisciplined lot of men. Dressed in buckskin or homespun, they made ribald jokes, drank homemade whiskey, and chewed tobacco. But there were few jokes in the canoes, which were not easily managed in the ocean swells, and they struggled desperately to keep them upright. MacGregor's oarsmen backed water with their oars, waiting until all his boats had gathered around *Neptune*. Despite the cold wind, they worked themselves into a sweat just keeping the boats in the same position. Swarms of other boats converged silently upon the area, and it was difficult for the sailors to row without entangling their oars.

At four o'clock in the morning, with all boats assigned to their respective divisions, dawn was breaking in the east, early as it did in the latitude of Louisbourg. A single deep-throated bell sounded faintly over the heaving ocean as a signal to launch the invasion. MacGregor was the first to lead his boats toward the beaches.

Bomb ketches began to fire their arching shells into the enemy shoreline while the closer frigates began a hot fire into the invasion beaches. As MacGregor's boats passed the British bomb ketches anchored near the head of the bay, guns belched fire and smoke, sending a heavy powder-filled ball directly over their heads. In the gathering dawn they could see the mortar bombs arcing high into the sky over their heads and exploding in the trees ashore. Now French twenty-four pound shells sent great geysers of water around the boats. Smoke drifted across the bay from the ships behind them, blowing toward the enemy beaches. *Bless that smoke. May there be much smoke on the beaches, amen.*

"Watch my white cape," MacGregor yelled. He urged his sailors westward, leading the contingent of boats westward, deep into Gabarus Bay. The invasion force of small boats, like a vast swarm of red insects, moved inland. Lieutenant MacGregor knew they coursed the distance rapidly, yet it seemed they sat motionless. *We are in range of the biggest French guns if they choose a long shot. Hopefully, French gunners will be blinded by that sun in their eyes.*

MacGregor looked behind him, into that rising sun, to see Wolfe's forces. On both sides of Wolfe's smaller force, the larger assembly of boats followed. He saw the promontory of White Point peninsula projecting into the bay on his right. He lifted his telescope to Coromandière Peninsula and its nearby cove, far to his left. *We must parallel the enemy beach, well within range of their guns. Easy targets we'll be!* With MacGregor's group of Highlanders and Rangers thrust farther ahead, a mortar shell sent a great white geyser in front of him, almost upsetting the boat. If it was French or English, he could not tell nor did he care. He continued ahead until he saw the tips of both points in line. "Steer west," he ordered. MacGregor lifted his sword in the air, holding the white cape aloft. A pipe issued a shrill call, signaling a hard charge in direction.

Yelling voices attempted to be heard over the cannons. "Row hard, men," MacGregor shouted. "We must remain in the lead as other boats are cutting the corner behind us." With his contingent rowing madly, he was able to keep ahead, and with motions of his sword, he rearranged the V formation. Now they paralleled the beach. English shells landed in the water behind them as well as in the dark, green forest beyond. French shells fell among the boats, but most were aimed at the larger assembly of boats behind them. MacGregor's marines and Highlanders rowed straight toward the dark, peaceful looking Coromandière Cove. American Rangers soon passed MacGregor's boats with their faster canoes, despite MacGregor's efforts to keep them in line. With his force nearing shore, English cannons ceased firing. All now seemed quiet in this area, disturbed only by distant guns. The last boats of his contingent made their final turn and the skirl of bagpipes sounded from a boat of Highlanders, the eerie sound echoing across the relatively quiet bay. The cove in front of MacGregor's invaders lay very still and silent. It was a soft blanket of evergreens surmounting a rocky beach and was untouched by English mortar and cannon shells. The quietness here surprised him. MacGregor's boats moved into shallow water and steeper waves. Surf pounded against the rocks ahead, sending salt spray through the morning air. MacGregor stood in the rocking boat, looking over the heads of his marines to see the deserted beach. He turned to look behind him where his contingent spread across the bay. Glancing back, he saw the main force of Wolfe's division still far out in Gabarus Bay. MacGregor could see another division behind Wolfe, moving slowly toward Flat Point. Off to the east he knew Whitmore's division moved toward White Point; none, however, would land before Wolfe. MacGregor waved his white cape in the air, and, on a broad front, the boats converged on the quiet little cove.

As MacGregor's boat moved toward the beach, Sergeant O'Bannion sat in the bow of the boat looking back at his marines. He called, "Patience, lads, you'll soon have a chance to stick some Frenchies with your bayonets."

Anxious and undisciplined, American Rangers strained their eyes for the enemy and sought to keep their canoes upright in the surf. Following closely behind, sailors rowed the Highlanders, faster still, trying to keep pace with the Americans. Surf pounding the rocks sent white clouds of spray into the dense green foliage of spruce boughs. Lieutenant MacGregor urged his sailors to row faster as American Rangers now gained the beach in their faster canoes, leaping in the water and wading toward shore. Nearing the rocky shoreline, the Highlanders began looking for a safe place to land in the pounding surf. More slowly now, they approached the rocky beach while sailors backed water with their oars in vain attempts to avoid collision with other boats. Oars became entangled and sailors cursed each other. Behind them the packed melee of boats bumped and jostled each other. MacGregor found himself barred from the beach as men eager to quit the ocean rushed ahead and cut him off.

Suddenly, the green spruce boughs fell aside on the beach, revealing the enemy. French cannons and swivel guns stood suddenly exposed. The enemy guns exploded in a roar of fire and smoke. At point-blank range they thundered a deadly hail of grape shot into the men on the beach and the closely packed boats. Lead balls struck boats with a dull thud and splashed the water like hail stones. They struck flesh with a sickening splat and men fell, sometimes silently, other times with a scream. Bloody soldiers slumped in the boats or fell in the water to drown with their wounds. Boats overturned in the rough water as men struggled to turn them around and row away. Curses, screams, and cannon fire deafened their ears. Oars, pieces of boats, floating bodies, and struggling men filled the churning water. Retreating boats plowed into other boats trying to reach the shore. More boats overturned. Drowning men splashed in the water near their comrades who had died from the cannons. Strong swimmers braved the pounding surf and climbed ashore, coughing and stumbling, to die on the bayonets of French marines. A few Highlanders pushed empty boats ahead of them and forced their way toward the beach. There the hail of lead cut most to pieces before their feet found dry land. Others leaped from boats to escape the hail of bullets and drowned.

From deeper in the bay, out of range of the French guns, General Wolfe saw the massacre and urged his reserves forward. With curses and orders from their officers, the sailors hesitantly rowed toward the hell now taking place on the bay. These men, the pride of the British Army, sat rigidly in their red tunics, their bayonets in the air. Their faces grew ashen as they reached the carnage. Bullets began splitting the air around them. Some in the lead boats fell to French rifle fire. Fear washed over them. Rowing through the dead and dying men, sailors balked at the oars. Soldiers called to turn back as swivel guns found their range.

MacGregor found himself trapped between boats fleeing the carnage and others rushing to storm the beach. Grape-shot whizzed around them. He urged his sailors to continue rowing toward shore. Valiantly the men tried, but they could not move forward. Overturned boats and struggling men barred their way. There was no retreat, for more boats still converged on the narrow bay. He turned to the signalman in a nearby boat and ordered, "Signal for cannon fire on Coromandière Bay." With fear in his eyes, the sailor slowly stood. He lifted his flag and began the laborious flailing of the long flag. Midway through the signal a rifle ball cut the man down; he splashed into the water. MacGregor felt his heart pounding in his chest and his breath labored as he stood in the tossing boat. MacGregor slowly lifted his signal flag. Expecting a musket shot to end his life at any moment, he began to signal the frigate *Kennington,* anchored in range of even the smaller French guns. Every second seemed an eternity as musket balls tore at his flag. With the boat tossing in the surf and a man writhing beside him, he continued to wave the flag, sending his message across the bay.

Henri Ouilette lay prone on a brow of Coromandière Point, a tiny peninsula jutting into the bay. He looked down on the death and destruction as he fired on the British boats. Many enemy boats were in easy rifle distance, and an officer with a white cape stood waving a signal flag. Henri Ouilette reloaded his rifle and charged the priming. The woodsman licked his thumb and rubbed it across the front sight of his rifle. A hail of musket fire splashed water around the boat with the waving flag. Falling to another rifle ball, a marine jerked forward and fell at the officer's feet. Henri inhaled deeply and exhaled half the air in his lungs, holding his breath. Aiming carefully, he slowly squeezed the trigger when his sights were covering the signaling officer's head. But at that instant another boat crashed into MacGregor's. He lost his balance and dropped on one knee. Henri's bullet tore MacGregor's hat from his head.

Sergeant O'Bannion saw sailors dropping their oars in panic. His surviving marines sat frozen in fear, failing to respond to his encouragement. To inspire them he suddenly stood in the boat while shouting, "Who would not spend a life in hell to listen to such music today?" Immediately O'Bannion's head jerked back, and he fell with a bullet in his head, his big body almost overturning the boat as it splashed into the water. MacGregor crouched in the boat, holding the gunnels. The flag pole rattled against the boat's sides as MacGregor fought to regain his footing. His marines now seemed completely demoralized. Jerkily, chest pounding, MacGregor fished the floating signal flag from the water. The wait seemed interminable until first one, than several, then many British cannons answered MacGregor's call. Gunners aboard *Kennington* and *Halifax* loaded and fired as fast as they could. A few shells sent large plumes of water skyward, among their own boats, before gunners found their elevation. But British cannons could not take the beach nor save the soldiers caught in the surf. Seeing a rout in progress, General Wolfe ordered his bugler to sound retreat. The bugler stood.. His loud notes mixed with the crash of cannons, popping of small arms fire, and screams of the wounded. Some rearward boats answered the recall immediately, but hammering fury of the cannons prevented others from hearing. Bullets swished past MacGregor's head and splashed water around the boat. Another sailor screamed and fell over his oar but a marine quickly took his place. MacGregor drew the telescope from his pocket and looked around the beach ahead of him. Despite the British cannons, French swivel guns still blasted a murderous fire from concealed positions. It would be suicide to land here. He raised his telescope, searching for an alternative site. MacGregor saw American Rangers rowing madly under Coromandière Point and then turn into a tiny bay on the other side. They disappeared behind a small headland which the French called *Cap Rouge* that formed the west side of Coromandière Cove. He remembered the small bay behind that point, but doubted it was large enough to hold even six boats and certainly not Wolfe's invasion force. They seemed to be protected there from French guns. He pointed his telescope in that direction and glassed the nearby trees. It seemed peaceful and quiet. Perhaps there were guns hidden in those trees too, but he must take a chance; landing in this place would be certain death for everyone who followed him.

MacGregor ordered his boat toward the little point. MacGregor called to Highlanders in nearby boats, "Follow me, men!" Those men too quickly recognized the relative safety offered by the point; they bent to the oars with renewed vigor, rowing furiously for that shelter and away from the rain of death. Their boats raced rapidly across the water, followed by many others. Arriving behind the point, it was like a lull in the storm, French cannons did not indeed reach them there. Only intermittent sniper fire, as deadly as that can be, struck boats and men. MacGregor ordered his boat ashore, not knowing if camouflaged cannons would again appear from the void or if there might be a place to land. They coursed toward the quiet area, finding a small rocky beach. American Rangers had abandoned their boats offshore and jumped in the surf. On the rocky beach the buff-clad men waded ashore, holding their rifles above their heads. There they slipped into the trees.

A French officer saw the British going ashore in this unexpected place and sent a force of one hundred soldiers hurrying to oppose their landing. But by now a force of perhaps a dozen American Rangers had taken cover in the trees. These men had dried their weapons and now waited to block the French counterattack.

Lieutenant Hopkins led his surviving Highlanders into the sanctuary and splashed into the water. With drawn saber he waded ashore, urging the

Highlanders out of the boat and into the surf. MacGregor directed his boat toward the beach until he felt it touch rocks and ordered, "Quickly, marines! Jump! Get ashore and take cover in the trees!" He drew his sword to prod those who hesitated. Standing in the boat, he waved his signal flag, motioning for other boats to join them behind the little headland, then leaped into the water after the marines. With his brogues slipping on the rocks below, MacGregor fought the surf and waded ashore, using his signal flag as a staff to keep his balance.

Meanwhile, on the bluff overlooking their landing, Henri Ouilette saw the enemy seeking safety behind the point of land where French cannons could not reach them. He picked up his rifle and worked his way to the west side. There, Henri lay down again on the soft evergreen needles and watched them landing on the beach without opposition. Henri reloaded his rifle several times, shooting red-coated Highlanders coming ashore.

Lieutenant Hopkins led his Highlanders into the trees, shouting, "Claymore! Claymore!" They charged the enemy. Soon the skirl of pipes sounded across the beach, stirring an inborn emotion within Scots whose ancestors fought Englishmen to that sound.

On the beach, MacGregor confirmed there were no French cannons guarding the area. He waded into the water until he could be seen by the boats offshore, then took cover behind a deserted boat. There he waved the coded message. With bullets zipping about him and thumping into the boat, he sent his signal to General Wolfe.

Wolfe quickly realized this force would flank the guns, barring him from his objective, and sounded the charge, leading his boats toward Coromandière Cove, their original target.

Lieutenant MacGregor dropped his signal flag. *Sergeant O'Bannion is dead. I must now lead his marines.* He drew his claymore and waded ashore. Now joined by Lieutenant Brown and Ensign Grant, leading their Highlanders, Lieutenant Hopkins said, "We are attacking the French guns from the rear."

MacGregor called to the ensign leading the American Rangers, pointing with his sword, "Guard our flanks on either side, and when we attack, fire into the French artillerymen."

The ensign spat a stream of tobacco juice, wiped his mouth and said, "Nobody 'ken that better'an us Rangers. Ain't no man in mah company who 'kaint shoot the eye out'a 'ol squirrel at a 'hundert yards. This will be a turkey shoot." The American silently directed his Rangers into position with hand signals.

When MacGregor was confident they were in position, he assembled the marines, now numbering less than thirty. Pointing at the brow of the low ridge with his claymore, he said, "The Highlanders will charge the enemy cannons from the rear; we can assist with a charge on the enemy flank. Let's show the Highlanders how the navy fights." Bent low and holding his claymore in the air, MacGregor moved them forward, leading the marines up the low ridge.

At the brow of the little ridge MacGregor stopped, looking down through the woods where he saw blue clad men through the clouds of gun smoke. He heard a bullet whizz past him as the marines lined up on the ridge. He lowered his sword and began to trot toward the French artillery. It was a thin red line that charged the guns. *I'm dressed like the French! I could be mistaken for the enemy.*

French irregulars concealed in the woods began a hot fire into their ranks. Several men fell and the thirty marines became less. As they neared the cannons, MacGregor called, "Ready a volley." Trotting forward, they cocked their flintlocks. He lifted his sword and hurried toward the busy artillerymen who were lost in the smoke.

Through the woods the Highlanders charged the cannons from the rear, their wail of bagpipes echoing through the woods. Still running forward, MacGregor ordered, "Fire!" A ragged volley erupted from the marine's rifles, but less than a dozen had fired. Their powder was too wet. Knowing his men would have no time to reload, MacGregor ran faster, yelling, "Bayonets! Bayonets!" The red-coated marines ran forward in a ragged rank, bayonets thrust before them. French soldiers now turned to see themselves under attack from the rear and side.

Running, MacGregor remembered playing soldier as a child; as he had yelled then, he now shouted his clan's battle cry, "Gregorach! Gregorach!" His breath came in short gasps, and his heart thumped in his chest. Tears formed in his eyes, and he expected the fatal bullet every second.

Across the hill, Highlanders charged down the wooded slope. American Rangers at the top of the ridge fired their rifles over the heads of the Highlanders, cutting down French soldiers who rose to challenge the charge. The charging Scots stopped in ragged lines. Their officers raised their swords, the front ranks kneeled, and all Highlanders lifted their rifles. Officers slashed downward with swords and barked their orders to fire. A thick cloud of white smoke engulfed the kneeling red ranks. Rifles rattled a hail of fire into the French artillerymen, but like the marines, many had wet powder. A few French soldiers dropped. Others attempted to return the volley, but it was with far too few guns. Indians, waiting in their hiding places until the Highlanders had fired their guns, now rushed at the Highlanders with tomahawks and knives. MacGregor's marines reached the French position, charging into the enemy with bayonets and rifle butts. French artillerymen left their guns to fight with shot rammers and pistols. The thinning French contingent sought to reload their swivel guns, but first one and then another fell to American sharpshooters. A French officer led a pathetic handful of brave French soldiers into the charging Highlanders, but they were quickly cut down. Americans now charged down the ridge, swinging tomahawks and screaming blood curdling yells aimed mostly at the Indians and irregulars. Highlanders thrust, parried, and fell while French artillerymen struggled to survive. More Scottish Highlanders poured over the hill, some charging the irregulars while others fell upon the already outnumbered artillerymen.

MacGregor raced past a French bayonet, deflecting it with his claymore. He fired his pistol into a French officer and slashed a blue-coated soldier with his claymore. Running through the melee of slashing, cursing men, he parried a bayonet thrust with his heavy claymore. He slashed the man across the throat and ran to attack another attempting to reload a swivel gun. But it was too late when he saw a man in blue charging him with a bayonet. MacGregor could not sidestep the soldier. He felt the bayonet thrust and the sharp metal plunge through his flesh. Leaping on the French marine, he twisted the bayonet, now entangled in his side. A blinding flash of pain blurred his vision as he felt his flesh tear. A warm trickle of blood ran down his side as the man's hands gripped his throat. MacGregor fell heavily on the ground with the marine choking away his breath. He was unable to swing the big claymore. He dropped his sword and shoved the man's face backward. With his free hand he reached for the dirk below his knee. Wrestling him to the ground, MacGregor freed the dirk and plunged it into the man's abdomen. He watched the man's eyes grow larger as he felt the steel sink into his organs. He twisted the dirk and felt the man convulse. He pushed the enemy aside to see another French soldier flying toward him. The man landed heavily upon MacGregor and gripped his dirk hand in a vice like grip. An American Ranger loomed behind the French soldier with upraised tomahawk. The Ranger's tomahawk sank into the man's skull, and he felt the French marine's grip slacken. Blood ran down his hands as he watched the marine's face turn ashen and lifeless. MacGregor felt terror while throwing the body aside. He leaped to his feet, holding only his dirk. A French soldier swung the butt of his rifle at MacGregor's head. While he ducked under the rifle, MacGregor thrust upward with his dirk. The soldier crumpled to the ground. He now saw a tall, gray-haired Frenchman in buckskins and blue toque take down a Highlander with his skinning knife. The gray-haired Frenchman shoved the dying Highlander aside and ran toward MacGregor, readying his knife for another attack. But in front of the charging Frenchman another wounded Highlander stumbled to his feet. Holding a hand over his bleeding side, the Highlander charged Henri Ouilette, holding his bayoneted rifle under his one good arm. He drove the bayonet deep into the abdomen of the French woodsman. With bayoneted rifle gripped tightly under his one free arm, the Highlander forced his bayonet deeper and twisted Henri to the ground. The French woodsman looked down in surprise to see the tip of the bayonet penetrating below his chest. Blood ran down his buckskin jacket and over the blue sash tied around his waist. He attempted to stand and slash with his knife, but the kilted soldier held the rifle firmly, preventing his rising. Henri dropped to his knees and rolled over on the ground. The wounded Highlander placed a foot against the old man's chest, withdrawing the bayonet. Henri turned on his hands and knees, slashing the blade of his hunting knife upward in a vain attempt to strike the Highlander as the man staggered away to fall on the ground.

Henri Ouilette lifted his head toward the sunlight, saying, "Mary, mother of God…" Slowly, painfully, Henri crawled into the dark, dense forest nearby. Leaving a wide trail of blood on the soft green floor of the forest, he stopped and the breath left his lifeless body.

Surviving French soldiers fought bravely but now saw the futility of their struggle. They broke and ran. Excited Highlanders took chase, running after the French with their piper following, blowing his bagpipes. Even some of the wounded staggered up again, struggling, and joined their comrades in the chase. Behind the British, Americans also charged wildly after the retreating French, yelling their blood curdling screams. With the murderous French cannon fire stilled, Wolfe perceived that the Highlanders had flanked the enemy guns on the landing site and led his boats back to the beach. General Wolfe himself was one of the first to jump from a boat and lead the soldiers ashore. Now wave after red-coated wave rushed ashore, the cream of the British Army with their Brown Bess muskets. These men could load and fire some four rounds every minute in volley, a feat well appreciated by their enemies.

French soldiers retreating from the Coromandière landing alarmed other French artillerymen that British were at their rear also. Now those French soldiers found British in front of them and others charging them from behind.

Men in blue threw aside their powder flasks and lifted bayonets to meet the charge. A few yards from the French the Highlanders renewed their yell, "Claymore! Claymore!" Bayonets flashed in the morning sunlight as desperate men thrust and parried with flesh yielding to steel. Men cursed and fought each other with bayonets, swords, gun butts, cannon rammers, daggers, bare hands, teeth, and fingernails. The French fought furiously against the overwhelming British charge.

On the bloodied and body strewn beach, newly landed British soldiers formed ranks. To the beat of drums they marched through the trees with fixed bayonets, their red jackets and white trousers brightly visible in the morning sunlight. They climbed the beach and through the trees in numbers the French artillerymen had never imagined. Rank upon rank of red-coated English soldiers marched up the long slope toward Louisbourg. They were joined by those landing at Flat and White Points. Outnumbered French soldiers, running out of ammunition and seeing the host of British charging from three directions, deserted their positions, often without spiking their guns. At first, a few, and then in a rout, they ran back to the safety of Louisbourg's walls. British troops swept past the outer French defenses and on toward the fortress. By the hundreds they came until more than 13,000 British soldiers and irregulars stood before Louisbourg.

Lieutenant MacGregor found the wounded Highlander who had saved his life. He cradled the wounded man's head in his arms. With his face drained of color and blood in the corner of his mouth, the man leaned heavily against Lieutenant MacGregor. "I'll sit 'ere an' take a bit 'o rest, if you please, Sir," he whispered, coughing, "...and be back to fightin'." The man coughed a painfully rattling cough, gasping for breath, and died. MacGregor looked down at the man's black-dyed kilt and found a corner that had not been stained by the black dye. It was a blue-green tartan which MacGregor had been taught as a boy to recognize. It was the tartan of the hated Campbells, mortal enemies of the MacGregors. He sat beside the Highlander's lifeless body as hosts of red-coated troops poured past his position, disappearing into the woods where the sound of firing receded ever farther away. British took up siege positions just out of range of French cannons on the walls of Louisbourg. Then guns fell silent.

As the setting sun splayed colors of yellow and gold, the bay lay strangely quiet. The call of gulls replaced the booming cannons. Sailors pulled at the oars as the ship's boat coursed Gabarus Bay. Surviving Highlanders, some with bloody bandages, sat amidships, quietly congratulating each other on their good fortune of survival. Peering over the side from where he lay, MacGregor watched the form of *Grenadier* grow larger as the boat approached.

Sailors lifted their oars and the boat scraped against the ship's hull. Lines dropped from above. A sailor caught the boarding ladder, gently pulling the boat to a stop. MacGregor stood and tried to pull himself up the rope ladder. When his strength began to fail, strong hands encircled him, pulling him upward. He regained consciousness to see the boatswain carrying him up the net ladder. On deck he looked up through a haze to see Doctor Abrams looking down into his eyes. MacGregor tried to comprehend the words Dr. Abrams spoke, but his mind could not sort them out. He drifted off into unconsciousness.

Chapter Twenty-Nine

Meanwhile, French defenders retreated behind the walls of Fortress Louisbourg. They drove a few water-logged British prisoners ahead of them, most fished from the ocean in front of the French cannons. Marched at the point of bayonets, the prisoners seemed uncomprehending and dazed after surviving the massacre. Tired, battle-weary French troops were little better than their prisoners. They too were lucky to have survived. Trudging inside the gates, they carried their wounded when they could. Madame Drucour, never far from any action, stood on the ramparts, watching the swirl of battle around Louisbourg. As always, Marie Gauthier stood close by the governor's wife. When the soldiers entered the gates, the two women hurried down to welcome them back. Madame Drucour waved at the soldiers as they entered the gate, calling out, "You have fought bravely, we are proud of you." To a wounded man who limped inside the gate with a bandaged leg she said, "You poor dear, don't worry. Our good doctors will have you good as new in no time."

A French Army lieutenant galloped inside the gates, his horse snorting foam and bellowing as it recovered its breath from the hard ride back to the fort. British rifle bullets had sought the horse and rider since they broke from the tree line. Marie's anxious eyes sought Henri Ouilette. He was not among the returning soldiers. Undeterred, she was sure that Henri would return safely as he always did. At last Marie saw Captain Renau's powder blackened face. Weary and disheveled, he led a group of sailors and Basque fishermen inside the safety of Louisbourg. "Captain Renau," she asked, "did you see an Acadian named Henri Ouilette?"

"There were Acadians with the irregulars, Marie," Captain Renau replied, "but I cannot say about any one man. We were too busy. Someone left Coromandière point undefended. The British landed behind the point and attacked us from the rear. We were hardly able to spike our guns before retreating ahead of their bayonets. Unfortunately, many officers failed to spike their guns. Now the British will use them against us." He saw that his words were being lost on Marie; she was desperate to find this old man. "God help your friend, Marie. Excuse me, please, I have wounded men to care for."

Marie saw an elderly Acadian whom she recognized from her village. She ran to the man who carried a rifle over his shoulder, walking silently with the soldiers. Marie asked excitedly, "Have you seen Henri Ouilette?"

The man slowly lowered the rifle from his shoulder and looked sadly into Marie's eyes. "Henri Ouilette? No, *Mademoiselle*, I did not see Henri Ouilette nor even my own brother. I only saw redcoats, everywhere redcoats… more than we can shoot, everywhere redcoats." He walked on, shaking his head.

Marie ran out the gate, pausing to look into the faces of men still hurrying back to the fortress. Any man wearing buckskins or homespun caught her eye. Marie hurried to the sound of gunfire until an officer caught her in his arms. "Please, *Mademoiselle*, where do you go? You must return to the fortress. English soldiers are close behind my men."

"I must find Henri Ouilette," she pleaded. "He's out in the forest somewhere, fighting the English."

The officer held Marie with one hand around her shoulders, his sword in the other. He lifted his sword, signaling to his men as he motioned toward Louisbourg. "Come, *Mademoiselle*, we must hurry to the safety of the fortress. Is the man you seek an Acadian?"

"Yes, yes," replied Marie. "Henri is from my village, Beaubassin. He's an old man. Henri shouldn't be fighting the English like young men. He's all I have left." Tears streamed down her face.

The officer pulled Marie back toward the fortress, soothing her as he hurried her along. "Your Acadian may be hiding in the forest. Perhaps he will slip into the fortress after nightfall. Come along, *Mademoiselle*, we must hurry."

The citizens of Louisbourg spent an uneasy night. Cannons and rifles fired from the ramparts as many expected the English to charge the walls in the darkness. Early the next morning, under a white flag of truce, French and English officers met in the open field outside the walls. A short while later men walked out of Louisbourg carrying stretchers. Later, they returned bearing the French dead. Marie hurried to the gate and ran beside every stretcher bearing a man in buckskins. Before noon she saw two Acadians carrying a stretcher that caused her breathing to stop. A blanket covered the body but a hand trailed below the stretcher, clad in buckskin. Marie knew the tall figure beneath the blanket must be Henri. Fighting blackness, she ran to the litter and lifted a corner of the blanket. Henri's ashen face was cold to her touch. With grief flowing from her heart, Marie moved her fingers over his face and closed his eyes. The soldiers carefully laid the stretcher on the ground as Marie laid her head on Henri's silent chest, loudly sobbing.

Fortress Louisbourg now lay open to English attack from both land and sea.

Over the next few weeks French and British cannons exchanged fire while sappers worked their way closer to the French walls with British trenches. From the sea, attacks were launched against the Island Battery as that strong point must be eliminated to gain entrance to the harbor. French battleships also came under cannon fire.

In the harbor of Louisbourg, a British shell penetrated the poop of the great French warship, *Célèbre*. The shell set off a fire in some cartridges stored aboard the warship. There being few men aboard, the fire quickly spread out of control. Sparks blown from her blaze set fire to the *Bienfaisant*, who was also undermanned. The fire on *Bienfaisant* broke out freely, and as her cables parted, she drifted down upon *Capriciaux*, setting that battleship afire as well. Loaded guns aboard the ships became hot and exploded, sending French shells into Louisbourg, along with those falling from English guns. The battleship *Prudent* escaped, being upwind of the other vessels. All night the fires roared, with smoke, flames, and explosions. Courageous men saved *Bienfaisant* from the fate of the others by skill and daring, but the fire left her of little use. The next morning despairing citizens viewed the carnage from the ramparts of the Dauphin Gate. Not even the strongest spirit could view the remains of the once mighty battleships without realizing that all was lost. Those who had dreamed of going aboard those ships and sailing back to France now knew that dream had become a nightmare. As the soldiers and citizens stood looking at the smoldering, skeletal remains of the once mighty ships, their faces reflected the despair in their hearts. Madame Drucour appeared on the ramparts with Marie beside her. She said to them, "Fellow citizens, why do we cry that some ships are lost? Who will be disappointed but those who planned to run from the English? I, for one, do not plan to run away. I know that you do not, either. Therefore, let us forget the useless ships and prepare to meet the foe, here, as we have all along."

Madame Drucour turned to the captain of artillery. "It's a pity the women of Louisbourg cannot vent their anger against the English."

"Madame Drucour," replied the captain, "we are instructed to fire at any target of opportunity. Let us find a target for you. I guarantee you will feel better after you have given the English a cannon ball." The captain lifted a telescope, surveying the English lines, now only a short distance away. He stopped the movement of his telescope and began to call out aiming instructions to his crew. He bent to sight the cannon himself, rising to smile at Madame Drucour. "Madame, the cannon is sighted and here is the glowing match; place it against the touch hole and you will fire a thirty-six-pound shell at the English."

Madame Drucour nodded at the captain with a self-satisfied smile. She placed the match against the touch hole and the big gun roared in a cloud of smoke and fire. Madame Drucour jumped and dropped the match. Instantly, a geyser of dirt and smoke rose from the English lines. Holding the slow match triumphantly above her head, Madame Drucour smiled broadly. The soldiers as well as the town's people watching cheered as if a great victory had been achieved.

The captain turned to Marie, asking, "Would the *Mademoiselle* care to fire the cannon?"

"No thank you, Captain, the cannon will be better used if you do it for me." She averted her eyes and stood with her hands behind her back.

The captain turned to his gunners. "Quickly, men, we will fire a shell for the *Mademoiselle*." He found another target with his telescope and called out the firing instruction to his men.

With a roar the cannon fired again. Across no-man's-land a geysers of dirt and rocks lifted a red jacketed body into the air then dumped it on the ground like a rag doll. "Look, *Mademoiselle*, you see the there! That one we have fired for you and killed an Englishman." Again the gunners cheered and Marie averted her eyes, thinking, *God forgive me. I only want a stop to this killing. Please don't let me be the instrument of more death and suffering.* Madame Drucour led the way to another gun position where the lady again fired the cannon against the enemy as Marie watched from afar.

Madame Drucour now walked the stone ramparts daily, firing the cannons at the English. The soldiers loved to see the great lady standing bravely on the wall, disdaining the English shells while returning the enemy fire.

Chapter Thirty

MacGregor's wounds were mending and the pain was gone, but he was tired of laying in Dr. Abram's sick bay. He yearned for the fresh air and open sea. It was with some happiness he answered the commodore's summons. Waiting on *Grenadier* for his boat, MacGregor saw the boatswain approach. The man, said, "Beggin' yer pardon, Lieutenant, but we know you lost yer hat on the beach. I found you a purty new one in the slops. Our armorer made you some of o' yer leaves from a sheet of brass. I hope you like it, Sir."

MacGregor nodded his approval and clamped the new hat on his head and descended the rope ladder to his boat. Soon he mounted the boarding ladder of the commodore's flag ship as the morning sun cast shadows across the deck. In the light westerly wind the commodore's pennant fluttered from the masthead. On deck, neatly dressed sailors spliced lines and set new halyards. A side party stood nearby, ready to greet visiting officers, and MacGregor doffed his new hat to the colors as he gained the deck.

Blowing across the deck, the cool breeze caressed MacGregor's face as he turned to look toward Louisbourg. MacGregor felt the familiar salt-tingle to his nostrils. He inhaled deeply of fresh sea air, thinking, *the air will not be so pure and fresh for the people in Louisbourg*. Air bursts exploding above the walls sounded like distant thunder and smoke smudged the sky. Lieutenant MacGregor put the thoughts from his mind and followed the midshipman to the admiral's cabin. He knocked on the polished oak door and self-consciously brushed at lint on the sleeve of his coat. The marine guard in red jacket opened the door in response to the admiral's call. With hat in hand, MacGregor entered, "You asked to see me, Sir?"

The commodore sat at a polished oak desk, furnished with leather binders, ink well and brass sand box. A ripe, yellow pineapple set on the edge of his desk. Holding a goose feather shaft in his hand, he read a document. With a flourish, the admiral signed his name to the bottom of the letter. Sprinkling a little sand on the wet ink, he emptied the excess into a waste basket. He looked up at the yeoman standing beside him, handing him the document. The commodore then turned to MacGregor.

"Mr. MacGregor, Admiral Boscowen would like your help in trying to end this siege peacefully. We are sending you to Louisbourg as emissary to

Governor Drucour. With your experience at the French court, they will more likely listen to you than anyone. They tend to look down their noses on the rest of us as you know. MacGregor's heart leaped. *My dreams have come true. I may see Marie again.* He heard the commodore continue, "We expect you can better express our desire for peace with the French." The commodore's eyes showed his thoughts were racing ahead. He stood, walked to a map hanging on the wall and stood looking at it for a moment then turned thoughtfully back to MacGregor. "Come, look at this chart, Mr. MacGregor. You see Louisbourg, here," he said, pointing with a letter opener. "Louisbourg is the sentinel at the door of Canada. Now," he moved his hand to the left and upward, "here is the fortress of Quebec, the citadel inside Canada. If we are to take Canada from the French, we must defeat the guardian inside Canada's door, Quebec. But first we must defeat the sentinel outside the door, and that sentinel is fortress Louisbourg." He tapped Louisbourg with his letter opener. "From their safety within Louisbourg, the French fleet can sally forth to harass our sea lanes of supply. Their warships could demolish our troop transports. We cannot bypass them. We cannot defeat Quebec without first defeating Louisbourg. The French Governor at Louisbourg, Drucour, knows that also. We think Governor Drucour will hold Louisbourg as long as he can. Mr. MacGregor, Prime Minister Pitt needs a victory. Our citizens are disheartened by the fall of Minorca. Colonists at Boston and Halifax live in fear of a French invasion. Therefore, we must have Louisbourg, and we must have it soon.

"Admiral Boscawen wants to avoid bloodshed and suffering among the civilians in Louisbourg. He feels he is losing the argument with Amherst over bombardment of the civilian population. General Wolfe says he wastes his ammunition on the stone walls of the fortress, that Louisbourg will never surrender until the people demand it. Drucour's surrender would spare the citizens of Louisbourg. We would allow the citizens of Louisbourg to return to France in peace. Persuade Governor Drucour to surrender and you can save many lives." He moved to the door, handing the pineapple to MacGregor. "Take this as a gift to Madame Drucour with the Admiral's compliments. He much admires her family, the Courseracs… great admirals. Good luck and hurry back with the governor's reply. Wolfe is anxious to begin his assault on the city." The commodore then narrowed one eye as he spoke softly to MacGregor, "Also, I want you to discuss our prisoners held by the French. Learn how many they still hold, their names, units, and where held if you can. Observe ships in the harbor, cannons on the ramparts and uniforms of soldiers."

Before noon MacGregor was back on *Grenadier*, cruising within sight of Louisbourg. He walked to the bulwark and looked across the water at its majestic spires. The brass buttons on his jacket shone like new money and his claymore glistened in the sunshine. Captain Walshingham shouted orders. "Mr. Sethford! Order crewmen in Sunday best and marines on deck. Prepare to make sail for Louisbourg Harbor under a flag of truce. Put leads men in the chains with midshipman above to record the depths and map the harbor. Mr. Farwell! Note and list all shipping within the harbor. Mr. Thomas, note the gun positions and their caliber. You have your orders, Mr. MacGregor."

Grenadier slipped quietly through the water into Louisbourg Harbor as officers carefully noted their assigned reconnaissance. High above the ship a white flag of truce flapped gently in the breeze. From their stern the white Ensign proclaimed them a ship of the British fleet. Tars lined the deck and yards while the marines stood stiffly in their scarlet coats. The slender spires above the fortress so often seen from a distance now stood majestically before them. The island battery with its big gun slipped peacefully astern. Ahead, French battleships lay at anchor, an awesome sight for an English navy man. Bright morning sunshine glittered on the surface of the water now reflecting the white clouds and blue skies above and mirrored the shimmering sepia reflection of idle French warships. Under the watchful eye of French shore batteries, *Grenadier* sailed leisurely into Louisbourg Harbor.

Walshingham nodded at his crew from the quarterdeck. Sailors jumped to activity. A loud, shrill whistle drifted across the deck from the boatswain's pipe. The helmsman spun the wheel. Slowly, the bow of the ship turned into the wind while men on the foredeck doused the jibs and sailors in the masts handed the sails. When the ship coasted to a stop, their anchor splashed in the water. Blocks squeaked and rope whirred through davits as the ship's boat dropped with a little splash into the bay. The boarding ladder rattled against the side and sailors quickly descended into the boat, holding it steady as Lieutenant MacGregor carefully made his way down the ladder.

With MacGregor sitting in the stern, sailors handed him his leather case, followed by the rough, yellow pineapple. Sailors dipped their oars simultaneously to pull the boat in perfect unison. Lieutenant MacGregor sat in the boat, holding the briefcase and the pineapple on his knees. As one, the men raised their oars, allowing the boat to gently bump the dock. MacGregor neatly stepped out of the boat with no more effort than arising from a chair, his pineapple held aloft.

Under the watchful eyes of French Marines, MacGregor spoke to a young

French lieutenant. "I'm here as an emissary of the British Crown, with a message and gift for Governor Drucour. Kindly conduct me to the governor."

With the French lieutenant marching in front and a contingent of French marines marching behind, MacGregor walked up the pier. Fishermen turned from their racks of drying cod fish to look at the spectacle of men marching past. Others stopped work on their boats, laying aside their mauls and caulking materials to watch the strange procession. The sound of birds singing reminded MacGregor that he now walked among landsmen, his feet no longer rising and falling with waves; a new gait was called for in walking on land. Here grass and thousands of yellow oxeye daisies grew underfoot. Barefoot children ran beside MacGregor, yelling and pointing at him and the strange fruit in his hand. Dogs barked. Women in wooden shoes watched silently as they passed. MacGregor hardly noticed them. *Will Marie be here? Will I find her if she is? I must ask about her, even if my questions endanger her.* An Indian warrior wearing a tattered scarlet coat watched MacGregor with expressionless eyes. MacGregor arrived at a massive wooden gate set in a high stone wall, the Dauphin Gate. Here a captain and a contingent of marines stood nearby.

The captain stepped forward with his hand outstretched. "Welcome to Louisbourg, Englishman. I presume you have a dispatch for someone at Government House?"

"Yes, thank you, I'm Lieutenant MacGregor. I would be grateful if you would conduct me to Governor Drucour, for whom I have a message from my Admiral Boscawen."

Arriving at the imposing stone site of French administration at Louisbourg, MacGregor was taken to a waiting room. There he sat, awkwardly holding his pineapple, while the Captain conferred with others behind massive oak doors. MacGregor hefted the pineapple in one hand as if it was a bomb and overcame an urge to throw it at the wall. Presently the door opened to reveal an ancient servant dressed in black. The servant's eyes opened wide upon seeing this strange man and wider still at the sight of his pineapple. He bade MacGregor to follow him. MacGregor lifted himself from the chair, holding the pineapple awkwardly away from his body.

Slowly the servant shuffled along the corridor to a large oak door where he paused to rap almost imperceptibly against the thick door with knuckles in worn white gloves. There followed a long pause of silence. The servant looked coolly at MacGregor and rapped again on the massive wooden door. He knocked a bit more loudly this time and placed his ear close to the door.

The servant's eyes, fixed on MacGregor, seemed to say, "I told you so," upon hearing some sound imperceptible to MacGregor. He tugged downward on his vest and opened the door. The servant held out his hand to MacGregor, who surrendered the pineapple. The servant followed behind MacGregor, his hat and pineapple in hand.

MacGregor entered the room to find the distinguished Governor Drucour rising from his desk. He stood stiffly before his desk, saying, "I'm Lieutenant Charles MacGregor of the Royal Navy with dispatches for the governor from my admiral."

Laying some papers aside, the governor rose from his desk. He glanced hurriedly up at MacGregor and took his hand warmly. With the hint of a twinkle in his eye, the governor said, "Perhaps the English are ready to surrender already?"

MacGregor immediately liked the man and answered with a smile, "Quite the contrary, I'm afraid, sir. I'm directed by my admiral to give you these dispatches. I think they may call for your surrender, Sir." MacGregor quickly added, "I'm also instructed to present Madame Drucour with this pineapple." *When could I ask about Marie Gauthier? Must I wait for a more appropriate time?*

"Well, well, a pineapple, a treat indeed since the English blockade our colony." Smiling at the servant, Governor Drucour said, "Emile, take the pineapple to the kitchen. I would like it prepared for our lunch, and set a place for our young emissary."

The governor turned back to MacGregor, offering him a chair. "I insist you join us for lunch. You will learn that we do not starve, despite your blockade. Sit, Lieutenant, while I browse through your government's correspondence." The governor sat behind his desk and put on his glasses. MacGregor opened the dispatch case and handed the letters to the governor, then looking around for the chair, reluctantly sat down.

MacGregor looked around at the elegance of the room. The governor picked up the letters and read them. At last he laid the letters aside. He pulled out a drawer and carefully tucked the letters in the back of the drawer. He took a key from his pocket, carefully locking the drawer. He stood for a moment, contemplatively, and then turned from his desk. "Well, I believe I understand your government's communication and can formulate a proper reply, but one should not work on an empty stomach. I'm anxious to show you, Lieutenant, we are not as near starvation as your government believes. Their blockade has achieved little. Come, meet Madame Drucour and present your pineapple."

He strode out of the room and walked down the hall to a sitting room. The governor walked in the open door and waited for MacGregor to join him. As MacGregor entered the governor said, "Ladies, may I present Lieutenant Charles MacGregor of the British Navy."

MacGregor looked across the room to see the two women standing inside. Madame Drucour was moving toward him when he looked beyond the governor's wife and saw Marie Gauthier. Marie was walking across the room with a vase of flowers in her hand. She dropped the vase on the floor with a crash. Marie put her hand over her mouth and gasped audibly. The governor and her lady quickly looked at Marie and then at MacGregor. Marie's eyes flashed. "Is it you, Charles MacGregor? You who put my father on your ship and took him away at Ft. Beausejour? You took my father away…"

MacGregor stood speechless for a moment. None of the words he imagined he might say to Marie could be found. *God, I would like to take her in my arms!* The governor and Madame Drucour looked from one to the other with questioning eyes. At last MacGregor was able to ask, "Did Count De la Court give you the message about your father? I asked him to tell you he was alive and well in Boston."

Marie shuddered and looked intently into his eyes. "You have seen my father since you took him away?" With misty eyes Marie turned to the governor and Madame Drucour. "As you know, my father and I were separated by the English," Marie's eyes flashed as she turned to MacGregor, "when the English came to take us away from our homes." A tear rolled down her cheek, but her words sounded defiant as she said, "Tell me about father, please."

"Your father is well, Marie. I will get word to him that I have seen you. We could not be sure if you survived the sinking of *Gladiator*. I have looked for an opportunity to come here and inquire about you. I dared not dream of seeing you."

Marie's face was a mixture of relief and astonishment. She locked her hands together in front of her breasts and lowered her eyes as if in prayer, then dropped her eyes as she said, "Many of the people from my village did not survive."

Madame Drucour's words filled an awkward void. "Lieutenant MacGregor, you speak our language very well, and you seem to have good manners. But I can't place your accent. Are you Scottish or American? Not English, I think. As I recall, there is a community of Scots who took refuge in France. Might you have been one of those?"

MacGregor tore his gaze away from Marie with difficulty. He looked blankly at Madame Drucour. "Yes, they followed Bonnie Prince Charlie to France. Our lands were given to the Campbells, and Clan MacGregor was ordered shot on sight." Embarrassed, he quickly changed the subject. "I'm happy to learn that Marie is safe here with you. We have been... her father and I have been worried about her." He tried to smile at Marie while assessing her reaction.

Madame Drucour's face lightened. "So, there, I was right. You are a gentleman, I can tell. And how did you come to serve German George of England?"

MacGregor hesitated a moment before replying, "My parents died when I was young. My uncle, landless and with little money, brought me to America as a child. He apprenticed me to the British Navy, where he told me I could become an officer and a gentleman." He looked at Marie, hoping she might understand. "That is how I came to know Gaston Gauthier... and Marie. My ship rescued them at sea long before the war. To my regret, another of my ships separated them from each other and their home." MacGregor looked for her understanding, saying, "I've done my best for your father. My last promise to him was to find you if I could. Now that I have found you, I hope you will let me take you to him."

Governor Drucour put a hand on MacGregor's elbow. "I see that our lunch is ready; let us go in." The governor turned to Marie. "I have asked that a place at the table be set for you, my dear; you will be so kind as to join us." Governor Drucour said to Marie, "You will take the chair beside Lieutenant MacGregor."

While servants poured wine, Governor Drucour plied MacGregor with questions about the British navy. "You see, I was commandant of our marine academy, and I am very interested in such matters. The British seem to have an advantage over our Navy, ship for ship. I'm curious to know why. I know our ships sail better than those tubs of the English, yet the English usually win. Why do you suppose that happens, Lieutenant?" Waiters served a codfish stew, with fresh garden vegetables as they talked.

MacGregor struggled to tear his mind away from Marie and concentrate on the governor's question. "Sir, I have not had a lot of experience in fighting French ships. My frigate did capture a French battleship recently, the *Chasseur*. Her captain came here upon his parole. She was loaded with cargo and had few of her guns manned. But I did observe, however, that her cannons were much longer than ours. They would serve better perhaps, at a longer distance, but we fought much closer. And our shorter guns can be run in and out, and reloaded much faster than the long guns. I expect we fired at least twice for every once of the French guns."

Governor Drucour replied, "That is interesting, but there is another intangible that I expect hinders our Navy and that is the appointment of officers based not upon merit but their social standing." He looked away thoughtfully. "However, such appointments are the exclusive pleasure of the Crown. I take it that is not the case in the British Navy, else a man named MacGregor would not be an officer." Forcing a smile he changed the subject. "Enjoy the fresh vegetables, Lieutenant. I expect you will not be having many aboard your ship."

There was fresh baked bread with another item to which MacGregor was not accustomed: fresh butter. To Governor Drucour's urging, Marie told her story of the coming of the English to Beaubassin, the burning of her home by Abbe LeLoutre and their refuge at Fort Beausejour. She related with misty eyes the deaths of her brother under LeLoutre's partisans and her mother's death with a broken heart. Marie quickly concluded her story and sat with her hands in her lap.

An aide entered the dining room, leaning over to whisper in the ear of Governor Drucour. The governor replied, "Tell the gentlemen to wait until we have finished lunch."

Madame Drucour said, "You will, I presume, tell them that you are the governor here and that you will reply to the Englishmen without need of their advice?"

Governor Drucour looked kindly at his wife. "Now, now, my dear, let us be patient with our good generals. I will inform them of my reply to the Englishmen; it is the courteous thing to do."

Madame Drucour looked away coldly. She shifted her gaze to Lieutenant MacGregor and looked away with tight lips and firm jaw. He pretended not to notice the awkward silence.

Governor Drucour rose from the table saying, "Perhaps you will excuse me; I will have a few words with my colleagues. Marie, would you kindly entertain our guest. Perhaps with your music, if you like, while I prepare a reply for his officers?" Marie rose from the table and curtsied her acknowledgment to the governor.

Lieutenant MacGregor stood as the governor rose and remained standing as he left the room. Madame Drucour slowly stood, looking at the retreating figure of Governor Drucour as she said, "Yes, Marie, you play for Lieutenant

MacGregor. I must defend the governor as he seeks to defend Louisbourg from its enemies, those from within and without."

MacGregor looked down uncomfortably at his hands. He searched for words and looked up to see Marie retreating to the music room. He hurriedly followed her slim figure. Marie sat at the harpsichord, saying, "Would you care to hear some music of Rameau? He's a very good *French* composer. I play Bach also but find French composers more to my liking. Handel may compose good music but he is, like you, a servant of that German George who rules England."

MacGregor ignored Marie's words, saying, "I would like to hear anything you play, but I would rather spend the limited time we have *talking* to you." MacGregor moved closer to Marie. "Now that I've found you, I will do all in my power to reunite you." He continued patiently, "I have told your father… that I… regard you highly."

MacGregor's words were interrupted as Marie answered, "Any… regard you have for me you can tell me before you tell him. I once thought I had… some feeling for you, but that was before you helped the English take my people away from their land. That was before you took Father away and before I watched my people die in the wreckage of your English ship. Now you are saying you have… what did you call it? Regard? Yes, you said you had regard for me. But how can you have any feeling for me and still serve the English who are intent upon destroying me and my people?"

He stepped closer and took her hand. "Marie, there will be much suffering here if the governor does not surrender. How could I help you here if I were not with the English? My position as an officer in the British Navy allowed me to help your father, and I hope it will save you as well. The French can't win here. The English will soon destroy Louisbourg, I'm sure of it. You must leave before they destroy the town."

Marie bristled, "Governor Drucour shall not surrender! This is not Beausejour. We have many soldiers and ships here. You English will be defeated." Her eyes softened. "I do want to be with my father. I hope we can be reunited, and your English will not separate us again."

MacGregor spoke reluctantly. "Your father is owed a large amount of money by a Boston trader. If he can recover the money, he can easily pay your ransom. If he can't… then I'll provide what money I have. You should join him in Boston. It would be much safer. Will you leave, Marie, if we can arrange it?"

Marie began playing the harpsichord and looked away. Over the music she said, "I want to see my father, but how can I leave my friends here and join our enemy?" She lifted her chin and looked away. "I can't abandon these people. I beg you… bring my father here." She looked at MacGregor with pleading eyes.

"Marie," MacGregor said, raising his voice, "the English siege has only begun. If Governor Drucour doesn't surrender Louisbourg to the English, many people will die, maybe you. Please, you must leave Louisbourg and go to Boston. If you will not come away with me, go to Paris; go anywhere, but get out of here."

Marie stopped playing. She rose and walked to the window. Standing with the warm glow of sunshine against her face, tears welled in her eyes. She asked, "Your English must have what is ours or many people will die? Is that not always their way? How could I betray my countrymen while they are threatened with hunger and death? I could never be so selfish."

MacGregor sighed loudly. "The English are not the only barbarians; there's barbarism on both sides. The things the French and their Indian allies do to the English settlers can't be told in polite company. But this is not your fight, Marie. This is a war between people in far away lands over issues we hardly understand. You are not French, Marie; you are Acadian. And I'm not English. What I am, I can't exactly say, but…"

Marie quickly interjected, "Then why do you fight for the English? You have killed Frenchmen, I'm sure. Why do you fight for these heretics?" He looked down at his shoes and squeezed the hilt of his claymore. "They are your mother's people," Marie continued with bitterness. "How can you murder innocent people? Why do the English covet our homes and our lands? Why can't they allow us to live in peace? They take our land and kill us, just as they killed my brother! What the Indians did to your settlers I do not know, but I know the English take land that does not belong to them." With determination in her eyes she said, "I couldn't live with myself if I left my fellow Acadians to the mercy of our enemy. I'll remain in Louisbourg and stand beside the Drucours, my fellow Acadians, and the brave soldiers who defend us. They are my people, and if what you say is true, they will need me. Yes, I know my father needs me also and I need him, but I will not run away from Louisbourg." Marie turned her back to him. She walked to the window and looked out over the town of Louisbourg. "Louisbourg is the only home I have now. I feel as strongly about Louisbourg as I once did about Beaubassin. These people are my family. I love Louisbourg and its people. Even the hardships brought on us by the English are not unbearable." Marie turned to face him defiantly. "And our fighting men are brave. You are wrong to think the English will beat us!"

MacGregor heard the adjoining door open. "Somehow I will get you out of here. I hope you come willingly."

Governor Drucour strode into the room saying, "I hope you two made good use of your time."

"It was all too short, Sir," replied MacGregor. "I'm trying to convince Marie to leave Louisbourg for her safety. With your permission I will take her to join her father in Boston."

Governor Drucour's eyes narrowed. He stood quietly looking at Marie. A furrow deepened in his brow as he turned to MacGregor. "Being governor of Louisbourg, I bear a heavy responsibility for the welfare of its inhabitants. I'm also responsible for Marie's safety. Before allowing Marie to fall into English hands, I must be assured her father remains in Boston of his own free will. This I do not know, and at any rate, I can't be certain Marie would be safe in English hands. No, it is better for all concerned if Marie's father joins us in Louisbourg. I can insure their safety here."

Lieutenant MacGregor looked at Marie before he replied to Governor Drucour. "Governor, already our army has your fortress under siege. Soon British cannons will be dropping shells in the heart of the city and many civilians will be killed. Please, avoid unnecessary bloodshed and surrender now."

Governor Drucour walked casually across the room to adjust a picture hanging on the wall as he answered. "You should not rush to such impulsive conclusions, young man. Conditions will be considerably different now that our King has, at last, chosen a course of action against the English and Prussians. All Christendom will join France against the heretics. England and Prussia can not stand against the entire world. You, Lieutenant, should take refuge here where you belong. Leave the English oppressors of your people and join us." Governor Drucour placed his hand on MacGregor's shoulder. "Join us in the fight against the heretics; help us restore the throne to the line of Stuart, God's rightful heirs and perhaps your MacGregor's to their stolen land."

A chill ran down MacGregor's back as he placed his hand on the hilt of the sword hanging at his side. "Governor, I will honor the oath I have taken to King George so long as I'm an officer in his Navy."

He stepped in front of Marie, reaching to take her hand that she hastily withdrew. He dropped his hands to his side as he said, "Believe me, Marie, the French can't win this war in America. Their navy can't supply these outposts, and Louisbourg will fall with all the others. Please let me arrange for your passage to Boston before you suffer the fate of Louisbourg."

Marie turned to him with eyes flashing. "These people gave me food and shelter when I was homeless. I love the people here, and if they suffer hardships, I'll suffer with them. I couldn't desert them, even to be with my father." She looked at MacGregor with pleading eyes. "Please help my father come here. Perhaps your place is with the English; I know mine is with the French."

He reached for the dispatch case in the governor's hand and his face reflected determination. "I hope you'll change your mind before Wolfe's shells rain down on Louisbourg. Pray about it, *Mademoiselle*, and be ready... if you have an opportunity, leave Louisbourg."

With impatience Governor Drucour interjected, "In my dispatch, Lieutenant, I have told your superiors that we are not interested in their proposal of surrender."

"I'm also instructed to learn of our prisoners and their welfare," said MacGregor.

Governor Drucour spoke without hesitation, "The English cannot be trusted to know the location of the prisoners, but I have a list which I have given your admiral with my reply. I gave him my personal assurance that all prisoners are treated with respect and dignity. And, they eat as well as all inhabitants of Louisbourg... deprived by your blockade."

"I'll so inform my commodore, Sir," replied MacGregor. Holding out his hand, his eyes softened and a thin smile showed on his mouth.

The governor shook his hand. "Marie will show you to the door, Lieutenant, and my secretary will hand you a gift for your commanding officer. A little fresh butter should be a welcome treat to the fare aboard a ship. It has been a pleasure meeting you and I hope we meet again, under more peaceful circumstances."

Governor Drucour turned to Marie. "See our guest to the door."

MacGregor put the dispatch case under his arm. As they walked down the hall she looked up at MacGregor with searching eyes. "Do you understand? I can't leave. Will you explain that to my father?"

He looked straight ahead. As they reached the outside door he stopped, took Marie's hand in his, and replied, "Marie, I'll try to understand, and I'll try to explain to your father. You're making a mistake, but I respect your loyalty to your people. Hopefully the governor will surrender Louisbourg before women and children are killed."

Marie spoke with moist eyes. "Tell Father I love him and miss him. Tell him to come soon."

With Marie's hand in his, an uncertain emotion swept over MacGregor. "I'll tell him, *Mademoiselle*, what you have said. And I will tell him how the light shines in your hair and how beautiful you are. I will tell him, as I tell you, I'll be taking you out of Louisbourg. Goodbye, *Mademoiselle*. God keep you well." Striding through the door, he stopped. Putting on his hat, he strode out the door.

Anger flashed in Marie's eyes and then they softened, with a tear falling down her cheek. Marie wanted to run and put her arms around MacGregor, but she also wanted to beat his stubborn chest with her fists. She stood watching as he joined a French escort waiting beside the front steps. They walked away down the path toward the docks. Marie continued to watch until his image grew faint from her tears.

MacGregor made his way back through an even bigger crowd of people who had gathered to see the English ship in their harbor. Insults and taunts came his way. He shouldered past angry soldiers with various uniform insignia which he tried to remember. He tried to remember gun positions on the wall and looked for ammunition bunkers but thought mostly about Marie. Followed by a throng of jeering people, he exited the massive stone wall. A few stones landed near his feet and dogs barked at his heels. He forced his way past French sailors to take his place in the stern sheets of his boat. English sailors who had sat placidly through French insults gladly bent their backs to the oars in rowing MacGregor back to the ship. Lieutenant MacGregor doffed his hat to the colors as he stepped aboard H.M.S. *Grenadier*, then turned to look back at the majestic spires of Fortress Louisbourg standing against the soft blue sky.

The windlass clanked loudly and men groaned against the oak in raising the anchor. Chains clanked against the bow while the ship moved away in the current. *Grenadier*'s sails filled to the afternoon breeze.

Lieutenant MacGregor's thoughts were still on Marie when Walshingham yelled, "Take the ship out to sea and let's find the flagship. I'm anxious to give the commodore our report on Louisbourg if you are not, Mr. MacGregor." With the dispatch case clasped in hands behind his back, MacGregor stood looking wistfully at the spires of Louisbourg. He did not answer his captain and seemed not to have heard. All sails full, *Grenadier* heeled to starboard, crashing through the waves. Hard over, the frigate sailed in search of the flagship. Just before sundown Walshingham lifted a telescope from the rack and pointed it at the commodore's white pennant. His battleship rode the blue Atlantic swells like a majestic temple, massive sails spread before the wind, orange-red in the evening light.

Soon MacGregor stood in the commodore's cabin with the dispatch case under his arm. The commodore asked with a smile, "Have you taken the surrender of Governor Drucour?"

"Madame Drucour expresses her thanks for the pineapple," Lieutenant MacGregor replied as he delivered the dispatch case, "and Governor Drucour replies that he will accept *our* surrender."

Again he smiled as the commodore took the case and said, "Well, we have done the Christian thing and offered peace." Turning his back to MacGregor, the commodore looked out his stern window and said, "Now general Wolfe will have his way. William Pitt demands Louisbourg be taken this year, and Wolfe will give it to him, the civilians be damned." The admiral turned back to look at MacGregor. "Have you news of our prisoners? Did you learn where our remaining prisoners are kept?"

MacGregor said, "The governor will not disclose the location of our prisoners for fear we will attempt to free them by some covert action. He says there is a list of our prisoners with his reply."

"Very well, perhaps I can learn the location of our prisoners and make his fear a reality." The admiral seemed lost in thought for a while but presently looked up quickly to ask, "And what, MacGregor, were your impressions of Governor Drucour?"

"I'm afraid, Sir, like Admiral Boscawen, he's prepared to fight."

The admiral nodded. "He has his orders, I'm sure. So, there will be more bloodshed."

Chapter Thirty-One

MacGregor reported to his captain's cabin. Walshingham rocked back in his chair and smirked as he said, "MacGregor, I have volunteered ye for another mission. Take that bottle of wine as my compliments and report to Captain Laforey aboard *H.M.S. Hunter* just before sunset this evening."

Setting full and red in the west, the sun cast long shadows as MacGregor pulled himself up the boarding ladder. He responded to the mystifying order to go aboard *H.M.S. Hunter,* carrying a bottle of wine. Feeling foolish but doing as he was ordered, he found the captain of the ship standing on deck, waiting for him. As if he had known MacGregor for years, Captain Laforey almost shouted, "Good day, Charles, I see you have brought a bottle of wine. Good, when old friends meet, it should be over a good bottle of wine. Our mutual friend, Captain Balfour, is already here and waiting in my cabin. He even brought a basket of fine cheese with his wine." He leaned closer to MacGregor's ear, whispering, "For reasons you will learn in a moment, this meeting is disguised as a party among old friends." Captain Laforey led the way as they walked below deck, saying loudly, "It is so good to see you again, Charles. I heard you were wounded during the landing, not too seriously I hope?"

MacGregor replied, "I'm a little weak from loss of blood, but my surgeon thinks there is no better tonic than lots of red wine to rebuild the blood." MacGregor smiled. "My good doctor forces me to drink wine incessantly. Mind you, my doctor matches me drink for drink."

Entering the cabin he shut the door and said in fluent French, "This is Captain Balfour, of the fire ship, *Etna*. Like you, he's also fluent in French."

Captain Balfour looked young, not much older than himself, thought MacGregor. Balfour extended a hand. MacGregor took Balfour's outstretched hand and speaking in French said, "I'm honored to meet you, Sir, but totally unaware as to why I have been sent here."

Captain Balfour replied in French, "Nor I, Mr. MacGregor but I'm sure Captain Laforey will tell us soon enough."

"I will explain everything, gentlemen," said Laforey. "I'm pleased to see you both speak the language very well, although I can't quite place your accents. But that is good! And I must tell you, you both are highly recommended for the mission by our commodore. I know a little about both of you, having read your Admiralty records." He turned to MacGregor. "A little strange, Lieutenant MacGregor, don't you think? Your family exiled in France and mine in England. My parents were French Huguenots. As your father and grandfather was exiled in France, so mine were exiled in England... during the rein of William III."

MacGregor answered, "Yes, you will know, I suppose, that I was born in France. My mother was French and my father was, as you said, a Scottish exile in France. It seems the MacGregors always support the wrong side in any difficulty."

Captain Laforey replied, "It's a strange world, my friend. All very confusing. I won't ask why you fight for England, but then, there are thousands of Highlanders now fighting for England. I prefer not to think too much about these questions. But it is a tribute to the greatness of the Royal Navy that former enemies can rise to high command."

Laforey looked serious as he poured the two men a glass of wine. "Gentlemen, if you accept it, we are going on a very dangerous venture, a cutting out expedition. It's a job for volunteers only; we may not come back. But I think it is a mission you will not want to decline. Our mission is to capture two French men-o-war anchored in the harbor. They are very special warships, laden with English prisoners. When you think of the danger in our mission, imagine you were a prisoner confined in the dark holds of that ship. You would expect us to do all in our power to free you, and rightly so. We must not disappoint them. It won't be easy but we can do it, with God's help. And, with a little luck, we may also come away with a bit of prize money for our pockets."

Captain Balfour nodded in agreement. "Just the thought of being imprisoned in one of those ships gives me enough courage to attempt this... and the resolve not to join our comrades in imprisonment."

Laforey nodded in agreement. "Our leaders want them back very badly. You see, our spies tell us the French are anxious about the prisoners and may move them. We must act before they do so. At the same time we must be careful that we don't get our prisoners killed in the process. Therefore, this cutting out expedition requires detailed planning, practice, and perfect execution. Fortunately, the French seldom make hasty decisions. The commodore thinks there is time to practice our mischief." Laforey produced a hand-drawn chart of Louisbourg Harbor and pointed with his dirk. "These two ships block the entrance to Louisbourg Harbor. The French are clever. We can't send fire ships against their fleet. Fire ships would kill our British prisoners and the French know that. Knowing that, I'm sure they worry we may try to free them. I expect they will have doubled the guard. At any rate, we must do all in our power to free those prisoners so that we *can* send fire ships against them.

"You, Mister MacGregor, know Louisbourg Harbor. You have charted it and visited as an emissary. We will be using one of your charts and your knowledge of the waters. You will lead us into the harbor. Captain Balfour will lead a contingent against the French man-o-war, *Prudent*. My hope is," he said to Balfour, "that you can capture it without bloodshed. That is why every man on this mission speaks fluent French, both officers and enlisted men. Also… it is dangerous, so every man is a volunteer."

"While you attack the *Prudent*, Captain Balfour, I will cut out the enemy man-o-war, *Bienfaisant*. It is the larger and, we think, more heavily defended of the two. It is also the outside ship. If we fail to take *Bienfaisant*, your chances of getting out of harbor with *Prudent* will be poor.

"However, if we board and remove it, not only will the harbor lay open to our fire ships but the prisoners will be free." Captain Laforey spread MacGregor's chart on the desk and looked up at the two officers. "Study this chart carefully and memorize it. We must know it by heart. The shoal waters, hazards, and wrecks must be clear in our minds. There will be no opportunity to study charts during the attack. We must quickly find the two enemy warships and know they are the correct ships. If the vessels have moved, we must be able to recognize the movement." Captain Laforey tapped the chart with his dirk, showing the position of the two ships. "These two ships are close to the channel and have distinctive lines. We will all be dressed in French uniforms. We will carry pistols, but hopefully we will not use them. If we are successful, we will gain control of the ships by subterfuge and blade. If we use guns, our chances become poor. However, we will take enough men and weapons to prevail in the event our subterfuge is unsuccessful."

Lieutenant MacGregor asked, "How many men will we take? There can't be many sailors who speak fluent French."

"You'll be surprised, Mr. MacGregor. We know of almost five hundred French-speaking men through Admiralty records, and I venture every man will volunteer. They will speak no English after leaving this ship. We will go under cover of darkness and let us pray for fog. Our army on shore will mount a simultaneous attack to provide a distraction. With a little luck, that will draw return fire from the French and create a distraction for our pistol fire should we need them.

"You, Mister MacGregor, will take the lead boat and lead us into the harbor. Hopefully I can gain the deck of *Bienfaisant* without a shot and Captain Balfour can do likewise with *Prudent*. Remember, the safe recovery of our British prisoners is paramount, that is our number one objective. Secondly, we would like to open the harbor to our fire ships. Taking either of the ships as a prize would be a bonus, but remember, that is not our main objective. We must bring our prisoners out safely, however we can do it." Captain Laforey handed the men each a packet. "I have made copies of MacGregor's chart for each of you. I also have also obtained plans for both French battleships. Take them back to your own ships and let no one else see what I have provided you or know of our mission. Memorize every detail of these ships. When we meet again I will question you both in detail, and you must know every mark and scratch on the chart. You must be able to find your way in the French ships in total darkness. We will meet again in three days to plan every detail of our attack. Be here at the same time for another reunion party as we will have everyone thinking. Be sure you have memorized every detail and can reproduce it quickly when asked."

With some trepidation MacGregor made his way back to *Grenadier*. He spent hours memorizing every detail of the chart. After a second meeting with Laforey they began interviewing volunteers. Any man found not fit for duty was immediately dismissed before he learned of the mission. For three weeks the officers practiced and drilled the men selected. Each man must know his designated job; every man must know the back up plans. Speaking only in French, they honed and polished their plan. Any man who failed to meet their measure was confined. The officers criticized the plan and argued over changes. Every suggestion was thoroughly explored, adopted or rejected. With the aid of paroled prisoners, they studied the layout of the ships. At last, when the operation had become painfully familiar, Laforey announced the mission. The following night, July 25, 1758, would be moonless. The time was right.

With some four hundred specially trained, French-speaking sailors in French uniforms waiting in the darkness, the officers met a last time aboard the flag ship of Commodore. MacGregor felt naked without his claymore and strange in the French uniform. With the commodore looking on, Laforey went over the details of the mission once more. Finding no questions from MacGregor or Balfour, he pulled out his pistol. Laforey held it near the lamp, checking the priming. "Gentlemen, you know your jobs. Our mission can't fail; there are too many people depending on us. If things don't go exactly as planned, I expect you to change the plans on the spot and still accomplish the mission. Let's go!"

Captain Balfour threw his cloak over his shoulders and tied it at the throat. With a broad smile he shook MacGregor's hand. "I'll meet you back aboard Hunter for a little drink." He checked the dirk in his belt and hefted his pistol, saying, "I'm ready for a dram."

"I'll be happy to lift a glass with you, Sir," replied Lieutenant MacGregor. He put on his hat, pulling it down tightly on his head. He too drew his pistol, checked its priming, and slipped it back under the worn leather of his belt and threw a black cape over his shoulders. He felt for his dirk in his right boot. MacGregor hefted his sword to be sure it was free in its scabbard and held out his hand to Laforey. "I'll be on my way."

Captain Laforey gripped his hand firmly and looked him in the eye. "Take care of yourself, Mr. MacGregor. We all wait for your success. As soon as your last boat is clear, we'll follow. If we are lucky we will take the enemy ships without firing a shot. If we are not lucky we will succeed because we are determined to do this thing correctly." They left the warm, damp, 'tween-decks and ascended, their boots noisy on the stairs, their voices silent in their own thoughts. On deck, a cool, gentle breeze blew across their faces. The night was very dark, moonless and with wisps of fog. There was only the swish of sea foam, squeak of blocks, and groan of wooden timbers. Sailors on deck moved away silently as the officers walked across the deck, stopping by the port bulwark. "Good luck, said Laforey in French, "God be with you."

MacGregor, swinging his boot across the bulwark, said, "*Mai Dieu regard avec la faveur sur ce que nous faisons ici ce soir.*" He descended the boarding ladder and looked around at the boats. Only the closest boats were visible. Grey and colorless, they bobbed on the black swells. In his own boat, the lead boat, ashen colorless faces looked up at him. All men carried cutlasses; some carried pikes and many held clubs. The most trusted men also carried pistols. As Lieutenant MacGregor stepped down into his boat, he knew every man looked in his direction, searching his face for the sign of confidence that would bolster their own. MacGregor prayed they would see no fear in his face... nor in his behavior. If the plan failed, the failure would be his. MacGregor paused before he sat the boat. He looked into the faces of his men, saying with a broad smile, "I'm happy to see this fine crew of brave Frenchman serving our good King Louis tonight. It's a fine night for visiting our friends confined on their ships. I want to wish you all success in our merry party. If you meet any persons at this party who meet your fancy, you may invite as many as you like to return as your guests." He stepped down into the stern sheets of the boat.

"Cast off," he ordered in French. "We will speak no English beyond this point. Until we return, we are French. We will think in French, speak in French, and fight in French. May God go with you."

MacGregor settled in the boat, his hand resting on the hilt of his French sword. Ocean swells lifted the boat gently and pushed it along toward the harbor. Grave men rowed in silence. Oars, wrapped in muslin, dipped quietly in the water. Behind them, MacGregor saw the lead boats he knew were filled with determined men, all rowing toward Louisbourg Harbor. Suddenly he sensed there was no longer fog. *Fog, fog is needed. Where is the fog?* Waves washed the boat along, leaving a foaming, sparkling phosphorescence in its wake. MacGregor's pounding heart settled down as he thought, *The absence of fog will at least make our course easier to navigate.* He searched for landmarks when he found the telltale black rocks looming before them. It was time to watch the depths. "Lead line," he whispered in French.

A lead line, swung by the man in the bow, chunked softly as it sank beneath the water. The man whispered the water depth in French as he read the line. They rowed more slowly. *Surely a French sentry will see us soon*, he thought. Yet the many boats moved quietly over the black water. MacGregor felt he had never experienced a boat moving so slowly. The cool, damp air sent a chill down his spine as they rowed across the still, black waters of the harbor. His breathing seemed loud in his ears and his heart pounded too loudly. He squeezed the hilt of his sword. He searched the distance where he felt ships should be visible. Fog! Blessed fog had again obscured the harbor. *That's wonderful*, he thought. On through the low, gathering fog they rowed, with the man in the bow softly calling the depths. The rear boats were no longer visible to MacGregor, so thick was the fog. He strained his eyes ahead. Could he miss the ship in the fog?

A silhouette loomed black in the distance. *A ship!* Its black masts lifted into the gray of the dark sky, disappearing into the drifting fog, and reappearing. He asked himself, *Am I in the right place? Is this one of the target ships? Don't think of it yet. I'll decide when we are closer. Concentrate! Listen to the calls of water depth from the man in the bow.* MacGregor envisioned the chart of the harbor. He ordered changes in direction. He listened to the changes in water depth. He changed direction again until he found the desired water depths.

Then, deep in the fog, he saw only tall masts rising stark and thin against black sky. The familiar masts of a battleship. The ghostly form took shape as a ship. "It's the *Bienfaisant*, target ship for Captains Laforey," he whispered. He ordered his men to row past the ship, directing their following boat to remain and meet Laforey.

"Forward," ordered MacGregor. As the battleship fell away from them, he looked behind. Behind his boats there was only fog. He would not worry. Laforey would soon be alongside the ship. He must hurry and not keep Balfour waiting for his.

MacGregor felt the loneliness of command as only his smaller group pressed deeper into the fog. Fog grew thicker; he could hardly see the boat behind. Their lead line chunked into the water; the leads man whispered depths; little wavelets slapped the side of the boat. Oar locks squeaked. Somewhere a man coughed. A foot or club clunked against the side of a boat. Surely the noise will betray them to the enemy. Time seemed suspended. He waited for a gunshot to signal their discovery or the challenge of a sentry. Yet their boats moved slowly over the bay, alone, unchallenged in the foggy darkness. Where was *Prudent*? Surely they must have passed it by now; it couldn't be this far. How far had they come? How long had they been in the boats? It seemed like hours. Where was the ship? Perhaps the French had already moved it; perhaps he was leading his men into the enemy bay to no avail.

Something, a dark shape, caught MacGregor's eye in the fog. He ordered a slight change in course. Quickly stealing a glance behind him, MacGregor could only see two boats. Would the others be lost? Would he have enough men to carry the mission? He quickly scanned forward. The form he thought he saw had disappeared. Where was it? Was there really something there or an apparition built of fear? Was it his imagination? Had he passed his target ship? Another little opening in the fog again revealed a dark shape. Lieutenant MacGregor ordered another course correction. A bulky shape loomed above them in the fog. He strained his eyes into the foggy darkness. It was a ship, but which ship? *Where was the mizzen mast? Does the ship carry a spanker sail? What's the shape of the fore peak?* He studied the ship's lines as best he could in the hazy fog. Yes, they match; this ship was the French man-o-war, *Prudent*.

MacGregor held his breath, listening for a sentry's challenge, and heard only the pounding of his heart. *Where were the sentries? Were French sailors so careless?* His boat moved silently through the water, the enemy battleship looming larger before them. Their boat bumped the side of *Prudent*,

French man-o-war. From above a voice called, "Who goes there?"

Lieutenant MacGregor did not respond but rushed up the boarding ladder and as he did so, he saw more of his boats coming out of the fog. MacGregor strode confidently on deck, explaining, "I have come from the town to inspect your defenses." He hoped the challenge had not come from a senior French officer. He must act officiously and keep his adversary on the defensive.

MacGregor strode back to the bulwarks of the ship, his footsteps sounding loudly on the teak. He called down to his boat in French, "Five or six of you men come aboard; I need your assistance in my inspection." He turned back quickly to the sentry, "Where are your compatriots? You should not be here alone; the enemy could come from out of the fog and overpower you. This is a disgrace! Take me immediately to your superior officer."

MacGregor turned the speechless sentry toward the passage below deck and moved him away as English sailors climbed aboard. At the stairs to the quarterdeck the hapless sentry turned to look at the sailors now walking along the spardeck, silent men appearing out of the dark, swirling fog. Before the man could speak, MacGregor lifted his dirk from his boot and placed it at the man's throat. MacGregor whispered, "One word and you will die with my knife in your throat."

MacGregor waited breathlessly, knowing that a scream would undo everything. The cool night air seemed suddenly warm; his palms felt sweaty. His mind raced as to his action should the sentry speak. Should he attempt to club the man with his pistol? Should he sink his fist into his abdomen? He could not plunge the knife into the throat of a helpless man.

MacGregor's questions were moot. The man quickly raised his hands, his eyes wide in fear as he felt the knife at his throat. He slipped a hand over the man's mouth and forced the man to his knees. MacGregor motioned for a sailor. The man placed his own dirk at their prisoner's throat. MacGregor hurried back to the bulwark and looked down at the boats. *Thank God!* He saw Balfour pushing his way through the boats. His contingent had found the *Prudent*. Quickly, he bounded up the boarding ladder, followed by his men.

Balfour whispered to his sailors, "Quickly, now, you have your assignments: a man at every hatch." He watched his barefoot men moving away and turned to a group of sailors waiting expectantly beside him. "Let's get the prisoners," he whispered. MacGregor led them to the main companionway leading below, pistol drawn. Carefully, he lifted the hatch, revealing a dim light inside. The smell of tobacco smoke drifted through the hatch with the sound of French crewmen, chatting in carefree voices. Assured, MacGregor thrust the pistol back in his belt and waved Captain Balfour forward.

Balfour, adjusting his hat, pulled back his shoulders and confidently descended the stairs. Every step of his shoes sounded like a cannon shot, yet the men below continued their banter. MacGregor followed, allowing his eyes to adjust to the light as he neared the bottom of the stairs. The French crewmen ceased talking as Balfour's shoes landed on the deck below. Balfour whispered to MacGregor, "It sounds like young midshipmen, perhaps drinking wine and playing cards." Balfour threw open the door and demanded, "Who is in charge here?" Without waiting for a reply he continued, "This is a disgrace! You are all sitting here drinking with only one sentry on deck. What if the English came? They could take this ship without a fight. Go on deck immediately. I may take you back in my boat where you will have a great deal of explaining to do. Quickly! Get on deck this minute."

MacGregor picked up a hat on the table. He thrust it into the hands of the nearest young man and moved aside as the midshipman hurried up the stairs. The others quickly followed, buttoning their coats and putting on their hats as they went.

As Balfour went about securing the ship, MacGregor inspected the lower deck. Moving forward in the darkness, he found a sailor confronting him with a belaying pin. He guessed the man might be a guard for prisoners. Indecision was apparent in the man's eyes as MacGregor confidently asked, "Are the prisoners ready to be moved?"

The guard looked puzzled, replying, "No one told us the prisoners were to be moved."

"I can believe that," replied MacGregor. "No one seems to communicate with anyone now! I have come to take the prisoners. Our officers are concerned the English may try to take them. You should have had them ready to leave already." MacGregor's voice softened as he continued, "However, I can't blame you. Those worthless midshipmen do nothing but drink wine and play cards. It is they who are to blame. You can be sure my superior officers will hear of their neglect. Let's get those Englishmen up on deck. I'm anxious to get ashore so we can all get some sleep." MacGregor turned and yelled up the companionway, "Men, come below. Let's get these prisoners out of here. I'm anxious to go to bed."

Muffled voices whispered questions inside the darkened cell. The guard looked apprehensive. "I need a paper… a pass, or something…" Bare feet pounded across the deck above.

MacGregor called out to his men, "Come quickly! We haven't much time.

We must move the prisoners before daylight. Our commodore doesn't want the English to see them being moved."

A painful frown crossed the guard's face as he watched the armed men descending the stairs. The frown turned to resignation as he saw the men surrounding the door. MacGregor lifted a key tied at the guard's waist. He withdrew his dirk from his belt and sliced the cord holding the key. MacGregor thrust the key in the lock. Clicking loudly, the lock snapped open. Hushed voices and whispers sounded from the English prisoners inside the dark hold as the door squeaked open. The guard moved aside as he pulled open the door. MacGregor hurried inside, followed by several sailors. He could see the dark forms of prisoners moving in the shadows. "Quickly, men," he spoke in English, "take your clothing and follow me. Do not speak. There's no time to get dressed. We must get you away from here before the shooting starts. Keep close together and walk quickly. If there are any who cannot walk, you must carry them, but be quick about it."

Lieutenant MacGregor heard a scuffle outside the door. Wood thumped on skull bone. The guard fell heavily to the floor. MacGregor hurried out the door to find one of his sailors standing over the guard. Prisoners stumbled and groped through the darkness. They blinked and squinted in the yellow lantern light outside. Some men carried blankets and pieces of clothing. Two men held a hobbling prisoner between their arms. Lieutenant MacGregor said to his sailors, "Take the unconscious Frenchman along with you and go on deck. Get the prisoners off this ship and aboard our boats." They rushed out the companionway and up the stairs. MacGregor continued alone with drawn cutlass, inspecting the ship by the light of a lantern taken from the midshipmen's cabin. Cautiously he shined the light on blackened ship's timbers. There had been a fire. Farther he found signs of hasty repairs, and looking up, he saw where a shell had passed down between the decks. The bilge was full of water. He knew now the ship was damaged. MacGregor hurried up the stairs and out onto the fresh air of the deck.

MacGregor noted that a breeze blew lightly across the ship. "Mixed fortune," said Balfour. "A breeze to allow us to sail out with the ship, but perhaps a breeze to blow away the light fog."

MacGregor returned, "A shell has penetrated the ship forward and passed between the decks. I would not be surprised if she is grounded and unable to sail."

Balfour replied, "We will soon know." He ordered, "Men, let's make sail." As the sailors hurried off in the darkness, MacGregor went to the bow of the ship. He heard Balfour call, "Axemen, cut her cables!" Lieutenant MacGregor watched as men hefted their axes, running to the bow of the ship. By the time MacGregor reached the head of the ship, he heard the thump of axes. He placed his hands on the dew-dampened bulwarks and watched the final swings of a sailor's axe. From behind him he heard the splash of water and knew one set of cables were parted. Two more thumps of the axe, and again a splash. *The ship is free in the water*, he thought. A whistle shrilled sharply in the damp air. MacGregor turned to the main mast and saw men moving across the yards. Canvas fell from the yards, slatting and banging in the breeze. He returned to the head of the ship and looked down at the dark water. A long boat sped away from the bow of the ship, its sailors rowing as fast and hard as they could. He watched the line they carried rise from the bay. Drops of water dripped from the line as it reached the end of its tether. The line grew taut as the sailors strained at the oars but the big ship failed to move. MacGregor turned to watch the sailors working the sails. They braced the yards around to catch the wind. The slatting sails filled and grew silent, billowing into fullness, yet the ship did not move.

At the back of the ship Captain Balfour called, "Set more sail." He ran to the bow and stood by Lieutenant MacGregor, watching the sailors straining at their oars. "Hoist the jibs," he ordered. The line from their boat looked like a metal rod, straight and rigid across the dark water. MacGregor turned to look up at the masts, his heart beating faster. His sailors hurried across the upper yards, loosening gaskets. Jibs blossomed in loud snapping and popping on the bowsprit.

Distant gunfire sounded from the direction of *Bienfaisant*. Explosions rumbled loudly ashore. Rifle shots sounded sharp and erratic. Bright flashes lit the sky in the distance. Cannons answered and soon a cacophony of explosions echoed across the bay. That would be the distraction organized by Wolfe's army units. Would French sentries see their boats in the flash of shell bursts?

He hurried to the bulwarks, leaning across the rough, damp wood as he looked into the fog. It was *Bienfaisant*; Laforey's men were in trouble. Shooting popped loudly through the fog. Somewhere an officer barked an order in French. Two or three gunshots sounded in quick succession. MacGregor heard the splash of water and knew that someone had fallen overboard. The French were battling Captain Laforey's boarding party.

MacGregor hurried away from the bulwark. Balfour stood on the ship's quarterdeck and watched impatiently as his sailors loosed the sail gaskets.

Another sail slatted noisily in the night. MacGregor watched the yards braced around and saw the sail fill. He felt the ship heel slightly to starboard. Off the bow a second boat now tugged at the ship with a tow line, yet the ship would not move.

Running to the base of the foremast, he opened a trunk and rummaged inside. Tossing aside a box of gun flints, MacGregor shoved his hands deeper into the trunk. He threw several pieces of line on the deck before he found the object of his search. A heavy tug on the end of the cord told him he held the ship's lead line. MacGregor rushed to the bow, loosening the line into loops as he ran. He vaulted the bulwarks and stepped out on the ship's head as more gunshots sounded in the night. A bullet whined over his head. He unconsciously ducked. He held the heavy lead over the dark water and let the line slip through his fingers, noting the fathom marks as they slipped past.

In a disappointingly short time the lead found the muddy bottom and stopped. MacGregor hauled the line up, counting the fathom marks. One, two, three, four, five… subtract the height of the ship… aground! He dropped the lead line on deck. He felt confident the ship was aground and would not move. He thought, *At least they had not failed completely; the prisoners were free.* Now he must get them to safety before they were killed.

The dark night reverberated with a staccato of rifle and pistol shots. A cannon boomed. MacGregor's mind raced. The plan called for them to sail out in the protection of the captured French battleship. Now they would have to row back where they had come, past the ship where Laforey's men battled, where they would be easy targets in the open boats. *Would there be enough boats for the freed prisoners and their new French captives? Would there be enough time?*

MacGregor ran back to the quarterdeck where Captain Balfour stood. "We are hard aground," he yelled. "We must burn this ship and get back to the boats."

Captain Balfour agreed. He ran forward and called down to the men in the boats, "Cut your line! The ship's aground."

Back on the quarterdeck, MacGregor heard a gunshot followed by the splintering of wood behind him. He looked up to a see a man reloading a rifle on a nearby schooner. The object of his attention was not the man, however. The schooner! It was floating freely with its bow pointed into the tide. He yelled to the sailors on deck, "Take the prisoners down to our boats."

When Captain Balfour came running back to the quarterdeck, Lieutenant MacGregor yelled, "Our open, overloaded boats will be easy targets if the

French have overcome Laforey."

Captain Balfour quickly agreed but could not stop to discuss the next step. He ran down the deck, blowing his bosun's pipe. He blew three loud calls on the pipe and shouted, "Get our prisoners off this ship; she's aground. Take the prisoners aboard our boats!" A flurry of activity sounded on the decks below. The dark shapes of men rushed across the deck and down into the boats. Balfour turned to MacGregor. "Get our men aboard the boats. Take this ship's boats if needed."

Balfour hurried down the companionway, his footfalls clopping loudly on the stairs, his sword rattling on the handrail. He jumped the last few steps, landing heavily on the deck below. He scooped up a lantern and ran down the hallway. Lifting three more lanterns from the gimballed holders, he ran down the dark passage. Reaching the next companionway he held four lamps loosely in his arms. Balfour stopped, lifted the latch and looked down the dark stairs. *The powder magazine must be close below*, he thought. He began throwing the lamps. They bounded down the stairs, spilling their burning oil as the fell. Oil spilled over his sleeves. The last burning lamp he threw with force. It shattered against another on the deck below. Orange-yellow flames billowed from the spilled oil. Balfour bounded up the stairs, two at a time, the wood pounding under his feet.

In the meantime, MacGregor looked down from the deck of *Prudent* to see his sailors returning the gunfire of the French from the open boats. Sailors could hardly pull their oars, so crowded were the boats. His men would be slaughtered in the open boats. Lieutenant MacGregor made his decision. Vaulting the bulwarks he descended the boarding ladder. He leaped the last few feet into the crowded boat. With the boat swaying under the weight of his leap he ordered, "Shove off!" Pointing his sword at the schooner in the darkness, he said, "Row to that French schooner, there. Cut her cables and raise sail. We'll be safer in the schooner, and she should take us to safety."

The boat moved slowly across the dark bay, sailors straining to work the oars in too little space. Oars splashed water as they hurried. Bullets zinged across their heads and splashed in the water. MacGregor blew a long call on the boatswain's pipe, watching as other boats followed. He looked up at the schooner looming larger in the darkness. Fire flashed from the muzzle of a single gun and the shot barked across the water. MacGregor prayed they could be up the ship's boarding ladder before the guard could reload. He hurried forward, climbing over men in the crowded boat. The boat bumped hard against the schooner's hull and he fell forward, picking himself up on the shoulders of other men and leaped into the bow. He swung up the boarding ladder. Pulling himself up quickly, he threw a leg over the side. On the deck a French sailor worked furiously at reloading his rifle. Seeing MacGregor climbing over the side, he dropped his ramrod. The sentry swung the butt of the rifle at MacGregor. Throwing his sword aside, he dove for the man's legs and pulled him to the deck as other French sailors rushed in their direction. Squeezing the man's knees together, he twisted until he felt the man tumble on top of him. He shoved an arm under the man's leg and another under his shoulder. Straining, he lifted the struggling man and took two quick, wavering steps to the side. The marine's rifle rattled to the deck. MacGregor heaved him overboard. The man splashed into the dark water. Meanwhile, his own sailors clambered up the side and rushed over the deck. The few seamen, most unarmed, were quickly overcome. MacGregor saw smoke with the orange hue of flames rising from the main companionway of nearby *Prudent*. He saw the British sailors climbing the ratlines while others ran to the bow, chopping at the anchor cables with axes. Again, sailors ran out on the yards above, loosening sail gaskets. Every man worked with a purpose. Below, Balfour was climbing aboard the schooner as he felt the bow of the ship turning to the wind in her sails. Sailors hauled the yards over as the sails boomed and thundered in the breeze. Sailors hauled a jib up the forestay while the mainsails were sheeted home. A shudder passed down the deck as the schooner came to life. MacGregor spun the ship's wheel as a breeze filled the sails. He felt the cool air in his face. The schooner slipped forward. Hatless, his hair blew in the breeze.

Captain Balfour joined him on the quarterdeck and MacGregor asked, "Will you take the quarterdeck, Captain?"

Balfour replied, "No, MacGregor, you have earned the right. Sail her down to *Bienfaisant* and let us see what has happened to Laforey."

MacGregor looked over his shoulder. A gaggle of empty ships boat towed behind. Flames leaped into the masts and rigging of *Prudent*. "That's a battleship that will never do battle again," he said. MacGregor turned back to his task, steering the schooner into the open sea.

Gripping the smooth wood of the ship's wheel, MacGregor felt the ship answering the helm. He watched the sails filling in the night sky and heard the canvas cease its pounding as wind turned them rigid. He felt the ship heel to the sails and course through the water. The schooner gathered headway, moving ever faster across the harbor.

A breathless midshipman approached the quarterdeck. The young man's eyes reflected the ship's fire in the darkness. A proud smile crossed his face as he said, "We've not lost a single man in the action."

"Aye, a fine job indeed," answered Balfour. "Now get the prisoners below for safety and muster every weapon you can find to defend the ship." The young midshipman bounded away, his bare feet pounding the deck.

MacGregor spun the wheel to turn the bowsprit away from a large, black ship looming before him. Slowly, the schooner's bow turned. Could he clear the ship? It would be a close call. He spun the wheel as far as it would go and watched the bowsprit slipping slowly to the side. Holding his breath, he watched as they cleared the anchored ship's long bowsprit. From the waist of the ship he could have touched the other ship. He patted the ship's wheel, thinking, *You are a beautiful ship, fast and agile.* He steered the ship away from the warship, making sail in the harbor entrance. MacGregor saw that the French warship with which he had almost collided was sailing toward open water. *Bienfaisant!* Captain Laforey had cut out the heavy battleship and now sailed her out to sea.

MacGregor felt the surge of the ship as his men sheeted more sail to the wind. The faster schooner skimmed out of the harbor and found the wind of the open sea. MacGregor watched the dark form of rocks to starboard and eased the wheel over, seeking the middle of the channel. Where ocean met harbor entrance, wisps of fog still hung over the black water. Breaking waves showed white on the black sea. Ocean swells lifted the schooner as MacGregor watched astern for *Bienfaisant.* There the slower battleship struggled to make way. With jubilant sailors shouting and waving, MacGregor sailed the ship out beyond the harbor entrance. The schooner seemed alive in his hands, responding instantly to the wheel. To himself, MacGregor promised, "Some day I will own a schooner just like this one. I will stand behind the wheel and sail her myself. I would sail her around the world and never fear."

Happiness came over him and he smiled at the sailor standing nearby. He saw their prize quartermaster and moved back from the wheel, holding it with one hand as he offered the ship's helm to the designated sailor. The man stood still with hands behind his back, smiling back at MacGregor. MacGregor nodded. He smiled and turned back to the wheel, taking it in both hands. He forgot the war and smiled as the ship heeled to the wind.

Balfour turned to a midshipman nearby, ordering, "Bring the prisoners on deck." The young man, flushed with joy as he bounded away, replied, "It's my pleasure, Sir."

The midshipman soon returned on deck, followed by cheering men. Balfour looked across the crowded deck. He waited until the British prisoners had all come on top, then called, "Raise the King's X over her."

"Aye, Sir," answered a sailor pulling a Union Jack from his coat. To cheers on deck, the man ran the flag up the mainmast.

When the cheering subsided, MacGregor quietly turned to his first mate. He ordered, "Go below and inventory her cargo. Bring back her log and manifest if you can find them."

When the man returned, handing MacGregor a log and manifest, he reported, "Sir, I've looked below. The ship's got a cargo of French rifles, among other things. The rifles were hidden under a cargo of cloth, tea, and spices. And that's queer, Sir, because it's English, registered in the port of Boston!"

MacGregor looked up quickly. "English? Port of Boston? Does the ship have English papers?"

"Aye, Sir. It has papers in both English and French, but all the ship's charts show Greenwich meridian. If it were French, they would be Paris meridian. Her English registry shows her master as an Edward Brumley, of Boston."

MacGregor's face registered surprise. He was quiet for a few moments, looking at the man closely. "Edward Brumley? Aye, you're right. The ship must be English, I know her master. But was this ship captured by the French and brought here? No, I think not. Its hull shows no sign of battle damage. I think it's a contraband trader doing business with the enemy. We surprised this ship in the harbor by our invasion, and it was afraid to come out, I think."

Balfour said, "This is a legitimate prize of war. There will be a lot of prize money that goes with it. Our prisoners are free, and we didn't lose a man in the action. Let's enjoy our victory." He held out his hand to MacGregor. They shook hands and watched the blanket-wrapped prisoners congratulating themselves on their freedom.

MacGregor opened the leather bound log book the sailor handed him. It was too dark to make out the writing. He thrust the log and manifest under his arm and walked to the ship's rail. MacGregor lifted his leg on the rail and sat enjoying the fresh air, his chin high and chest swollen. He had not captured *Prudent*, but this sturdy schooner would fetch a fair sum of money and a large part of it would be his.

They sailed through the English fleet blockading Louisbourg, recognizing *Grenadier* as he passed. Lieutenant MacGregor sailed past the sentry ring of frigates, passed the second raters, and rounded up in the wind near the Commodore's flagship. Balfour picked up the speaking trumpet and called out,

"Heave to!"

The schooner rode the swells smoothly, her blocks squeaking lightly as they turned. Men spoke in happy voices on the deck below. Again, cheers broke out as *Bienfaisant* hove to beside the two waiting ships. Slowly, the French battleship turned her bow into the wind and slowed to a stop, idling as the crew reduced sail. Dawn broke in the east while the two prize ships hove to beside the commodore's flag ship.

The rising sun bathed the ships in bright orange light. It was then that MacGregor saw the lone oak flag of Edward Brumley flying above, sharply visible against the pale sky.

This was indeed Edward Brumley's ship! He quickly tore the ship's manifest from under his belt and held it to reflect the faint light of dawn against its worn pages. He hurried across the deck and threw open the companionway door. His feet thumped loudly on the stairs as he hurried down. Turning aft he threw open the door to the captain's cabin and rushed inside. He held the leather bound manifest under the lamp and read, starting at the last page. Quickly, he flipped the pages, reading hurriedly toward the front of the book. "There's no mention of rifles, only cloth, tea, and spices for Boston."

MacGregor picked up the lantern. With the lantern swinging in the darkness, casting moving shadows, he left the cabin and descended into the cargo hold. Holding the lantern above his head he shaded his eyes. The light of the lantern fell on neat stacks of cloth, casks, and boxes of tea. In one area the stacks were leaning, revealing rifle boxes hidden beneath the cloth and tea. MacGregor walked to the rifle boxes. Running his fingers across the rough wood of the rifle boxes he lowered the lantern to read the course French letters, "Via *Chasseur* to Louisbourg." *Chasseur*! These were the missing rifles he had captured two years ago aboard the French battleship, *Chasseur*. Walshingham had stolen the rifles and sold them to Edward Brumley! MacGregor stood the lantern on a nearby cask and drew his sword. The metal scraped loudly out of its sheath in the quiet of the cargo deck. He placed the point of the sword under the board bearing the letters *Chasseur*. The nails squeaked as the board pulled lose. MacGregor stood looking at the loose board in his hands, reading the legend, "Via *Chasseur* to Louisbourg."

MacGregor returned the sword to its sheath and picked up his lantern. He bounded the stairs two at a time. On deck he saw a boat departing the flag ship.

Watching from the schooner's waist, he saw the Commodore climb the boarding ladder to *Beinfaisant*. From the deck of the schooner MacGregor and Balfour watched the Commodore greet Captain Laforey. The two toured the captured vessel. Later they both boarded the commodore's boat and crossed the short distance to the captured ship. With the look of success in his eyes, the Commodore, followed by Captain Laforey, approached Balfour and MacGregor. It was a meeting of victors, with congratulations and back slapping. Captain Laforey said, "We lost seven men killed and several wounded, but we freed twenty British prisoners and captured three enemy sailors! And you?"

Balfour answered, "We rescued sixteen prisoners and lost not one man while capturing this fine schooner."

The commodore spread his arms wide, exclaiming, "Magnificent!" He smiled at MacGregor. "A job well done." Smiling at Balfour and Laforey, he added, "And you are richer men today." He looked at MacGregor. "Is this a French merchantman?"

"No, Sir," answered MacGregor, handing him the ship's log. "It's an American ship belonging to Edward Brumley of Boston."

The Commodore's eyes grew wide. "Brumley's ship? How did Brumley's ship come to be in Louisbourg? There's been no report of a schooner lost to the French. Is there cargo aboard her, Mr. MacGregor?"

MacGregor handed the commodore the ship's manifest. "Aye, Sir. There's lead and powder from England." MacGregor squeezed the hilt of his sword, adding, "And model 1734 muskets made in Tulle, France. The same as those aboard *Chasseur*, the prize we captured last year and about the same number."

The commodore exclaimed, "Lead? Powder? Rifles from the prize ship *Chasseur*?" The other officers spoke to each other in hushed, startled voices. The Commodore looked puzzled. He quickly opened the leather bound manifest and thumbed through its pages. "Yes, here it lists the rifles, purchased from a trader in Boston."

"Here." MacGregor lifted a paper. "A French agent paid for the weapons, with instructions that they be shipped to Quebec. Edward Brumley of Boston has signed here for receipt of the money." The Commodore looked up in surprise and then read more as MacGregor handed him another paper. "And here the French acknowledge receipt of the items in Louisbourg where they sought shelter from British ships. Unable to sail on to Quebec, they were trapped by our blockade of Louisbourg." The Commodore tucked the book and papers under his arm and turned toward the companionway leading below deck. "Let's go below and have a look." Swords rattled, boots thumped on stairs, and officers spoke in hushed tones as they went below. Lifting a brass lantern from its holder, MacGregor led the way down the dark cargo hold. In the damp, smelly hold, MacGregor lifted the lantern high and led the group to the uncovered rifles. He handed the lantern to Captain Balfour as he lifted the lid on a box and took out a long French rifle inscribed with the arms of France, the year 1734, and its place of manufacture, Tulle. Taking the rifle from MacGregor's hands, the Commodore held it close to the lantern, reading the French inscriptions. He quickly thrust the rifle back into MacGregor's hands and took the lantern from Balfour.

Lowering it to the box lid he read, "Louisbourg via *Chasseur*." The Commodore looked up at MacGregor. "These are indeed the rifles that disappeared from your prize, *Chasseur*."

"There's little question of it, Sir, whatever." answered MacGregor. The Commodore looked into MacGregor's eyes intently. "How do you suppose, Mr. MacGregor, that these rifles were not found aboard *Chasseur* when it was assayed?"

MacGregor looked the Commodore in the eye. "Sir, I reported these rifles to be aboard *Chasseur* to Captain Walshingham. They were aboard that vessel when I delivered it to Halifax. I can tell you, and port records will verify the fact, I'm sure, that this schooner belonging to Edward Brumley was anchored near *Chasseur* in Halifax Harbor."

The Commodore turned to his chief of staff. "Inventory everything in this ship with the greatest of care. Take charge of the manifest and logs. There will be a full investigation of this matter, I assure you. Either it will be investigated by the Admiralty or by myself and I choose that it be me. We will immediately convene a court martial right here and end this little windstorm before it blows to London and becomes a hurricane."

Chapter Thirty-Two

Anchored in Gabarus Bay, not far from Louisbourg, the schooner captured by MacGregor lifted to the waves entering the bay. A British Jack flew over the mainmast. On the deck of the captured schooner a group of senior officers milled about uncomfortably. Their Commodore stood, shading his eyes from the sun as he watched his ship's boat slow approach. The heavy ship's boat rode low on the ocean waves, filled with rowing sailors and armed marines. The Commodore recognized his aide sitting in the stern sheets. He guessed that the man sitting in front of Captain Anderson was Mr. Farwell, Captain Walshingham's purser. The Commodore paced the deck with hands behind his back as he spoke, "Gentlemen, the reason I have called you here is to inform you of your duties in the upcoming court martial. You will recall that our own Captain Walshingham, in a brave and if not foolhardy action, captured a French battleship. As luck often smiles on Captain Walshingham, that battleship was so loaded with cargo, he could not open his lower gun ports nor had he enough men to man all his guns. As it turns out, a load of rifles in the hold of that battleship was stolen from the French prize while it was anchored in Boston. Now those rifles are in this schooner which Walshingham's own Lieutenant MacGregor cut out of Louisbourg Harbor." He paused, looking impatiently at the boat approaching. The Commodore squinted his eyes and frowned as if he found something very distasteful. "I expect evidence will show that Walshingham, not content with his share of prize money, stole those rifles with the help of our new prize master in Boston. Gentlemen, this is an embarrassment to me as it is to our fleet. To make a long story short, I'm asking your cooperation in a court martial of Captain Walshingham. I do not want Walshingham's case going to London for trial; it's better we look after our own dirty laundry. Brumley is London's problem, they can do as they please with him, but Walshingham is our problem. If the facts substantiate my belief, you must find Walshingham guilty, and I want you to decide quickly. By law, thirteen post captains must try Walshingham and the senior officer shall act as judge. Walshingham could be shot for his actions, but I do not want that, nor I'm sure, do you. We should allow him to resign his commission and walk away, where I do not care, so long as it is far away. After all, no great crime has been committed, has it? We have the rifles, do we not? Certainly Walshingham's intentions were evil, but we can't hang a man for his intentions." The Commodore smiled and looked around into the men's eyes, saying, "After all, most of us could be found guilty of evil intentions every time a pretty lass walks past." There was a murmur of assent and chuckles from the captains. The Commodore continued, "By right, command of *Grenadier* should be given to MacGregor, but unfortunately I think that can't be. The Admiralty always has a list of officers they wish to promote to post captain. To help sway the Admiralty toward our way of handling this affair, we should let them provide a replacement for Walshingham. Those are my thoughts on the matter and now I leave it up to you." The Commodore turned away as if he were unable to look his officers in the eye. Turning to his yeoman, he asked, "Do you have the logs and manifest ready?"

"Aye, Sir," answered the yeoman, "I have the ship's records here in my hand, and the rope is in the ship's stern cabin as you directed."

"Very well," replied the commodore, looking up at the men coming on deck from the boarding ladder. "I will now present the jury with what I expect will be some revealing information from the purser of the frigate, *Grenadier*. I ask that you listen carefully, gentlemen." The Commodore greeted the new arrivals. "Ah, good to see you gentlemen. Thank you for coming at my request." He turned to the gaunt looking man whose eyes looked searchingly from a bony skull. "You must be Mr. Farwell, purser to Captain Walshingham."

Farwell carried a stack of journals in his arms, leaning backwards as he struggled with the load. His thin throat revealed a bobbling Adam's apple covered with gray whiskers. "Ah, aye, Sir. Mr. Farwell, Sir." His eyes were wide and questioning while his gnarled fingers fidgeted nervously.

The Commodore replied, "I'm glad to finally meet the excellent purser from *Grenadier*, Mr. Farwell. I see you brought your journals as I asked."

The gaunt man's eyes widened even more as he answered, "Aye, Sir, I've brought my journals just as you ordered. All of them."

"Good," replied the Commodore. "Give them to Captain Anderson, Mr. Farwell." He put an arm around the purser. "You know, a ship of the Royal Navy is a little like a business in London. It operates on money and that money must show a profit. A good captain like Walshingham shows an excellent return on the Crown's investment. I have always thought that behind a good captain there stood a superb purser. Captain Walshingham's excellent financial results are, I suspect, partly a result of your good work. You must have had a great deal to do with those fine records."

Mr. Farwell's face broke into a nervous grin to reveal a mouth missing many teeth. "Aye, Sir, I've maintained a fine set of records for Captain Walshingham over the last ten years."

"Yes, I'm sure you have," replied the Commodore. "Do you ever remember writing a report regarding your assay of this schooner?"

Mr. Farwell looked around the ship as if seeing it for the first time. "Er, no, Sir. I don't think I ever saw this ship before, Sir."

The Commodore looked surprised. "No? Well, perhaps you have not, Mr. Farwell. But you may have seen some of her cargo aboard one your prizes, *Chasseur*. Let us go below and see if we can find anything you might recognize." The Commodore turned to lead the procession of officers down the companionway. A red-coated marine stepped aside as the men thundered down the stairs. Lifting a lantern over his head, the marine led the group down the dark hallway and down into the musty smelling cargo hold. Taking the lantern, the Commodore led the way past stacks of boxes to an opened crate. He lifted the lantern and removed a rifle, handing it to Mr. Farwell. "Do you know what this is?"

Mr. Farwell's forehead showed drops of perspiration in the lantern light. "Well, yes, Sir, this is a rifle."

"Yes, no doubt about that," replied the Commodore. "But look at the rifle carefully and tell me what kind it is."

Mr. Farwell's eyes never moved from the Commodore as he replied, "I'm a man of paper and records, Sir. I never had anything to do with rifles. I wouldn't know one from another."

The Commodore smiled. "Of course, Mr. Farwell. I might have known that most of your time would be spent in writing and keeping books. You couldn't be expected to be an expert on rifles.

"But, Mr. Farwell, look at the inscription on the rifle here in the lamp light and see if you see any clue about the origin of this rife."

The purser took a pair of glasses from his pocket, carefully spread them across his nose and took the rifle. He turned the rifle in the light and held it away from his body, peering carefully down his nose through the glasses. "Well, Sir, I make this here writing to be French. I reckon this is a French rifle."

"Very good, Mr. Farwell," replied the Commodore. "You are absolutely right, this definitely is a French rifle. Now let me have it." He took the rifle and handed it to Captain Anderson, saying, "Pass this around to the other officers." He turned back to the cargo and lifted a wooden lid to the box. Holding the piece of wood in the light for Mr. Farwell, he asked, "Can you read this?"

Again Farwell squinted in the light. "Well, er, I don't parley no French, but it looks like *Louisbourg via Chasseur.*

"You are indeed right again, Mr. Farwell," replied the Commodore. "This ship carries cargo for the French Army, including rifles stolen from a ship by the same name in Halifax Harbor. I don't suppose you would know anything about that would you, Mr. Farwell?"

The purser's mouth opened once, twice, three times, and his Adam's apple bobbled once or twice but sound eluded him. He swallowed hard, finally managing to answer, "Oh, no, Sir. I would know nothin' about that."

The Commodore smiled benevolently. "We will examine your journals, Mr. Farwell, very carefully. Yes, we will examine them very, very carefully." Mr. Farwell stood nervously rotating his hat in his hands. "We will compare them against the manifest and bills of lading. We are also examining the books of Mr. Edward Brumley of Boston, the prize agent. As good a purser as you are, Mr. Farwell, you know that all the accounts must tally."

Handing the lantern to the marine, the Commodore said, "Now, let us go to the captain's cabin." He led the group of men back to the main deck and into the captain's cabin where light flooded the room through the stern windows. Speaking in hushed tones, they crowded into the small cabin where the Commodore's aide sat at the captain's desk, examining Farwell's journals. Having waited for everyone to enter, the Commodore accepted a journal from his aide. Farwell's eyes opened wide and he swallowed hard.

The Commodore quickly thumbed through the pages, stopped, flipped back several pages and held the page to the light. "Ah, yes," he said. "So this is your signature, is it not, Mr. Farwell?"

Mr. Farwell peeked around the Commodore's shoulder and worked his mouth several times before an answer came forth. "Er, yes, Sir. I reckon... I mean, aye, Sir. That's my signature."

"Yes, I thought so," replied the Commodore. He snapped the book shut, handing it to his own secretary, and said, "Pass this around for the officers." Captain Anderson gave the Commodore another book. The Commodore took the book while looking at Mr. Farwell. "This is a manifest from this schooner, Mr. Farwell." He opened the book at a marker and looked at it carefully. "This manifest shows the consignor of those rifles as a man named Walshingham. The consignee's signature appears to be that of our prize agent in Boston, Mr. Edward Brumley. And here, you, Mr. Farwell, have signed as Walshingham's agent. This is your name and your signature, is it not, Mr. Farwell?"

Yeoman Farwell's mouth opened but his eyes lids closed. No sound came from his mouth and his hands trembled. All color drained from his face and he began to sway.

"Get him a chair," ordered the Commodore. An officer quickly shoved a chair behind the yeoman, who fell to a sitting position. With the officer holding him upright in the chair, Mr. Farwell looked up at the Commodore without words.

The Commodore leaned against the desk, looking down at Farwell as he asked, "Do you expect Captain Walshingham will acknowledge you were acting on his behalf in selling these stolen rifles, or do you suppose he will say you acted alone and without his knowledge?" Without waiting for Farwell's answer, he turned to his aid. "Captain Anderson, show Mr. Farwell the fate of traitors who work for the enemy in time of war."

Captain Anderson walked across the room, his slow, deliberate footfalls sounding loudly on the wooden floor. He threw open a closet, displaying a hangman's noose. In four quick steps he stood before Mr. Farwell. The noose hung a few inches in front of Farwell's nose. Farwell's wide eyes followed the swinging noose. Beads of perspiration glistened on his forehead. He stammered a few unintelligible sounds.

The Commodore stood with his feet wide apart, his hands on his hips, looking down at Farwell. "Mr. Farwell, a very quick hanging could be your fate unless clemency is granted. I'm prepared to recommend clemency if you provide a true and accurate account of just how these rifles came to leave Boston Harbor."

Mr. Farwell managed to stammer, "Please, Sir, give me clemency. I'll tell 'em all, true and straight. I took care to protect myself, ya' know. I always do. I know Captain Walshingham real good, and I don't trust nobody. I been cheated too many times by slick merchants packing sawdust in the bottom of flour barrels, rancid meat beneath the good, and every other trick in the book. I keep a truce record of ever transaction."

The Commodore turned his back to Farwell and stood looking out the stern window, his lower lip pinched between his thumb and forefinger. He answered, still looking out the window, "Mr. Farwell, there's an excellent chance you could be given clemency... if you cooperate fully and reveal all the details about these stolen rifles. Good pursers are hard to find, and we can't afford to lose a good purser like you."

With reprieve glowing in his eyes, Mr. Farwell began to talk. Like steam from a boiling kettle his words rose. "You see, Sir, Captain Walshingham turned the cargo over to our prize agent in Boston, Edward Brumley.

Everything aboard *Chasseur* was listed as prize except the rifles. Mr. Brumley wuz to sell the rifles separately and split the money with Captain Walshingham. Them rifles would bring more money than the ship and all the other cargo put together."

Bending low and putting his face near Farwell's, the Commodore said, "Who else aboard *Grenadier* knew that the rifles were stolen?"

With beads of perspiration on his forehead the purser answered, "So far as I know, no one knew except Captain Walshingham... and me, Sir. Since Edward Brumley was the prize agent, everyone that handled the rifles thought the movement of them rifles to Brumley's ship was legitimate. Lieutenant MacGregor, I think, suspected something but could not prove nothing. He asked me questions, but I told him he better go ask Captain Walshingham. I suspect that hard-headed Scotchman, not meanin' no offence to no Scotchmen, mind you, went and asked the captain about it. I think that's why the captain has been mighty hard on MacGregor lately, like nobody can understand how that Scotchman is alive today after everything the captain done put him through. He's mighty lucky to be still alive, that Scotchman."

Meanwhile, off Louisbourg, Captain Walshingham paced the decks of *Grenadier,* his oppressive brow pulling his chin down against his chest. Sailors gave him a wide berth. *The Commodore's removal of my purser was unheard of, it was unethical, by God! What could that sneaky chamber servant of the Admiralty be up to?*

Walshingham's heart skipped as he saw a hoy approaching, its small sail heeled in the wind. A young midshipman sat in the bow as it skipped over the waves. His clothing was too well kept; it was a bad omen. The hoy came along side the frigate and the young midshipman leaped to the boarding ladder.

Bounding up the ladder, he doffed his hat to the Union Jack. He stepped over the coiled cordage and ropes strewn over the decks. The young man doffed his hat to Captain Walshingham. Holding out a document sealed with wax and red ribbon, the midshipman wondered why this brooding captain looked as if he had been smitten with an axe.

Captain Walshingham's eyes radiated fire as he tore the document from the messenger's hand. He squeezed the document in his fists as he read the letter. Walshingham walked slowly across the busy deck, his chin resting on the top button of his lace-collared shirt, the letter in his hand. Slowly, he walked down the stairs of the companionway, and with bowed head, he trudged down the narrow corridor. The red-coated marine snapped to attention and drew open his cabin door as Captain Walshingham approached. Walshingham seemed not to see the marine. He entered the cabin, slamming the heavy door behind him. Slowly, he walked to his polished oak desk. Spreading the letter across his desk, he stood looking down at the paper. Walshingham stood. He moved across the room, running his hands lovingly across his many books. The captain moved farther down the book shelf to a rack holding his liquor. From the gimballed rack Captain Walshingham lifted a bottle of choice whiskey. It was one he drank only on special occasions. Captain Walshingham pulled the cork from the bottle. He lifted the bottle to his mouth. Before drinking, however, he looked slowly around the ornate cabin. His eyes fell on the glistening chandelier over his desk. He looked longingly at his lovely paintings, moving quickly across the room to straighten a gold leafed frame that had been knocked askew. Again, he lifted the bottle in a silent toast to his beloved possessions and drank from the bottle he would ordinarily have sipped. Wiping his mouth on the back of his lace sleeve, he walked to his desk. Setting the bottle carefully on his desk, he moved to his stern window and stood silently looking over the army investing Louisbourg. When he turned back, his face appeared lighter. The faintest trace of a smile appeared and his eyes sparkled. Captain Walshingham moved quickly to his desk and opened the bottom drawer. He withdrew a polished mahogany box gilded with gold leaf and adornments. Laying the box on his desk, he lovingly opened the lid to reveal a matched set of dueling pistols. Walshingham lifted a pistol and ran his fingers over the cold steel. He breathed on the brilliant gold leaf, polishing it to a luster with his lace sleeve. Pausing only for another drink of whiskey, he quickly removed his coat and laid it carefully on a chair. Walshingham hurried back to the box on his desk and removed the powder flask. He opened the flask and measured a full charge of powder into a special silver spoon from the box. The captain poured the powder into the barrel and followed it with a tiny square of waxed cloth. Walshingham opened the leather shot bag and chose a well rounded shot, holding it against the light as he examined it with one eye closed. Satisfied, he laid the shot on the muzzle of his pistol. Captain Walshingham slipped the rammer from the pistol and laid its blunt end on the gray-blue ball. In one smooth, practiced movement he forced the ball and patch down the barrel. Pulling the hammer back to half cock, he tilted the gun to one side and poured a little powder into the firing pan. With satisfaction in his glistening eyes he admired the loaded weapon. Pistol in hand, he raised his eyes to the ceiling, saying loudly, "My jealous enemies think they have finally brought me down, but I will defy them. Everyone will now know that I, Captain Walshingham, commanded to the end. Only I can decide my fate. I am my master and no man can bend me to his will. I am undefeated now and undefeated shall I die."

He laid the pistol on his desk, being careful not to spill the powder from the pan. After another drink from the bottle, he found a piece of paper in his drawer. Walshingham removed the cork from his ink bottle, setting the ink carefully in front of him. He opened his sand box and laid it nearby. Captain Walshingham lifted a quill, poised it over the paper and began to write. He stopped, thinking, *What better place to record my independence, my freedom, my right to choose the time of my own freedom.* Walshingham lifted the pistol to his temple and squeezed the trigger. Gently at first, he squeezed and closed his eyes, waiting, wondering if he would hear the blast, feel the pain. The captain pulled harder on the trigger, but it would not budge. He smiled as he remembered he had left it on half-cock, safety. Walshingham removed the pistol from his temple and pulled the hammer full back with his other hand. *I do not die easily*, he thought. He lifted the pistol again to his temple and sat there, thinking, *Could my jealous adversaries see my suicide as an act of weakness? Damn their eyes, they shall see no weakness in Captain Walshingham.*

He lowered the pistol and aimed it at a priceless marble bust. Walshingham pulled the trigger. The pistol roared with fire and smoke. The marble bust shattered. Walshingham laughed as he threw the pistol on top of the broken pieces of marble. He hurriedly dressed in his finest uniform, one of many he had designed himself. He put on all the medals he had awarded himself and wore only to nonmilitary functions. Walshingham adorned his fingers with his finest rings and stood looking at himself in the mirror as he strapped on his gilded sword with jeweled hilt. He strode across the room and jerked open the door. The marine guard stood with his rifle at the ready, unsure as to his next move. His captain brushed past him, saying, "Follow me, we are going to the flagship."

Walshingham clapped up the stairs and out onto the sunlit deck. "Bosun! Bosun," he shouted, "make ready a side party and lower the gig. Call my orchestra on deck." Walshingham paced the deck with his face set tightly like a mask. At times his eyes flashed and a trace of a smile showed as the marines hurried to their positions. He paused and watched his orchestra readying their instruments. "*Rule Britannia*," he ordered.

The boatswain blew a long call on his pipe and the drums rolled. The orchestra began to play and Walshingham followed his marines over the side. He took his place in the boat with red-coated marines sitting smartly ahead, their bayonets glimmering in the sunlight. His sailors pulled smartly at the oars while the strains of *Rule Britannia* drifted over the ocean waves.

At the boarding ladder of the flagship, Walshingham ascended. He moved his portly body up the boarding ladder and stood still for a moment, looking at the Jack on the mainmast. The portly captain doffed his hat to the flag and tipped it also to the sailors standing in awe. Sun glinted on his medals as he threw back his cloak and strode across the deck. His footfalls pounded on the stairs as he descended, and he walked loudly down the hall. His stare moved the marine guards aside as he entered the Commodore's cabin. Walshingham threw back his cape. "Surely ye did not think me afraid to come here, Commodore? I know no fear. I have come to confront the jealous worms who seek my destruction."

The Commodore rose from his desk, his eyes dark, his expression grim. "Walshingham, often have I defended you, knowing that most prize money in my purse came from you. I've prevented angry officers from tearing your head from your bloated body. I have covered your transgressions and lied to the Admiralty. I've defended you, thinking your zeal served the Crown more than it injured." The Commodore's face grew darker; his words cut between his teeth as he hissed, "But the gold you bring to my purse crawls with the same dark slime that exudes from everything you touch. Your greed is like the mold consuming the pumpkin. It knows no limits; it grows beyond its bounds and consumes itself. And so have you now. Most men would have been content with the capture of a rich prize like *Chasseur*, but not you, Walshingham. You want more. Not content with the money paid you by the Crown for the ship, you stole the rifles. You had the audacity to sell them back to the enemy, you and your cohort, Brumley.

"Well, Walshingham, those rifles are back in the hands of the Crown. Your Lieutenant MacGregor captured them in the hold of Brumley's schooner, taken in the expedition for which you volunteered him. The French decided they could better be used in Quebec, but our blockade prevented the schooner from sailing to the new destination. Those rifles, the ship's manifest, and the testimony of your purser convicted you before a court martial of your peers. Our court could have put a bullet in your head if they kindly disposed toward you, or a noose around your neck if not." The Commodore sat in his chair, the oaken rungs squeaking as he pushed backwards. The Commodore rang a small hand bell on his desk. The door opened and two marines marched inside, followed by the assembled fleet officers. The Commodore lifted a paper from his desk, saying, "Walshingham, a jury of your peers have been magnanimous with you. They have given you a choice. Here is your letter of resignation. You may sign that and walk away a free man to enjoy your riches, or disgrace. You have no other choice. I want you to sign this letter and walk away from the Navy. You may return to England or sail where you wish. Buy yourself a ship and apply for a letter of marque if you wish, but sign this letter and resign. The only other choice is disgrace and death." The Commodore lifted a quill from his desk and dipped it in the ink well. He stood, handing the quill to Walshingham.

Looking around the cabin at his fellow officers, Walshingham smiled. "You shall be denied the pleasure of my hanging. It is my choice and I shall resign my commission to the King. But you have not heard the last of Captain Walshingham. With a letter of marque I shall earn a hundred pounds for your every pence, and in your old age I might deign to offer you a crumb from my table." Walshingham took the quill and signed the resignation with a flourish. Throwing his cape over his shoulder, he pushed past the marine guards and walked out of the cabin.

Looking at the door which Walshingham had just slammed, the Commodore said, "And now I think I shall go and have a bath."

Chapter Thirty-Three

It was a Sunday afternoon and Marie stood near the Dauphin Gate of Fortress Louisbourg. A white flag of truce flapped lazily from a pole on the stone ramparts. After days of continual bombardment, the quietness of the day was strange. No shells had landed since noon. Marie held a message from Charles MacGregor in her hand. When she had read his letter saying there would be a truce, she could hardly believe the words. How could a vicious war be stopped for a Sunday afternoon? Should she meet her people's enemy? But an urge Marie did not understand hurried her to the gate. Perhaps it was to learn news of her father.

In the shadow of the gate, a wounded English prisoner, pale and comatose, lay near death on a gurney. Two aides from the hospital waited to wheel him across no-man's-land. Another English prisoner leaned on crutches, the stump of his severed leg concealed in his empty trouser's leg. A blinded companion waited with bandages around his eyes. A nun waited to help the men to the English lines.

Standing near Marie was a young noblewoman of Louisbourg. The noble woman said, "My cousin is a British Army officer. We are meeting for a picnic." Marie made no reply, but smiled thinly as she looked at this woman, so debonair despite the gravity of Louisbourg. *One should not have a picnic in the middle of a war*, Marie thought. She had thought of refusing to meet MacGregor, but waiting for the drawbridge to be lowered, her heart beat quickly at the thought of seeing Charles MacGregor. Yet she felt some guilt as if she betrayed her friends.

Again the young noblewoman spoke to Marie, "I always absolutely hated picnics in France, but I look forward to this one. I only hope my cousin brought plenty of food."

Marie thought perhaps she was being too critical of this woman. "I'm meeting a friend. He is a British naval officer who may have news from my father, who is a prisoner of the English." Embarrassed, Marie looked down, fussing with her dress nervously.

At last, the big drawbridge clanked down across the barachois with a crash and rising dust. Marie looked down at her gown, brushing at the dust. The two young women smiled quickly at each other and walked across the bridge, past the French marines who stood with rifles and bayonets. They lifted their skirts to step over a pile of fallen stones, carefully picking their way past the shell holes.

Across the battle-scarred expanse of no-man's-land walked a group of English carrying a white flag. Three young officers in red coats walked beside MacGregor, who was dressed in a civilian blue coat and buff trousers. Marie thought, *Thank goodness he is not wearing that awful big sword.* Charles carried a canvas bag of food. Behind them a group of French prisoners limped, hopped, and stumbled toward the French lines. English soldiers followed with a gurney bearing a man who could not walk.

The young French noblewoman beside Marie whispered, "My cousin has a big basket. I pray it's full… of anything but codfish. Good wine, freshly baked bread, and fresh fruit would be heavenly."

Marie was hungry too but decided she wouldn't admit it. "I'm lucky I enjoy codfish." She quickly turned her head. *What a fool I am! No one would believe such a lie.*

The women lifted their skirts to walk around a muddy shell hole. The noblewoman said, "I have seen you at the Governor's mansion; you probably do not know the hunger suffered by the others of us in Louisbourg. But I do not begrudge you any food you have. I would empty chamber pots in the mansion if it meant more food and a warm place to sleep. Is the young man you meet a relative or a lover?"

Marie stammered the answer, "He is… he may have news of my father, who was taken by the English," She fumbled for more words and began again, "He is… a friend." *She will not believe that either. Must you make such a fool of yourself?*

The noblewoman smiled at Marie, knowingly. "It doesn't matter so long as he has food. I see he has a canvas bag. Take any gifts he offers. If you don't like it, you can easily sell it."

Marie was glad she wouldn't have to continue the conversation as they approached the men. MacGregor walked away from the other British officers. Carefully keeping her eyes on the ground as she lifted her skirts off the muddy field, Marie walked slowly toward him. MacGregor removed his hat and walked to meet her. Wordlessly, he took Marie's hand, leading her around a shell hole. Still holding her hand, they walked beneath the sparse shade of a shell-devastated tree. MacGregor kept his eyes on Marie as he set the canvas bag on the ground. "I wasn't sure you would come," he said as he opened the drawstrings and took out a blanket, spreading it on the ground.

Marie still had not met his eyes when she replied, "I hoped you might have news of my father."

MacGregor took her hand again and helped her down on the blanket. He sat beside her. "I have been unable to leave my ship. But I hired a lawyer to look after him. He will be fine, I think." He removed a bottle of wine from the canvas bag, followed by cheese and bread. "Will you leave Louisbourg? I'm anxious to know because, and I have thought about this carefully, I have decided I... care for you, whatever."

Marie met his eyes searchingly. "How could you, as you say, care for me? You hardly know me." *If he loves me, why can he not say so?* "I have told you I can't leave Louisbourg... even if I also... cared for you." *Why do I want to hurt him when I would rather he take me in his arms and hold me? He is trying to be kind to me and help my father, yet I say things to him that are unkind.*

She hung her head and accepted a slice of bread carved from a long loaf by his knife. He poured her a glass of wine. MacGregor sliced a piece of cheese for her as he asked, "Perhaps you could learn to like me? Can you never forgive me for killing French soldiers who try to kill me?"

After a long pause of silence she looked away and said, "I must confess to you that I killed a French soldier once." She looked down at her hands. "It was in Beaubassin... the English and French were fighting. He broke into my cabin. He tried to... I had to defend myself. I did not mean to, but I killed him." Her eyes were flooded with tears when she looked up at him. "I'm sorry," she said. "I don't mean I'm sorry for killing the French soldier... yes, I'm sorry for killing the French soldier, but what I mean is... I'm sorry for saying things that might hurt you. You are kind. I should not want to hurt you."

He put his hand on hers, saying, "Marie, we do what we must to survive. Do not be sorry for killing the man who tried to... harm you. But I wish you would learn to like me. I would take you and find your father. I would make you happy again and help you forget the suffering."

Marie lifted her gaze; it was as if their eyes embraced. She held his hand. "Charles, I do not hate you, but I could not. I have this feeling of guilt. You are an enemy of my people. War is terrible. It makes monsters of us all. Life was simple before the war. My life is changed and perhaps will never be the same."

MacGregor took her hand. "I'm happy that you don't hate me too much. I think of you often. I can not get you out of my mind."

Her eyes softened. *Can he not use the word?* Marie lifted his hand against her cheek. He felt warm tears against his hand. Embracing her, their lips met.

Passion, suppressed by separation and war, flowed like a fountain. His lips left hers only long enough to brush away the tears and returned to the joy of love. Marie felt the bonds of her heart falling away. She returned his kiss with a feeling she had never known before. Hesitantly, she took his hand in her hands. She whispered, "I can't leave Louisbourg… you must understand. I can't abandon my people." And so the two parted, not knowing if either would survive the war. They both walked in opposite directions, stopping once or twice to wave. MacGregor saw Marie reach up and wipe her eye. Soon no-man's-land was clear of people, and the town gate slammed shut behind the returning French. MacGregor jumped down in a trench and greeted the British soldiers who watched him with expressionless eyes.

When the truce flags came down, explosions again ripped the muddy earth around Louisbourg. Cannons thundered from the walls, and English shells fell on the ramparts while dirty black smoke drifted over the city, smudging the clear blue skies. Alarmed citizens heard the rattle of musketry during the pauses of cannon fire. A furious new battle raged outside the fortress. French forces fought valiantly, but British soldiers moved inexorably closer to the walls. General Wolfe's troops seized a long coveted mound in no-man's-land. He was jubilant. Now he could fire his cannons into the inner reaches of the town of Louisbourg.

Wolfe's cannons moved ever closer and now reached any target in Louisbourg. He knew Louisbourg would not surrender if he only bombarded the fortress wall. He must make the people want to surrender. Hell now rained on Louisbourg's town of four thousand inhabitants. Homes vanished in a cloud of fire, dust, smoke, and flying timbers. Shells killed men, women, and children, burying them under the wreckage of their homes. Marie worked with Madame Drucour, taking wounded and injured to hospital. But at sunset Marie stood on the ramparts and looked across a coppery ocean at the British ships. Early the next morning Marie rose to accompany Madame Drucour on another tour of the ramparts. After exchanging words with soldiers on the ramparts, Madame Drucour led the way to the hospital once more. With rest and hardly any sleep, Madame Drucour and Marie continued their resistance and endured Wolfe's cannons. Daily Madame Drucour fired cannons at the enemy.

But the English returned a murderous cannon fire into the heart of the town. Daily they took their toll. The city became a shambles, with homeless people seeking shelter in the wreckage or wherever they could. Daily soldiers dug in the ruins to recover bodies. And all the while, British trenches inched closer to the fortress.

Back in Louisbourg with Madame Drucour, Marie walked among the people. The lady spoke softly to the soldiers of their loved ones back home in France while the once proud town of Louisbourg fell to Wolfe's cannons. Burned out shells of houses, charred black from fire, lay in heaps around the remains of chimneys that stood like tombstones over the corpse of the building. Dazed civilians rummaged through the wreckage, their anxious eyes searching for loved ones in the rubble.

Marie walked with her chin held high. A cheery smile hid her weary heart as she offered an encouraging word at every opportunity. During those trying times Marie visited the chapel where she found many citizens seeking solace. With a hug here and a handshake there, she greeted them. Children received a kiss or a smile. Marie lifted the veil over her head and walked inside. Dipping her finger in the baptismal font, she made the Sign of the Cross and entered reverently.

The gleaming white walls of the chapel, trimmed with sparkling gold leaf, presented an ethereal atmosphere of old world France. With golden sunshine flooding through the French windows, Marie knelt near the front of the chapel. Marie lifted her eyes to the painting of Christ the King and again crossed herself. Forcing the rumble of cannons from her mind, she rested her hands on the shining oaken pew ahead of her and prayed. A distant explosion shook the windows in the heavy stone walls. Marie's lifted her glistening eyes as she prayed. She crossed herself and remained on her knees for a long time, seemingly oblivious to the rattling windows and shaking ground. Again Marie crossed herself before rising from the kneeler.

Outside she found Madame Drucour waiting. The governor's lady placed her arm around Marie as they walked back to Government House. Madame Drucour whispered quietly, "I know the young British officer wants to take you away from Louisbourg. I know too that you are struggling with the decision to leave, but I have thought long about the matter. Hesitate no longer. Go, Marie! You are young. Leave with the young man and the fate which may await most of us here in Louisbourg. We have no choice but to remain. You are free to leave, the governor will not stop you."

Walking back to Government House Marie answered softly, "Madame, I care little for the glory of France, but I love these people. I can't abandon them. I see the eyes of the young soldiers standing on the walls of the fortress; they are ready to die for us. I see the hungry children, the mothers, the old men from Beaubassin, their vision would haunt me all my life if I left them to die alone."

"It is your decision, my dear," replied Madame Drucour, "and I will support you, no matter how you decide. Perhaps our fleet will bring reinforcements, but no one really thinks so. I no longer believe in a French victory; we are left in this wilderness like a pawn on a chess board."

Marie walked back to the little courtyard and sat in the shade, listening to the thunder of the cannons. Doubts filled her mind as she thought of the decision she had made.

The next day, Marie walked briskly to the hospital with a book under her arm. There, a young soldier, blinded by an English grenade, delighted in hearing her voice again. Marie resumed reading to him and no one knew of her inner turmoil. Outside the fortress, the cannons fired with a new intensity, and she hid in doorways from shells exploding overhead. Rifle fire crackled with renewed frequency.

Anxious French soldiers watched the English trenches moving closer to the walls. Soon the trenches were so close they could no longer fire into them with their cannons. They called their officers to the ramparts, who surveyed the enemy trenches with telescopes. The officers rushed their concern to Government House. Generals conferred with the governor long into the night. The English trenches promised a disaster. The big cannons could no longer depress to the level of the trenches.

* * *

Madame Drucour and Marie visited the busy artillery soldiers on the Dauphin Bastion. There they found Captain Renau standing on the ramparts. He examined a map held by an artillery captain in a dusty, soiled uniform. The commander of the Dauphin Bastion explained the problem to Captain Renau. "The English now hold that hill, there," he said, pointing. "From that promontory they can shell any target in Louisbourg while they move their trenches closer to the wall. They kill civilians and weaken their resolve to resist. The enemy trenches are so close, I can't depress my cannons to fire on them. Daily they extend their trenches closer to the wall. They now move their mortars into position to drop shells anywhere they choose. Next their infantry will move down their trenches and breach the gate. This can happen in a matter of days, and the battle will be over. Louisbourg will be lost."

Captain Renau surveyed the land with the officer's telescope. He lowered the glass and looked over the harbor. "I will bring my frigate broadside to the wharf, there," he said, pointing to a spot in the harbor. "From that position I can rake the plains in front of the walls with my cannons. There will be no Englishmen climbing out of their trenches to breach the walls as long as my cannons control the plains." Captain Renau said, "Thank you, Major," and quickly bounded down the steps, hurrying to his ship.

That night French sailors towed their frigate into position along the wharf. Captain Renau anchored the ship securely, fore and aft. He readied his cannons. Just before midnight, when the English engineers came out to work on their entrenchment, a crashing roar from his cannons rained deadly chain-shot across the plains, dropping English soldiers in a hail of steel. British survivors scampered for cover and brought cheers from the French soldiers on the ramparts. Throughout the night *Pélerine* loosed a deadly broadside across the English trenches. As air bursts from Renau's cannons exploded over the plains, all work on the British trenches stopped. The deadly cannons of His Majesty's Ship *Pélerine* mastered General Wolfe's battlefield throughout the next few days and nights.

With the English advance stalled, General Wolfe conferred with his artillerymen. They reacted quickly. Wolfe, who by now was making most of the decisions himself, brought a battery of big guns up from the rear. He positioned the cannons carefully to rain shells down on the French fleet in Louisbourg Harbor. Soon British cannons returned the fire of *Pélerine*. Not only that, but Wolfe's howitzers bombarded the entire harbor area. The entire French fleet now lay exposed to Wolfe's cannons. They especially sought the French frigate *Pélerine*.

Commodore Des Gouttes began to react against the British artillery danger to his fleet. Finally he evacuated the crews from his ships. The big battleships were virtually abandoned, leaving only a few sentinels, and even those were under the command of inexperienced young midshipmen. Only *Pélerine* and the men who manned the little frigate, remained in the fight. With Wolfe's shells dropping all around him, Captain Renau moved *Pélerine* farther away from land, but continued to control the ground in front of the fortress. The English could still not breach the walls.

Smoke hung over the town as Marie walked to the hospital with a novel in her hand. Concealed in a pocket was a small piece of cheese for her favorite patient. Marie loved to read to the blinded young soldier; he was always grateful and reminded her of her younger brother, killed by the English. Walking through the deserted, litter strewn streets, Marie thought of her dead brother. As Marie neared the hospital, distant cannons boomed. The sound of a whistling rustle filled the air. She turned to look over her shoulder, seeking the source of the rustling. The hospital exploded. In fire, dust, and splinters it disintegrated in front of her, but she did not hear the sound. Geysers of earth and stone rose in all directions. A nearby house disappeared into flying debris.

The explosion lifted Marie off her feet. It slammed her into the sand bags lining the nearby building. Her world went black as debris rained down on her. Later Marie opened her eyes but she could not see. Her ears hurt and her head throbbed in pain. Her entire body hurt. She struggled to breathe but no breath came. Blackness overcame her as her lungs gasped vainly for air.

When Marie again opened her eyes, she saw only a blur. Dust filled her nostrils and eyes. A section of brick wall lay on her. Dirt filled her mouth and choked her as she lay gasping. Marie tried to call out, but she could hardly breathe; she could not speak. Her ears rang with a deafening roar. Blackness overcame her again.

Later Marie heard voices over the ringing in her ears. She struggled again to speak but managed only a louder moan. She tried to move the debris pinning her to the ground, but she could not. A fallen wall pinned her to the ground. With much pain in her shoulder, she pulled the arm upward, feeling the rough bricks tear at the flesh of her hand. With determination she pulled the arm upward. At last she moved her hand to her face. Marie painfully rubbed the dirt from her eyes, and the blurred image focused to become rubble over her. She wiped the dirt from her mouth and nose. Gasping to fill her lungs, she managed a weak cry. The voices stopped.

Marie heard the voices again; they were closer now. She tried to scream. Her voice sounded as a pitifully weak cry. The voices seemed much closer now; she could hear the words. Bricks and mortar fell. New pains coursed through her body as the wall crushed down on her. Men were digging in the rubble around her. Marie moaned loudly and weakly waved her free hand. The noise stopped. She heard someone calling. Marie tried to focus on the question asked by the voice. What had he asked? Surely she must know the answer, but it would not come. Doing the only thing she could, Marie moaned loudly. The noise started again but much closer this time. Boards crashed. She felt something in her hair. Marie cried out softly. It was a hand pulling her hair. Desperately moving her free hand to her head, Marie weakly squeezed the hand, using her last vestige of energy. She thought, *I'll just rest...*

Marie awoke to sunlight in her eyes. A nun leaned over her, lifting timbers off Marie's body. She attempted resistance and then relaxed to the nun's efforts of wiping the dirt from her face. Her body ached and her eyes hurt while the ringing in her ears continued. Marie rose to one elbow but the nurse pushed her back. "Lie still, child, you may have broken bones. You were buried beneath the wreckage. You are lucky to be alive. Lay still now and the doctor will examine you when he can; I must go tend to others."

Marie lay back on the bricks and closed her eyes, still struggling for breath. The bricks cut her back; pains racked her chest with every breath. In agony and nausea she tried to sit upright. Struggling forward, Marie propped herself up on one elbow. She saw the wreckage of the hospital for the first time. Marie remembered the novel she had been carrying. It lay in the dust, its pages blowing in the wind. Marie remembered the blind young soldier. She struggled to her knees. Crawling over the ruins of the hospital, Marie tore at the rocks with bleeding fingers. Exhausted, with a searing pain in her side at every breath, she fell back to the ground. As soldiers uncovered the patients in the hospital, Marie rose to watch. Most were dead, but when a wounded soldier was found alive, they quickly dragged him from the ruins. The pale, dust-covered dead lay in a long line of mangled bodies. They lifted the unconscious, breathing injured to stretchers, taking them away to the citadel. Moaning, whimpering survivors painfully waited their turn. Doctors examined victims who lay silently and still, to decide if they were living or dead. Marie struggled to the line of dusty bodies. There she found the young blind soldier.

Marie sat on the litter strewn ground beside his body and lifted his young head into her lap. She brushed the dust away from his handsome young face and closed his unseeing eyes. Tears streamed down her dusty cheeks.

With shells still falling in the town, Madame Drucour walked bravely through the streets, accompanied by the governor's aide and two marines. She walked straight to the hospital. It was there she found Marie crying over the body of the young soldier. The aide lifted Marie to her feet as Madame Drucour comforted her. Madame Drucour pushed Marie's hair back and wiped her face of dust and tears with a fine lace handkerchief.

Madame Drucour said to the officer, "Take Marie to the citadel and see that she is cared for; my place is here with the people." They forced Marie to lie on a crude gurney and wheeled her around bodies and rubble, through the besieged and litter strewn town. Shells burst over the city, showering hot steel on the group as the aide took Marie to Government House. He shoved open the door and walked into the entryway where he laid Marie on a couch.

Berthe hovered over her, wiping away the dirt from her face and hair. The aide knelt beside Marie. She smiled weakly as he lifted her hand and, holding it to his lips, kissed it as he looked at her with affection. "I can't stay," he said, "I'm needed on the ramparts, but please promise you will stay in the shelter of the citadel. You are a heroine to our soldiers; it would not do to lose you."

Marie managed a smile and replied, "I promise to take no more risks than any of you."

Later Berthe removed Marie's torn and soiled clothing. Like a baby, Berthe lifted Marie into a bath. Marie's ribs, aching painfully with every breath, showed plainly under the thin, bruised skin. Hiding her tears, Marie choked back a whimper.

Late in the evening a doctor came to Marie's room. He wrapped a bandage tightly around her ribs, and she endured a night of bombing with ringing ears and painful breathing. The relentless shelling of the city itself continued while the bastions of the fortress received a reprieve.

A British shell landed in a geyser of dirt and smoke, causing a nervous and weary Des Gouttes to quicken his pace as he hurried to Government House. Government House showed the effects of British shelling. Ragged shards of canvas swayed in the breeze, replacing the fine French windows and creating a dark, cave-like atmosphere inside. He found the first family of Louisbourg having their meager lunch. Governor Drucour's eyes were red-rimmed. A stubble of beard showed above the soiled collar of his shirt. Marie had joined them in the dark and dusty dinning room when Commodore Des Gouttes came into the room.

Briskly the Commodore announced, "Good day, Madame, *Mademoiselle*," while nodding in the direction of Marie and Madame Drucour. His smile faded as he addressed the governor. "Governor Drucour, the English cannons have destroyed our best ships. I remind you that I am responsible for the ships, although you have overall command of Louisbourg. Soon, all my ships will be destroyed. I must not let that happen, they are too important to the King. I am removing them from Louisbourg."

Governor Drucour bolted upright. "Remove the ships from Louisbourg? To where would you remove the ships?"

"Why, to France of course. They must not be lost to the English," replied Des Gouttes. Madame Drucour noisily returned her water glass to the table as she sat in silence, watching Des Gouttes with fiery eyes.

Governor Drucour's spoke softly but firmly, "Those ships are our only link to France; people will panic at the sight of your ships leaving. They will feel abandoned. You will not remove the ships from Louisbourg until I give my approval, and as of now that approval is not given. Do I make myself perfectly clear, Commodore?"

Des Gouttes bowed ever so slightly and with a thin trace of a smile, replied, "Perfectly clear, Governor. I am delighted you have assumed full responsibility for the King's ships. It is a most heavy responsibility for which I am pleased to be relieved. Since D'Anthony commands the defense, there is nothing more for me to do. Neither the surrender of Louisbourg nor the loss of the ships will be my responsibility. Good day, Governor, Madam," said Des Gouttes with a bow and thin smile. He seemed light on his feet and happy, walking briskly from the room. Governor Drucour rose slowly from the table and walked to a broken window, looking over the crumbling fortress.

Outside his office, tired, sleepless soldiers ate thin soup while sitting in the sun beside their guns. Civilians assembled for their daily ration in front of the citadel. Pale, hungry faces with wide, empty eyes looked up in anticipation. And daily, at about the same time, Wolfe concentrated his cannon fire there. The death toll mounted. Hungry families faced a dismal choice: risk instant death or slow starvation. Only the citadel offered protection for the wounded, with other rooms reserved for administration. The basement shelters were crowded with sick, wounded, and dispirited citizens.

Captain Renau sought permission to join a conference at Government House on July 12, 1758. The governor, concerned that the British might attempt another "cutting out operation" against the warships in the harbor, ordered Des Gouttes and his staff to the meeting. The Commodore granted Renau's request to attend.

Captain Renau surprised the men when he said, "My frigate is of little use now. My cannons no more prevent the storming of the walls. There is nothing more I can do to defend Louisbourg, but I could carry dispatches to France as well as any valuables you might not want to fall into the hands of the enemy. I propose to sail immediately with dispatches and any of your valuables you want protected."

Des Gouttes stormed back, "No! You might yet be useful to Louisbourg."

Captain Renau answered hotly, "Yes, by God, if you will give me one of your battleships of the line that are laid up doing nothing, you will see that I will do much more than I have done hitherto with a little frigate."

Madame Drucour watched silently from the doorway. The governor glanced in her direction before he lifted his hand to silence the two men. "I am the King's governor here and I will decide if Captain Renau sails or not."

The next day Marie sat with a wounded child deep within the citadel. Hunger gnawed at her stomach and her head ached from long hours without food. A shell exploded above the shelter. It startled Marie with its nearness. She looked up at the ceiling where a crack appeared and dust fell. The children cried out. As the little boy beside her whimpered, she hugged him close, careful not to squeeze his bandaged arm. Slowly, she rose to her feet, and limping slightly, she carefully stepped through the crowded shelter where a little girl lay crying out at every shell burst. Marie sat on the floor beside her and held her bandaged head against her breast, singing to her softly. Again Marie heard the now familiar rustle of shells flying overhead. Instinctively, she fell flat, falling on top the little girl and covering her body with her own. A series of explosions again shook the building. Timbers split and walls fell. Plaster dropped in large chunks. Screams filled the dusty, smoky air. Marie struggled from beneath the debris and made her way to the door. With difficulty she forced the door open and looked across at the maid's quarters. That building had taken a direct hit.

Marie ran as quickly as she could. Smoke and dust boiled from the doorway. Debris, smoke, and dust filled the halls. Marie put a handkerchief over nose and went inside. There she found Governor Drucour and Madame Drucour, dirty and disheveled, digging in the rubble along with servants and soldiers. Madame Drucour said, "Berthe was in her room, I think."

Calling to soldiers for assistance, Madame Drucour struggled through the wreckage. She found the shattered door to Berthe's little room and with the help of the soldiers, tore the boards away to enter the wreckage of collapsed beams and fallen bricks. As a soldier lifted a fallen beam, Marie saw Berthe lying in the rubble. White dust covered her red hair and freckled face. Her eyes starred wide in the final fear of her life. Muddy little rivulets marked the path of her tears down either side of her face. In her arms she clutched the little doll that always lay in the center of her bed. Madame Drucour lifted her lifeless hand. Sobbing loudly, Marie kneeled beside Berthe. Together they cried for her.

Later that day Captain Renau found Marie in the casement shelter. She looked pale in her dusty, blood-stained dress, changing a bandage for a wounded soldier. Nearby, other soldiers screamed as surgeons removed crushed limbs without anesthetic. The air was heavy and putrid. Renau gently lifted Marie to her feet. "Please, Marie, come with me to the courtyard. I must talk to you immediately."

He put his arm around her, supporting her as they walked down the hall, also filled with wounded. Tired and weary, Marie leaned against him as they walked to a dusty, litter-strewn courtyard. Smoke and clouds obscured the sun. With shells exploding in the distance he said, "Marie, I'm leaving tonight aboard *Pélerine*. I have permission to carry dispatches and valuables to France. I'll be home in a few weeks. Come with me, Marie. Madame Drucour will give her permission. Neither you nor I can do anything more for Louisbourg. It is lost. Come with me now, while it is still possible to do so."

The crash of a shell landing nearby shook the ground and dust swirled in the courtyard. They both ducked instinctively. Marie trembled as she looked up at Renau with large, moist eyes. "Jean, I can't go with you. You know that you mean much to me, but I know now it is not love. I should have told you sooner. I love another man. He is here, and it is here I must remain. I pray God grants you a safe voyage and that one day our leaders will be wise enough to know what a valiant officer they have."

He took her hands in his. "I wish I could make you change your mind, Marie. But I can see you are determined. I beg you, stay in the shelters. If you can survive a few more days, it will all be over. Goodbye, Marie. I'll be leaving. Perhaps we will meet again someday, somewhere, one never knows. You will be in my prayers."

Marie stood on the tips of her toes and kissed him on the cheek, saying, "Goodbye, Jean, I will remember you always." Renau enveloped her tightly in his arms, then hurried away down the corridor.

That night, as rockets lit the sky, Marie stood on the ramparts of the Dauphin Gate watching the harbor where *Pélerine* stood out from the other warships by its smaller size. Marie knew Renau's ship by the white sails unfurled in the darkness. In an instant, masts blossomed with sails. The frigate moved slowly with wind and tide toward the harbor mouth. Rifle fire sounded sharp and fine across the harbor as the English saw the movement. But it was several minutes before British artillerymen slowly turned their cumbersome cannons around, away from the town of Louisbourg, and toward the fleeing ship. Marie watched intently and prayed fervently as cannons belched fire and roared at *Pélerine*. White geysers of water erupted behind the ship, but the frigate sailed onward while British gunners elevated their cannons and loaded for another salvo. *Pélerine* sailed through a string of geysers erupting in front of the ship while picking up more wind in the open air. British gunners reloaded and lowered their elevation. Now black cannons belched red fire and white geysers erupted on all sides of the fast sailing frigate. The ship sailed until a low fog bank engulfed them.

July 26, 1758, less than three leagues from the smoky town of Louisbourg, Lieutenant MacGregor, temporary captain of *H.M.S. Grenadier*, again answered a summons to attend the Commodore aboard the flag ship. He doffed his hat to the colors and followed a lieutenant to the Commodore's quarters. Dressed in his best uniform, MacGregor once again stood before the Commodore's desk. "Mr. MacGregor, both you and I know that you should be named a post captain in command of *Grenadier*. But for reasons that I shall not attempt to explain, permanent command will be given to a senior officer selected by the Admiralty in London. You will continue to act as captain, temporarily, until the new man arrives from England.

"However, you deserve just compensation for your valor and loyalty. Since Admiral Boscawen has approved my appointment as temporary prize agent to replace Edward Brumley who has resigned, I will use my position to reward you in some measure for your service. As acting prize agent I'm awarding you the captured schooner which formerly belonged to Edward Brumley and which you captured from the hands of the enemy. The schooner shall be yours alone, to do with as you wish, if that satisfies you. Laforey and Balfour will share the prize *Beinfaisant* with the other men; they both agree you captured the schooner and deserve its total reward. I hope you will continue in my service. If you do, I promise you future promotions and rewards. You can place your schooner in the hands of any good shipping company out of London, and they will earn you a handsome income from its chartering. Of course, there is always the other choice, which I hope you will not choose, and that is to sail the ship yourself in commercial trade. I have stood at the wheel of that lean, greyhound of the sea, and I could understand if you wanted to sail such a beautiful ship. There will be profit in commercial trade when peace is restored in North America under British rule. You need not give me an answer now, Lieutenant MacGregor. Think it over carefully. You have an assured future either way you decide.

"Now to the other matter, Admiral Boscawen has composed another letter to Governor Drucour which General Amherst has approved. I would like you to deliver it to him. There is nothing new in the letter, but more importantly, Admiral Boscawen has a verbal message he wants delivered. You see, he respects Drucour and understands his position. But within two days our soldiers will be inside the walls of Louisbourg. There will be hand to hand fighting there. A very bloody business, that! Soldiers who kill with the bayonet can become cruel. The admiral wants the governor and Madame Drucour to survive this siege. Tell him his life is endangered as well as the lives of thousands of innocent people. He has conducted himself admirably with no shame at all." The Commodore looked intently at MacGregor. "Will you tell him that, Mister MacGregor?"

MacGregor replied. "I'll do my best to convince the governor to avoid injury to himself and Madame Drucour... and others who may suffer, whatever."

The Commodore handed him Admiral Boscawen's letter and said, "Go then and quickly. Let the ship's boat that brought you here take you to Gabarus

Bay. You may land there and take an army escort to the front line with a white flag."

Amid the crowded tents and shelters lining Gabarus Bay MacGregor found the Army headquarters where there seemed to be little interest in Boscawen's letter. MacGregor was given a tattered and dirty truce flag and pointed in the directions of a tall wooden tower built above the front lines. Bending low to avoid French marksmen, he hurried through the trenches. There he kneeled in a trench below a tall wooden tower constructed to assault the walls of Louisbourg. Explosions sent clouds of dirt and rock into the air, falling to the ground in a hail of rocks and dust around his trench.

Swearing, an angry Highlander rose quickly to fire his musket at the walls of Louisbourg in retaliation. The soldier hurriedly ducked behind the safety of the trench as a hail of musket balls returned. Another Highlander picked up MacGregor's soiled and torn truce flag. "Ah, a visitor for the French! We thank ye, Sir, for any break ye be' givin' us in the fightin'. I see ya' ha' the turkey talkin' flag right handy."

Removing his sweat-stained hat, MacGregor wiped the perspiration from his forehead and smiled at the Highlander. "What is this thing you have built here? Surely no one here needs Jacob's ladder to get to heaven, not with all the French shot and shell flying around."

The Highlander turned to look up at the top of the log tower, replying, "Angus over here built it, hoping to have a jump to heaven before the devil grabs him." The other man replied with a derisive remark in the Gaelic as a French bullet struck the tower. Splinters fell on the men in the trench.

MacGregor replied in the little Gaelic he had learned as a boy, "That Jacob's ladder could be harmful to your health, think ye?" The two men quickly looked at him in a new light.

The first man asked, "Hoots! What be yer' name, man? Be ye from the Highlands?" Both men looked at MacGregor with blackened, sweat stained faces; their eyes reflecting the death and suffering they had seen.

"My name is MacGregor," he answered, "and because my name is MacGregor, I can't set foot in the Old Country."

Angus replied, "Aye, ye MacGregors are to be shot on sight in the Old Country." The man's dirty face broke into a smile. "So come ye here to be shot instead?'

"That's not my intention, whatever," answered MacGregor with a smile. "I have here in my pocket a letter asking for the French surrender to Louisbourg. I'm supposed to deliver it to the governor if they will stop shooting long enough."

The other Highlander's face brightened. "A surrender? An end to this hell? Fer' that I'll be yer' helper, no fear." He grabbed the flag of truce from MacGregor's hand and laid down his musket. The man made a quick sign of the Cross and bounded into the tower. In an instant he had ascended to the top and leaned the tattered white flag over the parapet while a hail of French bullets struck the logs. Not climbing, but falling, the Highlander collapsed in the trench. There he sat with his head back against the dirt, his eyes wide, and his breath coming in short gasps. Again he made the sign of the Cross before looking at MacGregor. "There ye be, MacGregor, my good horse thief! Now, let us go end this bleedin' war."

With the dirty white truce flag flapping in the breeze, he sat back in the trench to wait for the enemy cease fire. MacGregor listened as the French rifles slowly stopped shooting. At last MacGregor bounded up the log tower to retrieve the white flag. Several musket balls made a splat in the logs, then the firing died away again into silence. MacGregor climbed down from the tower and stood above the trench, the truce flag in hand. The Highlander jumped from the trench and took the white flag, saying, "I'll escort ye, MacGregor, and carry this white flag. If ye soil yer diaper, I'll use this rag to change it fer' ye."

MacGregor smiled and stumbled through the Gaelic. "It's too late, methinks." He wiped his brow and put his hat on. Together the two men walked toward Fortress Louisbourg, one in a muddy red jacket and black kilt, the other in blue jacket and white trousers. In the July sun, sweat ran down MacGregor's back under the woolen coat. The men picked their way across the pockmarked landscape, now plowed and pulverized by the shelling. An awful odor drifted from no-man's-land. He tried to hold his breath as they passed a dead horse. At the gate, Lieutenant MacGregor stopped. There they waited with the white flag for the gate to be opened. The creaking drawbridge lowered jerkily over the barachois. Dusty, unshaven French soldiers leveled their muskets at them.

MacGregor lifted his chin and crossed the drawbridge, followed by the Highlander with the white flag. They stood waiting as the drawbridge cranked slowly back into position, the chains sounding strangely loud in the relative quiet of the lull. Seeing an officer, MacGregor spoke in French, "I have a letter for Governor Drucour from Admiral Boscawen."

The officer looked at MacGregor sullenly then replied, "I will take you to him. Your escort can remain here at the gate; my men will not harm him." The officer motioned for MacGregor to follow and quickly marched away. With a nod to the Highlander, MacGregor followed his escort. Walking through the streets, he felt more hostility than on his prior visit. A young boy threw a stone at him and quickly ran behind a building, his thin, bony dog following closely behind. Smoke and stench filled his nostrils as MacGregor made his way past the ghoulish citizens of Louisbourg looking from hollow, deep-set eyes. The sight of the dazed, ashen, starving civilians caused MacGregor to quicken his pace. His escort hurried to keep up. They passed a collapsed home where soldiers dug in the ruins with their bare hands. A bleeding mother, her hair dusted white by fallen mortar, wailed for her lost children and nuns stood comforting her in torn and soiled habits.

The citadel appeared as a bombed torn hulk, stark evidence of Wolfe's shelling of this resistance symbol. Soldiers fought a stubborn fire in the building with a brigade of water buckets passed hand to hand. Lieutenant MacGregor mounted the dusty steps of Government House. There was no servant holding the door open for him on this visit.

He mounted the broken steps of Government House where a haze of smoke drifted from the broken windows. His French escort walked past the bewildered guards standing before the door. MacGregor hurried down the wall, now strewn with fallen plaster, past the startled guards and inside the governor's office. His escort calmed the French guards as he approached Governor Drucour. Without greeting Governor Drucour, MacGregor asked, "Marie? Is she... where is she?"

Governor Drucour looked up quickly. His appearance contrasted with his usually impeccable presentation. He looked drawn and haggard. Unshaven, he appeared to have slept in the dusty clothing he wore. The governor remained seated as he entered, his eyes looking over MacGregor's head. "She's alive," he replied. "I think you will find her in a shelter with the common women. They are in the basement of the citadel where I sent them for protection from your artillery. Marie will be with the commoners and their children, if I know her."

Lieutenant MacGregor drew the envelope from his packet and tossed it on the desk before the governor. "This is a final offer of terms from the British commanders. Please accept his terms, Governor, and end this insanity. Admiral Boscawen said that you have conducted yourself with the greatest honor. There is no shame in surrendering now. If you do not surrender, British soldiers will breach the walls within two days. There will be hand to hand fighting and many will die, perhaps even you and your lady. The admiral urges you to surrender now as he fears for your safety." He turned to look toward the shelters, concluding," I'll come back for your answer, whatever. I go now to find Marie." MacGregor strode out into the smoke-filled corridor.

A wounded officer, coughing from the smoke and dust, directed him to the shelters. The first, he said, protected wounded officers from Wolfe's cannons. Another protected ladies of the town. The outside shelter is for the commoners.

Smoke seeped from the door of the officer's shelter. Perhaps sensing a lull in the artillery bombardment, men inside struggled to free themselves. The door shook and rumbled from inside. As MacGregor arrived, the door burst open. Coughing officers, all showing signs of wounds, pulled the door away and let it fall on the rubble. Over fallen sand bags and rubble they crawled and stumbled blindly, dragging others who could not walk. He caught a fleeing officer, holding the wide-eyed man by his arm as he asked, "Where is the shelter for the common women and children?"

Coughing and gasping for breath, the officer lifted a bloody, bandaged hand to point down the litter strewn hall. "Down there somewhere, beyond the ladies' shelter."

MacGregor hurried past the ladies' shelter where a few men had begun to remove rubble from the door. Climbing over fallen timbers and masonry, he found his way to the next shelter. Pulling fallen sand bags away from the entrance, he tugged at the door. MacGregor picked up a charred timber, prying at the loose door through which smoke curled. He heard pounding on the door inside and children crying. Sagging timbers seemed ready to drop tons of mortar on the shelter. MacGregor pulled harder at the door; it was barred from the inside. Pounding on the door he demanded in French, "Lift the bar from the inside." He listened as a bar rattled from the inside. A wide-eyed woman slowly opened the door, peeking around its timbers with a cloth held over her nose and mouth. The open door revealed a dark, crowded, smoke-filled room of coughing, gasping, fearful women and whimpering, crying children. He stood aside as women and children rushed past him for the cleaner air of the corridor. Frantically he called Marie's name.

A frail, choked voice answered from the back of the dark shelter, "Charles?" Stepping over and between women and children lying on the floor, MacGregor found Marie holding an infant. She looked up at him with wide, dark eyes. He took the child and placed it in its mother's arms. He lifted Marie from the straw and carried her through the hot, smoky shelter. Stepping over children and mothers, MacGregor climbed over the rubble near the door. He tenderly carried Marie out into the hall. Marie's hair was disheveled. Her dress wet with perspiration and stained with blood. Drops of sweat stood on her pale, drawn face. She turned her face against his chest, coughing.

MacGregor kicked open an outside door and carried Marie to an open courtyard. There he put Marie's feet on the ground and held her against him. With half-closed eyes, breathing in short quick gasps, Marie held him with trembling hands. A pair of soldiers approached MacGregor with upraised muskets. He ignored their weapons and commanded in French, "You there! Step lively! There are women and children in the shelter down the hall. Carry them out into the fresh air. Quickly! The truce flags are flying and they will be safe for now."

The soldiers stood only a moment in surprise before rushing to obey. Hurrying down the hall, they pulled away the debris blocking the ladies' shelter. The door swung open. One of the first women to exit the ladies shelter was Madame Drucour. Looking disheveled but still bearing her regal composure, the Governor's wife coughed into a lace handkerchief. Plaster dust covered her black, silk dress. She picked her away around the fallen debris and out into the courtyard. She hurried toward Marie. Madame Drucour wiped Marie's brow with her lace handkerchief, saying, "You should have come to the ladies' shelter." She looked at MacGregor and seemed to apologize as she said, "But Marie insisted on looking after the common women and children. Thank God she is all right."

Presently Madame Drucour's attention turned back to Lieutenant MacGregor as she brushed Marie's dusty hair. "What are you doing *here*, Lieutenant MacGregor?"

"I delivered final surrender terms to Governor Drucour," he answered. "You must go and talk to him. Our soldiers will breech the walls in two days time and many will die here in hand to hand fighting. Angry British soldiers will not do well with your people if they win the city by bayonet. You must talk sense to the governor. Louisbourg is already lost but not all the citizens. You must stop the slaughter."

Madame Drucour's eyes widened. She stood erect, saying, "Then I must speak to that proposition!" With lifted chin she started walking toward the governor's office. The governor's lady lifted her skirts and stepped over fallen beams and mortar. With dignity she raised her chin and navigated the wreckage to the governor's office.

When Marie had recovered and breathed normally, MacGregor put an arm around her thin waist and helped her out of the courtyard and down the dusty, litter-strewn hall. They stopped at Governor Drucour's office. Madame Drucour stood behind her husband reading the surrender ultimatum over her husband's shoulder. Several senior French officers stood around the room. They muttered angry comments that there should be no surrender. Governor Drucour held up his hand for silence at the sight of Lieutenant MacGregor, saying to MacGregor, "I find this incomprehensible." In a shaky and agitated voice, Governor Drucour said, "The terms of this ultimatum are inhumane. That I should surrender myself a prisoner at discretion is humiliating beyond comprehension. How can I ask my army to surrender their arms and colors after so valiant a fight? How can I put their families at the mercy of the enemy?" Governor Drucour's voice rose in pitch, near breaking. "I will not accept terms of unconditional surrender. I will fight on." The governor appeared near collapse as he turned to General D'Anthonay, saying, "General! You must mount a spirited defense of the city. We will not let our people fall into the hands of those barbarians." D'Anthony said nothing, looking around at the other senior officers, then nodded his compliance toward Drucour.

The governor turned to Loppinot, the old general who had accepted Louisbourg back from the English tens years before, after the Treaty of Aix la Chapelle. He ordered, "General Loppinot! Go immediately to the English and tell them I have rejected their ultimatum. Tell them I demand surrender with honor or there will be no surrender." The old man's craggy face showed no emotion as he raised his hand in salute. With a little bow he called to his aide and left the room.

Governor Drucour walked slowly across the room and looked out the shattered window. There he saw and heard the voices of angry Swiss mercenaries, who in their long history had never surrendered unconditionally to any enemy. They yelled insults at their officers. They splintered furniture for a bonfire upon which they would burn their colors rather than surrender them to the enemy. Marie hurried to Governor Drucour's window, watching the soldiers scuffle with their officers. Soldiers doused oil on their bonfire and tossed a lamp thereon. With the flames leaping skyward, the soldiers prepared to throw their battle flags and weapons on the fire.

The men stopped their destruction only when General Loppinot paused by the bonfire and said, wiping a tear from his eye, "Your weapons and colors may be needed tomorrow. The English surrender terms are rejected."

Lieutenant MacGregor turned to the governor and said, "You may fight on, Governor, for another day or two." With anger in his voice he continued, "You will cause the death of many more of your people and then surrender to the same terms, whatever. But you will not subject Marie to such insanity. I'm taking her out of Louisbourg and God help anyone who stands in my way."

Marie took him by the arm. "Please," she said, speaking to all in the room. "Perhaps the English would change their minds if Charles MacGregor talked to them."

MacGregor looked at Marie and spoke with firmness, "No. I can't change the minds of my officers nor can anyone. Louisbourg has been defeated and everyone here knows that. It will be in British hands in two days, either by treaty or the point of a bayonet. There is only the question of how many will live to see the light of that sorry day." He turned to Marie. "I'm leaving Louisbourg and taking you with me. If you have belongings you want, get them now."

Lieutenant MacGregor slowly asked, "Would you sacrifice a thousand lives for your vanity?" He looked around the room in disgust. "May God forgive you, history shall not." So saying, he looked at Marie. "Get your clothing; we are leaving." He turned to the Drucours. "Governor, Madame Drucour, I pray you both survive this decision."

Madame Drucour looked at Marie and said, "Go, my dear, you have devoted more loyalty to our King than he deserves." She turned to MacGregor. "Lieutenant, please send a man back for Marie's clothing and jewelry as soon as the city falls. If the English brigands have not destroyed my precious harpsichord, take it for her as well... take everything that has not been destroyed; it's Marie's with my love. I hope I can talk to these men. Their pride has overcome their good sense."

Marie hurried to Madame Drucour. She hugged her briefly and for a moment the two stood embracing each other. Then Madame Drucour stood away and said to Marie, "Go, my dear, your man is waiting, and we have much to discuss, in private." MacGregor took Marie by the hand. Together they hurried out where they found his escort waiting. MacGregor ordered, "Take us to the Dauphin Gate, quickly before the truce flags come down." They walked over and around the rubble left by General Wolfe's cannons. In the streets they passed bewildered, shell shocked residents. There was arguing and shouting between the soldiers. Some demanded fighting to the end; others pleaded for surrender. Marie surveyed the scene with tears in her eyes.

They crossed the drawbridge to the relief of the Highlander, waiting in the shadows by two thin horses of excellent breeding. With a wide grin he looked up at MacGregor, saying, "Aye, and ye MacGregors must uphold your reputation for horse stealin' so ye may claim ye stole these fine horses. However, a Frenchman gave them to us. He said he loves his horses and would rather give them to the enemy than have them killed by the cannons. They be' skinny but can take us back in style." The Highlander turned his eyes to Marie and continued, "But I didna' know ye MacGregors be stealin' women too."

"Good horses and pretty women you see," MacGregor replied. "I'll be takin' this little lady back to be my wife."

Marie bristled, "You may ask me first, Charles MacGregor. I will decide who shall be my husband." MacGregor smiled, lifted Marie onto the saddle and climbed up behind her. The Highlander mounted with his white flag, and they quickly trotted out the gate. But behind them, there was shouting. They stopped as D'Anthonay came running to the gate.

Hatless, his uniform dusty, perspiration on his forehead, he exclaimed, "The Governor has reversed himself. He is persuaded to accept the ultimatum." He gave MacGregor the ultimatum signed by Governor Drucour. "Give this to Admiral Boscawen."

Lieutenant MacGregor tucked the letter under his belt and turned his horse toward the British lines. "We'll hurry. Let's hope no one is killed before the truce is accepted." They urged their horses forward, leaving D'anthonay standing in the war-torn field beyond the walls, shading his eyes from the low sun. MacGregor and Marie galloped away from the smoky battlefield, together.

THE END

[1] Quotation from a letter to Lord Sackville

[2] 2 The drinking water barrel.

[3] Jean Renau is fictional but patterned after Brevet Captain Jean Vauquelin who arrived in Louisbourg in June of 1758. His exploits aboard the frigate, *Aréthuse,* contrast sharply with those his commanders. The *Aréthuse* was a converted merchant ship previously called, *Pélrine.*

Brevet referred to a temporary commission given to a merchant officer in the French Navy

[4] *Julius Caesar,* Act IV, Scene 3

Fresh Water Cove
(Kennington Cove)

Gabarouse Bay

Flat Point

White Point